PULSE

PULSE

PULSE

FELIX FRANCIS

G. P. Putnam's Sons
New York

G. P. PUTNAM'S SONS
Publishers Since 1838
An imprint of Penguin Random House LLC
375 Hudson Street
New York, New York 10014

The Library of Congress has catalogued the G. P. Putnam's Sons hardcover edition as follows:
Names: Francis, Felix, author.
Title: Pulse / Felix Francis.
Description: New York : G.P. Putnam's Sons, [2017] | "A Dick Francis novel."
Identifiers: LCCN 2017022753| ISBN 9780399574733 (hardcover) |
ISBN 9780399574757 (ebook)
Subjects: | BISAC: FICTION / Suspense. | FICTION / Thrillers. |
FICTION / Mystery & Detective / General. | GSAFD: Mystery fiction. |
Suspense fiction. Classification: LCC PR6056.R273 P85 2017 | DDC 823/.914—dc23
LC record available at https://lccn.loc.gov/2017022753

First G. P. Putnam's Sons hardcover edition / October 2017
First G. P. Putnam's Sons trade paperback edition / July 2018
G. P. Putnam's Sons trade paperback ISBN: 9780399574740

Printed in the United States of America
1 3 5 7 9 10 8 6 4 2

BOOK DESIGN BY LUCIA BERNARD

For my granddaughter
Emma Grace Francis

*With grateful thanks to Simon Claisse, Clerk of the Course
at Cheltenham Racecourse, and to the members of the
jockeys' medical team at Cheltenham, especially
doctors Sue Smith, Andy Simpson and Lee Humphreys,
nurses Sarah Godfrey and Sue Denley
and physical therapist Jennifer (Rabbit) Slattery.
I promise them that all my characters are fictitious.
I hope they don't mind me taking some liberties.*

And, as always, my special thanks and much love to Debbie.

PART 1

NOVEMBER

1

I didn't expect the patient to die but, of course, he did, and it was my fault.

While my colleagues told me that it wasn't, and I shouldn't blame myself, I knew better.

I was a bad person, and my inadequacy and foolishness *were* the reasons the man died.

I felt wretched.

THE MAN HAD ARRIVED at the hospital by ambulance, unconscious but still breathing, and with a weak but rapid heartbeat.

"Unknown middle-aged male," said one of the paramedics loudly as he handed the patient over to the hospital emergency staff. "Found fully dressed but unresponsive in a cubicle of a male restroom in the main grandstand at Cheltenham Racecourse at about ten past seven this evening."

I looked up at the clock on the wall—it was now half past eight.

"There is no indication of how long he'd been there," the paramedic continued. "The last race today was at five after four, so it could have been a while. Both pupils large and unresponsive, blood pressure high but stable at a hundred and seventy over one-ten, pulse one-eighty. He has symmetrical breathing and O$_2$ saturation is at ninety-five percent. Body temperature high at thirty-nine degrees Celsius but not extreme. No obvious trace of trauma but fitted with a collar as a precaution and given supplementary oxygen at four liters per minute on-site and since, plus two hundred and fifty milliliters of IV saline en route. No sign of awareness throughout."

"Blood sugar?" I asked.

"Tested on-site at one-twenty. Retested in the ambulance. Same result."

One hundred twenty milligrams per deciliter was well within the normal range, so the man wasn't hypoglycemic—very low in blood sugar—my first guess for someone unconscious with such a high pulse rate.

"ECG?" I asked.

The paramedic pulled a long strip of pink paper from his pocket and handed it to me. "Shows typical SVT."

I glanced at the electrocardiogram trace on the paper and it certainly looked like SVT—supraventricular tachycardia—a malfunction of the heart's electrical system resulting in a resting pulse rate in excess of 150 beats per minute.

"Any medications?" I asked.

"Nothing on him and nothing given other than the saline."

"Right," I said. "Thank you."

The paramedics collected their gear and departed. Off to another Saturday night crisis.

I looked down at the man lying face-up on the gurney in front of me. He was probably in his early forties, just like me, and he didn't look unusual or remarkable, merely another patient.

He had olive-brown skin with black curly hair that was graying slightly at the temples, and he was clean-shaven under the oxygen mask. He was wearing a white shirt, spread open wide across his chest for the application of the ECG electrodes, together with navy pinstripe trousers, black socks and highly polished laced-up shoes.

As the senior physician on duty in the Cheltenham General Hospital Accident and Emergency Department, I was now responsible for his well-being and I could almost feel the penetrating stares of the three other members of my team burning into me as they waited for my instructions.

Anxiety and panic rose in my throat like a tidal wave.

I wanted to run away and hide.

I silently berated myself. *Get a grip. You can do this. This is what you do all the time. Every day. Take a deep breath. Calm down. CALM DOWN!*

The panic subsided—for the moment.

"OK," I said slowly and deliberately. "Let's get some bloods done—full count plus everything else. Check for external injuries, especially on the head and neck. Set up vital-signs monitors and we'll send him to CT as soon as we're happy he's stable. There must be a reason why he's unconscious."

It was fairly unusual for someone to remain comatose for so long without any visible sign of trauma, especially someone who must have been walking around at the races earlier in the afternoon. But it was also unusual for someone's heart to beat 180 times per minute.

A drug overdose came readily to mind, as did the possibility of a stroke or a brain tumor—the CT X-ray scan would indicate if it was one of those.

My team of two nurses and a junior doctor set to work removing the man's clothing and connecting him to various monitors.

One of the nurses inserted a cannula into a vein on the inside of his left elbow to draw some blood. Another shone a flashlight alternately into each of the man's eyes, watching for the pupils to react to the brightness.

"Still no response on either side," she said.

In a healthy person the constricting of the pupils due to light is an involuntary reflex reaction—it happens without the individual having to think about it—and the lack of it in both eyes could indicate abnormally high pressure in the head or damage to the brain stem, but it could also be the result of having taken certain drugs—barbiturates, for example.

"Ask the lab to specifically check for a drug overdose," I said to the nurse who was filling test tubes of blood from the cannula in the man's arm. "Can we also get a urine sample?"

Seeking to discover what was wrong with the man was a bit like a murder mystery in an Agatha Christie novel, with me taking on the role of the detective. There were many possible suspects for the cause of his condition and I had to determine the guilty one by eliminating each of the others in turn.

I let my team do the intricate work while I stood back trying to take in the bigger picture.

On the periphery of the group hovered a very young-looking uniformed policeman.

"Can I help you?" I said. "I'm Dr. Rankin, Chris Rankin. I'm in charge of A&E this evening."

"PC Filippos." He instinctively put out a hand but I didn't shake it because I was wearing sterile latex gloves.

"Filippos?" I said.

"Yes." He smiled. "Half Greek. I came in with your patient." He waved a hand toward the man on the gurney. "The racecourse called us first. They thought he was drunk. It was me who called the ambulance."

I had wondered why it had taken so long for the man to get to the hospital.

"Well done," I said to him.

"What's wrong with him?" the policeman asked.

"I'm not sure yet. We have to run some more tests. But I don't think he's drunk."

There was a slight trace of alcohol on the man's breath but not the usual overpoweringly sweet aroma of the unconscious drunk. I was well used to dealing with those on a Saturday night. We called them VIPs—*very intoxicated persons.*

"Any idea who he is?" I asked.

"None at all. I searched his pockets while waiting for the ambulance. All he had on him was eighty-two pounds in cash and one crumpled bookmaker's betting slip. No cards, no wallet, no keys, nothing."

"He must have had a coat," I said. It was far too cold in mid-November to be at the races in only a thin shirt.

The constable nodded. "He did, and a jacket and tie. I have them bagged up." He lifted a clear plastic bag to show me. "Shall I take the rest of his clothes to add to it?"

"He'll need them to go home in."

"If he does go home," the policeman said flatly.

I glanced at him. "Do you know something I don't?"

"No," he said, but I wasn't sure if he was telling me the truth.

One of the nurses interrupted us. "Dr. Rankin, we're ready for the CT."

"Excuse me," I said to the policeman. "I have to go with the patient."

"I'll wait here," PC Filippos said with determination.

I raised my eyebrows at him in surprise.

"It's probably not necessary," he said, "but I'll wait anyway. Then, if he does come round, I'll be able to inform his family. He reminds me a bit of my dad, you know, in looks and the way he's dressed. I'd want someone to tell me if my dad was found unconscious in a racecourse restroom."

"You can wait in the relatives' room," I said. "There's a coffee machine in there."

"Thanks."

THE CT SCAN WAS CLEAR—no visible clots or bleeds in the brain, and no tumor.

More suspects had been eliminated.

Now what?

I began to feel shaky again.

Stop it. Keep control.

I looked at the monitor that showed the man's heart beating 196 times per minute, even higher than when he was brought in. And the cardiac trace on the screen was becoming increasingly random, strikingly different from the nice smooth, repeating pattern produced by a healthy organ. But, in spite of the irregularity of his heart, his blood pressure was holding up, indeed it was far too high, and the oxygen saturation was steady at 98 percent.

"I'm worried about him," I said to my senior staff nurse.

We had been unable to obtain a urine sample for a dip drug test. Did that indicate that his kidneys were not working properly? I also thought his skin displayed the slight yellowing of jaundice, so was there a problem with his liver function?

Both could be a direct result of his cardiac arrhythmia.

In medicine, as in life, one initial problem could all too quickly spawn a whole raft of secondary troubles.

The blood-test results should give us the answers but we were still waiting for those to come back from pathology. Nothing, it seemed, happened quickly on a Saturday anywhere else in the hospital. But accidents and emergencies didn't respect the normal working week. Indeed, Saturdays and Sundays were by far our busiest days.

"His pulse is still far too fast and getting very irregular," I said. "His heart's clearly tiring. If it is SVT, then it's high time we tried to reset his rhythm back to normal."

I took a deep breath.

"We'll give him six milligrams of adenosine," I said decisively.

"We don't know what else he's taken," the staff nurse said with a note of caution.

Adenosine was an antiarrhythmic medication used to slow an abnormally high heart rate, but it could occasionally react badly with some psychotic drugs.

"I think we'll have to take that chance," I said. "Have you checked him for puncture marks?"

"I did, and I couldn't find anything obvious."

Puncture marks in the skin were telltale signs of an intravenous drug user—and we saw far too many of those.

"We could just wait for the results of the bloods," the staff nurse said. "They'll surely be back soon."

If it had been a weekday between eight and six, I'd have simply phoned a specialist from the coronary unit for some advice, but, at nine o'clock on a Saturday evening, they'd all be either at home watching television or out socializing.

Should I page the on-call duty cardiologist? Drag him into the hospital from his dinner?

Decision time.

I was the senior physician here. If I made the call, the duty heart doctor would be my junior. So it would be my decision anyway.

Do nothing or do something?

Which was right?

I could feel the ends of my fingers beginning to tingle and my right knee began to tremble slightly.

Breathe, I told myself. *In through my nose, hold for a second or two, and out through my mouth*—just as I'd been taught.

Breathe deeply, and again, and again.

The trembling in my knee slowly died away.

I looked again at the now-alarmingly uneven rapid trace on the monitor. Even if I paged the heart specialist, I was worried that the patient's condition might deteriorate before he arrived.

"I don't think we can wait any longer," I said.

"OK," the nurse said. "I'll get it."

"Also get someone in here with the shocker."

She went off, leaving me alone in the cubicle with the patient.

I glanced down at the man.

He appeared even more vulnerable than when he'd first arrived, probably because all his clothing had since been removed, replaced by a faded blue hospital gown that was not properly secured around his shoulders.

It was not that uncommon for unnamed trauma cases to arrive at A&E, such as lone pedestrians knocked down by cars, but I thought it was a little odd for someone wearing a pinstripe suit plus a tie to have no identification on him whatsoever.

I touched his forehead. It was damp with perspiration.

"Who are you?" I asked quietly into the stillness. "And what's wrong with you?"

He didn't reply. I hadn't expected him to. Instead the monitor above his head simply went on showing me his erratic pulse and over-high blood pressure.

The staff nurse returned holding a small syringe containing the adenosine and a much larger one full of normal saline solution that would flush the drug around to the man's heart.

She was followed in by one of the emergency junior doctors, who was pushing a small metal cart on which sat the shocker— the electrical defibrillator that would be used to give the patient's heart a restarting electric shock in the unlikely event that the adenosine caused a cardiac arrest.

The staff nurse connected both the syringes to the cannula on the inside of the man's elbow such that their barrels sat at right angles to each other.

"OK?" she asked, looking straight at me.

"Ready?" I said, looking at the junior doctor.

"Can I assume that the patient doesn't have a pacemaker fitted?" he asked.

"He does not," I confirmed. It would have been obvious on the CT scan. But it was a good question. Shocking someone who had a pacemaker was still possible but greater care was needed in positioning the electrode plates.

"OK," said the doctor. "I'm ready."

"Right," I said. "Go."

The nurse rapidly depressed the plunger of the small syringe and then immediately followed it with the complete contents of the larger.

Adenosine was rapidly metabolized by red blood cells with a very short half-life. Consequently, it was important to give it very quickly, together with a large bulk of saline, in the hope that enough of the active drug makes it to the heart to cause a temporary block in the atrioventricular node, which in turn should reset the heart back into a normal rhythm.

Our three sets of eyes were firmly fixed on the monitor screen. If the adenosine was going to work, it would do so almost immediately.

Initially, nothing happened, but then the trace went flat as the drug arrived at the heart and the block occurred.

I held my breath.

It was only a few seconds but it seemed like an age before any spikes reappeared. Erratic at first, then more regular, but still overly fast, the pulse counter almost immediately going back up to over 190.

The adenosine had failed to do the trick.

"Bugger," I said.

"Double the dose and try again?" asked the staff nurse. It was normal practice.

I nodded and she went off to fetch new syringes full of drug and saline.

"Are you sure it's SVT?" asked the junior doctor.

"No," I replied, "I'm not sure. We're still waiting for the results of his bloods to come back from the lab."

We stood in silence and waited.

"Double adult trauma call, six minutes," said a seemingly disembodied voice over the department public address system.

Saturday night in A&E.

Busier than an ice-cream seller in a heat wave.

2

Chris, we need you." It was Jeremy Cook, a fellow emergency physician.

"Coming," I said, without taking my eyes off the monitor screen above my patient's head. The second dose of adenosine had just been administered.

"Now," Jeremy insisted, tugging gently at my sleeve.

"OK," I said, turning toward him. There was a look of apprehension in his eyes.

"It's a really bad one," he said. "A motorcyclist lost control on London Road and hit a lamppost when doing nearly sixty. And he had a passenger. Both will be here in two minutes with multiple life-threatening injuries."

"OK," I said again. "I'm coming."

An incoming trauma casualty with life-threatening injuries demanded the undivided attention of an emergency senior physician and Jeremy and I were the only two currently on duty. I handed the comatose man over to the junior doctor.

"Keep me informed," I shouted over my shoulder at him as I hurried away.

The emergency department at Cheltenham General was known

universally as A&E, which actually stood for *Accident and Emergency* even though it was nicknamed *Anything and Everyone* by the doctors and nurses who worked there, and *Arse and Elbow* by some idiots who thought we didn't know the difference.

By the time the two motorcyclists arrived by ambulance we were ready for them with two separate trauma teams, each of six staff. In addition, I'd already paged the on-call orthopedic surgeon in the sure knowledge that he would be needed.

We would also likely require a neurologist. Even with modern full-face safety helmets, the forces acting on the head in such high-speed incidents nearly always resulted in some form of brain injury, often severe and debilitating, not to mention the likelihood of life-changing spinal cord damage.

But our job as emergency staff was to assess the patients, to ensure they were stable and not about to die. Only after that could the specialists deal with the further fallout from the accident.

The two patients were wheeled in on gurneys, each with a couple of paramedics in attendance together with a first-response doctor who had attended the scene. I took the female pillion passenger while Jeremy looked after the male driver. Both of them were in a bad way and close to death.

For the next hour or so my team and I worked feverishly to stabilize the young woman's condition.

She had arrived in a coma, medically induced by the doctor at the roadside, so there was no chance of asking her where it hurt. But it really didn't take any great medical skill to determine the extent of some of her injuries.

From the unusual angle of her feet it was clear that both her legs were broken and she had numerous gashes in her leather suit that indicated severe lacerations beneath.

But, in emergency medicine, the same mantra applies as in

first aid: ABC—airway, breathing and circulation. Without respiration and circulation a patient will rapidly die and intervention elsewhere would be fruitless.

So we initially concentrated on keeping her airway open, her lungs ventilated and her heart beating. Next we checked for signs of major bleeding, both external and internal, and in particular into the chest cavity. When we were confident that she wasn't about to die on us in the scanner, we took her to CT for a full-body scan that revealed not only the multiple fractures to her lower legs but also several cracked vertebrae in her back, together with a bruise and a small bleed into the brain.

If the bruising caused any swelling to her brain, then the pressure in her skull would need to be relieved. She would need dedicated specialist neurological treatment, something that was not available here at Cheltenham. If we hadn't been so close to the accident, she probably wouldn't have come here in the first place.

As soon as she was well enough, she would be transferred to the regional major trauma center in Bristol, some forty miles away. A dedicated ambulance was already standing by.

With her breathing and pulse finally stabilized, I had to be sure that she had an adequate blood supply to her lower limbs before she was moved. If the broken bones had punctured the tibial arteries through her calves, then her feet would start to die even before she made it to Bristol.

I studied the CT scan closely. It showed that there was a little internal bleeding behind the knees but not as much as would be expected from an arterial tear. In addition, I could feel a slight but steady pulse on the top of each foot.

"OK," I said. "She's ready to go."

A fresh team of paramedics connected her to their portable

monitoring equipment and then wheeled her gently out to the waiting ambulance.

My whole team took a collective sigh.

"Well done, everybody," I said. "Good job."

The young woman had been on the brink of death when she'd arrived but now there was every chance she'd survive. Only time would tell if her brain injury would be life-changing.

So preoccupied had I been trying to save the patient in front of me that I had temporarily forgotten about the unconscious man I'd left in the other cubicle—that was until I saw the junior doctor, who was standing to one side waiting for a break in the action. I could tell from his expression that things were not good.

"What is it?" I asked.

"He died," he said bluntly.

"He what!" I shrieked at him in anger. "How?"

"Cardiac arrest," he said. "Just after you left. We've been trying to resuscitate him for most of the past hour." He looked up at the clock on the wall. "I declared him dead five minutes ago."

"Why didn't you call me?" I shouted.

"You were busy," he said rather sheepishly. "And we received the results of his blood tests back from the lab."

"And?" I demanded.

"He'd taken a massive cocaine overdose. There was nothing anyone could have done to save him."

I felt the tingling reappear in my fingertips and my right leg again began to tremble.

THERE MUST BE WORSE PLACES to have a full-blown panic attack than in the emergency department of a hospital. However,

I was determined that none of my medical colleagues should be aware of it.

Thankfully, after the departures of the female motorcyclist to Bristol and her male companion to the operating theater to have a broken leg set, there was a brief respite of major activity. But I knew it was only the lull before the storm. That would occur later in the evening, when the pubs and bars closed, and the half-drunk, and worse, would turn up at our door with injuries caused by anything from vicious street brawls to simply falling over in the gutter. But our job wasn't to police the public's drinking habits, just to patch them up and send them on their wobbly way.

The tingling migrated up through my hands and into my arms and I just about managed to tell Jeremy Cook to cover for me for a few minutes before sneaking off and locking myself in the department linen store.

The shaking that had started in my right knee gradually spread all over my body and the tingling rolled right up my arms and into my throat.

It's OK, I said to myself as I crouched in the dark. *Keep breathing. This will pass.* Although it didn't feel like it at the time.

But this was not the first occasion.

I had been a doctor now for over eighteen years and had been a specialist in emergency medicine for the past ten. Hence, I believed I knew the workings and failings of the human body pretty thoroughly, but I had little idea what was happening to my own.

ABOUT A YEAR AGO, I'd been to see a gynecologist.

"Onset of menopause," he had said with a knowing nod.

"Surely not," I'd replied, emitting a hollow laugh. "I'm only forty."

"Slightly early, I'll admit, but that's what it is. No doubt about it. But it's nothing to worry about. Quite normal."

I had given him very low marks for patient sensitivity as he'd ushered me out the door of his consulting rooms. He was a busy man, he explained unapologetically. Lots of patients waiting.

Menopause.

I'd sat outside in my car and cried.

I cried for my lost youth and also for the lost future my husband and I had been planning.

We had twin boys, now aged fourteen, and we had recently been trying for another baby—maybe even the daughter that both of us so craved.

My husband, Grant, had been a soldier when I'd met him, my eye caught initially by the uniform rather than the man inside it. We'd been at a wedding where my female cousin was marrying his male one. We had spent the whole evening together, and then the night too, sans uniform.

He'd been a combat engineer and had remained in the army for the first twelve years of our marriage. Hence, he'd had frequent postings to Iraq and Afghanistan when the boys were small and he'd missed out on many of the things most fathers would take for granted. He'd been on deployment, building bridges in Basra, when the twins took their first steps. He'd also been away when they started school, for their nativity plays and concerts, and had been absent at too many sports days to remember.

But now Grant was back in civvy street and working nine-to-five as head of the product-research team of a local aerospace-instrument company. He'd been looking forward to helping at bath time and reading bedtime stories, to being the hands-on dad he'd been unable to be with the twins.

But I'd had trouble conceiving. I'd put it down to my age. But plenty of other women have babies after the age of forty. If Madonna and Meryl Streep could do it, why couldn't I? That's why I'd gone to see the gynecologist in the first place.

Menopause.

How could it be? I wasn't having hot flashes or night sweats. True, my periods were a bit erratic but they always had been. Everything else appeared normal. But the doctor had arranged for me to have a blood test, and he'd just given me the result.

No estrogen.

No eggs.

No fertility.

No baby.

Menopause.

I had sat in the car and cried for more than an hour.

But here I was holed up in the linen store, twelve months down the line, and things were worse than I could possibly have imagined. Much worse. Not being able to have another baby was now the least of my problems.

INITIALLY, Grant had taken the news pretty well, but I felt that I'd let him down badly.

I began to imagine that he would look elsewhere for a fertile woman to be the mother of his daughter and I became intensely and irrationally suspicious of his young unmarried secretary, all the more so when she started showing signs of being pregnant.

I even confronted Grant and accused him of being the father.

He just laughed and told me not to be so silly, but I couldn't throw the thought from my head. So obsessed was I that I later went to see the secretary in the maternity wing after she'd given birth. I was convinced the child would look just like Grant.

The secretary was there with her boyfriend, a large Afro-Caribbean man called Leroy, and the baby cradled in his arms had dark skin.

I had almost cried out with joy.

And I'd felt foolish.

But, by that stage, feeling foolish was one of my lesser worries.

Twelve months ago if you had given me a broken leg, a punctured lung or a ruptured spleen, I would have known exactly how to fix it, but a chemical imbalance in the brain and the impact it has on mental function had been a closed book to me.

Not that I really knew any better now, in spite of some extensive research, with me acting as the guinea pig.

During the year I had been referred to two different gynecologists, an endocrinologist and, in desperation, a psychiatrist. I also had so many blood tests that the veins in my arms were like pincushions.

Yet not one of those eminent physicians could point a finger and confidently say, "This is what is wrong with you." Each of them had their own opinion, and that seemed to vary with each successive set of blood results.

"Ah, yes," my endocrinologist would say, studying one of the readouts. "Your thyroid hormone level is too low. We need to boost that."

So I would take a pill every night. However, the next test would show that the thyroxine was now too high but my testosterone was too low. So another medication would be prescribed.

And so it would go on.

I was now taking a nightly cocktail of fifteen pills, plus applying various patches and creams, and still I didn't feel well.

It had taken me quite a while to accept a diagnosis of depression.

How could I be depressed? I had a loving husband whom I adored, two wonderful kids doing well at school, a nice house, roses in the garden, two cars in the driveway, a purposeful career and no financial worries. What did I have to be depressed about?

"It's not about what you have or don't have," the psychiatrist told me. "John D. Rockefeller was the richest man there has ever been and he suffered from depression. Acute anxiety caused him to lose all the hair on his body."

Was that supposed to make me feel any better?

It certainly had me scrutinizing my hairbrush each morning to see if I was losing mine. I would lie awake for hours at night worrying about it. In fact, I had become a chronic worrier. I could worry for England about an entire range of things about which I had no control, or any need to control. The whole process simply made me immensely tired and even more anxious.

Some days my mood was so low that I had difficulty getting out of bed. All I wanted to do was curl up in a ball and wish the whole world would go away.

But I had kids to get to school, a husband who liked his breakfast, and a job where people were relying on me to keep them alive. So curling up was not an option.

But, all the while, I was trying to keep my condition a secret—a secret from my children, from my mother, and especially from my work—not an easy task when I was surrounded on a day-to-day basis by highly trained and observant doctors. Indeed, there had already been a few questions asked, questions that I had successfully sidestepped and left unanswered.

"Why don't you just tell them?" Grant often asked. "I'm sure they would understand and be helpful."

Would they?

According to the Mental Health Foundation, some form of mental illness affects about one in four of the UK population.

So I was not as alone as I felt.

However, there was a stigma surrounding it, with many imagining that those with a mental disorder were likely to be violent and dangerous.

But perhaps the real reason I wanted to keep things a secret was because I believed that it would make me appear a failure and a liability, and I had a dread of being a disappointment.

I feared that, even if I didn't lose my job because of it, my colleagues would look at me in a new light, one that wasn't supportive. They would begin to doubt my competency and fitness to practice. I would be written off and downgraded at a time when my work was the only normality in my life, the rock to which I was still clinging.

Hence, here I was in the linen cupboard, hiding away while my mind played tricks with my body.

Panic Attack had always seemed to me to be a bad term. I didn't particularly feel that I had been panicking about anything. The symptoms simply appeared out of nowhere at times of stress. Perhaps *Stress Attack* would have been a better name.

Either way, the effect on my physical well-being was pronounced. Apart from the shaking and the tingling, my heart was pounding in my chest and I was hyperventilating. Both those things tended to make me even more stressed, to the point where there was a positive-feedback loop with every new symptom reinforcing the problem and making the situation worse and worse. I felt I was spiraling down ever faster into a bottomless pit.

I forced myself to breathe slowly—in through my nose and out through my mouth. I knew from experience that the attack *would* pass. Sometimes it would take just a few minutes, on other occasions it could last for hours.

I didn't have hours.

I repeatedly told myself to *get a grip*, but telling someone with a mental illness to *get a grip* was a waste of time and even counterproductive.

I couldn't *get a grip* any more than someone with cancer could somehow *get a grip* and use their free will to initiate a cure.

Depression is a disease, but one of the mind, not the body. There is no fever, no bleeding, nothing that shows up on X-rays or scans, indeed there are no visible signs whatsoever. But it is a disease nevertheless. It is like a worm that gets inside your head and burrows through your brain, eating your self-respect and laughter, while leaving nothing but frustration, pain, loneliness and misery.

It makes you feel worthless, ugly and a burden to those around you.

And it spawns the belief that you would be better off dead.

3

I emerged from the linen store cupboard about ten to fifteen minutes later.

Thankfully, it had been one of my shorter episodes and no one else in the department seemed to have been unduly concerned by my absence.

"There's a policeman looking for you," one of the staff said to me as she hurried past.

It was PC Filippos and he found me at the nurses' station.

"Ah, Dr. Rankin, there you are," he said with a slight trace of irritation in his voice. "I need to ask you some questions."

"I'm busy," I said.

Answering questions was the last thing I wanted to do.

He looked around at the surprisingly empty cubicles behind me. "It won't take long."

"I'll be needed if an emergency arrives."

"It won't take long," he repeated. "Can we go somewhere private?"

Something about his expression told me he wouldn't give up, so I went with him to the relatives' room.

"Coffee?" he asked, standing by the machine in the corner.

"No thanks." Caffeine was the last thing I needed in my present fragile state. He made himself one and then sat down opposite me on the hospital-issue pink chairs.

"I understand my patient died," he said.

His patient, I thought. That was a new one.

"Yes," I said. "He had a cardiac arrest and couldn't be resuscitated."

He took out a black police notebook and wrote something down. "What caused the cardiac arrest?"

"That will be up to the pathologist to determine and the coroner to confirm."

"You must have some idea, as the attending physician."

"I wasn't attending him when he arrested," I said.

If he was surprised, he didn't show it. "And why was that exactly?"

"I was called to attend another patient—a motorcycle pillion passenger arrived by ambulance with life-threatening injuries."

He nodded as if he had already known.

"But my patient also had a life-threatening condition."

My stress level notched up a little.

"As it turns out, yes, he did. But I didn't believe it was as critical at the time."

He went back to writing in his notebook. He sipped his coffee.

"Am I being accused of something?" I asked, my stress levels now reaching the stratosphere with the tingling returning to my fingertips.

"No, Dr. Rankin, nothing like that." He smiled and the tingling abated. "I just have to get the sequence of events accurate for my report."

He wrote some more then looked up at me. "You must have some idea what killed him."

"As I said, that will be determined by a postmortem examination."

"No ideas at all?" He was persistent.

"I understand that a blood test showed he had excessive cocaine in his system but I haven't actually seen the results myself."

The policeman raised his eyebrows. "Cocaine?"

"Yes. It seems that he had taken a massive overdose. One of my colleagues is of the opinion that no intervention by us could have saved him but the toxicology results will prove that one way or the other."

He wrote it down.

"Was there any indication of how the cocaine entered his system?"

"If you mean were there obvious signs of him having injected it, then no, there weren't. But the autopsy should determine that too. Some addicts are very ingenious at disguising the fact by injecting themselves in difficult-to-see places."

"I didn't see a syringe in the racecourse restroom."

"Shooting up is not the only method of taking cocaine, you know," I said. "Most users snort it up their noses and some smoke it. You can even take it orally."

"You seem to know a lot about it."

I'm sure I blushed.

"A misspent youth," I said with a laugh.

He wasn't to know that I had recently tried anything and everything to try to alleviate my feelings of despair. Drink, drugs, cigarettes—all had been my bosom pals at some time or another during the previous twelve months. Some still were.

"Is that all?" I asked. "I should be getting back."

"All for the time being," PC Filippos replied. "But can I have your home address just in case?"

Just in case of what? I wondered.

I gave him my address and he wrote it down in his notebook, which he then snapped shut.

"Thank you, Dr. Rankin," he said, standing up. "Most helpful. I suspect the coroner's office will be in touch in due course."

"What happens if you can't find out who he was?" I asked.

"Oh, I'm sure we'll do that. For a start, we'll check his description against people reported missing. That usually turns up the identity of the deceased. Someone, somewhere, will miss him when he doesn't return home, maybe not tonight but soon enough."

I shuddered at the thought of the man's wife and family waiting for him to get back for his supper totally unaware that his body was already cooling in the hospital morgue.

"Awful to die so alone," said PC Filippos, as if he had been reading my mind. He downed the rest of his coffee and looked at his watch. "Right, I must be getting along. I've got to get back to the racecourse. I need to check for evidence in the men's room where the man was found."

"What, now?" I said. "Surely it will have been cleaned."

"It was the cleaner who found him—the poor woman was very upset. The man was in a locked lavatory cubicle and all she could see were his feet under the door. I have given instructions for the whole men's room to be left alone so I'd best go back tonight. They'll need it available for the racing tomorrow."

He hurried away and I went back to caring for the sick and injured, all the while thinking about the unnamed man lying on a slab just along the corridor.

I worried about my decision to administer the adenosine. Why did I do that before having the blood results back from the lab? That had been reckless of me. At best, it had hastened his death. At worst, perhaps he would have survived if I hadn't been so foolish.

I soon convinced myself that it had been my stupidity that had killed him.

It was all my fault.

MY SHIFT ENDED AT TWO A.M. and I drove home afterward like a maniac.

It was a way to express the anger that was boiling within me.

I was angry with the man for dying, and angry with myself for letting it happen. But, most of all, I was angry at what had become of me—angry at this wretched depression and the way it was ruining my life.

I jumped a red light on the Evesham Road, passing straight through the junction without even braking.

It was as if I didn't care.

And I didn't.

On this occasion, late at night, the roads were clear and I sailed through without incident. I did it without thinking rather than as a conscious effort to kill myself. I didn't exactly think of myself as having a death wish, but if the Grim Reaper came along and hooked me with his scythe, it wouldn't have bothered me too much.

Maybe I was more suicidal than I realized.

But then I thought about those in another car that I might hit. I knew all too well the horrific injuries that occurred in high-speed car crashes. I spent my working life saving people from them.

I would never forgive myself if I seriously injured or killed someone else.

I slowed a fraction.

Perhaps I'd be better off just driving really fast into a nice big solid tree. That should do it.

"Single-car accidents," the police called them. "Tut-tut," they would say, "she must have gone to sleep after a long shift at the hospital. Such a shame. Such a waste."

But Grant would have known otherwise. What would he say to the boys?

The boys!

Oh God, I couldn't do it to them.

I slowed a bit more.

I MADE IT HOME in one piece.

Home was a modern four-bedroom detached house on a new estate on the outskirts of Gotherington, a village five miles to the north of Cheltenham.

I'd had to drive past Cheltenham Racecourse on my way.

I knew it well. I regularly acted as one of the racecourse medical officers, following the horses in a Land Rover, ready to leap out and treat any jockey injured as a result of a fall.

But my mind tonight wasn't on the track, the horses and the medical requirements; it was on the gentlemen's restroom under the main grandstand.

I imagined the unfortunate cleaner finding the man unconscious in one of the cubicles. It must have given her quite a shock. But at least the man was then still alive.

When I'd been at medical school there had been a story going around about a man who had died while sitting on the toilet. In the macabre humor of all medical students, we had laughed at the revelation that, by the time he was found, rigor mortis had set in and the ambulance crew couldn't lay him down flat on a stretcher. He'd had to be carried to the morgue on a chair.

I pulled into the driveway and parked my little Mini Cooper next to Grant's Audi.

That was a good sign, I thought. He's still here.

I had an intense fear that Grant would leave me—that he would have had enough of my erratic behavior and, one day, I would come home to find him packed and gone. I didn't have any hard evidence to make me think that way—no unexplained telephone calls or cryptic e-mails—but I still worried. Sex between us had become a distant memory and I'd have probably left me by now if I'd been him.

He repeatedly tried to reassure me that he wouldn't go but I knew that he was fed up treading around me on eggshells, saying nothing at all rather than risk uttering some throwaway line to which I would take exception.

I realized that I took even the slightest criticism straight to my heart; every cross word was a dagger in my side.

Didn't everyone?

No, they didn't.

I had tried hard to let things pass, to laugh them off as nothing more than mere banter between husband and wife, but God had wired my brain wrongly. I couldn't leave things be or let them go. I would demand to know what he meant and refuse to believe his answer of "nothing." It would end in tears, his or mine, and we wouldn't speak for hours.

I quietly let myself in through the front door. The light was on in the hall but the house was quiet. I imagined Grant had allowed the boys to stay up late to watch the soccer highlights show but they would be asleep by now, dead to the world as only teenagers could be.

I went through to the kitchen and, even at this late hour, I put out the breakfast things. It was like a ritual. Cereal packets, bowls, spoons, mugs, plates, knives, butter dish and marmalade—all had to be put in exactly the right place on the table.

I stood back and checked.

I'd always had a bit of OCD—obsessive-compulsive disorder—but the depression had made it much worse. I knew that it was irrational to arrange everything just so, but I couldn't help it. The house might burn down in the night if I didn't, or my mother would die in her sleep, or any number of other awful outcomes would occur simply because I hadn't put the spoons properly in line with the bowls.

I believed it. Totally.

I went upstairs and put my head around the door of each of the boys' rooms.

As I'd expected, they were fast asleep, the sound of their breathing like music to my ears. They were my *raison d'être*. My all, my life.

I took my pills, potions and patches in the bathroom and then slipped between the sheets next to Grant. He grunted, which I took to mean, "Welcome home," and then he went straight back to sleep, snoring gently.

It had been my first "late" shift of three in a row and I'd been up since six, almost twenty-one hours on the go and most of it on my feet. I was exhausted but, even so, I couldn't nod off.

I lay in the darkness listening to the sounds of the house cooling, as I did almost every night. My psychiatrist had given me pills to help me sleep but they didn't seem to work. Perhaps I should double the dose.

My mind was racing too much for sleep, worrying about the dead unnamed man, about the still-living girl I'd sent to Bristol, about whether I had put the marmalade in the correct place downstairs and if I should go and check, about how I would pay the mortgage if Grant left me, about famine in Africa and about nuclear missiles raining down on us from North Korea. I worried about anything and everything, most of which I had no control over anyway. But that didn't stop me worrying about it.

I turned over and tried unsuccessfully to switch off my brain. I was tired of worrying.

I was also tired of being angry all the time, tired of feeling worthless and tired of the emptiness I felt inside.

I was tired of being depressed while pretending I was fine.

But, most of all, I was just tired of being tired.

I MUST HAVE FALLEN ASLEEP eventually because it was light when I woke. And I was alone in the bed. I rolled over and looked at the clock on my bedside table. Eight-thirty. Not bad for me, I thought. I was usually awake at five.

Grant will have gone on his regular Sunday morning run, I said to myself. He'd put on a few pounds after leaving the military but he still liked to keep himself in reasonable shape. He wouldn't be back until nine-thirty at the earliest.

He was welcome to it. The last thing I felt like doing was exercise. I simply didn't have the energy to do *anything* I didn't absolutely have to.

I rolled over again and stuck my head deep into the pillow. A little longer wouldn't do any harm, surely, and I would be back at work at six that evening for another eight hours of picking up the broken pieces of other people's lives.

I just wished I could pick up those of my own.

"Mum, are you awake?" one of the twins shouted from the

landing. Even after fourteen years I found it difficult to tell their voices apart, especially when they were shouting.

"I am now," I shouted back.

"I need my soccer gear. I have a practice at nine."

Toby, I thought. The elder by two minutes. Mad keen on soccer and now on the village boys' team. "It's in the airing cupboard," I called back. "And your cleats are under the stairs."

"Thanks."

"Do you want any breakfast?"

"No time," Toby shouted back. "I'll have it after."

Oliver, the younger twin, meanwhile, would still be sound asleep. He hated soccer and only said he wanted to watch the soccer highlights so he could stay up late. The twins might look identical, but they had very differing opinions. Oliver maintained, often at great length, that soccer players were all overpaid prima donnas who should get a real job rather than playing a stupid game all the time.

But I thought we were all playing a stupid game, the game of life, and, when the referee's whistle blew, we would shuffle off this mortal coil and out of the floodlights only to be replaced by a new signing with an unpronounceable name from *Real Madrid* or *Juventus*. The never-ending match would go on, but without us on the field. And no one would notice.

The front door slammed shut as Toby left and I went back to trying to catch a few more winks.

The quiet before the storm.

4

It started raining heavily as I drove to the hospital on Sunday evening at a time when most sane people would be going home for the night.

The day had seemed to drag on interminably.

I'd failed miserably to get back to sleep and had finally dragged myself out of bed and into the shower just before Grant returned from his run, all hot and sweaty, demanding access.

There had been a time when we would have squeezed into the shower cubicle together, relishing our wet bodies being in such close contact. Things would have invariably progressed to another form of steamy action in the bedroom.

But not anymore.

It was as much as I could do to be naked and visible in the same room as my husband, let alone within his touching distance.

I hated my body and I felt sure he must too, in spite of him continually telling me he loved it. My once firm, fulsome and prominent breasts now sagged alarmingly toward my waist and, in spite of nightly applications of expensive anti-cellulite creams, the skin on my thighs was already giving a good impression of orange peel.

That alone was enough to make me depressed.

"What do you expect?" Grant would say. "You're in your for-ties having had two children. It's nothing to worry about."

But, of course, I did worry about it. And I was constantly desperate that he might trade me in for a younger model, just as he did every three or four years with his car.

I had finally made it downstairs just before ten and, of course, the marmalade had been in the right place on the table all the time. If it hadn't, then I would surely have known about it. The house would have burned down, or the boys been infected with some debilitating disease, or we would be involved in a world-wide nuclear Armageddon with only minutes left to live.

It was true, and all because of the position of the marmalade.

Toby returned from his soccer practice caked in mud and with a bloodied knee after being accidentally kicked by one of the other boys. But he wasn't about to let his emergency-doctor mother do anything about it.

"Leave it out, Mum," he said sharply when I tried to see ex-actly how deep was the cut. "It's fine."

"It might get infected."

"I said it's fine," he insisted.

Fourteen-year-old boys. Not yet men but so eager to be manly. A bleeding knee was a badge of honor, a war wound.

"Go and have a shower and put some of this on it." I tossed him a tube of antiseptic cream from my first-aid cupboard in the kitchen.

He rolled his eyes in irritation but he caught the tube and took it upstairs with him to the bathroom.

Lunch had then come and gone without any great fanfare, Grant and the boys mostly grazing on what leftovers they could find in the back corners of the refrigerator.

Only a year or so previously, I would have eagerly produced a proper Sunday lunch—maybe a roast chicken or a joint of beef with all the trimmings.

I had prided myself on my Sunday lunches, taking great pleasure in having the family sitting down at the dining-room table for one meal in the week with no TV, video games or cell phones allowed to interrupt the conversation.

Now, I simply didn't have the energy or the inclination.

Meals in the Rankin household had mostly become either *ready* or *takeaway*, with Grant now on first-name terms with the managers at both the local Indian and Chinese restaurants, even if they did rather embarrassingly call him Mr. Wankin.

I, meanwhile, had decided to stop eating altogether, existing on a meager diet of vegetable soup plus the occasional sliver of plain grilled fish. Not that it seemed to be doing much good. Even though our bathroom scale showed that I'd lost another seven pounds in the last month, I was yet to *feel* any thinner. I regularly spent far too much time looking at myself in a full-length mirror. Not that I liked what I saw. It was far too stressful.

I parked my Mini in a space in the staff parking lot.

It was ten to six in the evening but it might as well have been the middle of the night. The sun had gone down at quarter past four and it had been pitch-black for over an hour. The intense rain had also cleared the streets of all but the most hardy.

I hated the prospect of the coming winter. The ever-dwindling length of daylight reflected the lowering of my own mood. Just five weeks, I thought, until the winter solstice and then the days would start getting longer again.

Surely I could last out five weeks.

But then it would be Christmas.

The very thought made my toes curl inside my shoes.

How could I get through all that eating, drinking and bon-homie?

I was not ready for any form of socializing. All I really wanted to do was hide myself from everyone except my immediate family. Yet, perversely, here I was about to delve into the darker recesses of humanity, dealing with people at their most vulnerable, when they would be relying on me to make them better.

But they were strangers.

I don't know why it made a difference, but it did.

I would be more anxious about joining close girlfriends for a drink than of swimming in piranha-infested waters. But I felt able to deal quite easily with a waiting room full of prospective patients.

Not that I found myself dealing with any patients on that particular night.

THERE WERE TWO MEN and a woman waiting for me when I went in from the car to change. I could tell immediately that it didn't signify good news.

"Ah, Chris, there you are," one of the men said when he saw me. I knew him well. He was the Medical Director of the hospital. My clinical boss. What was he doing here on a Sunday evening? And in a suit too.

"Can we have a word?" He was clearly uncomfortable.

I looked at the three of them.

"Of course," I said. "Here?"

There were other hospital staff milling around, some arriving, some leaving.

"Let's go somewhere more private," said the woman.

The four of us walked together down a long stark hospital

corridor, brightly lit only by the cool glow of overhead fluorescent tubes. "On my way to the condemned cell" was the only thought that floated into my head.

I found I didn't much care as long as the end was quick.

We went into one of the consulting rooms in the now-closed outpatients department. There were only two chairs at a table, so we all remained standing.

"What's this about?" I asked.

"Um," said the Medical Director uneasily, "we have received a complaint concerning your clinical competence."

"From whom?" I said, but I knew who it must have been—either the staff nurse who I'd told to administer the adenosine, or the junior doctor who'd been standing by with the defibrillator.

"That's not relevant at this point," said the woman.

I personally thought that it was very relevant but saying so wouldn't have made the slightest difference.

I was surprisingly calm—not a tingle to be felt anywhere. I even wordlessly congratulated myself on my control in such a stressful situation.

"We have decided," the woman went on, looking around briefly at the other two, "that it would be best if you were suspended from duty while the complaint is investigated. On full pay, of course."

"Suspended?" I said. "But why? I used my judgment as a doctor to make a decision that I felt was in the patient's best interests. Are you doubting my ability to make future decisions?"

There was an awkward silence.

"We are also concerned by the state of your mental health," said the Medical Director.

I felt as if I'd been punched in the stomach.

I couldn't breathe.

How did they know?

"What about my mental health?" I tried to sound as calm as possible.

"We have reasons to believe that you are suffering from clinical depression."

Putting the word *clinical* in front always made something sound much more serious.

"What reasons?" I demanded, anger rising within me. "I don't know what you're talking about. I have a slight anxiety problem, that's all."

"Chris, please be reasonable," the Medical Director said. "Several of your colleagues have raised concerns, noting that you sometimes absent yourself from the department during your shift."

"A woman is surely allowed to go to the ladies' room."

"But you don't go to the ladies' room, do you, Chris? You go and hide in a cupboard. Jeremy Cook saw you do that yesterday."

He paused but I said nothing, so he went on.

"I was concerned enough to use my legal powers to gain access to your medical records. One doesn't have to take Prozac twice a day just for a slight anxiety problem."

"I thought personal medical records were meant to be confidential." It was almost a mumble.

"Not when patients' lives are at risk."

"Are you suggesting that my depression has something to do with the death of a patient?" I could feel the anger rising in me again and, this time, there *was* a slight tingling in my fingertips.

"No." It was the other man, the one who had so far remained silent. "We are suggesting no such thing. We are simply stating the fact that a complaint has been received and it is the hospital's decision that you be suspended from duty while the circumstances are investigated. No one at this stage is implying that you have done anything wrong."

Lawyer, I thought. I wasn't particularly reassured.

"Right, then," I said, almost in a daze. "What do I do now?"

"You go home," said the Medical Director.

"But first I would like you to sign this," the lawyer said quickly, removing a folded piece of paper from the inside pocket of his suit jacket and placing it on the table along with a pen. I sat down on one of the chairs and read the single paragraph printed on the hospital's official headed notepaper:

I, Dr. Christine Rankin, understand that, following a complaint made against me, I have been suspended from duty at Cheltenham General Hospital pending an investigation into my competence to practice. I undertake that, until that investigation is complete, I will not attempt to gain access to the hospital premises in the role of a clinician. I further undertake that, prior to any hearing that might take place, I will not discuss the details of the said complaint with any of my medical colleagues.

Signed _____ *Date* _____

"What was the complaint?" I asked. "I can't undertake not to discuss something I know nothing about."

"That you failed to consult with colleagues and administered medication to a patient without due professional care and in a manner likely to have hastened the death of the patient."

The Medical Director read it from another piece of official notepaper, which he now handed to me. It was the formal notification of my suspension from duty.

Someone *had* been busy, and on a Sunday.

I picked up the pen and signed the lawyer's paper.

What else could I do?

I believed that the complaint was justified, that the man's death had been my fault.

I was a bad person.

MY PHONE RANG. I looked down. It was Grant calling.

I ignored it and, after a while, it stopped.

The time readout on the phone showed it was 04:50.

What was Grant doing up at ten to five in the morning?

For that matter, what was I doing up?

After a few minutes the phone started ringing again. I went on ignoring it and after six rings it stopped once more. It rang again—six more rings, then it would go to voice mail. It stopped.

Beep-beep.

A text arrived. It was from Grant.

"My darling, PLEASE, PLEASE answer your phone."

I was sitting in my Mini. I had been all night.

I couldn't remember driving out of the hospital parking lot. In fact, I couldn't really remember driving at all but I must have. How else could I have come to be where I was?

And where was I?

I looked out through the windshield, past the raindrops on the glass to the view beyond.

Some rightly say that Clifton Suspension Bridge is the most beautiful creation of Isambard Kingdom Brunel although, in truth, it wasn't completed until five years after his death to the final design of two different civil engineers, and only based on Brunel's original.

But it certainly looked magnificent to me now, dimly lit only by occasional streetlights at this time of the morning. The bridge spans 702 feet across the Avon Gorge, crossing some 245 feet above the river surface. It said so on a notice near one end.

What was I doing here?

I had asked myself that question at least a hundred times.

Did I really intend to throw myself off?

That had been my plan, and that was why I'd driven more than an hour from Cheltenham to get here. I had even walked across the bridge, searching for the best place to go over the side, the place from where death would be most certain, most instant.

Was 245 feet high enough?

Surely it was, especially if I landed on the rocks rather than in the water.

But I had been back in the car now for the last six hours, just sitting here churning things over and over in my head, trying desperately to make sense of my life—or my death.

It wasn't that I was frightened of dying. I was much more frightened of living, of having to face up to what was happening to me.

The phone rang again.

This time, almost automatically, I picked it up and answered. "Hello."

"Oh, thank God! Thank God!" Grant wailed from the other end. He was crying. "Where are you?"

"Bristol."

"Bristol! What are you doing in Bristol?"

"Looking at Clifton Suspension Bridge."

The significance wasn't lost on him.

"Oh my God, Chris!" he screamed. "Don't do anything. Just stay calm. Please, my darling, don't do anything! Think of the boys. I'm on my way."

He disconnected.

Strange, I thought. He didn't ask me why.

I got out of my Mini and leaned against it, stretching away the kinks in my spine. I could do with a cigarette but I'd smoked my last one at least an hour ago.

The phone rang once more. It was Grant again.

"I'm in the car on my way to you," he said breathlessly. "Please, my love . . . don't . . ." It was a desperate plea.

"I'm fine," I said. "Don't kill yourself on the roads trying to get here too fast."

I inwardly laughed at the irony of what I'd just said.

But, if I were going to jump, I'd have probably done it by now.

"I'm fine," I said again, feeling dreadfully weak at the knees. "Please just come and get me."

A police car came hurtling around the corner with its blue lights flashing. Someone else was also having a bad day, I thought, but the car pulled up next to me and two young policemen climbed out.

"Are you Christine Rankin?" one of them asked.

I nodded, unable to speak from emotion and with tears streaming down my face.

I was saved—I was safe.

At least for the time being.

5

I spent the next four hours confined in a police cell at Bristol Police Station.

"But I've done nothing wrong," I complained.

"It's for your own protection," they said. "It won't be for long. We've sent for a doctor."

I sat on the solid concrete bed and stared at the stark gray walls. How perfectly they summed up my life.

For the last year, I may have been walking around and seemingly living a normal existence, but, inside, I was locked into a gray prison cell—closed in by four great walls created by my own consciousness. I was trapped and, like in the nightmare, the four walls were getting ever closer. I felt I could easily reach out and touch them all at once. One day soon they would undoubtedly squeeze the very breath from my body.

Grant arrived before the doctor, but, even so, not until nine-thirty.

"I'm sorry I've been so long," he said. "I had to get the boys ready for school and also arrange a day off from work."

I was not much placated. "You said you were on your way here over four hours ago."

"I know I did. I'm sorry." He was embarrassed. "I did set out to come but I also called the police and begged them to go and find you. I was still in Cheltenham when they called me back to tell me they had found you and you were all right." He was almost in tears. "So I went back home to see to the boys."

I sighed.

"What did you tell them?"

"I said that you'd had to stay at the hospital for an emergency."

"How did you know that I hadn't?" I asked.

"I woke just before five and you weren't in the bed. I tried calling your phone but you didn't answer, so I called the hospital. Someone told me you hadn't been working and you'd been sent home at seven o'clock last night. That made me desperately worried and very frightened."

Now he *was* in tears.

"Please take me home," I said.

"I can't. We have to wait for the doctor."

"I'm perfectly OK. I don't want to see another doctor."

"Darling, you're not OK. You just tried to commit suicide."

"I did not," I said indignantly. "If I *had* tried, I would be dead already. I admit that I did think about it but I didn't do it. I'm fine."

He shook his head. "Chris, you are not fine. You're just skin and bone. You won't eat. You don't sleep. You don't talk to me. You've cut yourself off from all our friends. You don't even speak to your mother anymore. You need help."

"What I *need* is to go home."

WE DID GO HOME but not until the afternoon, after I'd been seen by not one but two doctors.

Both of them recommended sending me to a psychiatric hospital.

"Why?" I asked them.

"For your own safety."

"But I am perfectly safe with my husband looking after me."

However, my husband wasn't so sure.

"Maybe it would be for the best to do as the doctors ask," he said.

"No. I want to go home."

The doctors had a conference between just the two of them.

I was worried.

I was all too aware that they had the ability to detain me against my will under the terms of the Mental Health Act. I had even occasionally used the powers myself for seriously disturbed patients, especially those brought in after self-harming. It is known colloquially as being "sectioned" because it refers to the various "sections" of the Act that allow for compulsory hospital treatment for individuals considered to be a danger to themselves or to others.

"Don't let them force me to go," I said urgently to Grant. "You are what is officially known as my Nearest Relative and you have the power to prevent it." I could tell that I was putting him in a difficult situation. "I promise not to do anything like this again." I grabbed his hand. "Darling, please!"

He looked at me.

"But you don't keep your promises," he said. "You're always promising that you will eat something but then you don't. So why should I believe you this time?"

"You must." I was almost begging. "I didn't do anything, did I? I would never do that to the boys."

Grant shook his head and, not for the first time, I wondered if he was on my side.

The doctors finished their discussion.

"It is our joint opinion," one of them said, "that you should be in the hospital. Are you prepared to be admitted as a voluntary patient?"

"No," I replied.

"Then we consider that you should be detained for assessment under Section 2 of the Mental Health Act."

"My husband is my Nearest Relative and he disagrees."

I stared imploringly at Grant and he looked long and hard at me then turned to the doctors.

"I am prepared to take Chris home with me and look after her there. I will ensure that she sees her psychiatrist as soon as possible."

The doctors would have known as well as I did that the patient's Nearest Relative could discharge a patient detained under Section 2 unless there were overpowering reasons why they should not. I couldn't think that any such overpowering reasons would exist in this case. It wasn't as if I'd threatened to harm any other person.

"I didn't actually attempt to kill myself, did I?" I said quickly. "I accept that I did think about it, but then I decided not to. So I am clearly not a danger to myself or anyone else."

They didn't look particularly convinced but the doctors and police finally agreed to leave me in Grant's care provided we signed some paperwork to the effect that we had both noted their advice and decided not to follow it.

GRANT DROVE HOME mostly in silence, no doubt worrying if he had done the right thing.

"Thank you," I said.

He didn't reply. He just shook his head slightly and appeared to concentrate hard on the road ahead.

I had been expecting the third degree, starting with *Why weren't you at work last night?* but there was nothing. In truth, he must already know. The complaint had only been the catalyst. The real reason was the mental-health issue and Grant knew from experience to tread carefully around that.

We stopped only once, at a motorway service station, to pick up a late lunch—a ham sandwich for him and a lentil salad for me that I didn't really want, or eat.

"What about my car?" I asked as we turned back onto the motorway.

"I brought Trevor with me from work. He picked it up using the spare keys."

My Mini was already in Gotherington when we arrived but it wasn't the only vehicle waiting for us outside our house. There was also a police car parked on the road, and a man in civilian clothes climbed out as we pulled into the driveway.

"What does he want?" Grant said with a degree of irritation in his voice.

I was worried that the Bristol police had changed their minds about allowing me home with Grant but it wasn't that.

"Dr. Rankin?" the man asked as we climbed out of the Audi.

"Yes." Grant and I both answered together. He was a doctor too, with a Ph.D. in mechanical engineering.

"Dr. Christine Rankin?"

"That's me," I said.

"My name is Detective Sergeant Merryweather." He briefly held up a police identity card. "I would like to ask you some questions concerning a man found unconscious at the racecourse on Saturday evening who subsequently died at the hospital under your care."

I didn't know whether to run away or to hold my wrists out for the handcuffs.

"Of course," I said, trying to keep the nervousness and panic out of my voice. "Come on in."

The three of us went into the sitting room and sat down.

"How can I help?" I said.

"We are treating this as an unexplained death," said the policeman. "We have had the preliminary results of the autopsy that was carried out early this morning. There was no cause of death given in the report, so we will have to wait for further analysis of the samples taken. But one of our constables told me that you did some blood tests while the man was still alive."

I nodded. "PC Filippos."

"Yes, that's right. He also said that you mentioned the possibility of a cocaine overdose."

I nodded again. "One of my colleagues told me that the blood test showed cocaine in the man's system. I didn't actually see the results myself."

I'd been too busy dealing with the sick and injured on Saturday night and had intended to look at them on Sunday evening, but other events had overtaken me.

"Could you get those test results for me?" asked the detective sergeant, "and also copies of the man's medical file?"

"Can't you get them yourself, direct from the hospital?"

"We only have your name as a contact and the hospital told us you were not working today. I have learned from experience that it is far better to approach a named individual than to try to navigate my way through health-service bureaucracy." He looked at me and raised his eyebrows.

"I'll see what I can do," I said. Not necessarily that easy when I was suspended from duty and barred from entering the hospital, but I wasn't going to mention that if he didn't. "Is that all?"

"No, not quite," said the policeman. "We are still having difficulty putting a name to the dead man and wondered if you had any further clues to his identity."

"Like what?" I asked.

"Did you remove anything from him that could assist us? An identification bracelet or other jewelry, for example?"

I shook my head. "There was nothing at all on him. PC Filippos said that he had searched the man's pockets while he'd been waiting for the ambulance. He took away the man's clothes and shoes after he died."

"Yes, I am aware of that. We have someone trying to ascertain where the clothes were bought. They don't appear to have been available for sale in this country."

"Have you checked a list of people who are missing?" I asked.

DS Merryweather looked at me as if I were an imbecile.

"That was our first line of inquiry. His DNA profile, photo, dental details and fingerprints have also been sent to Interpol and Europol but nothing has turned up so far."

I felt sorry for the poor fingerprint officer, who must have had to take the dabs from the dead man's digits.

"How about the betting slip?"

"The betting slip?"

"PC Filippos told me that the man had had a crumpled-up betting slip in his pocket. Have you asked the bookmaker?"

"Not yet." He wrote something in his notebook. "Do you happen to know the bookmaker's name?"

"No, but it should be printed on the slip. They all are these days."

He wrote it down then looked up at me.

"Can you tell us anything else about the man that might be useful?"

I thought back to Saturday evening. The details were clearly etched in my memory. I had spent much of the previous night in Bristol going over and over the events of those hours, wondering if I should have done anything differently.

"I'm sorry," I said. "He was in a coma when he arrived at the hospital and he never regained consciousness. Prior to the blood-test results, he gave all the indications of suffering from SVT—supraventricular tachycardia—and that is how we were treating him when I was called away by the arrival of two motorcyclists severely injured in a road-traffic accident. The man died shortly after that."

He nodded as if he knew. Then he stood up.

"Thank you for your time, Dr. Rankin." He handed me a business card with his contact details. "Please give me a call when you have the blood-test results or if you think of anything else that might be useful."

Grant showed him out of the house while I remained sitting on the sofa, shaking.

I had quite expected to be arrested.

The police obviously didn't know about my suspension from work or else they wouldn't have asked me to obtain the test results. Maybe they didn't believe I was responsible for the man's death. Or were they just waiting for the postmortem toxicology results?

As was I.

I SPENT THE REST OF THE DAY in bed. Not that I was able to sleep.

I should have been tired. I had dozed a little during the night and for the last half hour on the drive home but it had been thirty hours since I'd got up on Sunday morning. Somehow, it seemed longer.

The twins came home on the school bus at four-thirty and both of them came up to tell me about their day. They thought nothing of the fact that their mother was in bed in the middle of the afternoon. They were well used to me working shifts, leaving, returning and sleeping at odd times. Needless to say, I didn't enlighten them that I hadn't been at the hospital the previous night.

"So what did you learn at school today?" I asked them.

"Nothing," Oliver said. It was his usual reply to my common question.

"I did," Toby chipped in. "I learned that Mr. Harris can tell us apart."

"How do you know?" I asked.

"Well," he said rather sheepishly, "me and Olly sometimes swap, like."

"Olly and I," I corrected.

"Yeah, right." He made a silly face. "So me and Olly always swap PE and art on Mondays. I hate art and he can't stand PE, like, so we just swap. No one notices."

"Except Mr. Harris?" I said.

"Yeah. He grabbed me today in PE and said that he knew that I was Toby when I should have been Olly. Of course, I told him he was wrong, like, but he put his finger up against his nose and winked at me."

"He must have been guessing," Oliver said. "I assume you had my gear on."

"Yeah, of course." Their school PE gear had to have large

nametapes sewn on the outside to prevent "borrowing." "But he kept calling me Toby and told me not to do it again next week."

"Do you swap a lot?" I asked.

"All the time," Oliver said with a huge grin. "It's fun."

Physically, the twins were almost truly identical. Even I had difficulty telling them apart unless they were both together in front of me. Toby's left ear stuck out very slightly more from his head than Oliver's, due, I'd been told, to the position he had been lying in my womb when his ear had developed. Other than that I reckoned they were indistinguishable.

Mr. Harris must know something I didn't.

The boys went off, supposedly to do their homework but I knew that they would be playing computer games online first. Only when it was time for bed would they moan that they still had their work to do.

I smiled.

I had been just the same when I was their age, although I'd have been lucky to be allowed to play Pong on an Atari games console plugged into the back of the family television rather than on the ultra-HD virtual-world headsets with interactive surround sound that they had now.

I rolled over in the bed and thought about the boys some more.

They had turned fourteen in September, an age at which, I was reliably informed, they would instantly transform from the sweet and adorable children I knew and loved into spotty, rude and opinionated monsters that are all modern teenagers.

"Good luck," a friend had said to me last year. "I've only got one boy and he's a nightmare. You're in for twice as much. It's the surly behavior and answering back that I can't stand. It always ends in rows and name-calling. And he's now got piercings in his lips and even a dragon tattoo on his arm."

She had shuddered in disgust.

So far, clearly, Grant and I had been lucky. Or maybe our intentional plan of letting the boys have increasingly greater freedom was working. One of my therapists told me that most teenagers want to sack their parents from the job they have done in the past, only to rehire them a few years later, but as consultants, not managers—all the while maintaining their current account at the family bank.

But whatever our plan, I suppose we had been fortunate that our boys hadn't fallen in with a bad crowd where drugs were prevalent.

Drugs.

Cocaine.

The unnamed man.

Anywhere I might try to turn my thoughts, they always twisted back like a magnet in a solenoid. I was becoming almost obsessive about it.

Who was he? And why did he die?

6

At Grant's insistence, I remained in bed for most of Tuesday. I think he believed it was the right thing for me but it just gave my mind the time and space to worry about every conceivable minor family problem, as well as some of the world's major ones.

I was actually better when I was *doing* something.

Grant had taken a second day off work even though I'd told him it was unnecessary.

"I need to look after you," he said.

Keep an eye on me more like, I thought, in case I decided to disappear off to Bristol once more. But the aching desire to harm myself had subsided during that long night at the bridge, at least for the time being, so I didn't put up a fight. I simply stayed in bed as he requested.

However, on Wednesday morning, with some trepidation, Grant went back to work.

"You stay here all day," he instructed before he left. "I'm taking your car keys with me."

"But I need the car. I have an appointment with Stephen Butler."

Stephen Butler was my psychiatrist and Grant had given an

assurance to the Bristol doctors that he would get me to see my psychiatrist as soon as possible.

"Can't you get a taxi?"

"Grant, don't be ridiculous. I'm quite capable of driving."

I held my hand out for the keys and, reluctantly, he handed them over.

"Please, be careful," he said. "Don't do anything stupid."

As if I would.

I DON'T THINK Jeremy Cook was pleased to hear from me when I called him at eleven. After all, it had been he who had spilled the beans to the Medical Director that I'd been hiding in the linen cupboard.

"Ah, hello, Chris," he said when I called him, the embarrassment thick in his voice. "How are you doing?"

"Fine, thank you, Jeremy."

"How can I help?" he asked.

Help? I thought. That's a laugh. He'd hardly been much help so far.

"I need some information for the police," I said.

"The police?"

"Yes, a policeman came to my home on Monday and asked me to get him the blood-test results and a copy of the medical file for the man who died in the department on Saturday evening. Do you remember?"

"Yes," Jeremy replied. "The man with no name."

"Exactly. Normally I would come in and get the results myself, but, as you must know, I have been barred from entering the hospital."

That did nothing to lower the level of Jeremy's awkwardness.

"Why don't the police go direct to the hospital administration?" he asked.

"I have no idea," I said. "But they've asked me to get them instead. You're on ten till six today, right?"

"Yes."

"Good. Make copies and I'll collect them from you in an hour. I can't come in, so bring them out to me." I wasn't giving him a chance to refuse. "I'll be outside the main entrance in a light blue Mini."

"OK," he said unsurely. "If I'm not too busy."

"If you are, send somebody else out. I've told the police that I'll get everything to them by half past twelve today."

"OK," he said again. "In an hour, you say?"

"Yes. Can you make the copies straightaway?" I asked.

"I suppose so," he replied.

"Good. See you in a bit."

I hung up before he had a chance to change his mind.

It wasn't only the police who wanted to see those blood results. I was pretty interested in them too.

JEREMY COOK appeared right on cue dressed, as always, in physicians' blue scrubs. He looked around, saw me and rushed over and thrust a buff folder through the open car window.

"Must dash," he said. "There's a suspected myocardial infarction arriving in two minutes."

He hurried back inside without another word—and no awkward questions. Never before have I been pleased that someone was having a heart attack. As I drove out onto College Road an ambulance came the other way, lights flashing and siren blaring. Jeremy Cook was welcome to it.

I parked in a side street in Montpelier near the Queens Hotel and picked up the folder. My hands were shaking.

Jeremy had been busy. The folder contained not just the blood-test results and the medical file for the time when the man was alive, but also the preliminary report of the postmortem examination of his body.

I had told Jeremy I'd promised to get everything to the police by twelve-thirty but that had been just a little white lie to encourage him to make the copies. I had all the time I needed to study them.

It was the blood results I was most interested in.

I stared at the paper with my heart racing and there it was in black-and-white.

Cocaine.

The blood-plasma concentration was 0.7 milligrams of cocaine per liter. Normally a minimum reading of at least 1.4 was required to be considered a lethal dose but, assuming the man had been several hours in the lavatory cubicle before being found, the initial dose would have been much higher. Cocaine has a blood metabolic half-life of about ninety minutes. So, in a three-hour period, the level would have dropped to only one-quarter of the original. In four and a half hours it would only be one-eighth.

However, it was the level of benzoylecgonine, or BZG, in the blood that was the real clincher. BZG is the primary metabolite of cocaine and it has a much greater half-life, remaining in the system long after the drug itself has ceased to be detectable. It is BZG excreted in urine that is used by the police or employers to give a positive test for cocaine. Scientists even monitor the concentration of BZG in the River Thames as a means of estimating the amount of cocaine consumed by the population of London.

In this particular case, the BZG in the man's blood was over

8 milligrams per liter, indicating an initial cocaine dose several times greater than that required to kill him.

The junior doctor had been right: there was nothing we could have done to save him. The only surprising thing was that, given the levels, he had been still alive when he'd arrived at the hospital.

So I hadn't killed him. Giving the adenosine had made no difference to the outcome.

I suppose I should have been elated, but, in truth, I just felt empty.

I looked up from the papers and watched as a young mother came along the sidewalk with a tiny newborn strapped to her chest. It gave me an enormous pang of regret. Our baby would have been a few months old by now—if only I had managed to get pregnant.

I forced my eyes back down and glanced through the autopsy report.

It only showed preliminary results but did reveal that no puncture marks had been found in the man's skin, other than the one we had made in his elbow to take blood and administer the adenosine. A dip test of urine found in the bladder had confirmed the presence of a high concentration of benzoylecgonine, confirming the existence of a large dose of cocaine in the man's system.

The pathologist suggested that, most probably, the cocaine had been ingested orally, as he found no evidence of powder in the nasal passages, and no residues in the lungs as might be expected if that much of the drug had been smoked. He had sent samples for analysis taken from the lungs and stomach to confirm this opinion, along with other specimens from the man's liver, kidneys, heart and brain. A sample of hair had also been acquired to establish if there was a history of prolonged illegal drug use.

As DS Merryweather had indicated, there was no definitive cause of death recorded in the report even though the pathologist did hint that the urine dip test made it likely that a cocaine overdose was the culprit. His final conclusions would only be made on completion of the toxicology tests.

I put the papers back in the folder and placed it down on the passenger seat. For some considerable time I simply stared out the windshield, drops of fine rain periodically marking the outside of the glass.

Why did I worry so much about this man?

Sadly, death in a hospital was not uncommon. Dealing with the dying was one of the pitfalls of being an emergency-care doctor. Strokes and heart attacks were the most common causes. Accident victims who arrived alive mostly stayed that way, at least until they had passed through to specialist surgical teams. Nevertheless, I had witnessed hundreds, if not thousands, of my patients as they took their last breath and their lives literally slipped away through my fingers.

Not that I had become immune and unaffected by the process of death, especially if the victim was a young adult or, worse, a child. Over the years, I had shed more than my share of grief-driven tears for those I had never known before they had arrived in front of me with non-survivable injuries or untreatable disease.

Some of my colleagues tried to grow a thicker skin or build a shell of indifference around themselves, anything to allow them to continue to function when the natural instinct was to simply close one's eyes and run away.

But there was something about the death of this particular man that troubled me.

Maybe it was because no one knew who he was—his wife and family would still be unaware that their husband and father had ceased to exist nearly four days ago. Or perhaps it was that, in my experience, smartly groomed men in sober suits rarely presented at the hospital with massive cocaine overdoses.

Had he overdosed on purpose in order to kill himself, or had it been an accident? A cubicle in a men's room seemed a strange place to commit suicide, but who was I to talk? Was it really any more strange than the rocks below Clifton Suspension Bridge? Was shattering one's body with a high-speed fall in a public place somehow preferable to privately swallowing a cocaine-laced sandwich in a locked lavatory?

If one was so desperate to die, did the manner or the venue matter?

But, if the man *had* killed himself, why did he dispose of any form of identification beforehand? I knew that many suicides go to great lengths to ensure that their loved ones are not the first to stumble across their lifeless corpse. Did this man simply want to die without his family ever finding out?

It sounded like a sensible idea to me.

I READ THROUGH ALL THE PAPERS twice more before driving to Cheltenham Police Station and parking in one of the visitor spaces around the back.

DS Merryweather had asked me to phone him when I had the blood-test results but I had no real desire to speak to him again. I decided I would just hand in the folder at the reception desk, marked for his attention, and then leave. But it didn't quite work out like that.

"Dr. Rankin," called out a voice behind me as I climbed the three steps up to the back door of the police station. I turned around.

"PC Filippos," said a young uniformed officer. "We met at the hospital last Saturday."

"Yes," I said, nodding. "You're half Greek."

He smiled broadly at me, clearly pleased I'd remembered. "Can I help you?"

"I have a folder for DS Merryweather." I held it out. "Could you please give it to him?"

"Sure," he said, taking it. "Are these the blood-test results for the nameless man?"

I nodded again. "Have you still not found out who he is?"

"Not yet but I'm sure we will eventually."

"Did you find anything at the racecourse?"

He looked at me quizzically.

"On Saturday night, after the man died, you told me you were going back to the racecourse to search the men's room where he was found."

"Ah, yes," he said. "So I did."

"So what did you find?" I asked again.

"Not a lot. There was nothing in the cubicle and mostly just paper towels in the trash can by the washbasins."

"Mostly?"

"There was also some other general waste, you know, a few newspapers, a couple of discarded racing programs, some torn-up betting slips and one of those small flat quarter bottles of whisky."

I thought back to the slight smell of alcohol that had been present on the man's breath at the hospital. It could have been whisky.

"The man had definitely had a drink of alcohol at some stage. Have you checked the bottle for his fingerprints?"

It was clear from his expression that he hadn't.

"And did you test the contents?"

"It was empty."

"There must have been some residue left," I said. "According to his report, the pathologist thinks the cocaine was probably ingested orally. I wonder if it was in the whisky."

"Can you put cocaine in whisky?" he asked.

"Sure," I said. "It will dissolve in almost any liquid. I remember a case a few years back when someone drank rum laced with cocaine. It killed him."

"Are you serious?"

"Deadly serious," I said. "A man dissolved a large quantity of cocaine in a bottle of rum to smuggle it into the UK. His girlfriend carried it because he claimed he was over the duty-free limit but the man was stopped by customs and the girlfriend gave up waiting. She gave the bottle to a taxi driver without realizing its contents were lethal and he died after drinking a single shot."

"Couldn't he taste it?"

"Obviously not. Probably knocked it back in one go. And that's not the only time. Someone else died drinking pear juice laced with cocaine, again after it was smuggled into the country."

"But how can you get it back out of the liquid?"

"Simple," I said. "Gently evaporate it in a saucepan and you'll be left with the cocaine powder at the bottom."

"So you think our nameless man was a smuggler?"

"No," I said. "I didn't say that. I'm simply asking whether you've tested the whisky bottle as the possible source. Have you still got it?"

"Yes," he said with certainty. "Everything was bagged up."

I suddenly felt dreadfully light-headed and rocked slightly, grabbing hold of the handrail.

"Are you all right, Dr. Rankin?" PC Filippos asked. "You've gone very pale."

"I'm fine," I said automatically.

I was always *fine*.

But, in truth, this time I was far from feeling fine. I was dizzy, shaky and I couldn't focus my eyes properly. In fact, I was very close to passing out altogether. I slumped farther against the handrail and only the policeman's strong arms of the law stopped me falling over completely.

"I'm sorry," I mumbled. "Must be something I ate." Even though I doubted that. I hadn't eaten anything at all since the previous evening and, even then, I had only consumed a reduced-calorie cup of vegetable soup.

"Come on," he said, holding me tightly around my waist, "let's get you inside and sat down."

He all but carried me through the door of the police station. One of his colleagues rushed to help and, between them, they lifted me onto an upright chair in the reception area.

"I'll call an ambulance," said the colleague.

"No," I said, trying but failing to be forceful. "No ambulance."

I'd have had more chance of holding back the tide.

7

I was currently banned from entering Cheltenham General Hospital in the role of a clinician but, sadly, not as a patient.

However, my first embarrassment was that I knew the ambulance crew—I had seen them often at the hospital as they'd delivered other people.

"Hello, Dr. Rankin," one of them said cheerfully when he saw me sitting in the police station reception, "I'm Derek. What seems to be the problem?"

"There's no problem," I said. "I'm fine. Lot of fuss about nothing."

"Let me be the judge of that," Derek replied with a smile, crouching down to be on my level. There was something very reassuring about his manner—confident and in control. I leaned my head back against the wall and decided not to fight him. "Let's get you into the ambulance and do some tests."

The two paramedics lifted me onto an upright wheeled chair and took me out to their vehicle.

"I'll be in touch," PC Filippos said as he held the door open for us.

I nodded weakly at him. I really didn't feel very well at all.

My skin was clammy and I could feel more palpitations in my chest.

Doctors are notoriously bad at self-diagnosis, only surpassed by the general population at large, who predictably diagnose a bout of indigestion as a life-threatening heart attack and a blocked sweat gland as terminal skin cancer. Doctors, however, tend to err the other way, dismissing potentially serious symptoms in themselves as trivial when they wouldn't hesitate to refer to a specialist any patient presenting to them in a similar condition.

However, all of that notwithstanding, I had a pretty good idea what was wrong with me—lack of food resulting in blood-sugar levels that were too low.

Maybe skipping lunch, after having had no breakfast, hadn't been such a good idea after all.

In the ambulance I was wired up to their ECG machine. I was not having a heart attack, Derek assured me. I knew that. But, nevertheless, the trace was somewhat irregular from the palpitations.

"Blood sugar," I said. "It's probably too low."

"Are you diabetic?" Derek asked seriously.

"No. I'm not. But I haven't eaten much today."

In fact, I hadn't had as much as a cup of tea in the preceding twenty hours.

"Tut-tut," Derek said. "You should know better than that."

I did know better than that. I also knew that I was starving myself and that I desperately needed to consume more food, but it was as if I needed to get to the bottom of what was happening to me before I could start eating again. Not that I even knew where the bottom was, or whether I would realize it when I got there.

Grant urged me to eat all the time. Indeed, he begged me to.

But it wasn't as simple as just doing it.

There was a voice inside me that wouldn't allow it.

And I was terrified that, once I started eating, I wouldn't be able to stop and I would grow fatter and fatter until I became a completely round blob like Violet Beauregarde in *Charlie and the Chocolate Factory*.

Or perhaps, by continuing not to eat, I felt that I was still in some sort of control of what was happening to me. By selecting where and when I swallowed even the smallest amount of sustenance, was I trying to convince myself that I remained on top of my emotions and in charge of my life?

Maybe I even believed it.

However, my psychiatrist was alarmed that what had been an initial show of self-discipline and control had developed into a full-blown eating disorder.

"Don't be silly," I'd told him with a nervous laugh. "Surely anorexia is for teenage girls."

But the doctor in me knew that wasn't true. Loads of middle-aged women suffered from anorexia, and specialist eating-disorder wards in psychiatric hospitals were full of them.

But I was surely far from being one of those.

I was fat.

You only had to look at me to see that. So what that Grant said I was just skin and bone? I saw myself as fat and ugly.

"Fifty-five," Derek said, reading from the blood-glucose monitor. "Far too low. No wonder you're feeling faint and having palpitations."

He dug around in one of the ambulance's many lockers and produced a high-energy banana milk shake, chockablock with added sugar.

"Here," he said, tearing off the top of the carton and holding it out to me, "drink this."

I pushed it away.

"Come on, Dr. Rankin, please drink it," he said. "Your blood-sugar figure is dangerously low."

I took the carton and put it to my lips but there was no way I was going to tip it. I tried but I couldn't. The voice inside my head was now shouting, ordering me not to, and it was simply too strong to overcome.

"If you won't drink it, I'll have to put you on an IV glucose drip," Derek warned, almost aggressively. "Do you really want that?"

Not particularly, I thought, but, even so, there was no way I was going to swallow his sickly sweet banana concoction. It would have made me retch.

Derek was still encouraging me to consume his poison when we arrived at the hospital, but, far from that being the end of my troubles, it was only the beginning.

Things at that point descended from being bad to worse, much worse.

MAYBE IT WAS just fellow-professional courtesy, but I was taken straight through without waiting into Resus, that part of the emergency department where serious trauma and other life-threatening conditions were treated.

It was my customary place of work and I was among my usual colleagues; however, far from feeling relaxed in familiar surroundings, I was self-conscious, ashamed and humiliated.

A senior staff nurse, the very individual I suspected of making the formal complaint against me, was now the person wiring

ECG electrodes on my chest to the monitoring equipment. She did it without saying anything and with minimal eye contact. Maybe she was embarrassed too.

One of the other nurses took my right index finger and pricked it with a needle to get the drop of blood required for another blood-sugar test.

Then I was left alone in the cubicle lying on the hospital gurney, with the blue privacy curtains drawn around me.

The time seemed to drag but it must have been only a few minutes before Jeremy Cook appeared, sticking his head through a gap in the curtains.

"Hello, Chris." He said it almost with a sigh. "How can I help?"

"You can't," I said, swinging my legs over the side of the gurney. "I'm grateful for your concern, Jeremy, but I really don't need your help. I've no idea why I was brought here. I was a bit dizzy, that's all. I just needed a little sit-down."

He definitely sighed this time. "Your blood sugar."

"What about it?" I asked.

"It's dangerously low."

"That's simply because I didn't have breakfast and ran out of time for lunch," I said in my best "Don't make a fuss" voice. I even forced a laugh. "I'm sure it'll be back to normal this evening after my first glass of red wine."

He sighed again and shook his head.

"Don't lie to me, Chris," Jeremy said. "We've known each other for too long." He paused. "I've just been speaking to Grant."

"Oh," I said, understanding the significance. "Is he here?"

"No, I called him at work. He's on his way over here now. You stay right where you are until he arrives. In the meantime, I'm going to give you an injection of glucagon."

Glucagon was a glucose-increasing hormone. Many insulin-dependent diabetics have a preloaded self-injector of the stuff readily available just in case they suffer a "hypo," a sudden drop in blood sugar that, if left untreated, could rapidly lead to coma and death.

He held up the syringe in his right hand.

"Is that really necessary?" I asked.

"Not if you will eat this." He held up a chocolate bar in his left.

I shook my head and said nothing. I just stared at him.

He stuck the needle into my arm and, after a while, I did begin to feel a little better.

GRANT ARRIVED AT THE HOSPITAL about half an hour later but he wasn't alone. Stephen Butler, my psychiatrist, was with him. The two of them came into the cubicle with Jeremy Cook.

"I have an appointment to see you later today," I said to Stephen with a laugh.

"I know," he replied without a trace of humor. "Grant called me and explained the situation, so I came over now."

"What situation?" I said. "I just felt a bit dizzy, that's all."

Grant was staring down, saying nothing.

Stephen sat on a chair next to me and took my hand.

"Chris," he said. "We are all very concerned about you."

"You don't have to be. I'm fine."

I sounded like a broken record—I'm fine . . . I'm fine . . . I'm fine . . .

"You are not fine," Stephen said emphatically. "I've been talking to Dr. Cook and also to Grant. He has told me all about your trip to Bristol on Sunday night."

I looked across at Grant but he was still resolutely studying the blue vinyl floor.

Stephen went on. "He also tells me that you still won't eat anything and that it is getting worse. You have already lost far too much weight. Starving yourself is very dangerous, Chris, and Dr. Cook is very worried that you are putting your heart under undue strain. You need to eat. You *have* to take in more energy simply to stay alive."

"I have plenty of energy," I laughed. "I'm hardly fading away, am I? I'm still far too fat."

"You are not fat," Stephen said in an uncharacteristic moment of irritation. He collected himself. "Chris, listen to me. By not eating, you are seriously endangering your life. Your husband and your boys love you, and they don't want to lose you. Do you understand?"

He had been more talkative in the last few minutes than he had been in all the nine months I had been going to see him.

"Do you understand?" he said again.

"Yes," I replied, but I'm not sure I did. Surely I was not so ill that my husband and psychiatrist had to come rushing to see me in A&E. I had only felt a bit dizzy.

"Good," Stephen said. "Because Grant, Dr. Cook and I consider that it would be best if you were admitted to the hospital for a while. Just long enough to get you sorted."

Hospital? I was not sure I was hearing him right.

"This hospital?" I asked blankly.

"No, Chris. Not this one. We think you should go to Wotton Lawn."

Wotton Lawn was the acute mental-health hospital for Gloucestershire.

"No," I said firmly. "I don't need to go there."

"We think you do."

"Well, I'm not going." I was adamant.

Stephen was very calm. "We consider that it is essential for your own protection. I have already spoken to Wotton Lawn and they have a bed waiting for you in their eating-disorder unit. If you won't go voluntarily, you *will* be sectioned under the Mental Health Act, 1983."

I looked again at Grant but he steadfastly refused to meet my eye.

I could feel the anger rising again, grabbing me by the throat and trying to suffocate me.

How could Grant agree to this?

He knew how I hated the prospect of being a patient in a hospital.

"Grant!" I shouted at him. "Help me."

He finally looked up. There were tears in his eyes.

"I am *trying* to help you," he said.

I now wished that I *had* jumped off Clifton Suspension Bridge.

PART 2

MARCH

8

The arrival of March was always an exciting time in Cheltenham.

Everyone had only one thing on their mind—the annual Cheltenham Racing Festival. Four days of exhilarating action on the hallowed track at Prestbury Park when the stars of both Irish and English steeplechasing came together to establish who were the champions.

The Grand National might be the most famous steeplechase in the world, but, for horseracing folk, owning, training or riding a winner at the Cheltenham Festival would be the defining achievement of their careers, with the Gold Cup, on the final afternoon, being the really *big one*—at three and a quarter miles over twenty-two fences, with all the horses carrying the same weight, it was the true championship race.

Every hotel within fifty miles of the racecourse was fully booked months in advance, many by the tide of Irish punters that surged across the sea each year to gamble extensively, consume huge quantities of Guinness and cheer home their equine idols.

"So, Dr. Rankin, you can act as a racecourse medical officer for the Festival next week?"

"Yes," I said excitedly. "I can."

I was on the phone to the Clerk of the Course at Cheltenham. He had called me in some agitation on behalf of the senior racecourse medical officer. It seemed that one of their regular doctors, who had already been signed up, had carelessly collided with a tree while on a skiing holiday in the French Alps and had broken his right leg in six places. He was currently laid up in traction at the Hospital Center De Moûtiers, and was likely to remain so for the foreseeable future.

"Er," said the Clerk of the Course uneasily, "I'm afraid there is one question I am required to ask you."

"Go ahead," I said.

"If I remember rightly, I couldn't use you for the International meeting in December because you were suspended from your usual employment and therefore unavailable under the racing authority rules. Is that still the case?"

"No," I said. "It is not still the case."

There was a sigh of relief from the other end of the line. "Good," he said. "I thought so because you are back on the Authority's list of approved medics."

That was reassuring.

"I will send you all the details straightaway. Usual e-mail address?"

"Yes," I said. "Thank you."

He disconnected.

I sat calmly at the kitchen table and drank my coffee. Was this another example of my life returning to some degree of normality?

I sincerely hoped so.

———

GOING INTO WOTTON LAWN the previous November had been a nightmare but, in truth, it was only an extension to the nightmare that my life had already become.

Deep down inside I knew that the hospital *was* the best place for me, but that didn't stop me fighting against it.

I was angry and I took out my frustration on everything and everyone.

I shouted. I screamed. I even tried to run away.

I threatened to kill myself and was placed on a twenty-four-hour suicide watch.

They locked me in my room and tried to force me to eat three meals a day. Then they watched me like hawks to ensure I didn't nip off to the bathroom to throw the food back up again.

About the only thing they didn't do was truss me up in a straitjacket.

And I wouldn't have blamed them if they had.

I was what was known as a *difficult patient*.

I refused to attend the group therapy sessions and the first person I would speak to was Stephen Butler when he came to see me on the third day.

I quite expected him to tell me off for being so bloody tiresome but he didn't. Instead, as usual, he just listened tolerantly as I prattled on for ten minutes or more about how awful it was in there and how nasty the staff were to me.

"But what is the alternative?" he asked when I finally ran out of steam. "You claim you will kill yourself but do you really want to die? Do you want Grant and the boys to have to go on living without you? Do you think they would ever forgive you for being so selfish?"

That shut me up.

Maybe he *was* telling me off after all.

The trouble was that I felt like I was split in two. Half of me wanted to get better and put an end to this misery, but the other half was in control, trapping me in this horrendous existence, dictating my dreadful thoughts and actions.

I needed to break out—to be *me* again—but here I was fighting against the very people who were trying to help me.

Stephen came to see me every day for the next week—way beyond what would normally be expected within the health service. He was my friend—my lifeline to which I clung with all my strength.

Grant came too, but somehow we couldn't communicate.

I was terrified he was getting so pissed off that he'd leave me and, the more frightened I became, the less I was able to speak to him. Crazily, I was not even pleased to see him when he did come to see me. It was as if I was only waiting for the inevitable and preparing myself for the pain to come.

"What have you told the boys?" I asked him when he again arrived alone.

"The truth," he said. "I told them that their mum wasn't well and that she would be staying in the hospital for a while to get better."

"How are they doing? Are you feeding them?"

"Your mother is doing that," Grant said without any hint of emotion. "She turned up yesterday afternoon."

"My mother! Oh God, does she know I'm in the hospital?"

He nodded. "The boys told her. They needed to talk to someone."

Tears flowed freely down my cheeks. My poor boys.

"Will you please bring them in to see me?" I asked.

"Is that wise?" he replied. "Do you really want them to see you like this?"

"But I miss them," I shouted at him.

"They miss you too. And, if you start eating, you'll be home with them very soon."

I wondered if he was punishing me by keeping them away.

If so, I deserved it.

GRADUALLY, during the first two weeks in the hospital, the anger in me had subsided and I'd stopped shouting. The screaming had stopped too, at least on the outside.

But it had left me feeling somewhat vacant, almost numb.

It was as if the eating disorder had somehow taken control of my emotions—both the good and the bad. It had become a protective cloak around me, making me immune from worry and fear but also rendering me unresponsive to love and kindness.

I suddenly seemed not to care about anything anymore, although I had started eating, albeit on a very limited basis and under duress. However, it had been simple curiosity that took me to my first therapy session rather than any great urge to participate.

But that session was the start of my long journey to getting well again.

Not that I had realized it at the time.

Stephen had told me that there was another woman patient in her forties in the group and I wondered if she possessed the same feelings of hopelessness and guilt that plagued me, and there was only one way to find out.

I had initially only intended to listen—to sit there in silence—but it was like staring into a mirror of my own emotions.

Beth was the woman's name, and I found myself warming to her, verbally agreeing when she spoke of her fear of letting people down, especially her mother and father. Like me, she'd had parents who were very ambitious for their daughter and their expectations had far exceeded her ability to fulfill them.

It forced me to think back to my own early life.

Fortunately, in my case, I had found my schoolwork relatively easy and had always been at or near the top of my class. Not that my parents ever gave me any praise for it. I presumed they believed it was my rightful place and they regularly criticized me for not doing even better.

Looking back, I realized that the lack of praise then was the beginning of the emotional chasm that still existed between my mother and me.

Even as a small girl, I had never been particularly close to either parent and my childhood home was not one I remembered as being filled with love and happiness.

My parents had both been serious academics. My father had been a lecturer in medieval archaeology at Oxford University and my mother had been a Ph.D. student in the same department.

There had been an age gap of almost twenty years between them and, I now suppose, there must have been a touch of scandal at the time, but it was never spoken about. Flower power and free love were just about hanging on into the early 1970s, and people were perhaps more tolerant then of sexual peccadilloes between staff and students. Ten years earlier and the two of them would have undoubtedly been hounded out of the city. Ten years later and I would almost certainly have been aborted.

An aged aunt had told me stiffly and without elaboration at my father's funeral that he had always chosen the honorable path in his life. His marrying of my mother due to honor rather than for love had obviously been my misfortune.

Consequently, I had been an only child and I'd spent most of my life convinced that my arrival had been a mistake, perhaps the result of a momentary sexual indiscretion at a departmental Christmas party that had ended up with my mother becoming pregnant. The date would fit.

Not that I ever believed that my parents had been purposefully unkind or cruel to me as a child. There had been no abuse, but precious little love either. They lived for their work and both were infinitely more interested in the long dead than in the living, and that included each other and their offspring.

However, it had been listening to Beth and the realization of how the emotional wilderness of her youth had so clearly impacted her present state of mind that made me begin to understand who I was too.

It became the foundation of my climb back up to normality.

However, there were to be a few major hiccups on the way.

AT THE END OF MY SECOND WEEK in the hospital an assistant to the County Coroner had come to see me.

"I'm not dead yet," I said to him as we shook hands in the ward kitchen.

He smiled wanly. It was clearly not the first time he'd heard that little joke.

"No," he said, sitting down at the table and opening his briefcase. "I have come to ask you about a man who died at Cheltenham General nearly three weeks ago."

"The man found in the men's room at the racecourse?"

"Quite so."

"Have the police found out who he was?"

"No, they haven't." He made it sound like they couldn't have been trying hard enough. "That is our problem. The coroner opened an inquest last week and then adjourned it without establishing the identity of the deceased. Most unusual."

From his tone of voice it was obvious that he considered it a major failing.

"So how can I help?" I asked. "I have no idea who the man was."

"Did he not say anything to you at all before he died?" He was almost pleading for me to say yes. "Perhaps something you may have thought was not relevant at the time?"

I shook my head. "The man was unconscious when he arrived at the hospital and he never woke up."

The assistant coroner sucked his teeth in annoyance. "I've never had this happen to me before. It's very unsatisfactory." He made it sound more like poor service in a restaurant rather than the delicate matter of an anonymous corpse stretched out in a storage freezer at the county mortuary.

"Did the police have no luck with his clothes? I was told that they weren't available in this country."

"Both his suit and his shirt were made by a tailor in Singapore. His coat was from Hong Kong, and his shoes were handmade in Dubai."

"Won't the Singapore tailor have records?" I said. "Or the shoemaker?"

"Inquiries are continuing along those lines."

"How about his underwear?" I asked.

"Calvin Klein boxer shorts," the assistant coroner replied. "They could have been purchased anywhere."

Yes, I thought, but not cheaply. Add the handmade shoes, tailored suit and shirt—our dead friend had clearly not been short of a bob or two. Was that because he was a cocaine smuggler, ultimately undone by his own illegal shipment?

"What about the whisky bottle?" I asked. "Did it contain any cocaine residue?"

"You seem very well informed, Dr. Rankin." He made it sound suspicious.

"I'm just interested," I said matter-of-factly. "It's not often that a well-dressed, respectable-looking man with handmade shoes dies of cocaine poisoning whilst in my care."

But, if the truth were known, I was more than just interested— I was becoming seriously obsessed by the unnamed man, and why he had died. The obsession had been building in me ever since he had first arrived at the hospital, further fueled by the complaint against me and the strangeness of his passing.

The assistant coroner closed his briefcase and began to stand up. As far as he was concerned, the meeting was over.

"So did it?" I asked.

"Did what?"

"Did the whisky contain the cocaine?"

"We are still waiting for all the forensic toxicology test results. That one included."

I had the strong impression that he wouldn't have told me even if he knew, as if his own position of importance would have somehow been diminished if he couldn't withhold some snippet of crucial information from those he considered to be lesser mortals.

I shrugged as if I didn't care.

How I had moved on in only a couple of weeks.

Only ten days previously I would have shouted and screamed

at the silly man and probably found myself being sedated by the hospital staff with a jab in the backside.

Was I really getting better?

An examination of the complaint against my medical competence took place three weeks and two days after my admission and, as a courtesy to my situation, had been held in the dining hall of Wotton Lawn.

I protested that, as a hospital inpatient, I obviously wasn't well enough to defend myself against the charges and I'd had insufficient time to brief a lawyer to act as my counsel.

However, I was advised privately by the Medical Director to let the proceedings go ahead, as the complaint against me was to be dismissed as being without foundation and it would not be considered as a disciplinary hearing.

"How come?" I'd asked him.

"The nurse is now saying that she would have likely done the same thing as you in similar circumstances and her support makes all the difference."

"But wasn't it her who complained about me in the first place?"

"No. It was a junior doctor. It appears that he didn't like getting shouted at by you in front of everyone so he complained about your competence. He has now been persuaded of his error."

Little shit, I thought. He'd been responsible for everything.

But had he?

This disaster had been brewing for some considerable time. If it hadn't been his complaint that had tipped me over the edge, something else would have done.

The hearing took just a few minutes to complete and neither the nurse nor the junior doctor was present. The Medical Director acted as the chairman of the panel of three, and he was the only one who spoke.

"After further consideration of the events surrounding the death of an unknown man at Cheltenham General Hospital, this panel finds that there is no case for Dr. Christine Rankin to answer in relation to a complaint made against her. Hence, this panel hereby lifts the suspension from duty previously imposed on Dr. Rankin, and no report of the circumstances relating to this matter shall be forwarded to the General Medical Council."

The Medical Director may have lifted my official suspension but he made it perfectly clear that I was, instead, placed on long-term sick leave and it would need his personal approval for me to go back to work at Cheltenham General.

So I was not suspended, but I was.

I still couldn't do my job.

Did it make a whole heap of difference why?

It seems it did to the horseracing authorities.

9

In all, I had spent five and a half weeks in Wotton Lawn, coming out just before Christmas.

My official status had improved from being "dangerously ill" to "stable" and I had even managed to put on a few pounds. Not that I necessarily felt better for it.

Grant had collected me in the late afternoon and drove me home across the Golden Valley and through the center of Cheltenham.

I'd been struck by the beauty of the Christmas lights.

Everything in the hospital had been designed as being functional rather than aesthetically pleasing. And functional also meant that it could not be used to assist a suicide—showerheads were built right into the wall, towel rails were held up by magnets and, in the wardrobe, there wasn't a proper clothes rail, just a solid ledge for hooking hangers over. There had to be nothing from which patients might be able to hang themselves. Even the meager curtains were held in place by Velcro, ready to give way if a human body weight was applied.

The twins had made a huge banner for my arrival at the house, hung between two of the upstairs front windows, with

WELCOME HOME MUM emblazoned across it in big black letters.

I suppose they did it out of love but I couldn't help thinking that advertising to the neighbors that I'd been away in a psychiatric hospital was not something to shout about.

And it wasn't as if I hadn't seen the boys.

Grant had steadfastly refused to bring them into the hospital, but, for the last two weeks of my stay, I had been allowed out on accompanied visits to a local café and I had seen them there.

My mother had also been waiting for me at home, standing at the front door as we'd pulled into the drive.

"Hello, dear," she'd said, giving me a peck on the cheek, as she always did. There had been no hug, no grasp to her bosom, no tears of happiness, no joy. Had I expected there to be? I now saw all too clearly how such lack of affection had damaged me.

I would not do the same to my own children.

I had hugged them both, together and separately, and thanked them effusively for the banner.

"It was Dad's idea," they said.

So I'd hugged him too. The first time in months.

Not that coming home had been all sweetness and light.

It never ceases to amaze me how quickly patients become institutionalized by a stay in the hospital, and the same had clearly happened to me.

All the while I'd been away, I had wanted so much to go home and be with my family, but, with my wish finally granted, I'd hated it and longed to be back surrounded by the safe cocoon of routine and procedure. And what made it worse was that everyone else had been so pleased to have me there. Their delight had only seemed to add to my despair and isolation.

That first night, I'd cried myself to sleep.

———

I TURNED DS Merryweather's business card over and over in my hands. I had found it tucked behind the bread bin in the kitchen, where I'd placed it after his visit on the day Grant had driven me home from Bristol in November.

Should I call him?

The unnamed man was increasingly invading my consciousness.

Almost three months had passed since the assistant coroner had been to see me. Surely the toxicology results would be back by now? And how about his clothes? Had the Singapore tailor come forward with a name?

Something inside me *had* to know.

I rang the number.

"DS Merryweather," said the voice that answered.

"Ah, yes, hello," I said hesitantly, "this is Dr. Rankin. I was wondering if you had any news about the date of the inquest for the dead man from the racecourse men's room, because I'm busy during all four days of the racing festival next week."

It was the best excuse for calling that I could think of.

"As far as I am aware, no date has yet been set," the policeman replied very formally. "I am sure someone will let you know in due course, Dr. Rankin—that is, if you are required to attend. In any case, it certainly won't be next week. You would get more notice than that. But thank you for letting us know."

"Have you found out who he was?" I asked hurriedly before he had a chance to hang up.

"No," he said, "we have not."

"Didn't the Singapore tailor or the Dubai shoemaker provide you with a name?"

"No. Dead ends, both of them." If he was surprised I knew

about them, he didn't show it. "The tailor said he had no records, although I suspect he just didn't want to get involved, and the shoe man only knew him as Rahul."

"Surely that's a start," I said.

"Rahul is an extremely common name. For a start, there are about a million Rahuls in India alone. It's an Arabic name too. It is even prevalent in Southeast Asia. Buddha's only son was called Rahul."

"Do you have any idea where our Rahul came from?" I asked.

"Indian family origin seems the most likely. It seems that DNA testing can't positively determine race, but the odds are on India because the man's profile is similar to others from the sub-continent. But there's no way of telling from the DNA if he was born in New Delhi, New York or Newcastle."

I thought back and tried to remember if I'd assumed the man was Indian at the time. Not particularly so, but I could recall that his skin had been olive-brown and his hair black. He could have been Indian. But he could also have been Greek, or French, or Italian, or Spanish, or from any number of other countries where the sun shines brightly.

"How about the toxicology results?" I asked. "Do you know the definitive cause of death yet?"

"Respiratory collapse and heart failure brought on by cocaine overdose. The quantity of the drug found in the man's brain was extremely high, well over that required to kill."

I nodded. If the blood-test result had been accurate, then it had to be the case.

"Any suggestion where the cocaine came from?" I asked.

The detective sergeant hesitated as if deciding whether to tell me or not. "I believe you informed PC Filippos that cocaine could be dissolved into alcohol."

"That's right," I said. "It can be dissolved into almost anything."

"The empty whisky bottle found in the restroom trash can did contain cocaine. The tiny bit of liquid that remained in the bottle was tested and found to be at such a high concentration that just drinking a little of it would have been lethal."

"So you think that our Rahul must have drunk from the bottle?"

"It seems to be the logical scenario although, obviously, we have no idea if he did it on purpose or if it was an accident."

"Or murder?" I asked.

There was a slight pause from the other end of the line.

"Unlikely," he said. "There's no apparent motive."

"But you don't know who the man is. Don't you think that's suspicious in itself? There may also be a motive that you don't know about either."

"I agree but, for the time being, the man's death is being classified as 'unexplained' rather than 'suspicious.'"

"How about fingerprints?" I said. "Were his on the bottle?"

"Indeed they were."

"Oh." That stopped my dubious thoughts. "So what do you do now?"

"Keep on trying to discover his identity. We've sent his details over to our counterparts in India just in case he's from there, but their bureaucratic wheels turn so slowly it may be weeks or even months before we hear back."

"How about here?" I asked. "I haven't seen his photo in the press or on the TV."

"We've tried, but, when there is no apparent crime involved, the editors aren't interested. To them he was just another druggie found dead from an overdose in a public lavatory. The fact that we don't know who he was is irrelevant as far as they are concerned."

"You could always post his photo at the racecourse for the Festival next week and see if anyone recognizes him. After all, he was found there."

"We already have that in hand, Dr. Rankin."

HENCE, when I arrived at Cheltenham Racecourse the following Tuesday, one couldn't fail to see the man's photo stuck up next to every entry turnstile.

"DEAD MAN" said a caption underneath in large bold capital letters. "Do you know him?" There was also a telephone number to call if you did.

I wondered how they had got his eyes open for the photo, let alone appearing to stare straight into the camera. They had been firmly shut when I'd last seen him. I found knowing it was a picture taken of a dead man rather creepy, especially as his unseeing eyes seemed to follow me around as I moved.

There were more copies of the image in the weighing room where I went to present myself to Adrian Kings, the senior racecourse medical officer for the day. In his day job, Adrian was a GP in nearby Tewkesbury.

"Ah, hello, Chris," he said. "Welcome to the medical team." He looked at me closely. "Are you all right?"

"Perfectly," I said. "Why do you ask?"

"You just look rather pale and gaunt, that's all."

"I'm fine," I said. "And eager to get going." I smiled broadly at him.

"Good," he said, forcing back a smile. "Senior medical officer's briefing in ten minutes."

On each day of the Festival there were five official racecourse doctors on duty, including myself and Adrian, plus two nurses, a physical therapist and five ambulance crews, each consisting of two qualified paramedics. In addition, there would be a doctor representing the Irish Turf Club, someone who knew and was known to the many Irish riders who came over to compete at the Festival.

And all that was just for the jockeys.

Medical care for the rest of the vast crowd was provided elsewhere in compliance with the Sports Grounds Safety Authority regulations for sporting venues. That was not our concern, nor could it be. We were to concentrate solely on those brave souls balanced high on half a ton of horseflesh while jumping over huge fences at high speed, with no seat belts or air bags available in the event of a crash.

And they called *me* crazy!

Adrian's briefing took place in the jockeys' medical room with all nineteen members of the team crammed in around the two hospital-style beds and the physical therapist's treatment table.

Before he started, we were honored by a visit from Rupert Forrester, managing director of the racecourse, who came to give us a pep talk.

"Ladies and gentlemen," he said. "We will be very much in the public eye this week with extensive television news coverage. There are those who would try to destroy our wonderful sport of jump racing, so it is vital that we not only look after any injured jockeys and horses, but that we are seen to do so with care and professionalism. I am sure I don't have to remind you that your actions may be closely scrutinized by certain members of the press."

But he had done so anyway, I thought.

"Thank you all for your service," he said in closing.

"Thank you, Rupert," Adrian Kings said. "I am confident that we will all do our duty with diligence and competence."

The managing director nodded at him, and then at us, before departing to give the same speech, no doubt, to the veterinary team.

Adrian cleared his throat. "Right, seven races on the card today, including four chases. Lots of runners, so plenty of potential to keep us all busy." He smiled. Adrian liked to be kept busy. As a GP he saw very few, if any, trauma cases, so the more complex the injuries the more he liked it, short of anything spinal. None of us enjoyed dealing with those.

From my point of view, the quieter the afternoon turned out to be the better. I would be content not to have to set foot on the track at all. But I realized that I was also quite excited by the prospect of, once again, using my medical skills. I had not touched an actual patient in four months, but I hadn't wasted my time. I'd taken the opportunity to read all the latest medical journals and to catch up on some new techniques in emergency medicine. Now, maybe, I would have the chance to put some of them into practice.

Adrian handed out some racing programs and then he went through each race in turn, referring to a large map of the racecourse and detailing with a marker pen on a whiteboard where each doctor or ambulance was to be positioned.

He himself regularly chose either to remain with the nurses in the jockeys' medical room or to go up high in the grandstand with the "spotter," someone whose sole job was to watch for any fallers and call in veterinary or medical help if required.

I, meanwhile, would be out on the course with the other doctors, either on foot or as a passenger in a vehicle, following the horses as they ran, ready to give assistance to any faller.

"Do not forget," Adrian said to us seriously, "our primary task is to provide aid to every fallen rider within a maximum of one minute of him or her hitting the ground, but not at the price of putting yourselves in danger. Always keep your eyes and ears open for loose horses, and for any runners who are well behind the rest."

He went on to describe the arrangements for calling for a fence to be bypassed if an injured jockey could not be moved before the horses came back around on a second circuit.

None of it was new. We had heard it all before but it still had to be covered, just like the safety briefing on an airliner.

"Any questions?" Adrian asked.

There were none.

"OK," he said. "Please confirm to me individually that you have read and understood the latest racecourse medical standing orders and instructions. Also verify that your treatment kits are complete and all drugs and equipment are serviceable and in date. Lastly, let's do a radio check and, remember, no sensitive material over the airwaves, please. You never know who's listening."

We each in turn made some inane comment over our personal radios.

"Today is Tuesday and the weather is overcast," I said, and everyone nodded as they heard me loud and clear through their earpieces.

I read through the racecourse standing orders to see if there had been any changes since I'd last acted as a racecourse doctor the previous October. I smiled wryly at point six, which stated that one of the evacuation hospitals for an injured rider was

Cheltenham General. It would be ironic, I thought, if I had to accompany a casualty there.

The briefing broke up and I wandered outside, onto the red-brick terrace in front of the weighing room.

There was an air of huge anticipation all around. The whole season so far had been leading up to these four days, and they had finally arrived. It was the ambition of every owner, trainer and jockey to have a winner at the Cheltenham Festival. Hence, there was a degree of nervous tension mingled within the excitement, especially among those connected to the favorites.

I know it was silly but I found it exciting that people I would normally only see in the newspapers or on the television were here in the flesh, and actually talking to me as if I were one of them. It may have helped that I was wearing a green coat with "Jockey Club Racecourses" and "Doctor" embroidered on the left breast—my uniform.

In my experience everyone was polite to a doctor, at least when they were sober. You never knew when you might need one.

"Morning, Doctor," said a man standing in front of me. "Lovely day for racing—dry and not too cold."

I knew him, but only by reputation.

"Good morning, Mr. Hammond," I replied.

Peter Hammond was a household name even among those not the least bit interested in equine matters. He had been a champion racehorse trainer, both over jumps and on the flat, for almost as long as anyone could remember and had a waiting list for places in his yard that included kings, princes and presidents. And he had married a former Miss World, who was now an award-winning film star.

The Hammonds were definitely A-list celebrities, appearing

almost weekly on talk shows and in the society magazines, and yet here he was talking to me.

I was flattered.

"Any runners today, Mr. Hammond?" I asked by way of conversation.

"Only six here today," he said. "Plus three others at Sedge-field, and two more this evening at Wolverhampton on the all-weather."

He turned away from me to speak to a journalist who was hovering.

I looked through the program. Not only did he have six runners but two of them were in the big race of the day and well fancied.

I was embarrassed. How could I have asked him such a crass question?

I comforted myself in the knowledge that, while I didn't know much about the day's runners and riders, he probably wouldn't know that the most effective treatment for electrocution was mouth-to-mouth resuscitation.

I looked at my watch.

Still an hour to go before the first.

By now, the crowd would be pouring through the racecourse entrances in their torrents—tens of thousands of fans eager to choose their fancies and then cheer them home to victory, or otherwise, up the famous Cheltenham Hill to the winning post in front of the grandstands.

The bars were already doing strong business, particularly in the tented Guinness Village, where many of the Irish visitors were clearly well established, quenching their thirsts while listening to their favorite folk bands that had traveled with them across the water.

The numerous restaurants and private boxes were also packed with guests, the racecourse caterers producing literally thousands of gourmet lunches all at once.

A day out at the Cheltenham Festival was far more than just another day at the races. It was a special treat and one to be savored, and that included by the medical team.

I breathed deeply and soaked up the charged atmosphere around the parade ring. With it, all my troubles seemed to float away, at least for the time being, and I felt elated to be back in my role as a clinician.

Perhaps for the first time in eighteen months, I would have described myself as feeling reasonably happy.

Such a shame it wasn't to last.

My world was about to change once again, and not for the better.

10

There were one hundred and twenty horses running on that first day of the Festival, so we could assume that, on average, there would be about ten fallers during the afternoon. The record was nineteen. And we might statistically expect a couple of broken bones among the jockeys. Thankfully, major trauma was less common but we had to be ready for anything. And we'd all had experience at some time or another of having to call in the air ambulance.

Hence, I was in my position, eager and ready with my red doctor's bag by my side, sitting in a Land Rover at one-thirty when the famed Cheltenham Roar erupted from the enormous crowd to greet the start of the traditional Festival opener, the Supreme Novices' Hurdle race.

There was a dirt roadway running all around the inside of the racecourse to enable vehicles to follow the action and I hung on tight to the Land Rover's grab handles as we set off accompanied by an ambulance plus four more cars containing veterinary staff, horse catchers and a team of groundsmen with green screens. Horseracing was the *only* sport I knew of where the participants were actively chased by a full medical team of ambulances, vets and doctors.

In addition, other ambulances and more doctors were positioned at strategic points around the course, ready to take over if either I or the primary ambulance had to stop to attend to a fallen rider. Gone were the days of sixty or seventy years ago, when a solitary fence attendant had to wave an orange flag to signal for veterinary help for a horse, or a red-and-white one to request medical assistance for the jockey, which could then have taken upward of fifteen minutes to arrive.

"Hang on," my driver instructed as we bounced along the roadway at more than thirty miles an hour. It may not have been as fast as Formula One but, on the undulating single-width route, it was exhilarating enough as we followed the field of horses up the finishing straight for the first time, past the packed grandstands and onward left-handed.

"Faller," announced the spotter over the radio as we approached the third flight of hurdles down the backstretch.

It was now my time.

I grabbed my bag and had the Land Rover door open even before the driver had pulled off the roadway onto the grass alongside the hurdle. Then I was ducking under the white running rail and sprinting across the turf toward the prostrate figure wearing the now-muddied yellow-and-blue-diamond-checked silks.

As Adrian had instructed in his briefing, I looked around for the loose horse but it had already clambered to its feet and galloped away in pursuit of the other runners.

The jockey wasn't so much injured as angry and the presence of a female doctor clearly didn't inhibit him in expressing it.

"Fucking, fucking hell!" he shouted, spitting out grass and beating the ground in front of him with his hand. "I was going so well, I thought I'd win. Stupid nag should learn to pick up his bloody feet."

He rolled over, sat up and slowly rose to his feet, rubbing himself.

"You OK?" I asked in very non-doctoring language.

"Yeah," he said. "Just a slight kick in the nuts. Nothing more than a bruise."

"Do you want me to take a look?" I asked.

"Always, darling," he said, with a guffaw. "No, really, I'm OK."

We could hear the cheering from the stands as the race approached its climax and we both turned and looked in that direction, not that we could make out the individuals involved from so far away.

"Damn it," he said. "I should be over there winning this." The noise died away abruptly as the horses crossed the finish line. "Any chance of a lift back? I've got a ride in the next."

We were at about the farthest point on the course from the weighing room. He would be hard-pressed to get back in time on foot.

"Sure," I said.

We hurried back to the Land Rover, with him hobbling somewhat.

"Are you sure you're OK?" I asked. "You're limping."

"Old injury," he said. "I'm just back from a broken ankle that I did five weeks ago at Bangor. OK for riding but not a hundred percent yet for running."

"Completely mad," I said, shaking my head.

He laughed. "It helps."

He climbed into the back of the vehicle while I got in the front.

"Thanks, Doc," he said, leaning his head back and closing his eyes.

I wondered if he was in more pain than he was letting on. Jockeys were supreme experts at avoiding being stood down even for quite serious injuries when lesser mortals would have gladly taken weeks off work. For a jockey, not riding meant not earning, and there was no sick pay for the self-employed.

"Don't forget to report to the jockeys' medical room to get clearance before you can ride again."

"Sure," he said, not opening his eyes. "No problem."

All fallen riders had to "pass the doctor" even if there was no apparent injury. In particular we were looking for any signs of concussion. They had to answer seven specific questions known as the "Turner Questions" to test their memory function—the name or number of the horse they had just been riding, the trainer's name, the type and length of the race, the name of the racecourse, the name of the current champion jockey, the winning horse or jockey of the previous Grand National or Cheltenham Gold Cup, and the names of two other jockeys riding at the course on that day. The aim was to test both short- and long-term memory.

They also had to do the Tandem Stance Test, where they were required to stand with their feet in line one behind the other, hands on hips and eyes closed for twenty seconds without losing balance.

Any rider with a suspected concussion would be fully medically assessed, immediately stood down and not permitted to ride again until cleared by the Chief Medical Adviser (CMA) of the horseracing authority. They are also not left alone or allowed to drive and may well be sent directly to the hospital for a brain scan.

The driver dropped us off as close as possible to the enclosures and we hurried together across the track and up the horse-walk where the horses come out onto the course from the paddock.

The huge-screen TVs next to the parade ring flashed up the photo of the dead man with the bold DEAD MAN caption underneath asking if anyone recognized him.

The jockey beside me stopped abruptly. He was staring up at the screen.

"Do you know that man?" I asked.

He didn't answer.

"Do you know him?" I asked again, this time more forcefully while tugging on the arm of his silks.

"Er, no," he said, turning toward me. "Never seen him before."

He started moving forward again, briskly pushing his way through the crowd toward the weighing room. I stood and watched him go.

He had clearly been lying.

I took the program out of my coat pocket and turned to check the details of the first race. Yellow-and-blue diamonds, yellow cap—the horse was called Fast Broadband and had been ridden by one Richard McGee—Dick McGee.

He was one of the top twenty or so jump jockeys presently riding.

I made my way back to the weighing room but more sedately. I needed to register the details of the faller on the computerized Riders Injury Management System, known as RIMANI, even

though there was no real injury to speak of. Every patient encounter, however brief, had to be recorded.

"Hi, Chris," said Adrian Kings as he saw me enter the medical
room. "All well?"

"Yes, thanks," I replied. "Just filing my report."

I sat at the computer terminal and typed in the information.

"I see from this that you have already cleared Dick McGee to
ride," I said, spinning the chair around to face Adrian.

"Yes," he said. "He was in here a second ago." He suddenly
looked concerned. "Is there a reason why I shouldn't have?"

"No reason," I said. "I just wondered how you found him."

Adrian shrugged his shoulders. "Much like any other bruised
jockey who is trying to convince me it doesn't hurt when he's
actually in agony. These boys could give our soccer players a
lesson or two."

"But you still passed him fit to ride?" I asked.

"No medical reason why I shouldn't. Bruises may be sore but
they are not normally dangerous—not unless they're of the brain,
of course."

What I had really meant was more to do with the jockey's
demeanor. Had he been unduly agitated? Or overly concerned?

I was certain Dick McGee had recognized the dead man and
I intended finding out why he had denied it.

THE SECOND RACE was event-free as far as the medical team was
concerned.

The doctors rotated their positions on the course for each race
and this time I was down at the start as the twelve runners circled
while having their girths tightened by the assistant starters. I

stood by the rail watching Dick McGee go round and round. He was now wearing red-and-black silks aboard the favorite, a six-year-old gray called Oystercard.

He saw me looking at him, but, if that worried him, he didn't openly show it.

I climbed into the Land Rover as the starter called the jockeys into line and then the chase was on once more.

Ten of the twelve horses finished the race and the other two pulled up without incident when tailed off coming down the hill toward the third-last fence.

Oystercard won.

In the distance I could see the figure in red and black standing tall in the stirrups and saluting the vast crowd, which roared back its approval as he passed by the winning post, in front by two lengths.

The lows and highs of jump racing, I thought—a kick in the nuts and a mouthful of grass in the first, victory and acclaim in the second.

However, the third race, a three-mile handicap steeplechase over two complete circuits of the course with twenty fences to negotiate, was more challenging for the medical team.

Twenty-four runners went to post but only fourteen of them were to get to the finish. Of the remaining ten, four pulled up, four fell and the other two were brought down by tripping over another horse that had already fallen, both at the same fence, the second open ditch at the far end of the course on the first circuit.

Being "brought down" was always the worst way to fall. Not only was it no fault of the horse in question, but there was little or no warning for the jockey, who could easily be catapulted directly headfirst into the turf.

So it was with some trepidation that I ran across the track to a motionless form, while a second doctor plus one of the ambulance crews tended to the other two fallen riders.

To compound the problem, one of the horses was still lying on the ground nearby, its forelegs thrashing about violently. I feared at the time that it might have been fatally injured.

Taking care to avoid the flailing hooves, I reached my allocated jockey, who was lying on the grass curled up in a ball, gently moaning.

I took that to be a good sign. At least he was conscious.

I went down on my knees next to his back and gently touched him.

"Dr. Rankin here," I said. "Don't try and move. Let me assess you first."

"It's my left shoulder, Doc," he said, panting slightly with the pain.

"Dislocated?" I asked. Many jockeys knew from prior experience what the excruciating pain of a dislocated shoulder was like and, if you'd felt it once, it was difficult then to forget.

"Collarbone, I think," he said. "I've done it before."

"What's your name?" I asked.

"Dave," he said. "Dave Leigh."

I pulled up his racing silks and ran my hand down his spine inside his body protector. "Any pain here, Dave?"

"None."

Next I felt around his neck. "Anything?"

"No."

"Can you remember if you banged your head?" I asked.

"I know I didn't," he said with certainty. "I instinctively put my bloody hand out to break the impact. Stupid idiot. I landed on that."

The classic method of fracturing a collarbone.

"Wiggle your toes for me."

He did so. I could see them moving inside his wafer-thin riding boots.

"Can you sit up?" I asked.

I steadied him as he rolled toward me until he was sitting upright on the damp grass. He supported his left wrist in his right hand. I had a gentle feel around the joint. As far as I could tell, the head of the humerus was correctly located into the glenoid fossa, the shallow shoulder socket, so it didn't appear to be a dislocation, but the left arm hung down slightly lower in a manner expected with a broken collarbone. However, only an X-ray could confirm if that was truly the case.

My doctor colleague came over to join us, his fallen rider having hurt nothing more than his pride.

"Dave Leigh," I said. "Suspected fractured clavicle. Hospital job."

"Can he be moved?"

I looked around. The other two riders had already got up and gone and, much to my relief, even the horse was now on his feet and being led away, but the fence attendants were hovering nearby, getting ready to cordon off the fence for the remaining runners to bypass on the second circuit.

Our primary concern was always the welfare of the jockey and my decision had to be in his interests first but I would not be thanked if I didn't make every effort to clear the course if it was safe to do so.

"Come on, Dave, let's get you up," I said. "But tell me immediately if anything else hurts."

The other doctor and I helped the jockey to his feet and, together, we walked him off the track toward the waiting ambulance, and just before those horses still running in the race arrived back at the fence.

I turned and watched them again jump the open ditch, this time without incident, and, with the injured jockey now safely installed in an ambulance ready for the journey to the hospital, I jogged back to the Land Rover to continue the pursuit, smiling broadly.

Boy, it felt good to be doctoring again.

11

The fourth race was the big event of the day, the Champion Hurdle Challenge Trophy—not that any of the races at the Festival were small. But this was the one that made racing history. As its name suggested, this race determined the year's champion hurdler and the name of the winner would be painted on the racecourse honors board to be viewed in perpetuity.

The rotation of the doctors had me on foot on this occasion. I was to remain in the parade ring until the last horse departed, follow it down to the track and then stand close to the final flight of hurdles for the race.

Statistically, more horses fall at the final obstacle than at any other and that is not just due to tiredness. At the last, jockeys are urging their mounts forward for a final effort to the finish and are infinitely more likely to ask them for a large stride than to take a pull on the reins and put in an extra small one—that could be the difference between winning and losing and, in horseracing, winning is everything.

In many a jockey's mind, falling while trying to win was far preferable to being safe and finishing second, and to hell with the bruises. That's what separated the greats from the also-rans. It was also why a doctor was positioned close by to pick up the pieces.

I watched as the riders were tossed up onto the horses, the atmosphere almost crackling from the excited static from owners and trainers as they hoped and prayed that, this time, it would be they who would be hailed the champion. Even the usually ultra-calm Peter Hammond looked nervous as he gave last-minute instructions to his two jockeys, one of whom I noticed was Dick McGee, this time wearing green-and-yellow-striped silks.

Indeed, the calmest individuals were the horses themselves, who behaved impeccably by not throwing a rider, nor giving the doctor anything else to do.

I stood near the exit watching the horses file out of the parade ring before following them down the horse-walk toward the track. As he passed by, Dick McGee looked down at me from his lofty position, no emotion readable on his face.

I know he knows who the dead man is, I thought, and, what's more, he knows I know he knows.

I STOOD BY THE FINAL HURDLE watching the race unfold on the big-screen TV in the center of the course.

As one might expect from the best two-mile hurdlers around, the contest was run at lightning pace, all ten of the runners remaining tightly bunched as they passed the grandstands for the first time.

Cheltenham is an undulating track and the field spread out somewhat as they climbed to the highest point of the course, farthest from the finish line. Then they swung sharply left-handed and raced back down the hill with just three flights left to jump.

From the head-on camera angle, Dick McGee's green-and-yellow silks were clearly visible as the horse beneath him hit the top of the hurdle with its forelegs and went down on its knees. At that speed the animal had no chance to recover and, almost as if in slow motion, it keeled over onto its right side and went all the way to the floor, slithering along the wet grass and ejecting its pilot from the saddle as it did so.

"Faller third last," said the spotter into my radio earpiece, followed shortly thereafter by the reassuring words, "Horse and jockey both up."

The remainder of the field, unaffected by the loss of one of their number, clattered over the second-last hurdle and ran on into the finishing straight.

The four leading horses jumped the last flight in line abreast, the jockeys working hard with their hands, heels and whips to encourage them up the hill to the winning post and everlasting glory.

In fact, all the remaining runners jumped the obstacle without mishap, leaving me free to turn back to the big screen to watch the race climax.

"Photograph, photograph," called the judge over the public address as two horses flashed past the post with hardly a cigarette paper between them.

As the crowd hushed, waiting for the result to be announced, I turned and looked down the track the other way, where I could see a figure in green and yellow trudging slowly toward me. Dick McGee. He was still a couple of hundred yards away so I hurried back up the horse-walk to ensure I made it back to the weighing room before he did.

"First, number six," came the announcement from the judge to a huge cheer, "second, number two, third, number three. Distances were a nose and two lengths. The fourth horse was number eight."

A "nose" was the shortest official winning margin and could be anything from only a few millimeters up to about six centimeters. On such small margins great reputations were made, and others lost.

I removed the photograph of the dead man from the bulletin board in the weighing room and took it with me into the jockeys' medical area. Dick McGee would have to report there before he could be cleared to ride again and I would be waiting for him.

"I TOLD YOU, I don't know him."

"I don't believe you," I said. "When you saw this image before, you stopped as if you'd been shot. You *do* recognize him, don't you?"

Dick McGee was standing in front of me in the medical room, still wearing his green-and-yellow stripes, and he was holding the man's picture, which I'd just handed to him.

"What is this? The Spanish Inquisition?" he whined, looking around at the two nurses as if he expected them to help him. "Just ask me the standard questions and let me get back to riding."

Adrian Kings, the senior medic, came into the room and Dick immediately turned to him to try to get himself out of his current predicament. "Doc, will *you* check me out and clear me?"

Adrian raised his eyebrows in my direction.

"Is there a problem?" he asked.

"No problem," I said. "I was just asking Dick here some questions."

"Well," Adrian said, completely misunderstanding what questions I'd been asking, "if he can't answer them correctly, you'll have to stand him down and make a Red Entry on RIMANI. He will then need clearance from the CMA before he can ride again. Seven days, minimum."

Dick McGee looked horrified.

"Have you done the Tandem Stance Test?" Adrian asked.

"Not yet," I said.

"OK, OK," Dick said. "I do recognize him but I don't know his name."

Adrian looked confused, and with good reason.

"Where do you recognize him from?" I asked, wanting to get some more answers before the confusion was cleared up.

"I saw him with JC at the Open."

The Open Meeting had been back in November, the same meeting at which the nameless man had been found in the men's room.

"Where?" I asked, waving Adrian away as he tried to interrupt.

"In the jockeys' parking lot before racing. They were having an argument."

"Will someone please tell me what's going on here?" Adrian said loudly.

Dick looked at him. "I don't know what's going on," he said. "I only saw them arguing. I didn't even know he was dead until I saw this." He held up the man's photo with the words DEAD MAN printed underneath.

"Who is JC?" I asked, ignoring Adrian, who was shaking his head in frustration. "Not Jesus Christ, obviously."

"Jason Conway," Dick said. "And Mike Sheraton was with him too. They were both talking to the man."

"Anyone else?" I asked.

"There may have been. I can't remember."

I was worried that Adrian was about to explode.

"What were they arguing about?" I asked.

"I don't know," Dick implored, "but it must have been important. They were shouting like bloody blue murder at each other, but they stopped suddenly when they saw me listening."

"Excuse me," Adrian Kings said, finally stepping between us and facing me. "Is Dick McGee concussed or not?"

"Not," I said. "There is absolutely nothing wrong with his memory or his mental function."

"So can I go now?" Dick asked.

"Just one more thing," I said. "Does the name Rahul mean anything to you?"

"Isn't there an Indian cricketer called Rahul something?" he said. "Apart from that, nothing." He thrust the photo back into my hands and was still shaking his head as he disappeared into the jockeys' changing room.

I wasn't sure I totally believed him, but, short of injecting a truth serum, I'd be unlikely to get anything further from him at the moment, and sodium thiopental was sadly not included in the approved medical kits.

"What the hell was that all about?" Adrian said.

"Oh, nothing much," I said. "I was just asking him about the unidentified man."

"What unidentified man?" Adrian asked.

I held out the photo. "This man was found unconscious in a men's room at the Open Meeting and never woke up. I was the receiving physician at Cheltenham General when he was brought in."

"But what has it got to do with Dick McGee?"

By now we had been joined by all the other doctors, who

were listening intently to the exchange. And I could feel myself getting anxious.

"Nothing," I said. "I just thought he might know who the man was, but I was wrong."

"Don't the police know who he is?" asked one of the others.

"No," I said. "Nobody does."

"So why then would Dick McGee?" asked another.

"Because he recognized him as someone he'd seen before," I said.

I was getting very uncomfortable at being questioned like this. I could feel the panic beginning to rise in my chest. I tried breathing deeply. I was clearly not as well as I thought. But my fellow medics were now intrigued by the mystery and weren't about to let things go.

"What was the cause of his death?" one asked.

"Cocaine overdose."

I could feel a sudden drop of interest in the room. As for all medical personnel, we'd each had our share of dealing with drug-related suffering and death, most of which was self-inflicted and preventable. While doctors were not paid to comment on other people's behavior—their job was simply to treat whatever condition appeared before them—one couldn't help feeling that some individuals were more deserving of our care than others.

But was I really any different from a street druggie?

I had always been partial to a cigarette or two, especially recently when they had helped to calm my frayed nerves. I'd also dabbled with illegal drugs in an attempt to alleviate the persistent heavy ache of depression. As a doctor, I knew better than most that I shouldn't have—they were not good for my health—but I'd done it nevertheless.

So who was I to pass judgment on some cokehead or heroin junkie who had journeyed once too far into total oblivion, either by chance or by design? But there was something about the unnamed man that made me convinced that his death had been more than an accident or suicide.

"Jockeys, five minutes," came the call. Five minutes before they were due out in the parade ring for the next race. Time for me to get out onto the course once more.

With relief, I picked up my red doctor's bag and walked out.

THE LAST TWO RACES on the first day of the Festival were always busy ones for the medical team. Each were steeplechases, one over four miles and the other over two and a half, and both were for novice horses—that is, those that hadn't won a race prior to the start of the jump season the previous April. In addition, the longer race was for amateur riders only, many of whom were novices themselves.

Inexperienced horses with inexperienced jockeys on board was all too often the ideal combination for fallers and especially for the unseated.

Jockeys are very particular about the difference between the two. A "faller" is when the horse falls over and the jockey goes down with the ship, while an "unseated" is where the jockey falls off but the horse remains on its feet. There is an important distinction but the result is pretty similar as far as the rider is concerned—hitting the ground hard, and at speed.

Thankfully, not one of the seven discarded riders in the amateur race was seriously injured but that didn't stop me having to run back and forth across the turf several times to check on them.

"What a great fun way to spend a Tuesday," one of them said, laughing and rubbing mud from his face with the sleeve of his silks. "Certainly beats being stuck in the office. And I got almost halfway round before coming off!"

The amateurs were clearly as mad as the pros.

ONCE THE LAST FALLEN RIDER had been patched up and sent on his way, the medical team had a short debrief in the medical room after six o'clock.

"Well done, everybody," Adrian Kings said to us. "I'm sure the racecourse managing director will be happy with us. A good day's work. One broken collarbone, some cracked ribs, a few bruises, one suspected concussion and not a hint of controversy. Not bad for the first day of the Festival." He sounded slightly disappointed, as if he had hoped for something more serious. "And today's 'Doctor of the Day Award' goes to Chris Rankin for providing us with some innovative and unusual alternatives to the Turner concussion questions."

He slapped me on the shoulder while the others applauded politely. I was sure I blushed a little, but, rather than being congratulated for some worthy deed, I felt that I was actually being slightly reprimanded for not following the approved procedure.

"OK," Adrian said, clapping his hands together. "This is the official stand-down for today. Let's go and have tea."

I placed my red treatment bag on the shelf provided for the purpose and hung up my green doctor's coat on the appropriate peg, ready for the following day.

"I think I'll skip tea," I said to Adrian. "If that's all right with you?"

"Of course," he replied.

Going to tea may not have been an official part of the day but it was expected. It was when the team discussed ways in which our performance might improve. But I was eager to get off home to fix supper for Grant and the twins.

However, I never made it.

12

The doctors' allocated parking spaces were in a corner of the jockeys' parking lot, close to the north entrance to the racecourse, alongside those reserved for holders of blue disabled badges and conveniently close to the weighing room.

However, for the Festival meeting, I tended not to use them.

The roads around the racecourse were pretty busy for many hours after the last race but the main problem was actually getting to the parking-lot exits in the first place. The doctors' parking was about as far from the exits as it was possible to be and, in the past, it had taken me an hour or more simply to get to the racecourse gates. So I now regularly parked in a farmyard just across the Evesham Road, from where it was much easier to drive away. The twins had been to junior school with the farmer's son and we had been friends ever since.

I walked alongside the long lines of cars that were inching very slowly toward the exits and smiled to myself. It had been a good day, and tomorrow I would get here early to talk to the jockeys Jason Conway and Mike Sheraton, and to find out what they had been arguing about with the unnamed man.

According to a note in the program, the sun set at eleven minutes past six, but, on such an overcast day, it was almost pitch-black by the time I arrived at the Evesham Road only ten minutes later.

I remembered standing waiting for a break in the traffic, then the next thing I recall was being in the middle of the road with a huge bus bearing down on me. For some reason my legs and feet simply wouldn't work. I was rooted to the spot and transfixed by the vehicle's bright headlights as they rushed ever closer.

I heard the screech of the tires on the wet road surface as the driver stamped on his brakes but it was too late—the bus hit me, smacking my head against its windshield and throwing me forward into a crumpled heap on the ground.

It had all happened so fast. One second I'd been happy and content, the next I was unsure of *where* I was, *when* it was or even *who* I was.

I'd have had no chance answering the Turner Questions, or of passing the Tandem Stance Test. I found I couldn't even lift my head off the tarmac without losing my balance. So I lay it back down again and shut my eyes, hoping that the whole world would go away.

IN TRUTH, I was never completely unconscious even if I did purposely keep my eyes closed. Everything around me swayed less that way.

"She stepped right out in front of me," I could hear the bus driver imploring to anyone who would listen. "I had no chance."

"Doctor coming through," I heard a man's voice say loudly. "Please stand back and give me some room."

Amazingly, it was Adrian Kings. He must have decided to skip the tea as well.

"Oh my God, Chris," he said, crouching down beside me. "What happened?"

There was nothing wrong with my hearing, but, when I tried to reply, nothing came out. My tongue seemed to belong to someone else, moving on its own accord and not obeying my brain's instructions.

"She stepped right out in front of me," the bus driver said again.

Adrian ignored him. "Has anyone called an ambulance?" he shouted at the gathering throng.

It seemed that someone had, and the police too.

Adrian removed his coat and gently slid it under my head, while someone else put another one over me.

As always, I tried to say that I was "fine," but I clearly wasn't, and it came out as little more than a croak.

"Just lie still," Adrian said. "Help is on the way."

HELP ARRIVED with multiple sirens and blue flashing lights and I found myself, for the second time within a few months, arriving at Cheltenham General Hospital as a patient, this time on a scoop stretcher wearing a neck collar.

Even though the surroundings were familiar, everything appeared in a bit of a haze, as if blurry around the edges.

It was good experience, I kept telling myself, but then I would forget what the experience was like. It felt like I was fighting my way through a fog, round and round on the same piece of road, getting nowhere.

As chance would have it, Jeremy Cook was again on duty and I could see him speaking to a policeman. But I could hear only snippets of what he was saying: ". . . mental-health issues . . . psychiatric hospital . . . suicidal . . ."

"No," I tried to say, "I am not suicidal." But it came out all confused and unintelligible.

But I knew.

I hadn't been trying to kill myself by stepping in front of a bus. I'd been pushed.

PREDICTABLY, no one would believe me.

I spent the night in the hospital with a suspected concussion even though a CT scan had indicated no visible damage to my brain, or to any other part of my body.

Concussion is the most common brain injury but one the medical profession perhaps knows least about. It is often referred to as a bruise to the brain, but bruising implies bleeding into the tissues and most concussed brains do not bleed; indeed, they appear identical on scans to healthy ones. Concussion is more of a temporary disruption of normal function but no one is quite sure why it affects sufferers in so many diverse ways. Some have difficulty sleeping while others struggle to stay awake, many have headaches while others do not, and it can change emotions across a wide spectrum from high elation to deep depression. It all depends on how different areas of the person's brain react to the trauma.

In my case, the concussion seemed to have disrupted my ability to talk, while leaving many of my other cognitive faculties unchanged. That may have been due to my head colliding with the bus close to what was known as Broca's area on the left side of the frontal lobe, that part of the brain responsible for speech production.

Gradually, overnight, my ability to communicate returned and with it came the questions from the police.

At about nine o'clock I woke from a snooze to find a uniformed officer sitting by my bed.

"Good morning, Dr. Rankin," he said in a friendly manner. "How are you feeling today?"

I focused my eyes on the policeman's face. It was PC Filippos.

I must have looked surprised to see him.

"I volunteered to come," he said, "when I heard it was you who'd been knocked down. I thought a familiar face might help."

"Yes," I said croakily. "Very thoughtful of you. Thank you." I suddenly became rather panicky. "I'm meant to be on duty at the racecourse in two hours."

"You are not going anywhere," PC Filippos said. "I know the racecourse management are aware you won't be coming today. The doctors here have said that you must have complete rest for at least twenty-four hours." He smiled. "You were very lucky not to have sustained greater injury in the accident."

"It wasn't an accident," I said, trying to keep the emotion out of my voice.

If he was surprised, he didn't show it.

But I then realized why. He already thought it wasn't an accident because he assumed that I'd walked out in front of the bus intentionally.

"I did *not* try to kill myself," I said firmly. "I was *pushed* out into the road."

I could tell from his expression that he didn't believe me.

"It's true," I said. "Someone gave me a big shove forward just as the bus was approaching."

"Who?" he asked, the doubt clearly audible in just the one word.

"I've no idea," I said, getting quite agitated. "That's surely your job to find out. But, I'm telling you, someone last night tried to kill me."

"Why?"

"To stop me asking questions."

"Questions about what?"

"The unnamed man," I said. "Our friend Rahul."

I could tell from his demeanor that he now thought I'd completely lost my marbles.

"I found someone who recognized him," I said quickly. "He says he saw the man at the racecourse in November."

There was a tiny spark of interest. "Does this person know his name?"

"No," I said. "But he does know the names of two people he saw arguing with him."

I told PC Filippos about Dick McGee and what he had said to me about the unnamed man arguing in the jockeys' parking lot with Jason Conway and Mike Sheraton. The policeman wrote it down in his notebook.

"But why on earth would anyone want to kill you for knowing that?"

"I don't know."

It sounded bizarre even to me.

We were interrupted by the arrival of Grant and he had the psychiatrist Stephen Butler with him. That didn't bode well, I thought.

"Hello, Chris," Stephen said. "How are you feeling?"

"I'm fine," I said automatically, and Grant shook his head in obvious frustration. He too must have thought I had stepped in front of the bus on purpose.

"I'll be on my way," PC Filippos said, standing up. "I'll be in touch, Dr. Rankin. I'll check up on those things we discussed."

He walked out and I wondered if he would even bother. His body language told me he believed I was as nutty as a fruitcake.

But I wasn't.

The more I thought about it, the more convinced I became that someone had pushed me in front of a speeding bus in order to stop me asking questions about the unnamed man.

Indeed, Rahul had now become my full-blown obsession.

However, I managed to prevent a rapid return to Wotton Lawn, but only just, and not by continuing to insist that someone had tried to kill me. I worked out pretty quickly that no one would believe me and to persist in maintaining that I'd been pushed would have only resulted in a one-way ticket to the funny farm.

After a considerable amount of persuasion on my part, Grant and the doctors accepted my claim that I'd been just careless rather than suicidal. I promised to be more vigilant in the future and to allow myself to be chaperoned whenever possible, which would not be often during the week, as Grant was at work and the boys at school.

But I knew the truth.

Someone had definitely tried to murder me and I intended finding out why.

13

Grant took me home with strict instructions that I should continue to rest for another twenty-four hours, and he had taken yet another day of his annual leave in order to ensure I did.

As he drove us out of the town past the racecourse, I wondered if Adrian Kings had managed to rustle up a replacement doctor at such short notice. Not that it would have been critical. The five of us plus the Irish doctor of yesterday had been a luxury when the horseracing authority regulations stipulated a minimum of only three. But at Cheltenham in general, and at its Festival in particular, jump racing was shown in the full glare of a TV spotlight and minimum requirements would never have been enough if anything had gone drastically wrong. That was why the managing director and the racecourse executive always paid for more. Public perception was a very strong incentive.

"What about my car?" I asked as we passed the farm where I'd parked it. I seemed recently to have made quite a habit of abandoning it.

"Tom and Julie brought it back early this morning," Grant said. "They were worried last night when you didn't turn up to collect it." Tom and Julie were the farmer and his wife. I'd left the car's keys with them, just in case they'd had to move it.

Grant insisted that I went straight to bed but I equally insisted that I be allowed to watch the racing on the television.

"The doctor told me that rest meant both physical and mental rest," he said. "No television and no computer."

"But I need to see the racing," I replied. "It's part of my job."

In the end we compromised that I could watch it for a short while with me lying under a blanket on the sofa in the sitting room, propped up with pillows, but Grant still fussed around me like a mother hen in heat.

"For God's sake," I said at one point as he yet again asked me if I was all right. "Will you please just sit down and watch the Queen Mother Champion Chase?"

Grant was not interested in horseracing. "Silly sport, really," he would often say, "just running round a track, getting nowhere."

I, in turn, would point out that his preferred sport, golf, was an equally silly sport—hitting a little white ball with long sticks around the countryside into holes in the ground. Indeed, almost any sport, if analyzed sufficiently, could be thought of as silly and without value. And so might many other pursuits in the entertainment business such as acting, singing and writing. My tutor at medical school had proclaimed that medicine was the only true worthy profession as it was the one thing that, in the long run, made a difference. But that hadn't stopped him being an ardent Manchester United fan.

There were ten runners in the Champion Chase and my interest was heightened when I saw that not only was Dick McGee riding, but so were both Jason Conway and Mike Sheraton.

I sat up and leaned forward to get a better view of the screen.

Over the years, I'd had various encounters with all three jockeys in my role as a racecourse doctor, but on those occasions I had been dealing only with their physical form rather than with their minds and personalities.

Now I was interested in them as people, not merely as patients.

What did they know about Rahul and why was it so important to stop me finding out?

Whereas the Gold Cup on Friday would be the ultimate test over three and a quarter miles, the Champion Chase was the zenith for two-milers, the sprinters of steeplechasing. It was always run at a fast pace but, on this occasion, one of the runners set off as if it were in the Charge of the Light Brigade, establishing a lead of three lengths or more by the time it reached the first fence, only a few strides from the starting gate.

Even the television commentator thought it unusual.

"Jason Conway is certainly in a hurry on Checkbook," he said. "Perhaps he's acting as a pacemaker for the favorite, but no one is going to keep up with that gallop."

I watched as Checkbook jumped the second fence at least six lengths ahead of the rest of the field, which remained tightly bunched at a more sensible speed.

And so it went on. By the time they passed the enclosures and swung left-handed, Checkbook and Jason Conway were a good ten to twelve lengths in front but the others were already beginning to close, and they surged past on the run toward the water jump.

Checkbook did not even finish the race, pulling up when tailed off last at the top of the hill. Jason Conway would definitely not get my vote as ride of the day and I wondered what the stewards would have to say about it.

The others, meanwhile, swept downhill toward the three

remaining fences, their pace now picking up as the business end of the race approached.

Dick McGee went down at the second-last, his horse getting in too close and hitting the fence hard with its shoulders, forcing it to screw sideways on landing and unceremoniously dumping its jockey onto the grass. Dick had had no chance of staying on but it was clearly not going to be his week. That was the third time he'd met the turf face-first, and we were only halfway through the second day.

Mike Sheraton, however, went on to win the race in another tight finish, using considerable skill to coax the horse to the front just before the wire.

I lay back on the pillows and sighed loudly. I hardly had enough energy to keep my eyes open. How was I going to start investigating something?

Grant was alarmed by my sigh.

"Are you all right?" he asked for the umpteenth time, worry lines etched across his forehead.

"I'm fine," I said. "Just tired."

"Are you hungry?" he asked. "Shall I get you something now? We didn't have any lunch."

Was I hungry? Hunger was something I tried not to think about.

But I should be, I thought. Not only hadn't I eaten any lunch, but I'd had no breakfast either. And absolutely nothing to eat the previous day. I'd been too excited at the prospect of working again to have any breakfast and I simply didn't have time during the day to even grab a sandwich. I had intended having a chicken breast for supper, but I'd never made it home.

There'd been some improvement in my eating since my admission to Wotton Lawn but it remained low on my list of priorities, very low.

"How about a cheese omelet?" Grant asked.

"That would be lovely," I said. I smiled at him and he smiled back, but his was a smile full of worry rather than one of love.

What was happening to me?

Why couldn't I be well and normal?

I believed that I must have some resolution of my problems before I could even start to get better, but I still didn't know what the problems were, let alone how to resolve them. They had something to do with my parents and my childhood but I couldn't figure out exactly what.

Maybe there was no single cause, and no magic solution.

My psychotherapist continuously encouraged me to talk about my emotions with regard to my mother and father, but I would often leave the session more confused and distressed than I had been beforehand. It was almost as if talking about my childhood unhappiness stirred everything up again, like shaking up the sediment in a bottle of excellent vintage Bordeaux—it made the whole contents unpalatable. Perhaps it would be far better to leave things undisturbed, decant and enjoy the fine wine above and then cast away the bitter sediment with the empty bottle.

But I remained driven to find "the main cause," to run round and round in circles searching like a dog that has lost a ball in the long grass. Only maybe there was no ball to find at all. Somehow, even though I knew it was madness, I was impelled to go on looking, and all my other problems had to wait.

I desperately wanted to break out of this cycle of misery but no one had told that to my unconscious mind, which went on working in its own mysterious and enigmatic manner.

"Here you are," Grant said, placing a tray down on my lap. He had prepared not only an omelet but also a large bowl of fruit generously covered with Greek yogurt.

I smiled up at him. "Thank you, darling."

Grant did his best but he didn't really comprehend what was happening to me. Neither did I at times. From the outside, an eating disorder was impossible to understand and, from the inside, impossible to explain. Most of my friends grasped even less than Grant.

"Surely it's just a matter of free will," one of them said to me. "You must be able to eat if you want to."

But I did want to eat. If I had learned only one thing in the hospital, it was how dangerous my situation had become, and, without more food, I would certainly die, probably from heart failure. I had used up all the fat in my body and had started consuming my muscle tissue simply to survive—and the heart is a muscle. I was slowly devouring the very organ I needed most.

Eighteen months ago, for my fortieth birthday party, I had struggled to fit into my favorite dress—a low-cut sexy black number. It had been a struggle because, whereas the dress was a size 12, my body had, in truth, been closer to a size 14. But, as a fairly tall woman of five feet eight inches, I'd been rounded rather than chubby, weighing in at just over a hundred sixty pounds.

Things had all changed dramatically the following year.

I had started to view my body as gross and disgusting, as if it were some alien creature from another planet that had to be defeated by starving it to death, and over the next six months I had lost almost a third of my body weight.

That same sexy black dress now hung on my bony and protruding shoulders like a shapeless sack.

Yet the voice in my head still refused to believe the bleeding obvious and, with every mouthful I took, it became louder and more difficult to ignore.

Spit it out! Spit it out! it demanded.

Resisting the voice was a daily fight, and one I needed to win if I was to see my forty-second birthday.

Since leaving the hospital, I *had* been winning, but I couldn't let down my guard even for a day. I had been incredibly stupid not to have eaten anything on Tuesday and I was now paying the price.

Had I really been pushed? Or had I simply been too weak from lack of sustenance to notice the bus?

No one believed me and now I was beginning to doubt myself.

I ate the omelet and picked at the fruit. Grant urged me to finish it all but I was too full. I had been trying hard to gradually increase my daily intake but I still couldn't eat a big meal. And it wasn't safe for me to do so anyway.

Refeeding syndrome had been first recognized as a potentially fatal condition at the very end of the Second World War when some emaciated Japanese soldiers died after they had surrendered to the Americans in the Philippines. Too much food given to them too quickly had caused electrolytic disturbances in their red blood cells as essential minerals were diverted to their digestive tracts, resulting in insufficient oxygen being delivered to the brain and heart to maintain life.

It had been one of my biggest fears and had been further ammunition for the voice in my head advising me not to eat anything at all.

And it didn't help when everyone else tried to tell me what I should do. I already knew, and I didn't like being lectured, especially by those who had no comprehension at all of my problem.

"Can I get you anything else?" Grant asked.

"No, darling," I said. "Thank you. I'm fine."

I watched the rest of the racing on the TV until the boys came home from school.

"Hi, Mum," Oliver said, sweeping into the sitting room and dumping his bag on the floor. "What's to eat?"

The twins were always hungry after a day of studying and that clearly overrode any concern for their concussed mother.

"Have an apple," I said. "There are some in the fridge."

Oliver turned his nose up. "Got any chips?"

"You finished them on Monday."

I had meant to do an online food order but that was something else that had been sidelined by the bus.

"Leave Mum alone," Grant said. "She's meant to be resting."

"What for?" Oliver asked. "Are you on nights again?"

"No, darling," I said, smiling at him. "I'm just resting after banging my head."

He nodded as if he'd just remembered.

How wonderful, I thought, to be fourteen. Not only did Oliver believe he was immortal but he also believed it of those he loved. He wasn't worried that his mother had been almost killed by a bus, his concerns were more about his sexuality and whether the blond girl in his class he fancied also fancied him, and what he'd do about it if she did.

Toby appeared dressed in his Gotherington Colts soccer gear.

"Hi, Mum," he said. "I'm off for a team practice. We've, like, got a local derby on Saturday morning against Woodmancote."

Woodmancote was a nearby village—huge rivals, not least because both teams' members went to the same school.

"Be careful," I said to his departing back.

"Yeah," he said, as if he would.

Normal family life went on unchanged just as it had for years. It was me who was different, not everyone else—something that had taken me a long while to appreciate.

GRANT WENT BACK TO WORK early on Thursday morning and, as usual, the boys caught the bus to school from outside the village post office, leaving me alone in the house.

I'd promised Grant that I would take things easy all day, but, there again, I'd never been that good at keeping my promises. I had already rested for the required twenty-four hours and now I felt absolutely fine, without so much as a minor headache.

I tidied the kitchen and put away the breakfast things. I stacked the dirty cups and bowls in the dishwasher and set it going. Next I went upstairs and made the beds and picked up the clothes that the boys had dumped on their bedroom floors. Then I vacuumed the carpets, tied back the curtains, pumped up the cushions on the sofa and straightened the magazines on the coffee table. I put in a wash load from the dirty-linen basket, and then I sorted my medications, yet again.

Finally, I sat down on a kitchen stool and looked at the digital clock on the stove.

It read 9:40.

What shall I do now?

I tried to read an article on the internet about interior design but my mind wasn't on it.

At five past ten I put my coat on and went to Cheltenham Races.

14

This time I did park my Mini in the doctors' assigned spaces in the jockeys' parking lot. It was not so much that I didn't want to have to cross the Evesham Road again, it was just that I expected to leave before the last race, before the traffic became too bad.

"Hello, Dr. Rankin," said a voice as I climbed out of the car. "Thanks for your help the other day."

I turned to find Dave Leigh, the jockey who had broken his collarbone on Tuesday, his left arm now in a sling. He was parked right next to me and was still sitting in a BMW 3 Series with the driver's window down.

"Hi, Dave," I said. "How's it going?"

"OK, I suppose. But I'll be off for at least four weeks. Damned nuisance."

I decided not to say that, after such a crashing fall, he was lucky to be alive, let alone well enough to come racing only two days later, albeit this time as a spectator rather than a participant.

"At least you can drive," I said.

"Automatic," he said, smiling. "Only need one arm and one leg."

"Are you here just for the atmosphere?" I asked.

"Naah. The TV people have asked me to do a bit in the changing room about what it's like just before a big race, but, to be honest, I don't know if I can do it. I'm totally gutted. I should be riding Card Reader in the Gold Cup tomorrow. Best horse I've ever been on. Has a really good chance."

"Who rides him now?"

"Bloody Mike Sheraton," he said. "Switched from a no-hoper. Probably win on him too, and that will be the end of me riding him forever, in spite of all our past successes."

"Surely not."

"Surely will. No owner would jock off a Gold Cup winner."

"But won't Mike Sheraton tell the owner to reinstate you?"

He looked at me as if I were mad, which indeed I might be. "You must be bloody joking. Mike Sheraton is a complete bastard. He'd even put *you* through the wings if he thought it would be to his advantage."

"So you want him to lose?" I asked.

Dave gave me a long cold stare that I took to mean that yes, of course he wanted him to lose.

"Good luck with the TV," I said.

"Yeah. Thanks." He didn't smile.

At least I wasn't the only one feeling depressed.

WHENEVER the actual saint's day falls, Cheltenham decrees the third day of the Festival to be "St. Patrick's Thursday" and there were many in the entrance line wearing over-large green leprechaun hats, some with attached red beards. It was quite obvious that more than a few had been enjoying a drink or two, or three, in the parking lot even at this early hour.

I used my "Authorized Doctor" pass to gain entry and made my way toward the weighing room.

Even though I wasn't acting in an official capacity—I had received an e-mail from Adrian Kings telling me I wasn't expected back—I was sure he wouldn't refuse a little extra help if I offered it for free, especially as there were even more runners in the seven races on the card today than there had been on Tuesday. However, as soon as I walked into the medical room, I realized it had been a huge mistake to come.

Adrian Kings was not happy to see me, and that was an understatement.

"You shouldn't be here," he said crossly. "How did you get in?"

"I walked," I said flippantly. "I may have banged my head on Tuesday but I'm not an invalid. I'm here to help if I can."

"You're not wanted," Adrian said sharply.

That hurt. I could feel the tears welling in my eyes but I fought them back. I would not give him the pleasure of seeing me cry.

"You should not have hidden from me the fact that you spent a month as an inpatient in a psychiatric hospital with an eating disorder." He was loud, and he was angry.

I wondered how he had found out. Not that it mattered.

"I didn't hide it," I said. "I just didn't broadcast the fact. And it has no relevance to my competence as a doctor."

"Of course it's relevant."

"Why?" I asked. "Why does having a psychiatric condition make me less able as a doctor?"

He didn't have an answer. He just waved his hand in a dismissive manner.

But I wasn't finished.

"You of all people should know."

"And what do you mean by that?" he demanded furiously.

I had known of Adrian Kings for a very long time. We had both been students at Guy's Hospital Medical School in London during the 1990s, even though we had never actually met while there. He was some five years older than me and had already qualified as a junior houseman when I was still doing my pre-clinical studies. But stories of the "mad doctor" had permeated down to us lesser mortals. Adrian had suffered with obsessive-compulsive disorder, in particular to do with washing his hands. All physicians are taught to keep their hands clean and germ-free, but Adrian had taken it to extremes, washing his far too often and scrubbing them until they bled. It was said to be the reason why he had gone into general practice rather than becoming the heart surgeon that he'd intended.

"I was at Guy's in the nineties," I said.

He stared at me. He must have known to what I was referring, but if I thought that, as a fellow sufferer, he might be more understanding of my position, I was much mistaken. If anything, it made him more determined to be rid of me.

"I don't want you here, not now, not ever," he said loudly and adamantly. "Get out and stay out." He pointed at the doorway.

He was the senior medical officer and it was his prerogative to have whomever he wanted on his team. I feared that my days as a racecourse doctor might be over for good.

I took just one step out of the medical room, my mind trying to come to terms with how my situation had so suddenly changed when all I had wanted to do was to help.

The tears came back into my eyes, blurring my vision.

The door to the medical room was in one corner of the male jockeys' changing room and I stood outside it gazing into space, almost as if in a trance.

My life seemed to be moving in an ever-steepening down-ward spiral. I still wasn't allowed by the Medical Director to return to my day job, and now I had seemingly lost my most enjoyable distraction from hospital work.

I wiped the tears from my eyes and realized that I had been staring into the changing room in general and at Dick McGee in particular. He stood on the far side holding a set of red-and-white-striped silks while wearing just a towel around his waist. He must have felt that I had been purposely looking straight at him. He glowered back at me. I slightly lifted a hand in apology and he responded by removing the towel.

If he thought that a naked male form was going to offend me, he was wrong. As an emergency doctor, I'd seen more willies than he'd had roast lunches.

I laughed, and that didn't please him either. He made a rude gesture in my direction and mouthed a couple of very ungentle-manly words encouraging me to go away; instead, I looked around to see if I could spot Mike Sheraton or Jason Conway. Not that I particularly wanted to see their willies too, I was just curious to see if they were there so that I could ask them about the man in the photo. But there was no sign of either of them.

I knew they were both due to ride, as I'd looked it up on the Racing Post website, but there was still nearly two hours before the first race, so they may have not arrived yet, or perhaps they were lurking in the sauna trying to shed a pound or two before racing started.

I walked out onto the weighing-room terrace and sat in the sun on one of the wooden benches. I couldn't remember ever having been to the races before when I didn't have anything to do.

I felt lost and miserable.

Part of me wanted to stand up and go back into the medical room, to tell Adrian Kings not to be so damned stupid, and to carry on doing what I did best. I even briefly thought about threatening to make public his hand-washing problems of the past if he didn't reinstate me but . . . what good would it do? He was the most senior racecourse medical officer here at Cheltenham and he would simply not choose me again anyway. And the way my health was going at the moment, I could do with every doctor being more of a friend than an enemy.

I sat on the bench for the next half hour watching the comings and goings, jockeys arriving to change, trainers collecting saddles to take over to the saddling boxes for the first race, owners hovering nervously more in hope than expectation. And then there were the TV and radio crews hoping for an exclusive interview to reveal some golden nugget of information about a horse's chances in the big race. In fact, all the regular hustle and bustle around the weighing room on a Festival morning.

But I was now out of it, present here only in body.

I thought about going home.

My home had always been my castle, my safe retreat from the horrors of emergency medicine, but it had recently become my prison, the place from where I gazed out through the glass at the world beyond, wondering if I would ever be able to rejoin.

Whereas going home had once been a pleasure, it was now a torment.

So I went on sitting on the bench, that was until I saw Jason Conway walking across the parade ring. I pulled the photo of the unnamed man from my coat pocket and went forward to intercept.

"Excuse me, Jason," I said, standing right in front of him. "Do you know this man?"

I thrust the photo almost up to his nose so he couldn't avoid looking at it.

Jason glanced at the picture then at me. "I've already told the police that I don't know him," he said.

"Why did he die?" I asked.

No reply.

"What are you involved in?"

"Leave me alone," he said, pushing past me and disappearing up the steps and into the sanctuary of the weighing room.

Two things struck me. The first was that, contrary to what I'd believed, PC Filippos must have actually taken note of what I'd said to him in the hospital, and the second was that Jason Conway was lying.

As the mother of identical twins, who as children had seemed to communicate as much by telepathy as by the spoken word, I had become quite adept at reading body language and detecting vibes. And there had been vibes aplenty radiating from Jason Conway. He was a deeply worried man and that could only be because, not only had he seen the unnamed man but he probably knew his full name and why he'd died.

I went back to the bench to wait for Mike Sheraton.

Adrian Kings appeared on the terrace to my left, took one look at me, pursed his lips and retreated back inside, where I saw him speaking to Rupert Forrester, the managing director. Presently, another member of the racecourse executive came over and asked me what reasons I had for being in a restricted zone.

Kick me when I'm down, why don't you?

"No reason," I said.

So he asked me to leave the weighing-room area. At least he didn't tell me to leave the racecourse entirely.

I walked across the parade ring and on toward the Princess

Royal Grandstand. In spite of the sunshine, I was desperately chilly and I dug my hands deep into my coat pockets. Always being cold was one of the unfortunate consequences of having lost so much weight and a fresh gust of icy wind made me shiver. I went in search of the nearest warm shelter—the Vestey Bar in the base of the grandstand.

I hadn't had a single alcoholic drink for many months—far too many calories—but now I found myself standing at the bar swiftly gulping down a double Whisky Mac to ward off both the cold and the awful feeling of helplessness that had gripped me by the throat.

Living my life over those months had been like walking a tightrope. I'd had to concentrate intensely for every single second in order not to fall off—one way into full-blown anorexia, starvation and death, the other into a hedonistic self-indulgence of drink, drugs and excess leading to massive weight gain and a return to crippling depression. Just being me, and staying as I was now, had become a full-time occupation.

Yet here I was in a bar at barely eleven in the morning, knocking back a third shot of whisky and loving the warm glow that enveloped me as a result.

"Another double, please," I said to the barman, pushing a fresh banknote across the counter toward him.

Part of me wanted him to say, *No, no, you've already had enough,* but instead he took my money and measured two shots of Dewar's Finest Scotch Whisky into a fresh tumbler, before splashing in an equal quantity of Stone's Original Green Ginger Wine.

"Bugger Adrian Kings," I said to myself, lifting the glass in a silent toast before downing its contents in three great gulps.

"And again," I said, sliding the empty glass across the bartop. This time the barman did look at me with a questioning expression but I just nodded at him and waved my hand around in encouragement.

What on earth are you doing? the sensible half of my brain asked.

Getting drunk, of course, replied the delinquent half with a laugh. *Sod the lot of them.*

And I was getting drunk, and very quickly. Not only had I lost my long-established tolerance for alcohol but I'd had nothing to eat for breakfast. Unaccustomed booze on an empty stomach— the perfect recipe for disaster.

I watched the barman dispense two more measures of the golden liquor.

Whisky. Whisky.

My scrambled brain wondered if it contained dissolved co-caine.

Even in this state, every line of thought came back to the unnamed man, my friend Rahul, and why he'd died.

15

The sensible half of my brain started to win.

I was sitting on a stool in the Vestey Bar with my fifth double Whisky Mac untouched on the high table in front of me, almost as if it were goading me to drink it like the bottle of magic liquid in *Alice in Wonderland*. But this particular potion certainly wouldn't make me shrink—indeed, it would quite likely make me fall over—so I sat looking at it, unable to move and determined not to stray any further from my tightrope.

I stayed put throughout the first race, not daring even to let go of the table in case I should stagger around like an animal with mad cow disease. Surely, I thought, one should be able to *think* oneself sober if one focused hard enough. My medical training told me otherwise but I went on trying nevertheless.

I tried to watch the race on one of the many TV sets fixed to the walls of the bar but the jockeys' silks seemed to blend together into a colorful kaleidoscopic mass before my intoxicated eyes. Only when the horses had jumped the last and were on the run-in to the finish line did I distinguish the leader's red-and-white stripes—Dick McGee.

I remembered back to his massive reaction to seeing the picture of the unnamed man. He must know more than he was telling.

I REMAINED WHERE I WAS in the bar for the next two races as the worst effects of the alcohol gradually began to diminish and I found that I could stand unaided with only a minor wobble.

I asked a fellow drinker to save my seat and then slowly weaved my way to the ladies' room. I poured the last demon drink down the toilet before splashing some cold water onto my face at the sink.

I looked at myself in the mirror. I didn't think that I appeared very drunk, but appearances could be deceiving.

And I now realized I had another big problem.

How was I going to get home?

I couldn't drive in this condition and it would be many hours until the alcohol in my blood dropped to a legal level.

I seemed to have three choices: I could walk the four and a half miles home, I could call Grant and ask him to collect me, or I could get a lift from someone going my way.

Whichever method I chose, my car would have to stay overnight in the racecourse parking lot and Grant would be certain to find out that I'd been drinking again. It would give him even more reason to believe I should be back in Wotton Lawn.

God, you're a fool, I told my reflection in the glass.

A goddamn bloody fool.

I SAFELY MADE MY WAY back to the bar to find that the person I'd asked to keep my seat had gone and so had the stool I'd been sitting on, snaffled by a large group of young twenty-somethings having a great day out.

I stood by the table and looked across at them as they laughed and joked with one another.

Where had *my* youth gone?

When I'd been their age I'd spent all my waking hours working or studying. I don't remember having had the time, or the money, for days at the races, or anywhere else for that matter. I suppose that everyone over forty must eye the young with a touch of envy. They still have their whole lives ahead of them, their dreams and aspirations untainted by experience and disappointment.

The fourth race of the day was the Grade One Stayers' Hurdle, run over two complete circuits of the course. At three miles it was one of the longest hurdle races on the calendar, with all twelve runners carrying the same weight of a hundred sixty-four pounds. It was a true test of a horse's stamina, especially as the going was officially "soft."

I stood by the window of the Vestey Bar and watched over the heads of the crowd as the horses walked around the parade ring and the jockeys were given leg-ups onto them. Someone had left a program lying on the table and I looked to see who was riding: Dick McGee was not, but Jason Conway and Mike Sheraton were both present, Jason in a red jacket with yellow cap, while Mike sported blue-and-white checks. They were easy to spot as they made their way down the horse-walk toward the course.

Many of those in the bar, including the youngsters, went outside to view the race live and cheer home their fancies, so I reclaimed my stool and sat on it watching the contest unfold on the television screen, concentrating hard through the haze of intoxication.

Jason Conway was at it again.

As soon as the starter released the field, Jason was off at a great rate of speed, jumping the first hurdle a good four lengths in front. However, this time, he reined back and settled into mid-division, before his horse tired coming down the hill the second time around and was pulled up before the last.

Mike Sheraton, meanwhile, rode the whole race in about third, fourth or fifth place, never seriously challenging the winner, which went away from the others over the last two flights to win easily by six lengths.

I went outside to watch the horses come back into the winner's enclosure to unsaddle. By now I was just about able to walk in a straight line but I was still thankful to lean on the rail right next to the pole designating the space reserved for the fourth-place horse.

Mike Sheraton had finished fourth.

As the blue-and-white checks came in I held up the photo of the unnamed man high above my head so that Mike Sheraton couldn't fail to see it.

He stared at it, then down at me.

"Who is this man?" I mouthed at him.

There was a touch of panic in his eyes. There was also something else—a coldness. It sent a shiver down my own back that was nothing to do with the ambient temperature. Perhaps it had not been such a good idea to hold up the photo after all. The alcohol had clearly made me over-bold.

I stayed leaning on the rail as Mike Sheraton dismounted and removed his saddle. He glanced my way a couple more times before turning and walking away to weigh in. I watched him go and wondered what he and Jason Conway were involved in.

The police were not even considering the unnamed man's

death as suspicious, just unexplained, but, if the two jockeys' reactions were anything to go by, I reckoned there was quite a lot that was suspicious about it.

I remained standing there as the horses were led away and the presentations to the winning connections were made by the chairman of the sponsors. Then I made my way up the steps toward the crowd first-aid room.

Not that I was in need of any urgent medical assistance or anything. However, I vaguely knew one of the St. John's Ambulance volunteer nurses who was regularly on duty and she lived just down the road from me in Gotherington.

I was hoping she might be able to give me a lift home.

"Hello, Isabelle," I said, going in and thankfully finding her in her bright green St. John's uniform shirt and black skirt.

"Hello, Dr. Rankin," she said in her broad Welsh accent. "How can I help?"

"I was wondering if you could give me a lift home later?" I said. "Save me asking Grant to come and collect me."

"Well, I could," she said slowly, "but my Ian is having to come for me. My car wouldn't start this morning, see. Probably the cold. Damn nuisance too, I can tell you."

"Oh," I said. "I have a car here. Could you drive us home in that?"

She looked at me with her head slightly to one side.

"Why can't you drive your own car? I could come with you then, see."

"Well," I said, taking a deep breath. "I think I may have had one too many to be fit to drive."

She went on looking at me. "Aren't you here on duty?" she asked with a disapproving tone in her voice.

"Good God, no," I said with a laugh. "Merely a spectator

today. Met some old chums and they seem to have forced too much drink on me."

Isabelle relaxed a little. Whether she believed me or not was another matter.

"I suppose I could ring Ian and tell him not to bother," she mused. "He would be grateful for that, see. It's always hell getting back in when everyone else is trying to leave and he likes to go down to the Shutters early on Thursdays for the skittles."

The Shutters was the Shutters Inn, the local pub in Gotherington village.

"Great," I said. "Shall I come back here when you finish? What time?"

She looked around at the other two staff as if gauging their reaction. "I suppose I could get away about an hour after the last race. Say half past six."

It was much later than I'd hoped. I might even be half sober by then.

"OK," I said. "You call your Ian and tell him you are coming home with me and I'll be back here at six-thirty sharp."

Six-thirty. I looked carefully at my watch, trying to concentrate on the hands. Half past four. Two hours to wait. I could easily walk home in that time but it would mean leaving the car, and I now had a plan to ensure that Grant never knew of my indiscretions with my good friend Whisky Macdonald.

Isabelle would drive to her house and then I'd take a chance by driving the last hundred yards home. Easy. Surely all the police would be busy directing the traffic leaving the racecourse.

I texted Grant to tell him that I'd not be home until about seven and could he put the pizzas from the fridge in the oven for the boys' tea if they were back before me. They had made plans to go to a friend's house after school all this week, as I'd been expecting to be on duty at the racecourse anyway.

He texted back straightaway to ask where I was.

"At the racecourse," I texted back. "Helping out. xxx"

"Supposed to be resting," came the reply after a short but meaningful pause. I could tell from the curtness, and no added kisses, that he wasn't pleased.

"I'm taking it easy," I texted back. "See you later. xxx"

Taking it easy drinking, I thought, and was almost tempted to go back to the Vestey Bar for more.

Instead, I went up to the Racing Hall of Fame area—cozy, and no alcohol.

I stood in front of the roaring log fire warming my hands and wondering where I went from here.

The sensible half of my brain was telling me to leave it all to the professionals. *If the police don't believe the man's death was suspicious,* it said, *who are you to say otherwise? Let it go.*

But the delinquent side was adamant. *Something is up,* it said, *and you are the only person who knows it. Keep digging.*

First I turned one way, and then the other.

"What shall I do?" I said, almost to myself.

"I'd do the favorite, if I were you," said the man standing next to me, who had obviously overheard. "But I'm no judge, really. I'm down on the day. In fact, I'm down for the whole bloody meeting. Don't actually know how I'm going to pay my hotel bill tomorrow." He laughed. "Not unless bloody Conway can win this one. Last-chance saloon."

"Jason Conway?" I said.

He nodded. "Useless sod." The man said it with feeling.

"Why did you back him then?" I asked.

"I didn't. I backed the horse, big-time. Months ago and before I knew Conway was riding it."

"So why do you think he's a useless sod?"

"He just is. Did you see the way he rode Checkbook yesterday in the Champion Chase?" The man threw his hands up. "Absolutely hopeless. Far too free early on, then, unsurprisingly, the horse ran out of puff well before the finish. Then Conway trots out some cock-and-bull story to the stewards about being unable to hold him back. All bloody nonsense. Why didn't he just admit that he got it wrong? I had him at a damn good price too."

"So you expected him to win?"

"At least to place or show. Had him across the board."

"Is Checkbook normally a front-runner?" I asked.

"Not according to Timeform. Couldn't believe it when Conway set off as if he was in the bloody Nunthorpe."

The Nunthorpe Stakes was the fastest horse race in the UK—a five-furlong dash, run each year at York in August, lasting less than a minute with the horses traveling in excess of forty miles per hour.

"He did nearly the same thing today in the Stayers' Hurdle," I said.

"Did he?" the man asked vaguely. "I wasn't on him then."

A former colleague of mine, who had also been a passionate gambler on the gee-gees, once told me that, in a race, he only ever watched the horses he'd bet on. What the others did was not his concern, not unless it impacted on how his choices ran.

My newfound friend and I moved away from the warmth of the open fire in order to watch the race on one of the many TV sets. We were both interested in how Jason Conway fared, but for different reasons. I wanted to see if he started fast again, while the man was far more concerned with how he finished.

There were seventeen runners in the Mares' Novice Hurdle and all three of Dick McGee, Mike Sheraton and Jason Conway were riding.

But this time, Jason Conway seemed to be in no particular hurry at the start and, indeed, it was Mike Sheraton who jumped off fastest, easily in front over the initial flight of hurdles before settling down into the pack as the field came up past the grandstands on the first occasion.

As the horses made their way down the back of the course they remained closely bunched together. Meanwhile, the man next to me stared unblinking at the screen, his knuckles gleaming white as he gripped the edge of a table with such force that he was in danger of pulling it over. He really must have been right about not being able to pay his hotel bill unless Jason Conway won on the favorite.

As the horses came to the last flight, the man had almost stopped breathing, then he let out an audible moan of relief as Jason Conway's mount took two lengths off her rivals in a huge leap, and then ran away from them up the hill to win easily.

"Bloody hell!" the man said, still holding on to the table for support. "I'm not doing that again."

"Doing what again?" I asked.

"Staking too much," he said. "Far too much. Real shirt-off-my-back stuff." He laughed nervously. "God, I need a drink."

So do I, I thought, but I didn't follow him off to find one. Instead, I went back to the fire and stood there staring into the flickering flames.

Several recent scientific studies have shown that blood pressure is reduced by the hypnotic effect of flames dancing in a fire. It is believed to have something to do with human evolution and how the discovery of fire reduced the risks of the night by providing light and warding off predators.

Maybe President Franklin D. Roosevelt knew more than people realized when he delivered his famous series of "fireside chats" during the Great Depression of the 1930s and the Second World War in the forties.

For me, it simply gave me an opportunity to think.

Why would the jockeys deny knowing the unnamed man when they clearly did? What were they trying to hide? Was it to do with his overdose of cocaine? Or something else? Was the man's death not an accident or suicide as the police believed, but murder? Or did the jockeys at least think that?

Lots of questions but no answers.

Someone had to find them and I didn't hold out much hope that it would be the police. It wasn't that I thought the detectives were particularly incompetent. It was just that I felt they were overly convinced that the unnamed man had killed himself, intentionally or otherwise, so they weren't looking at any other scenario.

So was it down to me?

16

At six-thirty sharp I was back at the first-aid room to find Isabelle leaning over a man lying on the treatment table.

"Just coming, Dr. Rankin," she said. "Mr. O'Connor, here, had a bit of an argument with a flight of stairs and has cut his head. I won't be a second."

"Can I help?" I asked.

I went over to the treatment table.

I might have had a few drinks too many, but Mr. O'Connor had clearly had quite a lot more than that. In spite of being horizontal, he forcefully gripped the edges of the treatment table to prevent himself from falling off as Isabelle applied some Steri-Strips to close a small wound on his forehead.

"There you are, Mr. O'Connor," Isabelle said, standing back and surveying her handiwork. "Now you take it easy, see."

Mr. O'Connor stood up very slowly. "Tank you," he said, before swaying slightly and making a roundabout lunge for the doorway. And then he was gone into the night.

Isabelle laughed. "Don't you just love the Irish," she said.

"They're always so mellow when they're drunk. Unlike the English, who simply fight."

"Are you ready now?" I asked her. I was quite eager to get away, as the twins were due home at seven.

"Coming, dear," Isabelle said, and she collected her coat.

ISABELLE AND I walked together down the hill in the dark to my car, but we were going nowhere in it, not for a while anyway.

It was Isabelle who spotted it first, in the glow of one of the lights that were set up around the parking lots to help people find their vehicles.

"Oh dear," she said. "I think you've got a puncture."

But then we saw that not just one but all four of the wheels were down on their rims.

"Bugger," I said angrily.

Isabelle, meanwhile, was quite distressed by the discovery. "This can't just have happened accidentally," she said with a tremor of concern in her voice. "Someone must have done this on purpose."

"Indeed they did," I said pragmatically, and wondered who.

I knew that he was pretty angry with me, but surely Adrian Kings wouldn't have done such a thing?

No. I dismissed the notion almost as soon as I had it. Ridiculous.

So, who? And why? And was it directed specifically at me or at Mini owners in general? And who knew my car well enough to pick it out among so many others?

I then noticed that there was a piece of paper tucked under the windshield wiper. I reached forward and removed it. There were three words written on it in capital letters: STOP ASKING QUESTIONS.

So it *was* directed specifically at me.

I wasn't shocked.

I wasn't even surprised.

In fact, if anything, I was pleased.

It confirmed that my obsession with the unnamed man must be for a valid reason.

I spun round a full 360 degrees on my heel, trying to see if the person who had done this had also waited to see what would happen when I came back to the car. But, if he were still there, he remained hidden in the shadows.

So, what to do now?

Isabelle was still rather flustered. "Shouldn't we call the police, dear?" she asked.

"Maybe," I said.

I opened the car and removed the flashlight that I kept in the glovebox. Next I used it to inspect the tires. I was quite expecting them to be slashed but I could spot no obvious damage to any of them. On all four, the little plastic cap had been removed, a short length of matchstick inserted to hold the valve open, and then the cap had been loosely replaced, allowing the tire to deflate.

They had all been let down rather than punctured.

"I don't think we need the police," I said. "What we need is a pump."

Most cars had departed soon after the last race but there was still a steady stream of people coming through the exits, leaving the bars and hospitality areas, where the drink had continued to flow well after the horses had stopped running.

I walked the few yards back to the exit.

"Does anyone have a pump?" I shouted. "I have a flat tire."

"I have one," said a smart gentleman in a three-piece tweed

suit with a shock of white hair—my chivalrous knight coming to the aid of a damsel in distress. "I'll get it. Where's your car?"

"Just down here," I said, pointing.

"OK," he said. "I'm just over there. Back in a mo."

He hurried away and I worried that, when he got to his car, he'd change his mind and drive off. But I needn't have. He came trotting over with a smart electric model that plugged into the car's cigarette lighter socket.

"I say," he said, inspecting all four wheels. "This is a rum do. Did you forget to pay your bookie or something?"

I laughed. "Something like that."

It was amazing how a bit of alcohol could make one both confident and carefree at the same time.

ISABELLE AND I were on our way after only a twenty-minute delay, with her driving, and the wait had even allowed the worst of the traffic to dissipate. We turned straight out onto the Evesham Road with no problem whatsoever.

"I still think we should call the police," Isabelle kept saying.

"On what grounds?" I asked. "That someone stole the air from my tires?"

"Malicious damage," she insisted. "It *must* be against the law to let other people's tires down."

It was certainly antisocial, I thought, but I doubted that it was also illegal, not unless you were purposefully trying to put someone in danger.

Isabelle drove *very* slowly. Maybe it was because she wasn't used to the car, or perhaps she didn't like driving at night, but it took us at least twenty minutes to reach her house, a journey I usually did in half that time.

"Are you sure you'll be all right, dear?" she asked when I told her I'd drive the last hundred yards home.

"Perfectly," I replied.

But I was pretty sure that I was still over the limit. I'd had eight measures of whisky and the same again of ginger wine—a minimum of twelve units of alcohol in just a single hour, when the recommended maximum was fourteen for a whole week. True, it had now been some time since my last one, but, even so, I wouldn't fancy my chances with a breath test. But I fancied my chances even less with Grant if he found out I'd been drinking. He'd have me back in the hospital before you could pop a champagne cork.

I dug into my pocket for the packet of extra-strong mints I'd bought at the confectionery stall at the racecourse, and popped two of them into my mouth.

I then waited until Isabelle had disappeared through her front door before gently letting out the clutch and driving smoothly, and very carefully, along the road.

No problem.

Imagine my horror, therefore, to find a yellow-and-blue-checked squad car waiting outside my house with a policeman sitting in it.

In panic, I thought about going straight on, but that would have been even more suspicious. We lived in a cul-de-sac and I'd have had to turn around at the far end and come back.

So I pulled into the driveway, quickly crunched two more extra-strong mints between my teeth, took a couple of deep breaths and climbed out of my car.

"Hello, Dr. Rankin," said the policeman. It was Constable Filippos and he held a clipboard, not a Breathalyzer. "Your husband said you'd be home soon from the racecourse, so I waited."

"Didn't he ask you in?" I said.

"He did but I could tell he was busy getting food ready, so I waited here." He waved toward the patrol car. "Can you spare me a few minutes?"

"Of course," I said. "Come on in."

We went into the house with me trying not to breathe anywhere near him. Grant and the boys were in the kitchen so we went into the sitting room.

"Are you on duty?" I asked, waving a hand at his clothes. He wasn't wearing his uniform but chinos and a sweater.

"Absolutely," he said. "I've been transferred to CID. I'm a detective constable now."

"Is that a promotion?"

"More like a shift sideways." He smiled. "But one I wanted."

"Congratulations. Can I get you anything? Coffee or tea?" Glass of wine? No, perhaps not.

"Tea would be lovely," he said. "Milk, no sugar."

I went into the kitchen.

"Hi, Mum," Toby and Oliver said together.

"Hi, darlings," I replied with a wave. "Good day?"

In unison, they both raised their eyes as if to say, "Of course it wasn't a good day, Mum, it was a school day."

Grant was busy cutting up pizzas and I decided not to go over and kiss him. I didn't want to breathe alcohol over him either.

"There's a policeman waiting for you outside," he said.

"I know. He's now in the sitting room. I expect he's come to ask me some questions about that patient who died at the hospital last November."

"Trouble?" Grant asked.

"No, nothing like that. Probably just some more information

needed for the coroner. Could you make him some tea—milk, no sugar—and bring it through? Thanks."

I went back to DC Filippos.

"I was just passing," he said, "on my way back from Stow-on-the-Wold, so I thought I'd pop in and bring you up to date with developments."

"What developments?" I demanded. "Have you caught the person who pushed me in front of the bus?"

He was slightly taken aback. "Sorry, no. No progress on that one."

That was because he wasn't looking, I thought.

"But I did speak yesterday to those two jockeys that you said were seen arguing with the dead man."

I nodded. "One of them told me."

"Then you probably already know what I'm going to tell you."

"No, I don't," I said. "He only told me that he'd spoken to the police, not what he'd actually said."

"Right. Well, I interviewed them both at the racecourse on Wednesday after racing and they said roughly the same thing."

"Which was?"

"That they vaguely remember having an argument with a man in the parking lot but they do not know who he was."

"What was the argument about?"

"As far as they could recall, it was about the unauthorized parking of his car in the jockeys' reserved area."

"So where is it now, then?" I asked.

"Where's what?"

"His car."

He stared at me.

"And his car keys," I added.

The policeman went on staring.

Grant came in with the tea and I waited silently for him to leave.

"So do you still think the man's death is not suspicious?" I said, my voice thick with irony. "I am absolutely certain that both the jockeys were lying to you. They know a lot more than they are telling."

"Why are you so sure?"

"Well, for one thing, their reaction when I showed them the photo of the dead man."

"How exactly did they react?"

"There was serious concern in Mike Sheraton's eyes and Jason Conway was no less troubled."

"But did they actually say anything?"

"Not as such, no," I said. "But their body language was screaming loudly in panic." The constable didn't look that convinced. "I'm telling you, they know more than they're saying. You could at least ask them the make of his car."

"I could," he agreed.

"And do it separately so they can't simply agree on an answer."

He smiled. "You've been watching too many television dramas, Dr. Rankin. No one is a suspect in this case."

"Not yet, but they will be."

"OK," he said. "I'll ask them but they will probably say that they don't remember, and, after all this time, I don't think I'd remember either."

"Did you ask them why they didn't come forward on their own?"

"I did," he said. "But they both claimed they didn't realize that the man they had argued with was the same man as in the photo."

"Dick McGee did. When *he* saw the image, he stopped as if he'd been shot."

"Then I will have to have a word with him as well." The DC smiled in a manner that made me think he was humoring me, and I didn't much like it.

"Look, I know you all think I'm crazy because I've spent time in a psychiatric hospital, but I'm not. I suffer from depression and I have an eating disorder but that doesn't make me paranoid or a fantasist."

"I'm sorry," he said.

"And there's another thing," I said, pulling the folded piece of paper from my pocket. "Someone let down all four tires on my car in the racecourse parking lot this evening and left this stuck under the windshield wipers."

I handed the piece of paper over to him and he opened it.

He dropped it onto the coffee table as if he'd received an electric shock, the three written words facing uppermost: STOP ASKING QUESTIONS.

DC Filippos wasn't smiling now.

"And all my questions," I said, "were directed toward Dick McGee, Jason Conway and Mike Sheraton. No one else." I paused. "So now tell me those jockeys don't know more than they're saying."

17

On Friday morning I went back to the racecourse, in direct violation of Grant's express command.

He had told me firmly at breakfast that I must spend the whole day resting. I'd sat there emotionless as he spoke. I'd had no intention of obeying him, but I hadn't exactly said so at the time. In fact, I hadn't said anything at all.

I had things I wanted to do at the racecourse, but I did plan to be home well before Grant returned from work so he wouldn't know.

I debated with myself whether I should park in the same place as I'd done the previous day and then secretly watch to see if anyone came again to let the tires down. But, in the end, I decided to leave my Mini in Tom and Julie's farmyard, as I'd done on Tuesday, and I made my way into the racecourse parking lot on foot, taking special care when crossing the Evesham Road.

The previous evening, DC Filippos had taken away the piece of paper after carefully placing it in a plastic sandwich bag I'd given him from my kitchen, making sure that Grant was unaware of its existence.

"I'll inform DS Merryweather and get the paper tested," he'd said. "It may give us some idea who left it there, although that doesn't prove it was the same person who let your tires down. Do you have any witnesses to that?"

I thought of Isabelle. "There is at least one other person who will swear that all four tires *were* flat, but she was not a witness to them actually being let down." I wondered if I could also find my chivalrous knight in his three-piece tweed suit, not that he would know anything that Isabelle and I didn't.

I arrived at the racecourse really early, before the gates even opened, and I hung about close to the jockeys' reserved parking area.

I didn't really know what I was going to do but I was determined to confront the three jockeys and to give them a piece of my mind for letting down my tires. Perhaps I was hoping for a reaction from one or more of them, something that might give me a lead to further revelations concerning the unnamed man.

Or was I being stupid to get involved?

Leave it to the police, the sensible half of my brain kept telling me.

But the delinquent half was now winning easily.

Of one thing, I *was* sure—having the nameless man to worry about, together with the sure knowledge that my concern was not without foundation, had done wonders for my mood. I felt, suddenly, that I had a purpose back in my life and it gave me a terrific lift.

I suppose I had been initially drawn to a career in medicine by some altruistic belief that I could do some good in the world. I think all doctors are. Otherwise why would we continue as impoverished students for so long after some of our contemporaries from school are already out in the real world earning six-figure salaries, to say nothing of the long hours and manic workload of the junior doctor.

Unlike some of my specialist colleagues in private practice, my chosen specialty of emergency medicine was never going to make me hugely wealthy but it was at the forefront of "doing good" and, as such, had always been rewarding in other ways.

To have had that taken away from me over these past few months had simply compounded my problems with depression.

Various studies have shown that doctors in general are more than twice as likely to kill themselves than members of the general population, a situation that increases to five or six times for female doctors compared to other women. So why do medics, who strive to save the lives of others, kill themselves in such disproportionately high numbers?

It certainly has something to do with a greater knowledge of the methods, and an increased availability of the means to end their own lives, which result in a higher success rate. But I am convinced that it is also because we doctors tend to enjoy a more utopian view of the world, a world where we assume modern medical science can cure all ills. Hence, when reality kicks in and medicine actually fails, we are more likely to feel guilt and self-condemnation.

I had certainly suffered overwhelming guilt over the death of the unnamed man. He had arrived at the hospital alive and breathing, yet I still hadn't been able to save him. Medical science had failed, when I'd fully expected it to win through.

But now I believed I was absolving myself from that guilt by finding out who the man was and why he had died. Yes, it had become an obsession, but I considered that it was also the road to my salvation and recovery. Some might say it was foolhardy, even dangerous, to confront the three jockeys, but, for me, it was logical and necessary.

WHILE I STOOD WAITING, the phone rang in my pocket. It was Constable Filippos.

"Ah, Dr. Rankin," he said. "I have a message from Detective Sergeant Merryweather. We would very much like to have a meeting with you. Can you come in to the station this afternoon?"

"I'm at the racecourse," I said.

"Oh," he said. "So are we."

"Where?" I asked.

"Outside the jockeys' changing room. We're here to conduct some interviews."

"With McGee, Conway and Sheraton?" I asked.

There was a slight pause from the other end as if he was deciding whether he should tell me.

"Among others, yes," replied the policeman.

"They're not here yet," I said. "I'm waiting for them in the parking lot."

"Dr. Rankin," DC Filippos said seriously, "please leave us to do our job. There is no need for you to speak with any of them."

"Isn't there?" I said. "If it wasn't for me, you wouldn't have a clue what to do next. I have learned more in the last three days than you lot have in four months."

"That is not entirely fair," he said. "We have made considerable progress ourselves."

"What progress?" I asked, unable to keep the sarcasm out of my voice.

"If you come to the station later, I will give you all the details."

"Why not give them to me here, after you've spoken to the jockeys?"

I could hear him speaking to someone else, even though I couldn't catch the exact words because he'd placed something over the microphone.

"OK," he said, eventually. "DS Merryweather and I will meet you here at the racecourse after we have spoken to the jockeys, on the condition that you do not to speak to them first."

That was bribery, I thought.

The only chance I had of accosting McGee, Conway and Sheraton was as they arrived. I couldn't wait until they left later in the day—that would be impossible with everyone going home at the same time, and in the dark.

"OK," I said slowly. "I promise not to speak to them first. Where do we meet, and when?"

"There's a police control room in the foyer of The Centaur. Meet us there at . . ." There was a pause as he consulted. ". . . half past twelve."

I looked at my watch. It showed it was now ten-thirty.

"OK," I said. "I'll be there."

GOLD CUP DAY was always the busiest of the four days of the Festival, with an expected crowd of seventy thousand, and the parking lots were beginning to fill up fast even at this early hour.

Even though I had agreed not to speak to McGee, Conway and Sheraton, it didn't mean that I would not still wait for them in the jockeys' reserved parking area.

However, the first person to arrive that I recognized was not one of those three. It was Dave Leigh, he with the broken collarbone, arriving in his automatic BMW. I walked over to greet him as he climbed out of his car.

"Hi, Dave," I said. "How's the shoulder today?"

"Oh, hi, Doc," he said. "Fine. But it's a bugger to sleep with. Can't get comfortable. I've ended up sitting in an armchair all night."

"It will be sore for a week or so," I said. "Until the ends of the bone begin to knit together."

He didn't look very happy at the prospect of more nights in his armchair.

"How did the TV work go yesterday?" I asked.

"Really well," he said with a smile. "They've asked me back again today, otherwise I wouldn't be here. I've decided I don't enjoy sitting watching others ride when I can't."

I knew how he felt. I didn't much enjoy watching the duty doctors working when I'd been excluded from their team.

"Where's your car then, Doc?" Dave asked, looking all around him.

"What about my car?" I asked sharply.

"I just wondered where it was," Dave said. "We were parked next to each other yesterday."

I thought it strange that he knew what my car looked like.

"Do you recall seeing my car when you came out last night?" I asked.

"Sure, light blue Mini with a Union Jack roof," he said. "Very distinctive. Same as my missus—that's why I remember it. But I left early. After the Stayers' Hurdle. After I'd done my bit for the TV people."

"What time?"

"I don't know exactly. About four. Why?"

"Did you notice anything unusual about my car?"

"No. What sort of unusual?"

"Were all the tires flat?"

"No," he said. "Least, I don't think so. I'd have surely no-ticed." He paused. "Blimey. Who did that then?"

"I wish I knew," I said. "I'd give them what for."

"Did they do anyone else's?"

"No," I replied. "Just mine."

"That's really bad luck," he said. "Did they slash them?"

"No," I said. "Just let them down. And it wasn't bad luck. I was specifically targeted."

Dave Leigh suddenly looked troubled.

"What's the problem?" I asked.

"Nothing," he said. "I'd better get on in." He turned to go away but I grabbed him by his good arm and swung him back to face me.

"What's the problem?" I asked again, this time more forcefully.

He looked like a frightened schoolboy.

"Somebody yesterday was asking about you."

"Who?"

"I can't remember."

"Come on, Dave," I said angrily. "Don't give me that crap. Who was it?"

"I really can't remember," he whined.

"What were they asking about me?"

"I don't know. I just heard your name mentioned and I'd just seen you so it registered with me."

"Where did this take place?"

"In the changing room. I was getting ready to do my piece to camera. Someone mentioned your name and I remember saying that it was a coincidence because I was parked right alongside you in the parking lot. That's all."

"Who knows your car?" I asked.

"What do you mean?"

"Which of the other jockeys knows your car?"

"All of them. We all know each other's cars. Wives and girl-friends help get them home when one of us gets injured. My car was driven back for me by someone on Tuesday when I broke this." He pointed at his collarbone. "The valets organize it."

"Please try and remember who it was who was talking about me."

He put his head on one side and stared into space. "Sorry," he said. "It could have been anyone."

"How about him?" I said, pointing at Mike Sheraton, who was driving an Audi into a parking space about twenty yards away from us.

"No, not him," Dave said with bitterness but conviction. "I'd have remembered if that bastard had been the one."

"How about Jason Conway or Dick McGee?"

He thought some more.

"It could have been, but it might not. Like I told you, I can't remember."

"Who heard what you said about parking next to me?"

"Anyone in there. I was hardly quiet." He laughed. "I was also miked up."

"Did *he* hear you?" I pointed again at Mike Sheraton, who was removing a carryall from the trunk of his car.

"Might have done," Dave said. "I don't know."

I stood staring at Mike Sheraton. He glanced briefly in my direction and did a double take, turning up one corner of his mouth in a sneer, but I couldn't be sure that he was sneering at me rather than at Dave Leigh. There was clearly no love lost between them.

Mike slammed shut the trunk of his car and marched off toward the entrance without looking back.

"Why do you two not get on?" I asked.

"That man doesn't get on with anyone," Dave replied.

"Why not?"

"He's too competitive."

I laughed. "That's rich. All jockeys are competitive."

"Yeah, maybe, but Sheraton is overly so. And he cheats."

"How?" I asked.

"He'll swerve to take your ground at the last second as you approach a fence when there's no head-on camera. Bloody dangerous it is, but he doesn't care. And he uses his whip."

"Don't you all?" I asked.

"Not on the opposition. Horses and jockeys. It doesn't make the nags run faster when he hits them across the nose, and it bloody hurts when he catches you on the face."

"Don't the stewards take action?"

"Never see it. He's too quick and too clever. He's not the only one, mind. Cutthroat business, racing. Win at all costs—that's what matters. My trouble is I'm too bloody nice."

He smiled at me and walked off.

I wasn't sure if he was joking or not, but I didn't have long to ponder before another of my three of interest arrived.

18

At a quarter past eleven, Jason Conway swept into the parking area in a silver Jaguar F-Type with a personalized number plate, locking up his rear wheels on the loose gravel as he braked to a halt.

I suppose my plan had been just to let Conway see me, to rattle him somewhat before he spoke with the police. But I was too slow. Almost in a single movement he climbed out of the car and set off toward the racecourse entrance, without looking once in my direction.

I hurried after him, wanting so much to shout out, to ask whether he had let down my tires, but I was wary of my promise to DC Filippos.

However, Jason Conway didn't go directly to the entrance. Instead, he veered off to his right, heading for the cars and four-by-fours already lined up six deep in the members' parking lot.

I hung back, not wanting to be seen following him.

He moved swiftly along the second line of vehicles almost right to the far end until he came to a long black Mercedes with dark-tinted rear windows. He ducked down a little and knocked on the driver's window, which opened a couple of inches. As far as I could tell, there was no verbal exchange with an occupant, just a handing out of what looked like a small white envelope that Jason quickly stuffed into his trouser pocket before walking away.

I bent down behind another car in the next line so that he couldn't see me. Gone had my plans to rattle him. The handing over of the envelope had all the hallmarks of a clandestine exchange, furtive and unseen, and I had no desire to let Jason Conway become aware that, in fact, I had witnessed it at all.

What could be in the envelope?

Drugs was the first thing that came to mind, but why would anyone hand over drugs in a racecourse parking lot before racing, when the place was awash with people either arriving or having a couple of cocktails over a tailgate before taking on the bookies. Surely it would have been better at the end of the day when it would be getting dark and everyone was intent on just finding their vehicles and departing.

It had to be something that he needed straightaway, something that couldn't wait until the end of the day.

His next fix? Was he addicted?

But what about the drug testers? Cheltenham Gold Cup day would be a given for them to be on-site with their detested pee-sampling kits. The racing authority took a very dim view of jockeys caught using recreational drugs, including alcohol, cannabis and cocaine. In a palpably dangerous sport, anything that could impair judgment was a threat to the safety of all participants—much like Lewis Hamilton driving under the influence in a Grand Prix.

I stayed low and watched Conway walk back down the line of cars toward the racecourse entrance.

What should I do now?

Should I follow him? Or should I watch and wait at the Mercedes to see who emerged?

I suddenly felt really excited, like a schoolgirl who has discovered something that no one else knows. As a teenager, I had avidly devoured all the Nancy Drew mysteries, livening up my own rather tedious young life by imagining myself accompanying the youthful amateur sleuth on her thrilling adventures, and here I was now being a detective myself, and one step ahead of the police.

I decided to stay where I was and see who got out of the black Mercedes but I was to be disappointed. Almost as soon as Jason Conway had disappeared through the racecourse entrance, the Mercedes drove off. I stood and watched it go to the parking-lot exit and turn left onto the Evesham Road in the direction of Cheltenham town center.

How odd, I thought, to be in the members' parking lot but not stay for the racing. I now wished I had followed Conway, but maybe the occupants of the Mercedes had been watching to see if he'd had a tail.

At least I had taken a photograph with my phone of the rear of the car as it drove away, its license plate clearly visible.

I walked back to the jockeys' reserved car-parking area, which had filled up considerably in the meantime. There I found one of my erstwhile colleagues, Dr. Jack Otley, who was still acting. He had just arrived and was putting on his coat.

"Hi, Jack," I said. "How are things?"

"Oh, hi, Chris. I didn't think you were here today."

"I'm not," I said. "Least, I'm not here as one of the team."

"Adrian is not very happy with you," he said. "He was in a foul mood yesterday, saying you had deceived him."

"That's not actually true. But it might be best not to tell him you've seen me." I laughed. "Are the drug testers in today, do you know?"

Drug testing of the jockeys was performed by an independent organization that turned up randomly at racecourses in order to carry out either breath or urine tests. If it was a breath day, then all the jockeys riding were tested for alcohol with the limit only half of that permitted for driving, and, for a urine day, a minimum of ten riders, selected by draw, were required to give a urine sample before leaving the racecourse. Even though the testers were independent of the racecourse medical team, they did need to notify the senior medical officer of their presence.

"They haven't been here all week, so I wouldn't be surprised," Jack said.

"If they come, get them to test Jason Conway," I said.

Jack looked at me strangely. "Why?"

"Just ask them."

"Chris, if you have reason to believe that a jockey should be tested for drugs, then you need to go through the proper channels." He was being very formal.

"Via Adrian Kings?" I shrugged. "I don't think so."

He looked awkward. "I must go. Adrian wants everyone there early today."

Everyone except me.

Jack hurried off toward the entrance and my watch showed me it was half past eleven. Still two hours until the first race and an hour before I was due to meet with the police.

The police.

I made a call.

"DC Filippos," said the voice that answered.

"Ask Jason Conway about the envelope in his right trouser pocket," I said.

"Sorry," said the policeman. "Who is this?"

"Chris Rankin," I said. "Ask Conway about the envelope. Or, better still, search him."

"Dr. Rankin," he said with a somewhat exasperated tone, "we can't just search people without good reason. What is in this envelope?"

"I thought you could stop and search anyone."

"Only if we have reasonable grounds for suspicion. Now, what is in the envelope?"

"Drugs," I said, jumping to a conclusion. "I saw it being handed over from a black Mercedes in the parking lot."

"Are you sure?" he asked.

I hesitated. "No, I'm not sure, but why else would something be handed over in such a furtive manner so that no one else could see?"

"But *you* saw."

"Only because I was following him."

"Dr. Rankin," the policeman said in a rather condescending manner, "I have already told you to leave any investigating to us."

"I am," I said. "That's why I'm telling you about the envelope. So that you can investigate it."

I decided not to mention my photograph of the Mercedes license plate, not yet anyway. Best to see what was in the envelope first.

I HUNG AROUND for a while longer in the parking lot but either Dick McGee was late or he had slipped in during my excursion up the line of cars behind Jason Conway.

I was concerned that my "Authorized Doctor" pass might have been revoked but it allowed me to safely negotiate the entrance turnstiles.

I kept well away from the weighing room and the parade ring, and I carefully bypassed the Vestey Bar in making my way up toward The Centaur, a big indoor space that could be used for all sorts of events from weddings and dinner dances to live-band music concerts and conferences.

During the racing festival, the space was used simply as an extension of the grandstand with bars, food outlets and bookmakers catering for the many who preferred to remain inside away from the elements, watching the action on a huge-screen projection TV.

I was at the police control room in the foyer bang on the appointed time but I still had to wait. Indeed, it was almost one o'clock before detectives Merryweather and Filippos arrived, and they weren't particularly happy with me.

I was ushered into a small interview room containing a table and four chairs. I sat on one side of the table while the two policemen sat opposite.

"Am I under arrest, or something?" I asked with a hollow laugh.

Neither of them laughed back.

"Not at this time," said DS Merryweather seriously. "However, we are concerned that you are interfering with our investigation, something that has to stop."

"I'm only trying to help," I said sheepishly.

"Well, you're not," he said angrily. "And, if you don't cease immediately, I will have you arrested for wasting police time."

He was trying to bully me, and I didn't like it.

"How exactly have I wasted your time?" I said, robustly

defending myself. "If it wasn't for me, you wouldn't have found anyone who knew who the nameless man was."

"We still haven't," he replied.

"But those jockeys know who he is."

"They deny that. Two of them agree that they may have had an argument with the man in the parking lot but they maintain they have no idea who he was."

"They're lying," I said flatly.

"How do you know?" DS Merryweather said.

"From their reaction to his picture. They were worried. They must know who he was. Can't you do a lie-detector test on them?"

"The polygraph is not standard equipment for use by UK police forces."

More's the pity, I thought.

"And how about the envelope?" I asked. "It was me who saw that transferred in the parking lot."

"Ah, yes," the detective said sarcastically. "The envelope. You told my constable here that it contained drugs. Why was that?"

"Didn't it?" I asked.

"No," he said.

"What did it contain?" I asked.

"A train time," he said. "Nothing more. Just a piece of paper with the name of a London railway station and the time of a train."

"Which station?" I asked.

"That doesn't matter," he said, his anger again rising. "We searched Jason Conway on your say-so and you made us look foolish when we found nothing sinister."

"What about my tires?" I asked. "Did you ask him about those?"

"Indeed we did," replied the detective, the sarcasm still thick in his voice. "Are you aware that Jason Conway's horse won the sixth race yesterday?"

"Yes," I said, "I watched it." I remembered back to the man who had staked too much on him and was in danger of not being able to pay his hotel bill.

"But are you also aware that the horse kicked Conway in the knee as he was removing his saddle? He was in the jockeys' medical room receiving treatment from the physical therapist until nearly seven o'clock last night. He could not have let your tires down."

"Then it must have been Dick McGee or Mike Sheraton. Did you ask them?"

"Both denied any knowledge of the incident. They also were adamant that neither of them even knows what your car looks like."

"They're lying," I said again. "It has to be one of them. No one else knew I'd been asking questions about the dead man." But I could tell from their demeanor that neither of the detectives believed me.

"Do you think I put that note on my windshield myself?" I asked in exasperation. "What about fingerprints on it? Did you test for them?"

For some reason they were uneasy about it, which probably meant no, they hadn't.

"We can't just fingerprint anyone we want, you know, not unless we've arrested them first."

"You haven't even taken mine to eliminate them," I said with resignation. "Anyone would think you don't want to know who the nameless man was or why he died."

"Our inquiries are ongoing," said the detective sergeant in true police-speak.

"What inquiries?" I asked, my tone rather mocking. "You don't even rate the man's death as suspicious."

"We are treating it as unexplained. That means we still have an open mind as to the full circumstances of his death. However, we do know that the man died of a cocaine overdose that was most likely consumed from a contaminated bottle of whisky that had his fingerprints all over it. He was found in a lavatory cubicle that had been locked from the inside and there were no obvious signs of a struggle. Our inference from the facts is that the man died either by suicide or by an accidental overdose."

"But the very fact that he had no means of identification and you still can't find out his name is surely suspicious."

"You might be surprised how many unidentified dead people we have in our files."

"How many?" I asked. "Three? Four? Five, maybe?"

"Nationwide, well over a thousand."

I must have sat there with my mouth hanging open for several seconds.

"A thousand!"

"There were one hundred and fifty unidentified human remains found last year alone," DS Merryweather said. "The man in the Cheltenham grandstand restroom was just one of those."

"That's incredible."

"Many are decomposed but a sizable number are, like our man, alive when first found or, at least, have only just died. And only about one in ten of those turns out to be suspicious."

"Don't people contact you when a family member fails to come home?"

"We get those calls all the time. We've had nearly forty about this particular man but none of them have delivered a credible name. There've even been two visits to the morgue by families claiming the man was theirs but both have been excluded by DNA testing."

I felt slightly ashamed that I thought the police had done nothing.

"Many of the unidentified are completely estranged from families, while others are foreigners who die while over in the UK. Quite a lot are suicides. About half will have a name put to them eventually, but the others will simply remain on file as unknown."

"What happens to them?" I asked.

"There is no national agreed protocol. Some councils provide basic burials, but many are stored in morgues for years."

I shuddered slightly. My medical career had always been concerned with the living, not least because of my parents' infatuation with the dead. I'd never had any wish to move into pathology, even though I could appreciate the excitement of uncovering the mystery of the causes of sudden death.

"So where do we go from here?" I asked.

"*You* go nowhere," DS Merryweather said firmly. "We will continue our inquiries. We're trying a new technique called isotope analysis, which looks at the makeup of a body in terms of its chemical isotopes. On the basis that you are what you eat, we hope it can reveal where in the world our man had been living."

"So you think he was foreign?" I asked.

"It is an open line of inquiry."

"Any news from India?"

"Not as yet, but it's early days."

"Do you have any idea how he traveled to the racecourse in

the first place?" I asked. "You surely don't believe that nonsense about him parking his car in the jockeys' reserved section?"

"We have an open mind about that," the detective said again. "We have no evidence that he came either by car or by train. There were no train tickets found on him."

"Nor any car keys," I said.

"No. Those neither. But he could have had a lift from someone, even someone he didn't know."

"How about CCTV?"

"The racecourse system failed to spot him entering and the cameras at the train station were out of order on the day in question."

How typical was that, I thought.

"How about the bookmaker's slip in the man's pocket?"

"Dead end."

"Which bookmaker?" I asked.

There was a pause while the sergeant worked out in his own mind if telling me was a good idea or a bad one.

"Come on," I said imploringly. "Tell me. Which bookmaker?"

"Tommy Berkley," he said reluctantly. "We showed him the photo but he says he can't remember the man. Seems he only ever remembers the big winners and big losers, and our man was neither of those."

"How much was the bet?" I asked. That too would have been printed on the slip.

"Five pounds to win. Not very memorable."

"Which horse?"

"I can't recall," the detective sergeant replied with some irritation. "It doesn't matter which horse."

"Fabricated," interjected DC Filippos, the first thing he'd said all interview.

"Yes, that's right," said Merryweather. "The horse's name was Fabricated."

Just like the jockeys' story about the man parking his car in their spaces.

AFTER MORE THAN HALF AN HOUR, I was sent on my way with another strongly worded warning still ringing in my ears.

"Leave it all to us," DS Merryweather commanded firmly, "or else you will be arrested and charged with obstructing the police in the execution of their duty."

"But . . ."

"No buts," he said, holding up a hand to interrupt me. "Absolutely no buts."

But there were *buts*, I thought. Lots of them.

But I was certain that the man's death actually was suspicious.

But I was the only person who had actually seen the reaction from Dick McGee and the other jockeys when they had seen the image of the dead man.

But I was the only person who therefore knew they were lying.

And finally, *but* this was very important to me, and not just for the dead man's sake. My whole future mental well-being might depend on it.

So I had no intention whatsoever of leaving it all to the police.

19

Racing was well under way by the time I emerged from the police control room.

What should I do now?

I wandered aimlessly among the huge crowd, surrounded on every side by those having a good time yet feeling totally isolated and alone. Somehow, up until this point, I had considered myself part of a team that was trying to solve the mystery of the dead man. Suddenly, I had been cast out, unwelcome and unappreciated.

Not wanted at the hospital, not wanted as a doctor at the racecourse and now seemingly "not wanted" in any capacity, I would have had every right and excuse for descending once more into a depression-fueled abyss. However, far from feeling miserable about my situation, I was spurred on by it.

I *would* discover why the man died.

I may have failed him in life, but I would not do so again in death.

I WATCHED THE THIRD RACE from the jam-packed viewing steps of the grandstand, crammed in between a group of six young men on a day trip from Birmingham and another of five, over from County Cork across the Irish Sea. I knew this because they introduced each other at length, every one of them insisting on shaking hands with all the members of the other group, something not easy when we were all squashed together like sardines.

I was unintentionally swept up in this example of international friendship, shaking my hand with all of them and even receiving a few beery kisses along the way.

It made me laugh, and it was just what I needed.

The favorite won the race to a great cheer from the crowd and was greeted into the winner's circle like a returning war hero.

I, meanwhile, made my way through the throng to the betting ring, that open space in front of the grandstand where the majority of the bookmakers stood at their pitches, their price boards glowing brightly with red and yellow lights.

"Let's be 'aving you," one of them shouted enthusiastically at the milling mass of prospective customers, "eleven-to-four the field for the Gold Cup."

The punters moved up and down the lines of bookmakers looking for the best-offered odds for their selected horse. The odds could vary slightly from bookie to bookie, and also in time as the race approached. Odds would shorten if large bets were made on a particular horse, while others might drift longer on less-fancied runners.

It was the way the bookmakers controlled the total bet with them on each horse, to maintain their "book" in profit whatever the outcome. The official "starting price" was the most frequent odds on the boards in the betting ring at the moment the race started.

However, the only odds I was really interested in were those displayed on the board of bookmaker Tommy Berkley.

I stood and watched him as he took banknotes from his customers, adding them to the large bundle of bills in his left hand. He shouted out the bet to his assistant behind him, who entered it into a computer. A printer produced a slip showing the bet details, which was then passed to the punter. Each transaction took only a second or two to complete and Tommy was looking for his next customer even before the slip was handed over—a slip just like the one DC Filippos had found in the unnamed man's pocket.

All the bookmakers were doing brisk business as the time approached for the main event of the day—indeed, the main event of the week, if not the whole year. The Cheltenham Gold Cup was the absolute pinnacle of jump racing, the stuff of dreams and legends, and the atmosphere in the betting ring was alive with the static of hope and expectancy.

I looked closely at the names and odds on Tommy Berkley's board.

Card Reader was quoted at three-to-one, his name flashing on and off to indicate he was the favorite in the market. I wondered how Dave Leigh was feeling, doing his piece to camera in the jockeys' changing room for the TV broadcaster with his broken collarbone, while Mike Sheraton donned the silks that Dave believed were rightly his.

But it was another horse's name on the board that really caught my eye.

I looked something up in the program, then took out my cell phone and dialed a number.

"DC Filippos."

"What was the name of the London railway station on the piece of paper in the envelope?" I asked.

"Dr. Rankin," he said firmly, "DS Merryweather told you to leave everything to us. Please do as he asks."

"I only want the name of the station."

"I'm sorry," he said. "I can't tell you that."

"Was it Liverpool Street?" I asked.

There was a long pause from the other end of the line.

"And was the train time three-thirty?"

Another pause.

"Yes," he said finally. "How do you know?"

"It's not a station and a train time," I said. "Liverpool Street is the name of a horse running in the Gold Cup, a race due off at three-thirty."

I waited while the information sank in.

"And Jason Conway is its jockey."

THERE WAS THE CUSTOMARY HUGE CHEER from the crowd as the starter lowered his flag and set the twelve runners in the field for the Gold Cup on their way at three-thirty precisely.

Jason Conway went straight to the front on Liverpool Street, jumping the first fence a good two lengths clear of the rest of the field before reining back and settling down at the front of the pack.

The race is run over two complete laps of the course, three and a quarter miles with twenty-two fences to be jumped, and the twelve runners remained well bunched throughout the first circuit, which was run at a steady tempo.

Only going down the backstretch on the second circuit did

the race begin to finally unfold with the pace hotting up as the jockeys made their bids for glory.

Card Reader led the field rapidly down the hill toward the third-last fence, stealing a lead of three or four lengths on the rest. This was where the race could be won and lost. Taking the downhill fence without a heartbeat of hesitation could gain an advantage that a rival could not recover in the run to the wire.

Mike Sheraton asked Card Reader for a long stride, to stand off from the fence. The horse responded, clearing the obstacle in a huge leap that took it farther away from its pursuers, and the crowd cheered their approval. Just the final straight to go and glory would surely be his.

But horseracing is a funny game and has a well-deserved reputation for producing the unexpected.

Card Reader cleared the second-last with ease and was quickly into his stride. He was now some six or seven lengths in front and going away.

His race was won.

The other runners were nowhere.

Just one fence to go.

Mike Sheraton asked the horse again for a big jump, but carrying a hundred sixty-four pounds over three and a quarter miles in soft ground saps the stamina of even the greatest of steeplechasers.

Card Reader caught the jockey unawares by putting in an extra stride. To indrawn gasps from the crowd, the horse was now far too close to the fence and it plowed through the top eighteen inches of the birch, catapulting Mike Sheraton forward out of the saddle, before following him down in a sprawling mass onto the bright green turf.

Horse and rider were quickly up on their feet but their chance of winning had long gone as the others swept past.

Dave Leigh and his collarbone would be delighted, I thought.

Those behind, who had previously thought their chances of victory were nonexistent, were suddenly spurred on by the realization that the big prize was still up for grabs.

Liverpool Street ran out of puff just twenty-five yards short of the winning post and was caught on the finish line by two other horses in a thrilling blanket finish that had the crowd in raptures.

I stood and watched as the horses walked back down in front of the packed grandstand, the winner being led in by his beaming trainer, Peter Hammond. They received a deserved standing ovation. It may not have been the favorite, but it had been well backed and was a popular winner.

Popular, that was, with the crowd.

Jason Conway, however, looked anything but happy as he went past. He must have thought he would win until the very last stride of the run-in, and had actually finished third. I wondered if the horse might have been able to hang on to win if he hadn't wasted his energy at the start by setting off so quickly.

Tommy Berkley was again busy when I went back to his pitch. I watched from about three yards away as he peeled notes from his wedge, handing them out to a line of successful punters before instantly encouraging them to reinvest in the next race.

He had spotted me earlier and now he looked across at me and raised his eyebrows in a questioning manner while continuing to pay out and take new bets.

I removed the photo of the dead man from my pocket and held it up so he could clearly see it.

"Wait a minute," he shouted across. "This rush will die down soon. Not so much interest in the Foxhunter's."

The Foxhunter Challenge Chase was the race that immediately followed and was run over exactly the same course and distance but was for amateur riders only. It was affectionately referred to as the Amateurs' Gold Cup.

Gradually the bookmaker's line of waiting customers diminished to zero.

"Kevin," he shouted over his shoulder. "Hold the fort a minute."

Kevin appeared and took his place on the pitch.

"Bill Tucker," he said, holding out his hand to me.

"Not Tommy Berkley?" I asked, shaking it.

"My late father-in-law was Tommy Berkley. I took over the business when he died. Who are you?"

"Dr. Chris Rankin," I said. "I treated this man when he was admitted to the hospital, where he later died." I held out the picture to him. "A betting slip with 'Tommy Berkley' printed on it was found in his pocket."

"I've already told the police I don't remember him."

"It was a five-pound bet on a horse called Fabricated."

"When?"

"Saturday of the International Meeting, last November."

"Blimey," he said. "No wonder I don't remember. I've seen an awful lot of punters' faces since then."

"Do you remember the horse?" I asked.

"Fabricated? Of course. Damn good chaser. Sadly didn't run in the Ryanair this week due to injuring himself in the King George on Boxing Day. Fell at the last. Three miles was probably a bit far for him, if the truth be told. Better over two and a half. He might be back for the Melling Chase at Aintree in three weeks. Do you want a price on him?"

"No thanks." I smiled at him. "What race was he in, back in November?"

"That would've been the Mackeson, or whatever it's called these days. The big race of the day anyway." He stared over my head for a second as if he was thinking. "Won by Price of Success at fifteen-to-two. Fabricated was third at eights, beaten a short-head for second by Medication at twelve-to-one, that's if I remember right."

I didn't doubt his memory for a second. In my experience, bookmakers might not remember their customers but they knew most things about the horses, especially their breeding and form. Profit margins depended on it.

"Do you remember who rode Fabricated?" I asked.

"Jason Conway usually rides him. I expect it was him."

"Good jockey?"

"Sure, as good as any of the other top ones. That's if he's making an honest effort."

It was presumed by most bookmakers that all jockeys were bent. The reverse was also the case.

"Can you remember anything else about the race?" I asked. "Anything unusual?"

He was silent for a moment.

"Sorry, love. Too long ago. But you could watch a replay of it, if you want. Bound to be on YouTube by now and, if not, it'll definitely be on the Racing UK website."

"Can you watch any past race on that?" I asked.

"Yeah. Most of them anyway. Either on the Racing UK or the At The Races websites. Depends on which racecourse. I do it all the time, but you might have to pay."

"Thanks, Bill. How do I contact you?"

"Hold on."

He went over to Kevin and said something that I didn't catch, then he returned and handed me a slip of paper.

"Free bet," he said. "Fiver to win on the favorite in the Fox-hunter's. My phone number is on the slip. If it wins, I'll give you another." He laughed.

"Thanks," I replied, laughing back.

Bookmakers were clearly not all bad.

I stuck the ticket into my pocket, just as the unnamed man must have done in November.

THE FAVORITE in the Foxhunter's finished fourth. Win nothing. Lose nothing.

I had stood by the big screen near the parade ring to watch the race but now I hurried out through the exit gates. It was past the time I had intended to leave and I was desperate to get home before Grant. True, it was only twenty past four, but Grant had a habit of leaving work early on Fridays—especially on Gold Cup Friday, when the traffic all over Cheltenham would soon be grid-locked for hours.

Even though I was much earlier than on Tuesday, and it was still light, I took extra care as I approached the parking-lot exit onto the Evesham Road. I turned through 360 degrees at least four or five times to be certain that no one was sneaking up on me ready to push me in front of a bus.

If I hadn't been so watchful, I'd have probably missed it.

The long black Mercedes with the tinted windows was back and parked in one of the expensive reserved spaces close to the parking-lot exit, and I could see through the windshield that there was a dark-suited man in the driver's position. He had re-clined the seat and was lying back with his eyes closed. Not that that was an unusual sight. There were quite a few other cars nearby with chauffeurs in them, waiting for their employers to emerge. Lucky them, I thought. An afternoon of good sport and fine wines, and no worries about having to drive home afterward.

I went over to the Mercedes and rapped hard on the driver's window with my knuckles.

The man inside sat bolt upright with a start and glared through the window at me with a strange look in his eye that I couldn't quite read. Perhaps he had thought it was his employer knocking on the window, and he wouldn't have been happy to have found his driver asleep.

The electric window slid down a few inches.

"What do you want?" he asked gruffly through the gap.

London accent, I thought. East Ender.

"Whose car is this?" I asked. "Who owns it?"

"That's none of your bleeding business," said the man. "Go away."

"I'll find out anyway," I said. "I've got your license plate."

"Sod off," the man said, and he closed the window to indicate that the conversation was at an end.

I stood looking at him through the glass. I reckoned he was in his thirties and very athletic, the arms of his dark suit bulging as they tried unsuccessfully to obscure his oversized biceps. He had slightly receding brown hair and a fashionable three-day stubble. He waved a dismissive gesture at me then lay back again in the seat but, this time, he didn't close his eyes.

He went on watching me as I walked off toward the parking-lot exit. I knew because every time I turned around to look, I could see him staring at me through the windshield.

I took extra care crossing the Evesham Road—not a bus in sight—and then walked down the track toward the farmyard where I'd parked my car.

I suddenly stopped and a shiver ran down my spine.

The man hadn't asked my name.

He hadn't needed to.

That look in his eye hadn't been concern over his employer finding him asleep—it had been his surprise at finding *me* standing there.

He had known exactly who I was.

I was sure of it.

20

I was home well before Grant.

I was tucked up on the sofa under a blanket drinking peppermint tea and watching a game show on the television by the time he arrived at ten to six.

"How are you doing?" he asked, leaning down and giving me a peck on the cheek. "Have you eaten anything?"

"I'm fine," I said automatically. "I had some soup for lunch."

That wasn't actually true. I'd had a one-egg omelet for breakfast, supervised by Grant before he went to work, but I'd had nothing since apart from the cup of tea I was holding. Eating was not a priority in my life at present, so I hadn't even thought about it.

"So you've had a good day?" Grant asked.

"Yes," I said. "Very restful. I watched the Gold Cup."

That bit was not a lie, even if Grant did assume it had been on the television rather than live at the racecourse.

"Bloody races," he said. "The traffic everywhere is already horrendous. I nearly came home about two hours ago to avoid it but Trevor wanted me to go through some new dial designs with him."

That was lucky, I thought, with an inward smile. And exciting. I could get quite hooked on this clandestine investigation malarkey.

Live dangerously, or not at all.

SATURDAY MORNING dawned cold, bright and sunny.

"Why don't we tidy the garden today?" Grant said over breakfast. "Get it all ready for the spring?"

"OK," I said with some resignation. My enthusiasm level for gardening was always rock bottom and my current condition hadn't improved it any.

"Not until after my game, like," Toby said forlornly. "You are coming to watch?"

"Of course, darling," I said. "I wouldn't miss it for the world." And especially not for gardening.

"What time?" Grant asked.

"Ten-thirty kickoff."

"OK. We have time to do the front before then."

Grant was in one of his "let's get going" moods, so we were all ushered outside in our coats and Wellington boots to tidy the front flowerbeds while he cut the grass.

"I bet Cristiano Ronaldo doesn't have to do the weeding before he plays a match," Toby whined unhappily, leaning on a spade.

"He'd get someone else to do it for him and just pay," Oliver said. "What a good idea! Dad, Dad," he was shouting, "are me and Toby getting paid for doing this?"

His father ignored him as if he hadn't heard, which he may not have done due to the lawn mower.

Happy families. Although, to be fair, the front garden looked a lot better after only forty minutes or so of work, when we were dismissed by Grant to get ready for the soccer.

IT WAS A MIXED OUTCOME for the Rankin family.

Gotherington Colts lost by three goals to two, but Toby did score both for the home team. However, in spite of his personal success, he was distraught about the overall result.

"How can I possibly go into school next week?" he said, trying to hold back the tears. "It will be, like, awful."

"Darling," I said to him, putting my arm around his shoulders, "don't get so upset. It's only a game."

He looked at me as if I were mad.

"Mum, how *can* you say that?"

How could I explain to my fourteen-year-old son that there were more important things in life than winning or losing a soccer match?

If there was only one thing that being an emergency doctor taught you very quickly, it was that acute illness and life-threatening injury put everything else into proper perspective.

When I'd first started working in emergency medicine, I'd found it difficult to tear myself away from patients at the end of my shift, even when I'd been so tired that I'd almost been unable to keep my eyes open. How could my mundane existence outside of work—shopping, eating, socializing, even sleeping—be more pressing than caring for the critically unwell? One had to become immune to the number of people in the line and the length of time they'd been waiting for treatment. It would never be that working a little longer would significantly decrease the backlog, as new patients would always arrive just as fast as others were seen, and an overtired doctor was a dangerous doctor.

But, thankfully, Toby hadn't yet had experience of any of that. For him, the match result *was* the most important thing in his life at present and the longer I could shield him and Oliver from the nastier things the better.

We went back home as a family, the four of us arm in arm, three in coats with hats and scarves, and one still in his soccer gear with muddy knees.

Such moments were so precious. The boys were quickly changing into young men, and, all too soon, the time would come when they would fly the nest forever. They were my motivation to carry on living. How would I cope when they were gone? I was determined to relish every second while I still had them.

There was a black Mercedes parked outside the village post office and my heart missed a beat or two before I realized this one was shorter and had a different registration to that I'd seen in the racecourse parking lot.

"Can you find out who owns a car from the license plate?" I asked.

"Sure you can," Oliver said. "The police do it all the time. I've seen it on those traffic-cop TV shows. When they stop cars, they always check who the owners are, and whether they're taxed and insured."

"Yes," I said, "I know the police can do it, but could I? Would the licensing agency give me the details if I asked them?"

"I doubt it," Grant said. "Data protection and all that stuff. You would have to ask the police, and then they probably wouldn't tell you. Why? Which car do you want to know the owners of?"

"None, really," I lied. "I was just wondering, that's all."

We walked on through the village and turned into our road.

"I suppose, like, I did at least score our two goals," Toby said as we reached the driveway.

On his way to recovery, I thought.

Much as *I* felt on days like these, like.

ON MONDAY MORNING the boys went to school and Grant went off to work, leaving me alone in the house.

I was bored.

It had now been some four months since I'd been placed on sick leave by the Medical Director and, even though I was technically still employed, and being paid, by Cheltenham Hospital, I wondered if it was time for me to look for a new job elsewhere. Not that finding one would be easy—my clinical references would hardly be likely to be encouraging for a prospective employer.

I'd had two medical assessments since being discharged from Wotton Lawn just before Christmas.

The first, in early January, had been a complete waste of time. I'd been at my lowest ebb and had been so dosed up with anti-anxiety medication that I'd hardly been able to stay awake or follow what was happening.

The second had been six weeks later, in late February, and I'd been wide-eyed and eager, putting my case for an immediate return to duty. I was fed up with doing nothing and I wanted to be back doing my job, not least because I believed that working was the best therapy for my depression.

However, a panel of two distinguished physicians and one psychiatrist had concluded that my recovery was not yet sufficiently advanced for me to be trusted with the lives of others, and had signed me off sick for another month.

My third and final assessment was due in another ten days. Either I would then be invited back to work or I would be designated as permanently unfit for my role as a specialist emergency physician, and fired. Then I would be forced to look for employment elsewhere, and maybe not even as a doctor.

So far, amazingly, I had managed to keep my professional record intact on the General Medical Council's List of Registered Medical Practitioners, but that would surely change if I lost my job.

I sighed.

I would have to cross that bridge if and when I came to it but, in the meantime, I would use my spare time to try to get to the bottom of whatever was going on with respect to the death of the unnamed man.

It gave me a goal and a sense of purpose.

So I sat at the dining-room table with my laptop and searched through the Racing UK website.

As the bookmaker Bill Tucker had suspected, I needed to purchase a subscription in order to view all past races, even though quite a few were available free. Next I tried the At The Races website and found that their videos were all viewable without charge but they had the rights to less than half of British racecourses. The others were covered by Racing UK, including Cheltenham.

But what did I need to look at?

I was certainly interested in horses ridden by Jason Conway, but how did I find out which ones those were? I could hardly ring him up and ask him.

But I could ring up and ask Bill Tucker.

I found the Tommy Berkley betting slip and called the number printed on it.

"Hello," said an echoey voice.

"Bill," I said, "it's Dr. Chris Rankin. I saw you on Friday at Cheltenham."

"Yes," he replied. "Sorry your free bet didn't win."

"Thanks anyway," I said. "Have you got a minute?"

"Fire away. I'm in the car on my way to Southwell races. There'll only be two men and a dog there on a wet Monday after Cheltenham but . . . it's a living. How can I help?"

"Is there any way of finding out which horse a jockey rode, and in what race?" I asked.

"Which jockey?"

Did I tell him?

Why not?

"One of Jason Conway, Mike Sheraton or Dick McGee."

"Ah, the terrible trio," Bill said with a laugh.

"Why are they terrible?"

"Because they're always costing me money," Bill said, still laughing. "Especially that bloody Sheraton. Never know whether he's on or off."

"What do you mean?" I asked.

"He can be damn good but he can also be dreadful. Depends on whether he's trying or not."

The age-old gripe by every bookmaker about every jockey. To be taken with a pinch of salt, and not backed up by the evidence.

"So how do I get the horses and races?" I asked.

"Your best bet would be to use one of the websites. At The Races, Racing UK and Racing Post all have a results service. You can easily see the rides each jockey has had in the last few weeks. They'll be listed when you click on their names. If you want to go back earlier, then check the results for a date and just look through until you find the jockey's name. It's quite easy but a bit time-consuming."

Time was something I had plenty of at the moment.

"Thanks," I said. "And you were right about needing to pay to see the full race on Racing UK. You can only get the finish for free."

"But that's the important bit," he said with yet another laugh.

"Not for what I'm looking for."

"And what is that?"

"I'll tell you if I find it."

"I'll hold you to that," Bill said. "How long do you want access to the site for?"

"Just today and maybe tomorrow. Depends on what I find."

"Use my log-in," he said. "I need to change the password anyway so I'll do that on . . ." He paused. "I'll change it on Thursday. That'll give you three days if you need it."

"Thanks," I said again.

"My user name is tommyberkley, all one word, all lowercase. Password is 6to4theField, all one word, the six and four as numbers with a capital *F* for *Field*."

"Got it," I said, writing it all down on a notepad.

"But you have to let me know if you find what you're looking for."

"It's a deal," I said. "Many thanks."

But did *I* even know what I was looking for? Not really, but searching might at least pass some of the endless hours of nothingness.

I LOGGED ON TO the Racing UK website using Bill Tucker's details and started by watching a rerun of the race at Cheltenham in November when Fabricated had finished third, the race on which the unnamed man had bet five pounds.

Jason Conway had indeed been riding Fabricated that day.

As I almost expected, Fabricated had jumped the first fence in front.

I stopped the video and sat staring into space.

Then I called Bill Tucker again.

"Hello," he said. No echo this time.

"Bill, it's Chris Rankin again."

"Are you having problems logging on?"

"No," I said. "That's fine, thank you. But I have a question for you about betting."

"Fire away," he said with his now-familiar laugh. "There's not much I don't know about that."

"Would you take a bet from me about which horse will jump the first fence in front during a race?"

There was a long pause from the other end.

"Bill?" I said. "You still there?"

"Yep," he said. "Still here. I'm just thinking. Someone asked me that once before. You've just reminded me of it."

"Who?" I asked.

"Can't remember."

"When was this?"

"Some time ago. Last year maybe."

"Last November? At Cheltenham? Were you asked by the man in the photo I showed you?"

There was another pause.

"Sorry," he said, "I really can't remember. I know I said that I wouldn't take the bet. I'm usually taking regular bets right up to the off, and sometimes even after that. Then I have to get my brolly down so as not to block the view for those in the grandstand. Hence, I never even watch them jump the first. It's bad enough getting to watch them finish at some courses, those without big TVs. So I only take bets on official results, those called by the judge."

"No good, then, asking you for a fiver on there being a white Christmas?"

"Too bloody complicated," he said. "And too many arguments about what constitutes a white Christmas—snow in the air, snow on the ground, and where. I prefer to stick to things where the outcome is black and white." He laughed. "If you'll excuse the pun. Look, I must dash. I'm now at Southwell and I must go and set up my pitch."

"OK, Bill," I said. "Thanks for your time."

We disconnected.

Maybe not with Tommy Berkley, but there were other bookmakers or betting websites where it was possible to bet on almost anything—not only the weather at Christmas, but election results, the Oscar winners, even the likelihood of intelligent alien life being found somewhere during the next year.

And "spread betting" on both financial markets and sports fixtures has been around for many years, allowing wagers to be made on such things as the gains or losses in the stock-market index, or even the number of corners or throw-ins during a game of soccer.

Was there somewhere a gambler making bets on a horse to jump the first fence in front, and then arranging for it to happen?

Spot-fixing is what it was called. Fixing not the result, which was difficult and would usually require a conspiracy with other participants, but fixing a minor occurrence during a race or a match, something that could be achieved by a single individual working alone, and one that no one would notice.

Three Pakistani cricketers had famously been imprisoned for arranging for two "no-balls" to be bowled at specific times in a match between Pakistan and England at Lord's Cricket Ground in 2010, to corruptly allow others to profit from bets laid with a bookmaker in Pakistan.

Did the unnamed man have anything to do with spot-fixing races?

And was he perhaps not Indian, but Pakistani?

I SPENT THE NEXT FEW HOURS watching videos of races in which Jason Conway had ridden, making a list of those where he had jumped the first fence or hurdle in front.

So preoccupied had I become that I failed to have any lunch and completely lost track of time, only realizing how late it had become when the twins arrived back from school at four o'clock.

"Hi, Mum," they said in unison, "any food?"

I'd meant to go out and get some, hours ago.

"I've got some fruit," I said, knowing that was not at all what they wanted. "Or you could go along to the village shop and get some bread."

"I've got a match debrief, like, and a team practice in twenty minutes," Toby said. "And I've got to change yet."

"I'll go," Oliver said chirpily. "Can we have chips?"

"OK," I said, and gave him a ten-pound note from my purse. "Just one small packet each, mind. Also get a large sliced loaf and a dozen eggs, plus some milk. I'll make scrambled eggs on toast for supper."

I stood at the front door and waved as he rode off down the road on his bicycle.

"Take care," I shouted after him. "And come straight back."

"Leave it out, Mum," he called back. "I'm not a child anymore."

He was to me, I thought, but, in truth, he was now almost as tall as I was, and beginning to grow stubble. As I watched him go, I realized that he'd also outgrown his child bike. Maybe it would be time for a new one next birthday.

I went back into the dining room, back to my computer and to the next race in which Jason Conway had ridden. I was totally absorbed.

"WHERE'S OLLY?" Toby said, coming into the dining room in his soccer gear. "I want the chips, like, but I've really got to go now. I'm already late, and he should've been back ages ago."

Oh, my God!

Oliver!

21

I sprinted down the road, the tears welling in my eyes so much that I couldn't see properly.

"Oliver! Oliver!" I shouted his name over and over desperately as I ran.

There was a main road he had to cross to get to the village shop, a road along which cars regularly drove too fast.

Why had I let him out alone? Why? Why? Why?

He was only a boy.

I'd tried his cell phone but it had rung on the kitchen counter. He hadn't taken it with him.

I arrived at the main road. There was no sign of Oliver or his bicycle, no bloody mess, nothing.

I crossed over and ran on, cursing myself for not having brought the car. It would have been so much quicker.

It was almost exactly a quarter of a mile from our house to the village shop and an Olympic athlete would have had nothing on me.

There was no sign of Oliver's bike outside. I burst into the shop, frightening Mrs. Atherton, who owned it.

"Where's Oliver?" I shouted at her.

She looked at me quizzically.

"Oliver, my son," I said. "He was coming here to buy bread, eggs and chips."

Mrs. Atherton nodded. "He's been. Served him myself."

"So where is he now?"

"Sorry, dear, I've no idea," Mrs. Atherton replied. "He took his change and left."

"How long ago?"

"Not more than ten minutes."

Ten minutes! A quarter of a mile on a bicycle would take just one, two at most. He should have been home ages ago.

I ran out of the shop and retraced my steps. I surely couldn't have missed him.

"Oliver!" I shouted as I ran. "Oliver!"

I was now in full panic mode and I could feel myself shaking with fear.

I looked over every garden fence and wall between the village shop and our house but there was no sign of Oliver or his bike.

When I arrived back, Toby was standing at the open front door.

"Is he back?" I shouted at him.

I could see fear in his face as he shook his head.

I was beginning to go into meltdown; I could feel the tingling in my fingers.

I rushed past Toby and grabbed the house phone, my fingers seemingly huge on the buttons as I dialed Grant's cell phone number. He answered at the second ring.

"Oliver's been abducted," I shouted down the phone at him.

"What?"

"Oliver's been abducted," I repeated breathlessly. "He went to the shop for some chips and he's disappeared."

"How long ago?" Grant asked.

"Twenty, twenty-five minutes. I ran to the shop. Mrs. Atherton says he was there but left ages ago. He never came home. Oh my God. Where is he?"

I was crying uncontrollably.

"Calm down, darling," Grant said. "He's probably stopped off at a friend's house."

"Why would he?" I screamed. "He knew we were waiting for him. I'm telling you, he's been snatched." I was sobbing. "I'm calling the police."

I hung up and immediately dialed 999.

"Emergency, which service?" asked the operator.

"Police," I shouted down the line. "My son's been abducted."

I HAD TO GIVE THE POLICE some credit.

The first squad car arrived with blue flashing lights and a blaring siren in only five minutes. It contained two uniformed police officers and I ran down the drive to meet them.

"We were already in Bishop's Cleeve," one of them said. "Diverted from another job. Shall we go inside? To take down the details."

"Inside?" I screamed. "He's not inside. We need to find him."

"Mrs. Rankin," said the policeman, "we understand how you must be feeling but we have to get the details correct."

Understand? Neither policeman looked old enough to be out of school, let alone be parents. How could they possibly *understand* how I was feeling?

One of them took me by the elbow and guided me into the house and then through to the kitchen. We sat down at the table.

"Now," the policeman said, extracting a notebook and pen from his stab-proof-vest pocket, "how old, exactly, is Oliver?"

"He was fourteen last September," I said. He looked up at me sharply as if he'd been expecting him to be younger, then he wrote it down in a notebook. "And what does he look like?"

"Like that," I said, pointing at Toby, who was standing by the door into the hall, still in his soccer gear. "They're identical twins."

"And how long has he been missing?"

"He went to the village shop on his bike to buy some bread and chips but he didn't come back. I've searched for him but . . . ." I broke off, trying unsuccessfully to hold back the tears.

"And when was this?"

"About half an hour ago."

"Half an hour?" He didn't quite sound incredulous, but close. "Do you not think he may just be taking his time?"

"No," I said. "I've searched everywhere between here and the shop. And I told him to come straight back."

"And does he always do what you tell him?"

I could tell from his tone that he was rather skeptical.

"Well, no, not always, but he would have done this time. He knew his brother was waiting for him."

The doorbell rang and I jumped up but it was only two more uniformed policemen, one of them a woman, who joined their colleagues in the kitchen. Child abduction was obviously taken very seriously.

"What was he wearing?" asked the same policeman as before.

"His school uniform," I said. "White shirt, dark gray trousers, navy pullover, with his school crest over the heart. Toby, go and get yours to show them."

Toby disappeared, presumably up to his room to fetch his uniform.

"Jacket and tie?" asked the policeman.

"No," I said. "Just a pullover these days."

"Any coat?"

I thought back. "No. He was only going to be gone a few minutes."

"Type of bike?"

"Raleigh. Kid's mountain bike. In blue. Toby's is red."

Grant arrived, throwing open the front door with a crash and rushing into the kitchen. I stood up and hugged him. He pulled away from me and turned to the four police officers.

"Why aren't you out searching for my son?" he demanded.

"All in good time, sir," replied one of them. "We need to get all the details first and a photograph. Do you have one we could show to our officers?"

"We have one upstairs that was taken at school," Grant said. "I'll fetch it."

I was getting even more agitated.

"We *must* go and look for him," I shouted at the police. "Why are we all stuck in here when he's out there somewhere?" I was openly sobbing and losing control. "My poor baby."

Into this intense scene of acute maternal hysteria walked Oliver.

He came through the open front door, down the hall and into the kitchen holding a white plastic shopping bag.

At first I thought it was Toby, assuming that he'd put his school uniform back on to show the police, but then I saw the bag.

"Mum," Oliver said with a slightly worried tone while looking around at the four police uniforms crowded into the kitchen, "what's going on?"

My first emotion was one of relief but this very quickly turned to anger.

"Where have you been?" I shouted at him.

"Looking for my bike," he said rather tearfully.

"What?" I screamed.

"I've been looking for my bike," he repeated. "Someone took it while I was in the shop."

Grant came into the kitchen clutching the photo and instantly grasped the situation.

"Where the hell have you been?" he asked loudly, turning to Oliver.

The poor young boy was now in floods of tears.

"I've been looking for my bike," he said once more between sobs. "It's been stolen."

"What do you mean, stolen?"

Gradually, over the next half hour, the full story came out.

Oliver had cycled straight to the shop and had gone in, leaning his bike against the wall outside. He had bought the items, but, when he came out, the bike was gone.

"I was only in there a couple of minutes," he said miserably. "I thought someone was playing a trick on me. So I looked to see if it'd been moved. But I couldn't find it anywhere. Then I thought Jamie Williams must have taken it."

"Jamie Williams?" asked one of the policemen.

"From school," Oliver said. "I thought I saw him on my way to the shop, near the phone box. He lives at that farm up the hill on Gretton Road."

"But why would he take your bike?" another of the policemen asked.

"Because he doesn't like me. And he's always nicking my stuff at school—pens, sports gear, stuff like that. Anyway, I walked all the way up to the farm to see if he had it."

"Why didn't you come back here first?" I asked angrily. "We were desperately worried."

"I was afraid," he said. "I thought you'd be cross that I'd lost my bike."

He might have been right.

"So did Jamie Williams have your bicycle?" the policeman asked him.

"No. At least, he says he hasn't. So I had to walk home."

"Perhaps we'll go and have a word with young Mr. Williams. What's the name of the farm?"

"Stoop Farm," Grant said. "On the right, about a mile out of the village."

"Right," said the policeman. "We'll leave you in peace now. I am pleased that the young man is back home safe and sound. We will go and see the Williams boy to check on the bicycle, and let you know."

"Thank you," I said. "I'm very grateful. And I'm sorry I was so emotional earlier."

"That's all right, Mrs. Rankin. As long as the boy is unhurt. That's what really matters."

Nevertheless, I was embarrassed that I'd shouted at them, so I let Grant show them out.

"I'm sorry, Mum," Oliver said, coming over and giving me a big hug.

"It's all right, darling," I said, hugging him back and stroking his hair. "As the policeman said, you being back home unhurt is the most important thing. And you're too big for that bike anyway."

"It's too late for me to go to soccer practice," Toby announced loudly. "So can we have the chips now?"

Crisis over. Proper priorities had been restored.

———

THE POLICEMAN CAME BACK while I was preparing the scrambled eggs.

"No luck, I'm afraid," he said when I opened the front door. "I'm satisfied that the Williams boy knows nothing about your son's bicycle."

"So who did take it?" I asked.

"Sorry," he said, holding his hands open, palms uppermost. "I went and asked the lady who runs the village shop but she had no idea either. She's agreed to keep an eye out for it. In the meantime, I'll make out a stolen-property report so you can claim it on your household insurance."

"Won't you go and look for it?" I asked.

"Sorry, ma'am," he said, not sounding it. "We don't have the manpower. We would definitely search for your child but not for his bike. But the details will remain on file in case it's found and handed in."

I suppose I couldn't blame him. The police could hardly go door-to-door asking about a child's mountain bike, even in our small village.

LIFE IN THE RANKIN HOUSEHOLD returned to what might be considered as normal for a Monday night but there were clearly underlying tensions.

Grant was never normally at his best on Mondays, when the whole week of work seemed to stretch ahead of him interminably. It wasn't that he hated his job, just that it was mundane and predictable compared to his years in the military, and I knew that he sometimes hankered after the excitement and adrenaline generated by being in mortal danger.

Oliver spent the evening very morose, apologizing at least every ten minutes for causing such distress to his mother. And he wasn't helped by Toby, who gave him no quarter, constantly accusing his brother of ruining his life as he was certain that, having missed the team practice, he would surely be dropped for the next match.

I, meanwhile, was desperate to get back to my investigation of races ridden by Jason Conway and Mike Sheraton since the previous November. By the time I had been interrupted by the suspected abduction of my son, I'd looked at races up to the end of January and had a list of forty-two in which Conway had jumped the first fence in front, with twenty-six others where Sheraton had done the same.

But was that significant? After all, someone had to be in the lead at the first fence.

Over that three-month period, Jason Conway had ridden in just over two hundred races. So he had led over the first fence in only a fifth of them.

Was that by chance or by design?

I could see that I would have to spend many more hours studying videos of races, even those in which Jason Conway had not been riding, to see if his numbers were significantly greater than anyone else's. But there was something about the determination he often showed to be the one in front that I found suspicious.

Not that I'd get any chance to continue my research on that particular evening. To say that Grant would not have approved would be a gross understatement. He was determined that I should do nothing but rest, as if that alone would solve all my ills, both physical and mental, while I felt I needed a goal, a target, something to occupy what Hercule Poirot always referred to as "the little gray cells."

After supper, the boys went up to their rooms to do their homework while Grant and I sat together on the sitting-room sofa in front of the TV, testing our general knowledge by attempting to answer a question or two on *University Challenge*.

Over the past year, watching television had seemingly become our way of not having to speak to each other. It was easier to allow the shows to wash over us, filling the void, than to address the one thing that was most important in our lives—the elephant in the room—my mental state, and whether I was continuing to recover.

I was certainly in a better place than I had been in back in November. For a start, I no longer believed that taking my own life was the inevitable outcome, and *that* was a major step in the right direction. Admittedly, I still thought about suicide now and then, but, since coming out of Wotton Lawn Hospital in December, I felt that I was able to rationalize my thinking and positively decide against any form of self-harm.

Not that I didn't sometimes feel the weight of gloom and depression hanging on my shoulders, when a fear of being self-indulgent was the only thing preventing me wallowing in tears and despair. But those episodes were now more rare and less intense, helped, I was sure, by a regimen of regular weekly blood tests and targeted hormone therapy. At last I could begin to appreciate how fluctuating amounts of thyroxine or testosterone, estrogen or progesterone, could affect my mood—not that I fully understood why.

However, I was becoming increasingly frustrated that I had to go on taking medications in ever-greater numbers. Every trip to a doctor seemed to add another tablet to my lengthy list. But I wanted to stop pill-popping altogether, to stop ingesting man-made chemicals and to become "organic" once again.

I was fed up with my body and its continuously changing hormone levels.

I was fed up that, in spite of the drugs, I never felt happy.

Indeed, I was just fed up.

"I think I'll go up to bed," I said to Grant at a quarter to ten.

"Are you OK?" he asked with concern. Quarter to ten was very early, even for me.

"I'm fine," I said. "Just tired."

"I'll be up in a while."

"I may be asleep," I replied. "Night-night."

"Good night." He didn't lean over and give me a kiss, he merely waved a hand in my general direction as his eyes, and his concentration, returned to the TV screen and the end of a murder-mystery drama that I hadn't been following.

It was hardly married life as I'd expected it.

I WAS WOKEN BY OLIVER, shouting outside our bedroom door.

"Mum, Mum. My bike is back. It's out on the drive."

"Great," I said, turning over and looking at the clock on my bedside table.

Six-forty. Not too bad. The alarm was due to go off in only a few minutes anyway. I turned on the light and sat up on the edge of the bed.

"What time is it?" Grant asked, sleepily. I hadn't heard him come to bed, so I expected he'd stayed up watching a movie until midnight, as he often did these days.

"Almost a quarter to seven," I said. "Oliver says his bike is back and lying on the drive."

"I bet that Williams boy had it all along," Grant said. "I imagine he's handed it back before the police returned to ask him a second time."

I heard both the twins running down the stairs and the front door being thrown open. But there was no joy or delight at the discovery.

"It's all bent and broken," Oliver said gloomily as he came back up the stairs. "Both the wheels are twisted and the frame is all out of shape."

He was close to tears again. It was bad enough for him to have lost his bike in the first place, but then to believe it had been returned safe and sound only to find it ruined was almost more than the poor boy could handle.

Grant put on his dressing gown and went downstairs and out onto the drive.

The phone rang and I immediately picked it up using the handset beside the bed.

"Hello," I said.

"Dr. Rankin?" asked a quiet male voice.

"Yes," I replied.

"You were told before to stop asking questions. I'll not tell you again. Next time I'll run over your kid, not just his bike."

22

I was still standing by the bed with the phone in my hand when Grant came back upstairs.

"Who was that?" he asked.

I didn't answer. I couldn't.

I was shaking too much.

Grant looked at me.

"Darling, are you all right? You look like you've seen a ghost."

I tried to reply that, as always, I was fine, but the words wouldn't come out. I felt sick and I pushed past him into the bathroom, where I threw up into the toilet.

"Good God, darling," Grant said. "What has happened?"

I shook my head. I couldn't tell him. My mind was racing around in ever-decreasing circles and my heart was thumping away, nineteen to the dozen.

I was simply too frightened to repeat what I'd just heard.

"I'm calling an ambulance," Grant said, worry etched deeply onto his face.

I shook my head.

"Call the police," I said, managing at last to get three words out together.

————

DETECTIVE SERGEANT MERRYWEATHER and Detective Constable Filippos sat on one side of our kitchen table while Grant and I sat on the other.

"What exactly did the man say to you?" asked the senior detective.

"He said that next time he'd run over my kid not just his bicycle."

Even three hours after I'd first heard them, repeating the words made my heart race.

"*Next time?* A rather strange turn of phrase. Why do you think he said that?"

I glanced at Grant. He was still unaware of the STOP ASKING QUESTIONS piece of paper previously placed on my windshield and I would have preferred it to have remained that way.

No chance.

"Did it have anything to do with the message you received before?" asked DC Filippos.

"What message?" Grant said immediately.

I sat silently, looking down at my hands.

"What message?" Grant repeated.

"Your wife found a message placed on her windshield," DC Filippos said.

"What message?" Grant said for a third time.

I said nothing but the detective wasn't finished. "The message said to stop asking questions."

Grant turned and looked at me. "Why didn't you tell me this?"

That was a good question and I didn't have a satisfactory answer.

"I didn't want to worry you," I said.

Grant shook his head in frustration. "So what questions were you asking?"

"Just questions," I said inadequately.

"Questions about what?" He was beginning to get angry and I could feel the stress growing in me too.

It all came out—it was bound to—everything, that was, except my flirtation with the Whisky Macs. I did at least manage to keep that quiet from both Grant and the police.

But all the rest came out, all the things I had tried so hard to keep from Grant. Not just the message on the windshield but also the flat tires, my approaches to the jockeys, the note in the envelope, and, most worrying of all, my belief that I'd been pushed in front of the bus.

Grant was horrified.

"Why didn't you tell me?" he said again.

"I knew you wouldn't like it."

"You're dead right there," he said forcefully. "I don't like it. Not one bit. In future, you must leave any investigating to the police."

I glanced across the table at the two policemen. "But they don't know what I do."

"And what is that?" asked DS Merryweather.

Did I say? Was I sure? Did I have enough evidence?

"I think someone is spot-fixing races and I believe it involves the jockeys Jason Conway and Mike Sheraton. And I'm sure it has something to do with Rahul, our unnamed man, who died in Cheltenham Hospital in November."

"What do you mean by spot-fixing?" asked DS Merryweather.

"Fixing which horse jumps the first fence in front."

I could tell instantly that he thought I was crazy.

"But why would that make any difference to the outcome?"

"It doesn't. That's the point. But if you could gamble on which horse jumped the first fence first, then it would be corrupt to fix it."

"But who would gamble on such a thing?" the detective asked, the disbelief clearly audible in his voice.

"Some people will gamble on anything," I said. "Especially, it seems, in India and Pakistan. If they gamble on when the first throw-in will occur in a game of soccer or when a no-ball is bowled in cricket, then why not on which horse is in front at the first fence?"

"What evidence do you have?"

"I've been watching videos of races in which Conway and Sheraton have been riding. I believe a pattern is emerging."

"What videos?" Grant asked.

"On my computer," I said. "There are racing websites that have videos of past races, and I was studying those all day yesterday."

"Is that why you had to send Oliver out to do the shopping?" Grant was cross again, and with good reason. It was exactly why.

I nodded and hung my head in shame.

"So, I ask you again," said the detective sergeant, "did this incident with Oliver's bicycle have anything to do with the previous message?"

I nodded again.

"The man on the phone said that I'd been told before not to ask questions and he wouldn't tell me again. Next time he'd run over my kid, not just his bike."

Grant was now really angry.

"How could you have put our son in such danger?" he demanded.

"But I hadn't asked any more questions," I said unhappily. "Not to the jockeys anyway."

"To who then?" asked DS Merryweather.

I thought back to my encounter with the driver of the long black Mercedes with the dark windows.

"The only question I've asked was of the driver of a certain Mercedes. I asked him who owned it."

"Which Mercedes?"

"The one from which Jason Conway had been given the piece of paper with the name of a London railway station and a time."

"Liverpool Street at three-thirty?" said DC Filippos.

"Quite so," I said. "Liverpool Street at three-thirty. Not a train time but the name of a horse that ran in the Gold Cup at three-thirty last Friday."

"But why go to the trouble of passing a piece of paper with the horse's name on it?" said DS Merryweather. "Why not just e-mail or call him?"

"Because e-mails and telephone calls leave records of contact that can be traced," I said. "I expect Conway now wishes he'd destroyed the paper as soon as he had read it." I paused and looked at the three of them. "Liverpool Street may have finished third in the race. But it started fast and jumped the first fence in front, and Jason Conway rode it."

THE DETECTIVES stayed for another hour, making notes while I showed them some of the race videos. Not that they were convinced, even then, that anything untoward had been going on.

"It stands to reason that *someone* has to jump the first fence in front," DS Merryweather said. "And it's not as if the same jockey does it every time."

"That would be too suspicious," I pointed out. "But there are certain races when it looks very much by design rather than by chance."

"But don't some horses just like to run at the front?" the detective sergeant said dubiously after I'd been through everything I'd found. "There's insufficient here to build a credible legal case. We know from experience how difficult it is to get a conviction for corruption in racing. About ten years ago, we thought we had irrefutable evidence of race-fixing by three jockeys, including a former champion, but the trial judge still threw it out after deciding the three had no case to answer—and we had a lot more on them than this." He waved his hand dismissively at my computer. "The same would certainly happen here. It's all circumstantial and coincidental."

"There was nothing coincidental about running over Oliver's bicycle," I said. "That was deliberate and intentional."

"But what is there to connect it to your allegation of spot-fixing in races? And how is it linked to the death of our nameless man from a cocaine overdose? Are you not guilty of simply piecing together several random situations into a single narrative because you want that so much to be the case?"

Was I?

I thought back once again to the reaction of the jockeys to the image of the unnamed man, to the certainty I'd felt about the Mercedes driver knowing who I was, to my collision with the bus and the telephone call of that morning.

"No," I said. "I'm not. I know I'm right."

"Could you prove it beyond a reasonable doubt in a court of law?"

"But I'm telling you the truth," I asserted with frustration.

"As may be," said the detective, "but the truth is no guarantee of justice."

"Isn't that rather cynical?" I said. "Especially from a policeman. Surely justice is all about finding out the truth."

He shook his head in disagreement. "Justice is determined by the facts, and those facts are decided solely by the jury based only on the evidence presented to them in court. Whether or not the events actually took place is irrelevant. In my experience, the truth doesn't usually enter into it."

If I couldn't even convince the police, what chance did I have with a jury? And what danger would I be placing my family into in the meantime?

I could feel the stress rising in me once again.

Grant had been listening carefully to everything that had been said and he had clearly not been impressed.

"Chris," he said, turning to me. "You *have* to let the police do their job and not get involved. The safety of our children is far more important than some suspected corruption in horseracing, or a dead man we don't know."

He was right. Of course he was right. But something inside me was telling me not to let it go.

I was like a drug addict who knew perfectly well that what he was taking was harmful to his health, even critically dangerous, but that didn't stop him doing it. Addiction was a major characteristic of obsessive-compulsive disorder and I was well wedded to that concept.

Maybe Grant could see the determination in my eyes.

"Darling," he pleaded, "you must stop. Promise me you will leave all this alone."

I looked across at the policemen.

"Don't you even want to know the license plate of the Mercedes?"

PART 3

APRIL

23

"Adult trauma, six minutes."

The hospital public address call caused a surge of adrenaline through my system—a rise in my heartbeat and a mixed feeling of excitement, fear and nervousness. Especially nervousness.

It was just my second day back.

Only a week previously, I had passed the assessment of my competence to return to work at Cheltenham General, although I hadn't thought so at the time.

Initially, the assessing panel had been interested in what I had been doing with my time since I'd been discharged from Wotton Lawn just before Christmas.

I decided against telling them anything about the unnamed man or the spot-fixing, concentrating more on how I had taken the opportunity to catch up with advances in emergency medicine by reading specialist publications. And I told them that I'd spent a day as a medical officer at the racecourse, without actually elaborating on what had happened later.

They had appeared impressed by all that but then they still spent quite a lot of time asking me about the medications that I was taking, and about my ongoing consultations with the psychiatrist Stephen Butler.

"We have to be so careful," the lady chairman of the panel had said in explanation. "We can't take any unnecessary risks. We have to be satisfied that your medical condition poses no threat to the welfare of our patients."

It had been at that point I'd become certain that I would fail whatever I said, so I'd thrown caution to the wind and told it how it really was.

"I have a mental-health problem," I said to them. "I repeat. I have a mental-health problem."

I stared at the three of them, one by one.

"Do you have any idea how difficult it is for me to say those six words to complete strangers?"

I took a deep breath.

"I've been off work now for four months but I've been ill for far longer than that, well over a year, probably longer. Initially I denied it, especially to myself. I made excuses for my strange behavior and hid myself away so that others couldn't see. But denial is very damaging. It may be the natural defense mechanism against acceptance of a painful truth but it makes things worse. Getting anxious because one is fearful of displaying that very anxiety is self-perpetuating. It is a chain reaction like an atom bomb that, if not defused, will detonate and destroy not only you but everything you hold dear—your marriage, your family, your house and your job. Everything, including your life itself."

I paused.

No one said anything. They just waited for me to go on.

"Acceptance is the key. Acceptance that one is ill is the very first step toward being well again. Instead of hiding away, acceptance allows one to seek out those who can help. But it is not just acceptance by me that's important, it is acceptance by others, by my family, my friends and my colleagues. Acceptance provides a sense of belonging that is vital to recovery, a purpose that is essential for healing."

I took another deep breath.

"I have been a doctor for nearly twenty years and I have been a specialist in emergency medicine for the past ten of those. I know my job and I am sure I would not be a threat to the welfare of patients. Quite the reverse."

I paused once more and looked at them.

"I want my job back. I want it back because I feel able to provide a worthwhile service to society. But I also want it back because I need it. I need it to become properly well again."

I fell silent with my hands lying in my lap.

After a few seconds the lady chairman cleared her throat.

"Thank you, Dr. Rankin," she said. "Most interesting. We will let you know our decision in due course."

And they had, and quickly too.

I'd received a letter only three days later stating that I was cleared to work again in the Accident and Emergency Department at Cheltenham General Hospital. The only caveat being that, provided I agreed, I would be working for the foreseeable future under the supervision of the other senior physicians rather than as one of them, although I would retain my outward status, and my salary.

I'd swallowed what little pride I still retained, agreed to their terms, and had gone gleefully back to work the following Monday—i.e., yesterday.

"A sixty-four-year-old man has fallen fifteen feet off a ladder," said the nurse who had taken the trauma call from the ambulance service. "Seems he was trying to fix his TV aerial. Stupid idiot. Fell onto a concrete path."

"Head injury?" I asked.

She shook her head. "Landed on his feet. The ambulance service think he may have broken both ankles."

Painful, but it shouldn't be life- or limb-threatening providing the breaks hadn't disrupted the blood supply to his feet. That would be the first thing I would check on his arrival.

"You take this one, Chris," Jeremy Cook said over my shoulder as I sat at the desk. "I'll just be on the periphery if you need me. Glad to have you back."

"Thank you, Jeremy," I said. "It's good to be back."

The patient arrived and I set to work stabilizing his condition and confirming that there was a detectable pulse in each foot. Next I sent him for X-rays as well as a full-body CT scan. It was clear from their positions that he had indeed broken both ankles, but it was vital to ensure that there were no other critical injuries, such as internal bleeding, which might be easily missed until it was too late. A fall from fifteen feet onto a hard surface would have resulted in large forces acting on all the major organs, maybe enough to cause a rupture.

Thankfully, however, the CT scan showed nothing out of the ordinary, no obvious further injuries.

I had already paged an orthopedic specialist and together we now set about realigning the patient's ankles and placing them in temporary plaster casts. There was every likelihood that he would require surgery to have one or both of them fixed properly but that would be for tomorrow, after the initial damage to the surrounding soft tissue had been given a chance to settle.

As the man was wheeled away to one of the hospital wards, I breathed a small sigh of relief. The first major trauma I'd dealt with in almost five months and I'd felt completely at home, with not a tingle detectable anywhere in my fingers.

"Well done, Chris," Jeremy Cook said. "Good job. Exactly according to the book."

I smiled.

I was back in business.

THE FOLLOWING MONDAY I appeared as a witness at the reconvened inquest of the unnamed man at Gloucestershire Coroner's Court.

Except that he was no longer an unnamed man. Police inquiries had finally produced a result.

"Good morning, Dr. Rankin," said DS Merryweather, meeting me in the glass vestibule of the brand-new coroner's court complex. He was with DC Filippos and they shook my hand in turn.

"Thank you for coming," said Constable Filippos. "How are you?"

"I'm fine, thanks," I said. "I'm back at work."

"I'm delighted to hear it." He smiled as if he really meant it.

I wanted to ask him about all sorts of things—in particular, if he'd discovered who owned the long black Mercedes—but I'd promised Grant that I wouldn't get involved. I'd assured him I would leave everything to the police and not ask any questions of anyone to do with the dead man or anything else that had happened at Cheltenham Racecourse.

So I was here only to *answer* questions from the coroner and not to ask any. As Grant had reminded me only that morning. But it didn't mean I wasn't interested. Perhaps I would just have to wait for information to be offered.

"You may have heard that we have identified the dead man," said the detective sergeant.

"So I believe," I replied. The summons I had received to attend had given the man's name as Rahul Kumar but no further details beyond that.

"As we had suspected, he was from India, from Delhi. The authorities there came up with a name and DNA comparison tests have confirmed it."

An usher came into the vestibule and loudly announced the inquest for Rahul Kumar. The two policemen and I filed into the courtroom and took places on one of the rows of blue-covered seats at the back.

I'd attended many inquests before in my professional capacity but I never forgot the reasons why we were here. An inquest was held solely to ascertain the answers to four simple questions: who, what, where and when?

Who was the deceased? What caused him to die? Where did he die? And when did he die? Nothing else. Long gone were the days when an inquest could apportion blame to someone responsible for causing a death.

Unlike in a criminal court, where prosecution and defense counsel argue about the facts of the case in an adversarial system while the judge remains mostly silent, dealing only with points of law, the coroner's proceedings were inquisitorial, with the coroner asking questions of the witnesses from the bench in order to reach his conclusion.

Juries only sit at inquests under certain limited circumstances, for example if the deceased died while in custody or if the coroner considers that there is particular public interest.

In this case, neither of those applied and the coroner sat alone, calling DS Merryweather as the first witness to give evidence of identification.

"The deceased's name is Rahul Kumar," the sergeant said loudly and clearly from the witness box while consulting his notes. "He was an Indian citizen and his home was in Narela, in the northern district of Delhi. Positive identification was confirmed using DNA comparison with his mother and brother."

"Did he have any family other than a mother and brother?" asked the coroner.

"Yes, sir," said the sergeant. "He has two sisters and various nieces and nephews."

"No children of his own?"

"No, sir. Mr. Kumar was unmarried."

"Is the family represented in any way at this hearing?"

"No, sir," said the detective. "His family were unable to travel. Full details are included in the report we submitted to your office."

"Yes, thank you," said the coroner. "I have read the report. Most interesting. May I congratulate you, Sergeant, on your efforts to discover who this man was. Quite a puzzle. Do you have any further information to add?"

"I have, sir," he said. "Since the report was written, we have determined that Mr. Kumar arrived in the UK seven days prior to his death on an Air India flight from New Delhi. His whereabouts during those seven days have yet to be determined and any belongings he may have brought with him have yet to be located."

"Did he have a profession?" asked the coroner.

"New information has just arrived from India that indicates Mr. Kumar had previously been an officer in the Indian Police Service but had retired some time ago to become a member of a private security organization."

"Is there any reason to believe he was working while here in the UK?"

"None, sir," replied the sergeant. "But there is no evidence at all of the purpose of his visit. He obtained a standard visitor visa in person using the twenty-four-hour super-priority visa service at the British visa application center in New Delhi on . . ." He consulted his notes. ". . . the third of November last year and booked his flight on the same day via the internet. He left India the following day, arriving at Heathrow on the morning of the fifth."

A very sudden decision, I thought. There had to have been a pressing reason for his trip.

The court had answered the "Who?" question.

Next into the witness box went Constable Filippos, who described how the man had been found in a cubicle in the gentlemen's restroom at the racecourse by one of the cleaning staff.

"And the cubicle was locked from the inside?" asked the coroner.

"Yes, sir."

"So how was access gained?"

"The cubicles were constructed of prefabricated panels that didn't go all the way to the ceiling. One of the racecourse staff leaned over from the adjoining cubicle and used the cleaner's mop handle to slide the lock open."

"Was that before or after you arrived at the scene?" asked the coroner.

"Before, sir. The method was described to me with a demonstration. The police were only called because the racecourse staff initially thought the man was drunk."

"Do we have the people present who found the man?" The coroner looked around the court expectantly.

"No, sir," said the constable. "The racecourse staff member was a young man on a short-term work exchange from Racing Victoria, in Australia. He has since returned home."

The coroner pursed his lips in obvious disapproval.

"And the cleaner?" he asked in an acid tone.

"The cleaner gave a statement to one of your assistants," the policeman said. "It should be with your notes, sir. She had originally thought the unresponsive man was already dead and she was badly shaken up at the time by the experience. It was not thought necessary for her to attend today."

The coroner shuffled the stack of papers in front of him and found the statement, but he clearly didn't like being seen to be put in his place by a young constable.

DC Filippos went on to describe how he had called for an ambulance and had then accompanied the man to Cheltenham General Hospital. He also told the court how he had returned to the racecourse later that evening and had discovered a whisky bottle in the trash can, later found to bear the fingerprints of the deceased.

"Do we have any indication where this bottle originated?" the coroner asked.

"No, sir," said the constable. "The bottle was branded as Bell's Blended Scotch Whisky. The size was twenty milliliters, a fraction more than a quarter bottle, and it was made from plastic, not glass. Such bottles are available as duty-free sales at airports or on board aircraft but we have no indication of exactly where this particular bottle was purchased or where it had been prior to being found in the trash can."

The coroner made some notes. "Thank you, Officer."

Next it was my turn. I collected my papers and walked to the witness box.

I took the Bible in my right hand. "I swear by Almighty God to tell the truth, the whole truth and nothing but the truth."

I sat down on the chair provided.

"My name is Dr. Christine Rankin, fellow of the Royal College of Emergency Medicine and senior physician at Cheltenham General Hospital. I was the receiving doctor in the A&E department on the night Mr. Kumar was admitted."

I went on to describe the treatment given to the man, referring regularly to the medical notes I had brought with me. I told the court about the suspected supraventricular tachycardia, how I had prescribed adenosine to try to bring down his heart rate, and how he had subsequently died of a cardiac arrest.

"Did the administration of the adenosine cause the cardiac arrest?" the coroner asked.

"No, sir," I said, keeping my breathing as even and calm as possible.

The truth, the whole truth and nothing but the truth.

But I was telling the truth.

"Supraventricular tachycardia is caused by improper electrical activity in the upper part of the heart. Adenosine causes a momentary block in the atrioventricular node, which should reset the heart rhythm. However, in this case that did not occur."

"Because the man was not, in fact, suffering from supraventricular tachycardia?"

"The man's heart did not respond to the adenosine due to the extent of the cocaine overdose," I said, not quite answering the coroner's question.

"Had you consulted with a cardiac specialist before administering the adenosine?" the coroner asked.

"No, sir," I said. "None were available in the hospital on a Saturday evening and I was of the opinion that to wait for the on-call cardiologist to arrive would be detrimental to the well-being of the patient."

"You thought he might die if you waited?" asked the coroner, looking me directly in the eye.

"Yes, sir," I said.

"But he died anyway."

"Yes, sir."

It didn't sound particularly good, even to my ears.

"Thank you, Dr. Rankin, you may step down now but please remain in the court. I may wish to re-call you later."

I went back to my seat while the coroner called the next witness, the senior county pathologist who had performed the postmortem examination of the man's body. His report was already on the coroner's bench.

"Please tell the court the cause of death," the coroner said after the pathologist had introduced himself.

"Acute cocaine poisoning," the pathologist said confidently, "resulting in cardiac arrest."

"Did the administration of adenosine at Cheltenham Hospital have any effect on his death?" the coroner asked.

I held my breath.

"I very much doubt it. I suppose it might have hastened it a fraction—by a few minutes, that's all. And if the patient had indeed been suffering from simple supraventricular tachycardia, the adenosine might have saved him. In my opinion it was a risk worth taking."

The coroner was looking at me and saw me sigh in relief.

"And was the absence of a specialist cardiologist at the hospital a factor?"

"No, sir," said the pathologist. "The amount of cocaine in the brain tissue was incompatible with life. In fact, I'm surprised he lived as long as he did."

The coroner wrote something in his notebook, then looked up at the pathologist. "Have you seen the report from the police forensic laboratory concerning the whisky bottle found in the trash can in the gentlemen's restroom?"

"Yes, sir," replied the pathologist. "I have. The concentration of cocaine found in the residue would be consistent with it being the source of the drug in the cadaver. Only a single teaspoonful of the liquid ingested orally would have been sufficient to cause death. Analysis of stomach contents was compatible with the deceased having consumed such a lethal dose."

"Thank you, Doctor," the coroner said.

"What?" had now been covered.

The last witness was the junior doctor who had certified the death, the doctor that I had shouted at, and the doctor who had made the initial complaint against me. I looked at him with contempt as he made his way to the witness box. What more was I now going to have to suffer from his mouth?

No wonder the coroner had told me to remain.

But, much to my surprise, the doctor restricted himself solely to the "Where?" and "When?" referring only to the facts recorded on the man's medical records indicating at what exact time and place life had ceased and the patient had been declared dead.

"And were you present at that point?" the coroner asked.

"Yes, sir, I was. I had been leading efforts to resuscitate the patient for the preceding hour but without any success. It was me who called a halt to those efforts."

"Was Dr. Rankin not present as well?"

"No, sir. Dr. Rankin was dealing with a young woman who had been seriously injured in a motorcycle accident."

"Was it usual for a seriously ill patient to be left unsupervised by a senior clinician?"

The junior doctor glanced briefly across the courtroom at me.

"Dr. Rankin was busy saving the life of another patient."

"I asked you if it was usual," the coroner said.

"No, sir, not usual, but certainly not unique."

The coroner made some more notes.

"Thank you, Doctor," he said. "You may step down."

The junior doctor left the witness box and walked back to his place at the back of the court, seemingly taking extra care not to look in my direction.

There was a lengthy silence as the coroner wrote some more in his notebook.

"Ladies and gentlemen," he said eventually, "I am satisfied as to the identification of the deceased as Rahul Kumar, citizen of the Republic of India. I am also satisfied that the direct cause of death was acute cocaine poisoning as a result of consuming contaminated whisky. There may be speculation that the death of Mr. Kumar was due to suicide but I am unable to come to that determination. In spite of him being found unconscious in a self-locked cubicle, and the existence of his fingerprints on a duty-free whisky bottle in which cocaine was found in extreme concentration, there is no evidence that Mr. Kumar intended to consume a dose sufficient to end his own life. Therefore it is the conclusion of this court that the death of Rahul Kumar was due to misadventure."

There was a slight murmur in the courtroom but the coroner wasn't quite finished.

"Furthermore," he said, "I will be writing to the Secretary of State for Health asking for clarification on some of the processes in our hospitals."

Good luck with that, I thought. Doctors had been trying to get that sort of clarification from the Health Secretary for decades.

"All stand," shouted the usher.

The coroner stood up as well, bowed toward us and then departed.

"Misadventure," said DS Merryweather, turning to me. "I'm happy with that."

I wasn't. Misadventure implied that Rahul Kumar's death had been unintentional—an accident or mishap brought on by his own actions.

Why was I the only person who believed that it was murder?

24

Anyone fancy a coffee?" I asked as we exited the courtroom. "I'm buying."

I saw DC Filippos hesitate and look at his boss.

"We just about have time," said the sergeant.

The two of them sat at a table at one end of the vestibule while I collected three cups of coffee from the vending machine in the corner.

"So you were happy with that verdict," I said, sitting down to join them.

It was not a question but a statement.

"It seemed reasonable in the circumstances," said DS Merryweather. "There are too many holes in our knowledge to be sure it was suicide."

I shook my head. "It was surely not suicide. I think he was murdered."

"He was found in a locked cubicle," the detective said with more than a trace of frustration.

"We heard how the lock was slid open using a cleaner's mop. Why couldn't it have been closed in the same way?" Now that *had* been a question. No doubt about it. "And why would anyone fly all the way from India just to kill himself?"

Another question.

My promise to Grant had clearly been thrown to the wind.

"People do funny things," replied the detective. "I knew someone who bought a new house when he had terminal cancer. Cost him a small fortune and then he died just two days after moving in."

That I *could* understand. It was called denial.

"And we don't know what he'd been doing in the seven days after he got here," said DC Filippos. "Maybe something happened during that week that made him do it."

"Perhaps it was a girl," said his boss. "Maybe he flew all this way and then was rejected. Enough to drive anyone to suicide."

"That's just wild speculation," I said.

"So is your notion that he was murdered."

"But, if you're right, where's the girl now? There was enough press coverage. She would have surely come forward."

"Not necessarily. The Indian community in this country can be very secretive, especially if he was coming here expecting an arranged marriage and was rejected. The family honor would mean they would all close ranks and say nothing."

It all sounded very improbable to me, but so did my theory that he'd been murdered.

"But where did he get the cocaine from?" I said, all pretense at not asking questions now completely gone.

"Maybe he brought it with him from India," DC Filippos said. "After all, it was you that told me about smuggling cocaine through customs by dissolving it in alcohol."

"So what happened to the rest of it?" I asked.

"Perhaps he'd already taken that beforehand," DS Merryweather said, "during the week he was here. Maybe this last time he just took too much."

I wondered if a test on the man's hair had revealed whether or not he'd had a long-term cocaine habit. It hadn't been mentioned in court. I looked to see if the pathologist was one of the people still milling around outside the courtroom to ask him, but there was no sign. However, I did spot Rupert Forrester, the racecourse managing director. He was talking with the usher. Probably checking that Cheltenham Racecourse wasn't to blame for anything.

"And why aren't any of the jockeys here as witnesses?" I asked. "They saw Rahul Kumar at Cheltenham Races on the day he died. They admit that they were arguing with him in the parking lot, even if they lied about why."

"We have no evidence that they were lying," said DS Merryweather.

"Trust me," I said. "They were lying. All that nonsense about parking his car in their spaces. If it was true, where's the car now?"

But, if not his parking, what had the man and the jockeys really been arguing about?

Was it to do with the spot-fixing?

Had Rahul Kumar been an illegal Indian bookmaker who had been trying to set up the "fix"?

But, if that was true, why was it still going on after his death?

Maybe he'd been trying to stop it.

"What sort of private security organization did Kumar work for?" I asked.

"According to his sister, it was a firm in New Delhi," said DC Filippos.

"Didn't you find out its name?" I asked.

"We sent a request to the Indian Police Service but heard nothing."

"Shouldn't the inquest have been adjourned until you found out? Don't you think it might have been relevant?"

"No," said the detective sergeant decisively, standing up. "All these questions are *not* relevant. The coroner has given his verdict. Rahul Kumar died from misadventure. End of."

"Inquests can always be reopened," I said.

"Not after a misadventure verdict, not unless there's a judicial review by the High Court, and only then if significant new evidence comes to light. It has taken us five long months even to find out who he was, so that's unlikely."

Especially if they weren't going to be looking, I thought.

Dead end. But I wasn't giving up that easily.

Giving up!

What was I thinking of?

We walked out to the parking lot.

"I suppose this investigation is now over for you two," I said.

"Definitely is," replied DS Merryweather, "and good riddance too. I only have another twenty-two open files on my desk."

Should I ask? Should I?

Why not? I'd already broken my promise to Grant. In for a penny . . .

"Who owns the black Mercedes?"

"I'm not allowed to give you that information," he said, "due to data protection."

"I promise I won't tell anybody."

Not that my promises were worth anything.

"I still can't tell you."

"Can't or won't?"

"Either and both," said the detective sergeant. "Leave it, Dr.

Rankin. Go back to treating your patients and concentrate on staying well. This is over."

The two policemen climbed into their car.

"How about my son's bike?" I shouted at them as they drove off. "Who did that?"

It may have been over for them but it wasn't for me.

GRANT ARRIVED HOME from work as I was sitting on the sofa, sipping tea and watching the six o'clock news on the television.

"How was it?" he asked.

"OK, I suppose," I said. "I took a bit of a grilling from the coroner over hospital procedure and that was quite uncomfortable, but, apart from that, it was fine."

"I'm sorry. I should have been with you."

Grant had intended coming with me to the inquest, but then he'd been asked to make an important presentation at his work— something to do with new instrumentation for a jet fighter being made for an Arab country. The ruling sheikh was going to be there.

Grant had been in two minds and, in the end, it had been me who'd insisted that he should give the presentation, because I knew that was what he truly wanted.

"It was OK," I said. "I was fine, and I think I coped all right. How did your presentation go?"

"Really well," he said, smiling. "The sheikh seemed very happy, which was the most important thing, as he holds the purse strings, and my bosses were delighted too."

"Good. Well done."

"Do you fancy a glass of wine to celebrate?" Grant asked.

"Not for me, thanks. I have my tea, but you have one."

"Are you all right?" Grant asked with some concern.

"Of course," I said. "I'm fine. I just don't want a drink."

Too many calories, I thought.

He went out to the kitchen to open a bottle while I thought back to my time in the witness box during the inquest, in particular when the coroner had seemingly implied that I had somehow failed to keep an eye on what was happening everywhere on the night the man had died.

I really had been fine about it.

A couple of months earlier and I would have probably broken down in tears or descended into a full-on panic attack. I might even have ended up back in the hospital myself.

I had recently made progress in my recovery, not that I could consider myself as being completely well. For a start I still wasn't eating properly, taking every available minor excuse to skip a meal.

Even though Grant and my family kept telling me I was far too thin, I still couldn't see it when looking in a mirror.

All I saw was myself as big, fat and ugly.

Going back to work had helped, if only because I couldn't spend the whole day studying my reflection. But I was still taking far too many damn pills, and trying to balance my hormone and thyroxine levels was still proving difficult, if not impossible.

I was still seeing Stephen Butler every other week and we had been working on my emotional state.

He considered that the lack of a loving relationship with either of my parents when I'd been a child was still somehow hindering my ability to fully interact emotionally with friends and family, and especially with my husband.

I loved Grant, and I was sure he loved me, but there was an emotional disconnect between us that I felt had recently widened. I couldn't exactly put my finger on the reason, and it may have been more in my head than in reality, but I believed we were drifting slowly apart. Maybe it was nothing to do with my illness, perhaps it was just what happened after eighteen years of marriage but, either way, it frightened me.

In the past, I would never have made a solemn promise to Grant not to ask questions and then so easily broken it, as I had done earlier. And I often found myself lying to him about my weight and especially about my eating, telling him happily that I'd had a big lunch when, in fact, I'd consumed nothing at all.

And what worried me most was that it was so easy, and I felt no guilt afterward.

My cell phone rang and I picked it up.

"Hello," I said.

"Ah, yes, hello, Chris," said a voice. "Er, Adrian Kings here, from the racecourse. How are you keeping?"

He sounded all sweetness and light. Too much so, in fact.

"I'm fine, thank you," I replied without any warmth.

What did he want?

"I hear you are back working at Cheltenham General."

"Yes," I said, and wondered how he knew. But it was not a secret and there was a healthy grapevine in local medical circles.

"I'm delighted that you are back to full fitness."

"Thank you."

I wasn't yet completely at *full* fitness but I wasn't going to tell him that. To say that I was slightly wary of this conversation would not have been an exaggeration. The last time he'd spoken to me he'd been spitting blood with anger.

"Er," he said.

I realized that he was embarrassed—I could tell from his voice. Clearly, he could also remember our last encounter.

I remained silent. I wasn't going to help him out.

"Chris?" he said finally.

"Yes."

"Would you be interested in acting as a medical officer at the upcoming April Meeting on Wednesday?" He said it in a rush as if trying to rid himself of the words as quickly as possible.

"At Cheltenham?" I asked.

"Yes, of course at Cheltenham."

Did I detect a hint of irritation?

"I don't know," I said. "Last time you spoke to me, you told me in no uncertain terms that you didn't ever want me to act for you again. In fact, you shouted at me to get out of the jockeys' medical room and stay out."

"Yes. Well, er, I may have been a trifle hasty."

It was as close to an apology as I was likely to get.

"Short, are you?" I said.

"No," he said firmly, too firmly. "Nothing like that."

I didn't believe him, and I was right.

"What with Easter being so late this year, it's just that some of the usual team are away on holiday with their children and I thought you might like to step in."

So he was short.

But I didn't care about the reason why. I was just pleased that he wanted me at all. I was even off duty at the hospital until Friday night and therefore available.

"I'd be delighted to," I said.

"Great," he said, the embarrassment finally banished. "I was talking to Rupert Forrester earlier and he said that he'd seen you giving evidence at an inquest this morning. It seems that he was impressed."

Was he telling me it had been the racecourse managing director's idea to ask me to act rather than his? Maybe he was, but I wasn't bothered. I'd thought my days as a racecourse doctor were over and now I was looking forward to them again.

"Who was that?" Grant asked as I disconnected. He had come back in from the kitchen with a glass of red wine and had caught only the tail end of the conversation.

"Adrian Kings," I said. "Senior medic at the racecourse. He wants me to act as a medical officer on Wednesday."

I could tell that Grant wasn't pleased. "Wasn't he very rude to you last time? I'm surprised you agreed. And, to be honest, I'd much rather you didn't do it. In fact, I would prefer it if you never went near that damn place ever again."

"But I drive past it going to work every day," I said flippantly.

"You know what I mean."

He knew better than to try to order me not to act as a racecourse doctor, persuasion rather than proscription always being the best method, but there was definite worry etched on his face.

"I'll be fine," I said, trying to reassure him. "Maybe I wasn't ready when I went back last time. But I'm better now. And all that other stuff is firmly behind me."

Little did I realize that it was also still firmly out in front, and it was about to come head-on at me like a runaway train.

25

There was a real spring in my step as I walked in through the racecourse entrance on Wednesday morning.

Things had been going well at the hospital and I had rediscovered my enthusiasm for emergency medicine. True, I was still being monitored by others, but I had been given more and more responsibility and, best of all, I hadn't once had to go and hide in the linen cupboard.

At home, things hadn't been quite so good.

The twins were doing well at school and seemingly unaffected by their mother being ill. However, relations with Grant had recently clearly been on the slide. He had confided in one of my girlfriends from the village that he was fed up at always having to be careful around me in order not to cause an upset.

The girlfriend had reckoned that he was telling her in the hope and expectation that she would pass it on and she had done so almost immediately.

Whereas in the months before Christmas, my reaction might have been one of panic and dread, I was now more calm and pragmatic. I was even able to speculate on whether Grant had really told my girlfriend because he fancied her. Maybe, in spite of what he had said, he actually wanted me to starve to death so that he'd be free to pursue her.

I knew I'd annoyed him by insisting that I was going back to act as a racecourse doctor. Had I gone too far? But I hadn't realized how much those days meant to me until I thought I'd had them taken away forever.

Even at breakfast that very morning, he had still tried to dissuade me.

"I couldn't possibly let them down at this short notice," I'd said. But I had no intention of letting them down at all because I loved it so much.

In order to remain on the approved list, I had to act as a racecourse doctor for a minimum of eight days per annum and, due to my illness and absence, I would struggle to fulfill the requirement for the current year if I only worked at Cheltenham. Hence, I already had plans to make myself available to other local courses, such as Worcester, Hereford and Stratford.

Not that I'd mentioned it yet to Grant. He was angry enough already that I was going back at all.

CHELTENHAM RACES at the April Meeting was nothing like that for the Festival. It was a much more low-key affair with an expected daily attendance of only ten thousand, a mere seventh of the crowd that had witnessed the Gold Cup the previous month.

Much of the tented village of shops and restaurants had been removed and the site where, in March, thousands of Irish visitors had sung along with live bands and poured copious pints of Guinness down their throats was now simply a flat empty space.

The temporary grandstands and glass-fronted restaurants that had stretched down the finishing straight well past the second-last fence were nothing more than a distant memory and the grass on which they had been erected was already recovering in the spring sunshine.

But, after the hurly-burly of the racecourse at the Festival, when getting from one place to another involved pushing through a crowd at every corner, there was something rather nice about the open spaces and the gentler pace of the April Meeting.

Jump racing was winding down toward the end of the season, and, even though some jumping continued throughout the summer months at the smaller courses, Cheltenham definitely had an "end of term" feel about it. Not that the racing would be any less competitive, with plenty of horses going to post for the seven races on each of the two days.

I was early, very early, such had been my eagerness for the day to begin.

The first race was not until almost two o'clock but I was in the medical room well before a quarter to twelve. I had tried to stay at home for most of the morning but I'd done nothing but continually look at my watch, urging the hands to hurry up and move around to my chosen leaving time. At eleven o'clock, I'd given up waiting and had driven to the racecourse a good half an hour before I'd intended, parking my Mini in the doctors' reserved spaces adjacent to the jockeys' parking lot.

With so many fewer spectators, I had no concerns about exit lines at the end of the day, so there had been no need on this occasion to park in Tom and Julie's farmyard.

I was busily checking through the medical kits when Jack Otley came sweeping in.

"Morning, Chris," he said. "You're here early."

"Hi, Jack," I replied. "So are you."

"I'm going for a spot of lunch with some friends who have a

box," he said. "Just dropping off my coat. Will you tell Adrian I'll be back in an hour and ask him to hold off his briefing till I get back? I'd appreciate it."

"OK," I said, "will do."

Jack hung up his coat on a hook outside the medical-room door and departed at a trot for his lunch.

Lunch? I hadn't really thought about lunch.

I wondered if I should get some now before we got busy.

But, in truth, lunch had been a problem for some considerable time. I simply *had* to eat some breakfast, as Grant and the boys were watching and they would get very agitated if I didn't eat something with them each morning at the kitchen table. And the same was true for dinner. However, at lunchtime I was nearly always on my own, at least during the week, so the "food police" were unaware of whether I ate anything or not.

Mostly not.

Two meals a day were about as many as I could stomach.

One would have been better.

Eating, or rather the lack of it, was the one thing still holding back my recovery. I still saw myself as too fat in spite of what the bathroom scales might say to the contrary. Grant had threatened to remove all the mirrors in the house so that I couldn't see my reflection but I'd told him not to be so silly. But it wasn't really silly. I looked at myself in those mirrors all the time, and I didn't much like the view.

I decided that, on balance, I could do without lunch. Again.

Instead, I walked out onto the terrace in front of the weighing room and soaked up some rays.

As was often the case in the United Kingdom in recent years, this April had so far been one of the best months for sunshine, with warm days and cool evenings, and today was no exception.

I stood facing the sun with my eyes closed, allowing its heat to soak deep into my soul.

"You look happy, Doc," said a voice in front of me.

I opened my eyes. It was Dave Leigh, he of the broken collarbone.

"Oh, hi, Dave," I said. "How are things? Are you working for the TV people again?"

"No," he said with a laugh, "I'm back riding."

"So soon?" I said with surprise. It had only been a month since he'd broken it. "You must heal very quickly."

"Had my first ride back on Monday at Huntingdon. It was a winner too."

"Well done," I said.

"I've got three more here today so I arrived good and early. Didn't want to miss out due to a breakdown or a traffic jam."

"Where do you live?" I asked.

"Lambourn," he said. "Center of the universe."

Lambourn was a large village nestling among the rolling Berkshire Downs between Newbury and Swindon. It was a major training center for racehorses, especially jumpers, with over thirty active trainers having yards in and around the village. And it was only about an hour's drive from Cheltenham.

Dave Leigh was clearly almost as eager as I for the day's racing to begin.

But he was not the only person on the terrace that I recognized. Rupert Forrester was also there, no doubt checking that all was in order. He looked in my direction and then came over.

"Dr. Rankin," he said, "good of you to help us out at such short notice."

He extended his hand and I shook it.

"No problem," I said. "Lovely day for it."

"Thank goodness," he said. "It makes a huge difference to the gate."

I could imagine. No one wanted to go racing in the rain.

"I saw you on Monday," he said. "At the inquest of that poor man."

"I spotted you there as well."

He nodded. "I was there to represent the racecourse. Fortunately, I wasn't called by the coroner. Always difficult when someone dies on the premises."

"The man actually died in the hospital," I said.

"Yes, so he did. But there have been others. We had three in one day last year, at the Festival. Two heart attacks and a burst aneurysm. The racing must have been too exciting for them." He laughed at his own inappropriate joke. "Ah, well, I must get on."

He disappeared into the weighing room while I went back to enjoying the sunshine. But he had made me think.

Human life was very fragile. I knew that only too well from my work. No one expected to go for a day at the races and not make it home again afterward. But it happened all the time. Not just heart attacks and burst aneurysms but also strokes, cardiac arrhythmia and pulmonary embolisms. All were common causes of sudden and unexpected death, to say nothing of road accidents and other forms of trauma.

Yet some people's bodies could take all sorts of punishment and still continue to operate almost normally.

And jockeys like Dave Leigh were clearly in that category.

JACK OTLEY was late returning from his lunch and Adrian Kings wasn't particularly pleased at having to wait to give his briefing.

"I hope you haven't been drinking," Adrian said acidly when he finally arrived.

"Of course not," Jack replied, somewhat aggrieved.

Good job too, I thought. We were the only three racecourse doctors on duty, the absolute minimum requirement and one less than was customary at Cheltenham due to the intersecting nature of the track. No wonder Rupert Forrester had been so pleased that I was able to step in at such short notice.

Adrian, however, was never going to admit that he was steering his ship too close to the rocks, and certainly not to me.

"All three of us will be out on the course," he said. "Plus we have four ambulances. That will provide plenty of cover."

The racing authority rules were quite simple. Irrespective of the number of ambulances available, not enough doctors would result in racing having to be abandoned.

Briefing over, I went out to fetch a coffee from the cafeteria and came face-to-face in the corridor with Jason Conway.

He looked at me and I at him from a distance of about eighteen inches. I was quite calm.

"Hello, JC," I said.

"Doc," he replied, not batting an eyelid at my use of his nickname.

"How many rides do you have today?" I asked.

"Three." He didn't move.

I stared deep into his eyes. Then I looked away. I wasn't going back there.

"Good luck," I said. "I hope I don't have to see you later."

"No chance," he said.

In spite of overwhelming evidence to the contrary, jockeys were always supremely confident that they wouldn't get hurt. They had to be, otherwise they'd never do the job in the first place. The fact that, when doing their work, they were actually chased by an ambulance didn't seem to faze them at all.

Jason pushed past me, back into the changing room.

I breathed out slowly through my mouth and walked on to fetch my coffee.

I had made a promise to myself not to ask any of the three jockeys anything about spot-fixing in racing, and this was one promise I intended keeping. No one else seemed to think it was happening anyway, and Grant had tried to convince me that I must be mistaken.

Except that I wasn't.

26

The first race of the afternoon was uneventful as far as the medical team were concerned, but, nevertheless, I relished being back in the Land Rover bouncing along behind the horses in a two-mile novice hurdle.

However, the second race, a handicap chase over three and a half miles and twenty-four fences, stretched us to the limit, even beyond it.

Eighteen runners went to post in a competitive Class 3 contest but only half were still standing at the finish. Of the other nine, three pulled up but six fell and four of the jockeys were injured.

The field was tightly bunched as they came past the grandstands with two complete circuits still to cover. My Land Rover was the second vehicle in the following train, immediately behind the lead ambulance.

"Two fallers, first fence in the back straight," came the voice of the spotter in my earpiece. "Horses up, jockeys not."

The Land Rover driver pulled the vehicle over onto the grass and I was quickly out the door and running. The lead ambulance had also stopped.

"Doc two attending," I called into my radio.

"And ambulance one," someone said into my ear.

"Ambulance two taking over the lead."

"Doc one joining." I recognized that as Adrian.

I ducked under the running rail and sprinted across the grass to one of the two jockeys, while the paramedic team from the ambulance went to the other and the groundsmen followed on with their green privacy screens.

I went down on my knees next to the moaning figure.

"Dr. Rankin here," I said. "Where does it hurt?"

"My left leg, Doc. I think I heard it go crack."

It was a woman's voice.

Female jump jockeys had been riding against men since the Sex Discrimination Act of 1975 finally forced British racing to allow it, but they were still rare, there being only a handful of female professionals among several hundred of their male colleagues.

I smiled.

I too was a member of a profession that had initially tried to exclude women until Elizabeth Garrett Anderson had broken through the prejudice to become the country's first female doctor. More than a hundred years later some 60 percent of British medical students were now women. Female jockeys clearly still had some way to go.

"What's your name?" I asked.

"Ellie Lowe," she said.

"Did you hit your head at all, Ellie?"

Legs could wait but head and neck injuries could kill quickly.

"No," she said. "It was an easy fall but my lower leg got landed on by one of the others."

Ouch, I thought.

Horses were generally pretty good at avoiding human beings

lying on the ground but sometimes there was nowhere else to go and the weight of a landing horse, acting through a slender metal-shod hoof, could do a lot of damage.

I gently examined her leg and she winced.

"It'll need an X-ray," I said. "I think you may have fractured your fibula above the ankle."

"Fuck," she said in a very unladylike manner. "Does that mean they'll cut my boot off?"

"Quite likely," I said.

"Fuck," she said again. "They're brand-new and were bloody expensive."

She seemed more concerned about her riding boots than her broken leg.

"Doc two to spotter," I said into my radio. "Another ambulance needed here."

"Roger," came the reply. "On its way."

The attendants were already placing barriers in front of the fence so it would be bypassed by the other runners next time around.

I looked across at the other fallen rider about four yards away, and the two paramedics who were still tending to him as he lay on the ground. I thought there was something quite urgent about their movements.

"Faller, downhill open ditch. Jockey still down." The spotter's voice was loud in my ear.

"Doc one attending," came the call from Adrian through the radio.

"I've ordered an ambulance and stretcher for you," I said to my lady jockey. "The horses are bypassing this fence. Will you be OK for a second, Ellie? I want to check on *him*."

I pointed at the other fallen rider.

"Yes," she said. "Go ahead. I'm sure I can hop."

"No," I said firmly. "No hopping. Wait for the stretcher."

I'd once had a patient arrive at A&E who, having broken one ankle, hopped across the waiting room when called and, while doing so, snapped the Achilles tendon in the other. The result had been both legs in plaster and eight weeks before he could walk again.

The other rider was Dick McGee and he wasn't swearing about not winning this time. He was conscious but with wide frightened eyes.

"Back injury," one of the paramedics said quietly to me as I went down on my knees next to him.

"Hi, Dick," I said. "Dr. Rankin here."

"Oh great, that's all I need," he replied sardonically, which I took to be a good sign.

"Stay still," I said to him. "We're going to put a collar around your neck, just as a precaution."

"I can't feel my legs, Doc," he said, the worry etched deeply across his forehead.

"It may just be spinal shock," I said, trying to be comforting. His back didn't appear to be out of shape. "Sometimes a bang to the spine causes things to stop working for a short while. Don't worry. Just let us look after you."

One of the paramedics slid a plastic immobilization collar gently under Dick's neck and fastened it with Velcro under his chin.

"Can you remember what happened?" I asked.

"Bloody nag hit the top and I went arse over tit. Landed flat on my back. Drove the bloody breath out of me, I can tell you."

Flat was good, I thought.

I felt down his legs to check that there was no major injury there. If he couldn't feel them, then he wouldn't be aware if one or both of his legs were broken.

I couldn't detect anything wrong.

"My feet have started bloody burning," Dick said, panic causing his voice to go up at least an octave. He was even trying to sit up.

"Lie still, Dick," I said urgently. "You don't want to do yourself any more damage, do you?"

"But my bloody feet hurt," he said.

"That's a good sign," I said. I ran my hand down his left leg and squeezed each side just above his knee, just like I used to squeeze the legs of my twins to make them laugh. "Can you feel that?"

"I can feel something," he said. "Pressure."

That was a very good sign.

"Do you need anything for the pain?" I asked him.

"Just about OK at the moment," he replied. "Thanks, Doc."

He looked up at me and I looked back down at him.

The paramedics had collected a scoop stretcher from their vehicle and they started sliding it under him. The two-piece construction of the stretcher allowed it to be slid in from each side before being joined together, thus reducing the amount the patient had to be moved unsupported.

I turned to one of the paramedics.

"Give him some supplementary oxygen at five liters per minute," I said. Added oxygen in his system would aid any recovery. "Or Entonox if he needs it." Entonox was a fifty-fifty mix of nitrous oxide and oxygen—gas and air—for relief of acute pain. Ask any mother.

"I'll be back in a sec."

The horses still in the race galloped past the fence on their second circuit as I went back to Ellie Lowe. The second ambulance crew were helping her onto their stretcher.

"You OK, Ellie?" I asked.

"Will be," she said. "And I managed to pull my boot off."

Amazed, I looked down at her ankle. "Didn't it hurt?"

"Like bloody murder," she said with a laugh. "But not as much as cutting it off would have hurt my bank balance."

She'd do, I thought. Jockeys were clearly made of stern stuff, male or female.

"Take her to the medical room," I said to the paramedics. "We'll arrange onward transportation from there." I turned back to Ellie. "I'll leave you with these guys now, if that's OK. I need to get back."

She nodded. "It's Dick McGee, isn't it? How's he doing?"

"Not great," I said.

"Is he paralyzed?"

It was the one thing that frightened every jockey.

"I don't think so. It may be too early to tell but I'm hopeful he's just jarred his back. But we can't take any risks."

She nodded and was carried away toward the waiting ambulance.

"Two fallers, fence after the water," said the spotter into my ear. "One jockey still down. Doc three, are you available?"

"Doc three on my way," I heard Jack Otley reply over the radio. He would have been stationed at the start and then have moved to the last fence.

I, meanwhile, went back over to Dick McGee, who was being strapped to the scoop ready to be lifted into the ambulance, which had been driven onto the track close by. In addition, he was now wearing a mask attached to a portable oxygen tank.

"You OK, Dick?" I asked.

"What do you think?" he replied, his voice somewhat muffled by the mask.

I considered it a good indicator that he was still able to engage me in his usual banter. If there had been a highly critical trauma to his spinal column, such as a complete break, I might have expected him to have had difficulty breathing let alone talking.

"How about the air ambulance?" one of the paramedics said.

Big-call time.

I put my hands onto the toe ends of Dick's lightweight riding boots.

"Dick," I said. "Wiggle your toes for me."

I could feel the slightest of movements through the wafer-thin leather.

"No need," I said to the paramedic. "There's movement. If it becomes necessary, we'll transfer him to Gloucestershire Royal. They have a spinal injury assessment unit, and it would take longer to get the air ambulance up here than to go by road."

I would have called the air ambulance if I'd thought his spinal column was severed or for a major head injury. He would then have had to go to Bristol.

"Faller, second-last," said the spotter into my ear. "Jockey down. Any doctor available?"

There was no reply.

"Can you cope here now?" I asked the paramedics.

"Sure."

"Take him to the jockeys' medical room for further assessment. Check his blood pressure and call me immediately on the radio if he deteriorates."

"Will do."

"Doc two. On my way," I said into the radio as I ran back to the Land Rover. It wasn't ideal, I'd have liked to remain with Dick McGee, even traveled with him all the way to the hospital if that was required, but it would leave us shorthanded.

I jumped into the Land Rover.

"Second-last fence," I said to the driver. "Quick as you can."

We set off at breakneck speed along the vehicle track.

"Doc two to medical room," I said into the radio as we bounded along.

"Medical room. Go ahead."

I gave the two nurses there a very brief account of both Ellie Lowe's and Dick McGee's condition and that both were on their way to them for further assessment.

"Doc one here," Adrian said over the radio. "On my way back to the medical room now."

I arrived at the second-last fence and was quickly out of the Land Rover and running.

The jockey who was down was being tended to by two paramedics from one of the remaining ambulances. I joined them.

"Jason Conway," one of the paramedics said to me as I approached. "Claims he's all right but he can't stand up properly."

First Dick McGee. Now Jason Conway.

Who would believe that was a coincidence?

I went over to him.

"Hello, Jason, what seems to be the problem?"

He looked at me but seemingly without any recognition.

"No problem," he said, trying to get up.

But his words were slightly slurred.

Concussion. I knew. I'd been there.

"Just lie down and let me examine you," I said.

I could tell that he wasn't keen. "I'm OK," he insisted.

"Jason," I said firmly, "I will need to examine you and if you refuse I will have to stand you down from riding anyway."

I wasn't sure that his brain was in a position to work out the logic but he stopped trying to get to his feet and lay back on the grass.

"Which horse were you riding?" I asked as I knelt down beside him.

He looked up at me blankly without answering.

"Where are you?" I asked.

"At the races," he said confidently.

"Which racecourse?"

Again there was no answer.

I turned to the paramedics. "Put a neck collar on him and we'll take him on a stretcher to the medical room. We'll decide there but I strongly suspect he'll need to go to the hospital for a scan."

While the paramedics collected their stretcher I examined Jason for any other injuries but there were none I could see. That didn't mean there weren't any. Unseen injuries were often the most dangerous.

To say that there was pandemonium in the medical room when I arrived back would not be an exaggeration. The two beds plus the physical therapist's table were already occupied by injured jockeys, hidden from view by the blue privacy curtains, and Jason Conway was still outside in the ambulance being cared for by the paramedics.

"Bloody hell," Adrian said. "It's like Piccadilly Circus in the rush hour. Speak to me."

"Ellie Lowe has a suspected broken fibula," I said. "Dick McGee took a blow to his back and initially couldn't feel his legs but some sensation and movement returned while I was with him. I've also got Jason Conway outside in the ambulance with suspected concussion. He couldn't stand properly and didn't know where he was or which horse he'd been riding. I think he should go for a scan."

"OK," Adrian said, taking a deep breath. "Ellie Lowe is having a support bandage fitted but will have to go to the hospital, so will Jason Conway. Both to Cheltenham General. Dick McGee says he's now fine and all sensation and movement have returned to normal and he should be able to ride in the fourth race. It's as much as I can do to keep him lying down. I've told him if he gets up, I'll sign him off riding for a month."

"I still think he should go for a scan, to be on the safe side," I said. "Who's in the other one?" I nodded toward the blue curtains nearest the door.

"Mike Sheraton," Adrian said. "Gashed his right knee. The nurse is just putting in a few stitches. He'll be fine."

I stared at him in disbelief.

Dick McGee, Jason Conway and Mike Sheraton, the three jockeys I had vowed to have nothing to do with, were all here, and all injured.

27

"Jockeys, five minutes," came the call through the changing-room loudspeaker system.

The next race.

"Can we cope?" Jack Otley said to Adrian.

"We'll have to," he said. "There are only eight runners in this one. Jack, you and I will be out on the course. Chris, you stay here to monitor our guests but listen out on the radio in case you're needed. With one ambulance stuck outside with Jason Conway, we still have three available. That's more than enough. Let's just hope we have no fallers this time."

Adrian knew fully well that we needed to act according to our clinical decisions and not allow financial or racing operational considerations to override our judgment. But, equally, we wouldn't be thanked if we canceled racing for no good reason.

"We do need to send Lowe, McGee and Conway to the hospital," I said.

"Could one ambulance take all three at once?" Adrian asked.

I shook my head. "I think both Jason Conway and Dick McGee should be kept horizontal. Ellie Lowe could sit on a seat as long as her left leg is up."

"Then call for an off-course ambulance," Adrian said, picking up his red doctor's bag. "Use that and the one outside."

"I'd really like to go with them," I said. "I don't trust either McGee or Conway not to simply walk away at the other end."

"Threaten them with a long suspension if they do."

He started for the door but was blocked by Rupert Forrester coming in.

"Everything all right in here?" he asked, standing in the doorway. "I hear we've had several injuries after that race."

"Yes, Rupert, we have," Adrian replied. "But we're coping." He sounded a lot more confident than I was.

"So racing can continue?"

"Absolutely," Adrian replied. "We meet the minimum requirement."

"Good," Rupert said. He started to leave but turned back. "Who's actually in here?" he asked, indicating toward the blue curtains.

"Mike Sheraton, Dick McGee and Ellie Lowe. Jason Conway is being treated outside in an ambulance."

"Any of them serious?"

"Serious but not critical," Adrian said. "One possible fractured fibula, one back spasm, one likely concussion and some stitches in a split knee. Nothing we can't deal with easily. Dr. Rankin, here, is going to call an off-course ambulance to assist with a transfer of a couple to the local hospital."

In my opinion, Adrian was downplaying the magnitude of the problem.

"Jockeys out," was called over the speakers.

"I must go," Adrian said. "I have to get down to the start or the race will be off late."

The regulations stated that racing was unable to proceed until the doctor at the start had confirmed to the official starter that at least the minimum required medical provision was in place.

Rupert Forrester stepped aside to let Adrian and Jack out but came back into the doorway.

"Dr. Rankin," he said, "are you happy that you can cope here on your own? Would you like me to stay? I'm no doctor but I could surely do something to help?"

"I'm fine, thank you," I said. "I have the nurses to help me and everything is under control." If Adrian wanted to talk down the seriousness of the injuries, I could do the same. I also decided not to point out to him that non-medical staff were not permitted to be in there anyway, not when we had patients present, due to compromising their medical confidentiality.

He nodded, took one more long look around the room and then departed.

"OK," I said almost to myself. "Where do I begin?"

First, I went outside to check on Jason Conway in the ambulance. He was still lying on the stretcher with one of the paramedics sitting next to him. He had been wired up to a heart monitor and had a blood-pressure cuff on his arm, but he had recovered somewhat, at least to the extent that he knew who I was, and he wasn't happy about it.

"I want another doctor," he said belligerently.

The paramedic gave me a sideways questioning glance, which I ignored.

"There isn't another doctor available," I replied calmly. "Now, Jason, can you answer some questions?"

"Not more bloody questions," he said, lying back on the stretcher and closing his eyes.

Not those questions, I thought. I needed to ask him the Turner concussion questions.

He did slightly better this time insofar as he could remember both that he was at Cheltenham Racecourse and the name of the horse he'd been riding. But as for who was the current champion jockey or the winner of the Grand National, which had only been run the previous Saturday, he wasn't even close.

"Jason," I said, "I consider that there is evidence of concussion and I will be making a Red Entry to that effect. You will not be able to ride for a minimum of seven days and, even then, you will need clearance from the Chief Medical Adviser before racing again. Do you understand?"

He looked at me somewhat vaguely. Fortunately, we had a prepared printed sheet to give to concussed riders that set out the rules and the procedure for obtaining clearance to ride, along with a voucher to help them purchase a new helmet. I gave him a copy.

"You are now going to go to the hospital," I said to him, "for a scan."

"No need," he said, trying to sit up but having difficulty doing so.

There was every need, I thought. I turned to the paramedic. "Vitals?"

"All good," he said.

"Never mind. Cheltenham General and now," I said. "I'll call ahead to warn them he's coming. I want an urgent head CT to check for any bleeds."

I turned back to the patient.

"Jason," I said, "you are going to the hospital now. I will talk to your valet and get your stuff sent on."

"No need," he said again, but he lay back on the stretcher and closed his eyes.

I was suddenly quite worried about him.

"Quick as you can," I said to the paramedic.

"No problem."

I climbed out of the ambulance and it set off with its blue lights flashing. I watched it go. Perhaps I should have gone with him, but I had more patients to deal with. I went back into the medical room.

The blue screen curtains had been pulled back and the three jockeys were all watching the current race on the television attached to the opposite wall. I glanced up at the screen as I made a call to A&E at Cheltenham General.

"I have three customers for you," I said. "One on his way now, two more to follow."

Jeremy Cook was on duty and I spoke directly with him, filling him in on the details of each expected patient.

"Thanks, Chris," he said when I'd finished. "We'll look after them."

Next I called the ambulance service requesting an ambulance.

"Thirty minutes OK?" said the operator. "There's been a big accident on the motorway and we're a bit stretched at present."

"Thirty minutes will be fine," I said, and wondered if the ambulance I'd just dispatched might be back sooner than that.

"Get out the fucking way," Mike Sheraton shouted at the nurse. She had just finished stitching his knee and had inadvertently stepped into his line of sight to the TV while fetching a dressing.

I turned and stared at him. "That's no way to speak to a lady."

He didn't reply. He didn't even look at me.

As Dave Leigh had said, Mike Sheraton was not a nice person. All the medical staff had their favorites among the jockeys but he wasn't on anyone's list.

I checked his RIMANI entry on the computer. Adrian had not stood him down from riding.

"Let me have a look at that knee before you cover it," I said to the nurse.

She had done a fine job. There was a tidy row of four small knotted stitches across the front of Sheraton's right knee. I studied the wound closely as the owner of the leg concentrated only on the televised finale of the race.

Simple suturing alone did not warrant a Red Entry and was, hence, not a reason to prevent someone from riding, but this injury was over a joint.

As the nurse applied the dressing, I filled out some paperwork and handed a sheet of paper to Mike Sheraton.

"What's this?" he demanded angrily.

"Notification of Red Entry form," I said. "You must have seen one before."

It gave the details of the injury and the reasons for the Red Entry.

"I know what it is," he said loudly, "but why are you giving it to me? This is nothing more than a scratch."

"It's a laceration that required four stitches, and it's over a joint. If you bend the knee too much, you will split it open again. Hence, I've made a Red Entry on the computer. You will need to give the form to a racecourse doctor and get clearance before you can ride again, and that won't be today."

"I'm not accepting that," he said, throwing the paper down angrily onto the bed.

He may have been furious, but I remained unmoved.

"You will," I said. "You'll not be cleared to ride again without it—or would you rather I reported you to the stewards?"

He knew he had no choice. If he refused to accept the form, the stewards could impose a much longer suspension from riding than the Red Entry would warrant, plus a fine on top. He scowled at me but he picked up the form and took it out with him into the changing room.

I could be just as nasty as him if I wanted to.

"You OK, Ellie?" I asked with a smile, turning toward my lady jockey, who was currently sitting up on the treatment table with her injured leg straight out in front of her. "An ambulance has been ordered to take you to Cheltenham General for an X-ray."

"I can't believe this," she said gloomily. "I'm meant to be my sister's bridesmaid on Saturday."

"You might still be able to," I said. "The hospital may just ensure the ends of the bone are aligned properly and put your foot in a walking cast. Your weight is mostly taken by the tibia, the other bone in your lower leg. Is the bridesmaid's dress long?"

"Yes," she said, suddenly more cheerful.

"Well, there you are, then," I said. "Wear a high heel on your good leg and no one will ever know, although dancing might be a problem."

Or else she might need surgery to have a metal plate put in, I thought silently. Only the X-ray would determine that.

The third occupant of a bed was Dick McGee, lying back with his arms behind his head. I looked at him.

"So, Dick," I said, "Dr. Kings tells me you believe you're fit enough to ride in the next race."

"I certainly am," he replied. "Watch."

He stood up quickly and started repeatedly touching his toes next to the bed before I had a chance to prevent him. He certainly looked all right. Was I being overcautious in believing that he needed a scan?

"It only hurts a bit," he said. "I can easily ride through that."

I didn't believe him for a second. I could see the pain etched plainly in his face.

"Stop it," I said to him urgently. "Just forty minutes ago you couldn't feel your legs. Don't you remember how frightening that was?"

He suddenly stopped the exercises and looked at me.

"Do you want to go back there?" I said. "I think it's best to have a scan to check that everything really is all right and your back is stable. You obviously gave it quite a hefty clout. Is one ride now worth a lifetime in a wheelchair?" I stared at him and raised my eyebrows. "Please lie down flat again for me."

He immediately lay back down on the bed like a scolded schoolboy.

Adrian Kings and Jack Otley walked into the medical room together.

"No fallers, thank God," Adrian said, dumping his doctor's bag on the floor. "How are things here?"

"Jason Conway has gone to Cheltenham General for a brain scan. I've spoken to the hospital. I've also ordered an ambulance for Ellie Lowe and Dick McGee." I looked at Dick, who made no objection. "And I gave Mike Sheraton a Red Entry on RIMANI. I told him he couldn't ride again today."

Adrian looked surprised. "Did his injury warrant that?"

"I had a good look at it," I said, "and in my opinion it did. He has a deep laceration over a joint and I consider that, if he flexes his knee to its full range, the stitches will probably rupture."

"I agree with Dr. Rankin," said the nurse. "Nasty cut."

Good girl, I thought, and winked at her.

"What did Sheraton say?"

"He didn't much like it," I said.

"Did you give him a Red Entry form?"

"I did," I said, without elaborating.

Adrian needed that information for his report, which would be telephoned through to the racing authority's Chief Medical Adviser at the end of the day, giving details of any rider transferred to the hospital or otherwise deemed medically unfit to ride.

The off-course ambulance arrived and the crew agreed to take both Ellie and Dick together, the latter being transferred from the medical room to the vehicle by stretcher even though he clearly thought it was unnecessary.

"Brainless doctor," I overheard him say to one of the paramedics as he was lifted from the bed onto the stretcher. "She doesn't know one end of an effing thermometer from the other."

I ignored him and went out to the ambulance with the jockeys' notes, which explained the causes and apparent nature of their injuries.

"A&E at Cheltenham General is expecting them," I said to the ambulance driver. "I've already spoken to Dr. Cook, the senior physician on duty."

"You're not coming with them, then?" he asked.

"No. I'm needed here."

The ambulance drove away, without flashing its blue lights, and a degree of calm returned to the jockeys' medical room, at least until the next race.

28

It was just one of those days.

When you're shorthanded, you hope for a nice quiet time, but, of course, fate has other ideas.

Three fallers in the fourth race had the doctors again stretched to the limit but, thankfully, there were no significant injuries other than a few bruises to both bodies and egos.

I was once more out on the course in the Land Rover and my first customer was a red-and-white-clad individual who had been unceremoniously dumped onto the turf when his mount had pecked deeply on landing, going down onto its knees, before recovering and galloping away unaccompanied.

It was Dave Leigh, and, by the time I reached him, he was sitting up on the ground more frustrated than injured.

"Stupid, stupid, stupid," he said.

"You or the horse?" I asked.

"Both," he said with a smile. "More me, I suppose. I shouldn't have fallen off. It was a spare ride and he won't ever ask me again."

"Who won't?" I said.

"Peter Hammond. Not often I get to ride for such a prestigious stable and now I've blown it."

"Never mind, Dave," I said. "Be thankful you haven't damaged your collarbone again."

I helped him to his feet and we walked off the track together.

"Whose ride was it meant to be?" I asked.

"Dick McGee's," he said. "But he had a fall and got hurt in the second."

And he was now in the hospital, I thought, probably still complaining about the brainless doctor who'd sent him there.

"Fancy a lift?" I asked. We were a long way from the weighing room.

"Thanks," Dave said. "But there should be a jockey transport somewhere." He was looking around for it.

"I waved it on," I said.

We climbed into the Land Rover and set off along the vehicle track.

"So, Doc," Dave said, "what on earth did you do to Mike Sheraton? He was mouthing off all sorts of obscenities about you just now in the changing room. I can't tell you what he said. It would make me blush to repeat it."

"I gave him a Red Entry for a perfectly legitimate medical reason. He didn't agree with me, that's all. Not a problem. I've got a thick skin."

I surprised myself by saying that.

At least for the past six months, my skin had actually been pretty thin. Even the slightest criticism would have been likely to cause me to burst into tears and descend into a deep hell of self-doubt. Going back to my job at the hospital had helped and I also relished the literal rough-and-tumble of the racecourse work.

Was I on my way back to normality?

Not until I could eat again, I thought. Stephen Butler even

reckoned that sorting out the anorexia was only the first step. Without that, he said, there could be no proper recovery at all.

"If you don't eat, you *will die*," Stephen had told me bluntly at our most recent session. "It's not a game. It's a reality. Anorexia kills far more people than any other psychiatric disorder."

But it didn't seem real.

Surely I was fine, wasn't I?

I didn't feel like I was dying. Yet, even the intimation that I was somehow playing with God was in itself both exhilarating and illusory.

Most anorexics don't want to die. They simply remain in denial, not paying attention as the severity of their condition creeps up on them, and then death snuffs them out before they even have a chance to shout, "Give me some food!"

It wasn't that I didn't *want* to eat. It was more that I physically couldn't. Something seemed to go wrong with the signals from my brain to my hand holding a fork that wouldn't allow it to travel to my mouth.

I'd taken to forcing myself to eat only a poached fish fillet, sea bass or sole, for most of my meals, with perhaps a little fruit for dessert, and even I was getting fed up with the monotony.

And, since I'd gone back to work, I was losing weight again.

I had tried hard to eat more but . . . I couldn't. I simply couldn't. Not eating had become a habit, and I was addicted to it.

"Don't forget to report in at the medical room," I said to Dave as we climbed out of the Land Rover. "You'll need to be checked and cleared."

"Don't worry, Doc," he said. "I know the rules."

He jogged off up the horse-walk toward the parade ring and the weighing room while I followed him at a more sedate pace.

My GP had advised me against doing any unnecessary exercise so as not to put too much strain on my heart. "Anorexics don't die from lack of energy," he had told me bluntly, "they die from heart failure."

Thanks, I'd thought, that was all I needed to hear.

THE REMAINDER OF THE AFTERNOON was quiet in comparison, with no more fallers in any of the last three races.

"Well done, everybody," Adrian said in his debrief to the medical team. "A busy afternoon but I think we coped rather well. Time now for tea. See you all tomorrow."

"Do you need me tomorrow?" I asked. "You only asked for Wednesday."

"Did I?" Adrian said. "Sorry. My mistake. Can you do it?"

"I'll have to check with Grant," I said. "We have children on Easter holiday as well."

"We really need you," he said.

It was nice to be needed, I thought. "I'll do my best."

"Good. And could you also give the hospital a quick call? See how everything is? Then I can phone through my report to headquarters. Best if you do it. You know the staff there better than me."

I wondered why that mattered but I did as he asked.

I caught Jeremy Cook just as he was going off duty.

"How are our jockeys?" I asked him.

"Mixed," he replied. "The girl with the broken fibula shouldn't need surgery. Simple fracture. She's been fitted with an Aircast walking boot and sent home. I've referred her to see a specialist at the Nuffield Orthopaedic Hospital in Oxford on Friday."

So she might get to the wedding, I thought.

"The young man with the head injury . . ." He paused.

"Jason Conway?" I said.

"Yes, that's right, Jason Conway. We did a CT and there's no evidence of bleeding into the brain but he still seems confused, so he's been admitted for observation. Classic case of concussion, if you ask me."

I was asking him.

"And Dick McGee?"

"He's a lucky lad, that one," Jeremy said.

"How so?" I asked.

"T-six and T-seven cracked right through from top to bottom. Severe instability."

T6 and T7 were thoracic vertebrae in the middle of the spine. I went hot and cold just thinking about his toe-touching antics. They could so easily have paralyzed him. I hadn't been such a brainless doctor after all.

"How is he now?" I asked.

"Contrite," Jeremy said. "He was complaining like crazy when he arrived. Claimed it was a waste of time his being here. Calling you all sorts of names too. Never seen anyone go so white when I showed him the results of the scan. As I say, he's a lucky man."

"Where is he?"

"Lying completely flat upstairs on a board in the orthopedic ward. I sent the results of the scan by e-mail to the top spine man in Bristol and he doesn't feel it needs any surgery. McGee has already been measured for a TLSO and it should be fitted tomorrow. He should be out of here by the weekend, but it will be a lot longer than that before he can ride again. At least six weeks."

A TLSO was a thoracolumbosacral orthosis, a lightweight

molded-plastic body cast that fitted tightly around the patient from shoulders to pelvis. It would allow him to walk while giving support to the back and preventing any relative movement of the damaged vertebrae while they healed.

"Thanks, Jeremy. I'll pass on the details to the racing authorities."

"One more thing," he said. "McGee's asking to see you. Probably wants to thank you for saving him from paralysis."

"I doubt that," I said, remembering back to some of our previous encounters.

"He also wants his clothes and stuff, his cell phone in particular."

"I'll see what I can do," I said, and disconnected.

I relayed the news to Adrian.

"Well done, you," he said, "for insisting McGee went to the hospital for a scan."

"I was there at the fence," I said. "I saw the initial distress."

But it had been touch-and-go and, if truth be told, I'd only really insisted because he'd previously been so rude to me.

"He's now crying out for his clothes. And he wants his phone."

"The valets will arrange that," Adrian said firmly. "It's not our problem."

Nevertheless, I went into the changing room and asked the valets working there which of them looked after Dick McGee.

"That would be me," said a wiry-looking man wearing an off-white shirt with rolled-up sleeves under a dark blue cotton apron. "Jim Morris by name, but most folk call me Whizz."

We didn't shake hands as he was in the process of removing a clod of Cheltenham Racecourse mud from a saddle.

Jockeys' valets are like the engine room of an ocean liner, totally hidden from the paying public but essential to the smooth running of the ship. They are not valets in the gentleman's gentleman manner of a domestic servant, and they are certainly no Jeeves to a jockeyed Bertie Wooster, but, without them, racing would unquestionably grind to a halt.

In short, they are responsible for ensuring that each jockey in their care is properly dressed and presented to the Clerk of the Scales before a race wearing the correct, clean silks and carrying a saddle, number cloth, etc., such that rider plus equipment are at the precise weight specified in the racing program.

To achieve that end requires many hours of unseen preparation with valets arriving at a racecourse at least four hours before racing begins to wash, dry and iron the silks and britches from the previous day, sort and soap saddles, polish boots, check and launder girths, plus a hundred other tasks, before even the first punter passes through the turnstiles.

"How can I help?" Whizz said, tucking his hands inside the top part of his apron, which had a line of spare safety pins fastened down one side.

"Dick McGee wants his things sent over to Cheltenham General, especially his cell phone."

"Is he staying in?" Whizz asked with surprise. "I thought he was fine."

I shook my head. "Fractured two vertebrae clean through. He's a lucky boy not to be paralyzed."

"Shit," Whizz said with feeling. "He'll be off for a while, then."

"Sure will," I said. "Can I leave it to you?"

He hesitated. "Does he need everything this evening or will tomorrow do?"

"I've no idea," I said. "I'm just passing on the message."

"It's my wedding anniversary today," Whizz said. "Promised the wife I'd be home early. Got some friends coming over for dinner and the hospital's in the wrong direction." He paused as if thinking. "I'll do it in the morning before I get here."

"If you pack up his things, I'll drop them in," I said. "I have to go into town anyway. My sons have been at an Easter holiday sports club at Cheltenham College. I'm picking them up soon and the hospital's just across the road."

"That would be great, thank you," said Whizz. "I'll try to get someone to drive his car home." He picked up a Tupperware box containing several sets of car keys and rifled through it. "Dick's will be in here somewhere."

"Do you also look after Jason Conway?" I asked. "He's in the same hospital with a concussion."

"Sure do," he said. "Got his car keys in here too. In the old days, back when I was riding, wives and girlfriends always came racing to drive us home if we got injured, but now they all have jobs, or kids to look after." He made it sound like a retrograde step. "I may have to leave the cars until tomorrow now but they'll be safe enough overnight in the parking lot."

While talking, he'd been stuffing things into two large plastic shopping bags.

"This one's Dick's," he said, holding out the bag in his right hand, "and this is Jason's." He held out the other. "Tell them I say hi and not to worry about their cars. I'll make some calls and get someone to share lifts here tomorrow to drive them home after."

"Thanks, I'll tell them," I said, taking the two bags.

Acting as a delivery girl for Jason Conway had not exactly been on my agenda but, I supposed, in for one, in for them both.

"How about the girl?" Whizz said. "Ellie. Someone told me she'd broken her leg."

"Simple fracture of the fibula," I said. "She's been sent home wearing a boot."

He nodded and went back to removing the mud from the saddle. "She'll sort herself out then. Tough old bird, she is."

Tough? Yes. Old? No. Bird? Maybe.

I left Whizz and his fellow valets busily packing gear into large rectangular wicker baskets. At least, with a two-day meeting, much of it could remain here overnight stacked ready to be washed and dried in the laundry room adjoining the changing room, in time for it to be worn and dirtied once again, and so the cycle went on relentlessly, day after day.

Horseracing was now a seven-day-a-week business with some 1,500 days of racing annually, spread across the sixty official British racecourses, to say nothing of hundreds of point-to-point meetings in addition. Indeed, there were only a couple of blank days in the whole year, at Christmas.

I took the two plastic bags into the medical room to find that only one of the nurses remained, everyone else having already gone to tea.

"I'm just locking up," said the nurse.

"I just want to check that everything's been entered on the computer," I said. "I'll only be a minute. You go on. I'll lock up."

She handed me the bunch of keys and put on her coat over her uniform scrubs.

"See you in a minute then," she said. "You know where to put the keys?"

I nodded. "In the key safe in the Clerk of the Course's office."

I checked that all three of the jockeys sent to the hospital had been given a Red Entry on RIMANI and that they were all CMA-Red, meaning that each would need clearance from the Chief Medical Adviser before riding again.

Satisfied all was in order, I checked that all the equipment cupboards were closed and also that the medicine cabinet on the wall was properly secured. It was where we kept our supply of morphine, the ultimate painkiller.

Then I picked up the bags from Whizz, locked the door, put the keys in the Clerk of the Course's office and went to tea . . . not that I ate anything.

I smiled.

Another highly interesting and rewarding day at the races.

Little did I realize that the excitement wasn't yet over.

29

I walked into Cheltenham Hospital at a quarter to eight as the setting sun cast long shadows of the college buildings across the open expanse of their cricket ground.

I adored the coming of summer when the days were lengthening and the evenings getting warm enough to sit outside in the garden, sipping chilled white wine spritzers with ice cubes clinking in the glass. Every year it did wonders for my mood and, this year in particular, it was a welcome release from the misery and gloom of the preceding winter.

I'd already picked up the boys and I left them sitting in my Mini in the staff parking lot while I took the bags in through the hospital main entrance. "I won't be long," I said to them. "Just dropping off some things."

Dick McGee was the only occupant of a two-bedded side ward and he appeared to be asleep when I quietly walked in.

Thank goodness, I thought. I can just dump his stuff and go.

I placed the bag gently on the floor next to the wall but he obviously sensed my being there and opened his eyes.

"Hello, Doc," he said.

"Hi, Dick," I replied. "How are you doing?"

"Not great, but I'll live. And I'll walk again thanks to you. It seems I owe you an apology."

"Just doing my job," I said.

"Thanks anyway."

"I brought your stuff," I said, indicating toward the bag on the floor, "and Whizz said to not worry about your car. He'll get someone to drive it to your home tomorrow. He also asked me to say hi from him."

Dick smiled but it turned into a grimace of pain.

"Hurts?" I asked.

"Only when I breathe," he said, trying to make a joke of it. "It comes in waves and it's got worse since I got here."

"Pain is sometimes like that, especially in the back. The bruising causes swelling that comes on later and presses on the spinal nerves. Haven't they given you something for it?"

"Doped to the bloody eyeballs," he said. "It'll soon pass."

He closed his eyes but the pain was still clearly visible in his features.

I looked down at him lying there, small and vulnerable in the hospital bed, very different from his godlike status as a fearless champion when sitting astride an impressive charger.

"Right," I said. "I'd better be off."

Dick opened his eyes and then his mouth as if he was about to say something. But he closed it again without uttering a sound.

"Your phone's in the bag," I said. "Do you want it?"

"Yeah. Great."

I took it out and handed it to him. "Bye, then," I said, and turned toward the door.

"He was some sort of investigator," Dick said quietly but clearly.

I turned back. "Who was?"

"The man in the parking lot, the one who died. The man in the photo."

TEN MINUTES LATER one of the nurses came to tell me she'd had a call from the hospital main reception desk. My son was there and he wanted to know how much longer I was going to be.

I'd completely forgotten about the twins.

"Not much longer," I said. "Please tell him I'm sorry and will he wait in the car."

The nurse went away and I turned back to Dick McGee.

"Will you tell the police or the racing authorities what you've just told me?"

"No way," he said. "I'd tell them I've no idea what you're talking about. Do you think I'm stupid or something? My life would be over. I'd be hounded out of the jockeys' changing room for a start. No one likes a snitch."

"So why are you telling me?" I asked.

"Because I reckon you've earned it," he said, waving a hand at his supine body. "If I'd had my way earlier this afternoon, I'd have ended up in a wheelchair or worse, although I'm not sure being dead *is* actually worse than being paralyzed. Anyway, I reckon I owe you, but I'm not telling anyone else and I'll deny ever having said it."

"So what am I meant to do with the information?" I asked.

"I don't care, just don't involve me."

"But you *are* involved," I said.

"No, I'm not," he said firmly. "I'm totally clean and above-board. Always have been and always will be. OK, I'm fiercely competitive, but I'm fair with it. Not like some others I could mention."

"Mike Sheraton, for example?"

He stared at me. "I've said enough. I think you'd better go now."

I walked out of the room into the main body of the ward and then along the corridor toward the elevator thinking about the conversation I'd just had with Dick McGee.

"The man was an investigator working for Indian racing," he'd told me. "He was looking into an allegation that an Indian bookmaker was paying jockeys in Britain to fix races."

"How do you know?"

"He said so. He was asking if anyone knew of a man called Geronimo. I remember because it seemed odd—a Native American Indian rather than an Indian from India as I'd thought."

"Was Geronimo the bookmaker?"

Dick shook his head. "Apparently he's some sort of intermediary. According to the dead man, Geronimo is English. The fixer."

"But the dead man was an Indian from India, not from America or England. The police finally found out who he was. His name was Rahul Kumar from Delhi."

"So the name Geronimo must be just a joke, a nickname. A play on the Indian thing."

"What else did the man say?"

"Not much."

"So why were Mike Sheraton and Jason Conway arguing with him?"

"I don't know but it wasn't the first time. He'd been at Sandown the previous Saturday asking questions and both JC and Sheraton had been arguing with him then too."

"Why didn't you tell me this before? Or tell the police? Why did you lie?"

"I didn't lie. You only asked me the man's name and I told

you I didn't know. And I don't. I'm no grass. I don't want to get involved. It's none of my business."

"But the integrity of your sport is at risk."

"Integrity! Don't make me laugh. Far too many people in racing are on the make."

"But not you?"

"Not me."

I wasn't at all sure I believed him. But he hadn't had to tell me what he knew. My question now was: what did I do about it? Did I tell anyone else? Would it make any difference? If Dick McGee would deny ever having told me, then any evidence would be dismissed as mere hearsay and not admissible in a court.

I was still pondering these questions when I arrived back at the Mini. So preoccupied had I been thinking about what Dick had said that only then did I realize I was still carrying the bag containing Jason Conway's clothes.

"Sorry, boys," I said to the twins, "I've got to go back in for something else, but I promise I won't be as long this time."

"Oh, come on, Mum," Toby whined. "We're starving."

"How about us stopping at McDonald's on the way home?" I said.

That cheered them up.

"I won't be long."

"That's what you said last time," Oliver complained.

"I mean it this time," I said. "I promise."

I went back into the hospital main entrance and found out from reception which ward Jason Conway was in. Needless to say, it was the farthest away.

As a concussion case, he was also in a side ward with the light dimmed. *Total rest* read the sign on the door. I'd been tempted just to leave the bag of his things at the nurses' station but things had a habit of disappearing, especially phones, so I slipped into his room as quietly as I could.

Jason was lying on his back in the semidarkness but he wasn't asleep. He rotated his head toward me.

"What the fuck do you want?" he asked.

Charming, I thought, and wondered why I'd bothered to come back. I was beginning to wish I'd just dumped his stuff in a trash bin in the parking lot and driven the boys straight home.

"Whizz asked me to bring in your clothes," I said, holding up the bag. "Your phone's in here too. Whizz says not to worry about your car. He'll get someone to drive it home for you tomorrow."

"I intend being out of here first thing in the morning. I'll drive it home myself."

"You'll have to sort that out with him," I said. "He has the keys."

I put the bag down on the end of his bed.

"You can sod off now," he snarled, without a hint of thanks. "If it wasn't for you, I wouldn't be in this bloody dump of a hospital."

"You were concussed in a fall," I said. "It had nothing to do with me."

"You sent me here."

"Not just me," I said. "The ambulance crew said you were concussed before I even got to you."

"You could have stopped it." He was angry.

"Now, why would I do that when you were clearly confused? It was for your own good. You are just lucky that the scan showed no bleeding into your brain."

Maybe, if the scan had showed something amiss, it would have improved his temper, if not his prognosis.

"If you want my advice, you should just rest and do what the medical staff tell you. The quicker you try and get up and about, the longer it will take for you to recover fully and get back to riding."

It was good advice—not that I'd taken it myself back in March when I'd been hit by the bus.

"I don't need *your* fucking advice," Jason said with real venom. "Now get the hell out of here."

The ungrateful, good-for-nothing, spot-fixing scumbag, I thought.

Now *I* was getting angry—furious, in fact.

I started to go but my anger got the better of me.

I turned back to him.

"Who is Geronimo?" I asked.

I knew instantly I'd made a big mistake.

Jason Conway stared at me with such hatred in his eyes that my anger transformed from rage into sheer terror, and a shiver ran down my spine.

I wished I'd never asked the question. Indeed, I more than wished it. I longed to have that moment back again, to be more composed, more controlled.

But, of course, I couldn't.

What was done was done.

I HURRIED ALONG the endless hospital corridors, back toward the main entrance, my feet seemingly unattached to my body.

How could I have been so foolish?

I had promised, not just to Grant but also to myself, that I'd ask no more questions.

Stop asking questions. Next time I'll run over your kid, not just his bike.

What had I done?

I rushed out into the parking lot desperate to get back to my boys, to check that they hadn't been kidnapped, or worse.

They were both in the car, of course they were.

Calm down, I said to myself. *Get a grip.*

I stood by the open Mini door, scanning the parking lot through 360 degrees, trying to convince myself I wasn't searching for a long black Mercedes with dark-tinted rear windows.

I was hyperventilating and could feel the beginnings of a panic attack in my fingers.

Calm down.

Breathe—in through my nose and out through my mouth—long deep breaths.

Slowly, things began to recover.

"Come on, Mum," shouted Toby. "Get in the car. Olly and I are, like, ravenous."

"Sorry, boys," I said, sitting down in the driver's seat and forcing a smile. "So, who wants a McDonald's?"

"We do," they chorused, bouncing up and down excitedly on the seats.

They might be fourteen but they could still be little boys again when they wanted.

They were my pride and joy. My reason for living.

How could I possibly have put them in so much danger?

30

We went to the McDonald's drive-thru on Tewkesbury Road for a double order of Big Mac, large fries and banana milk shake.

Identical meals for identical boys.

"What are you having, Mum?" Toby said.

"Nothing. I'll get myself some fish when we get home."

But, if the truth be known, I was feeling too ill to eat anything, and especially not a Big Mac and fries. The very thought of it made me feel sick.

"How about Dad?" Oliver shouted from the backseat. "Hadn't we better get something for him?"

"Your father's at a work do this evening," I said. "That's why I had to pick you up."

I drove home as the boys ate their food and noisily slurped their milk shakes. I spent almost as much time looking in the rearview mirror as I did watching the road ahead but, by now, the sun had long gone and it was almost totally dark, so all I could see were headlights anyway.

I drove all the way around the roundabout twice at Bishop's

Cleeve to check if we were being followed, and received a very strange look from Toby for doing so.

"You all right, Mum?" he asked.

"Perfectly," I said. "My mind was just on something else."

I could tell it didn't reassure him much. Whereas Oliver had pretty much taken my psychiatric hospital stay in his stride, Toby had been seriously concerned that I would die.

For many years as a child, Toby had equated being in the hospital with dying, ever since the mother of a good friend of his at primary school had gone into the hospital for a supposedly routine hernia repair only to perish on the operating table from complications with the anesthetic. The fact that I worked at a hospital didn't seem to shake this conviction and he was desperate that I shouldn't have to be readmitted as a patient.

So it did nothing to relieve his anxiety when, immediately after turning into the lane toward our village, I quickly pulled over and switched the lights off.

"What are you doing, Mum?" he asked with concern.

What could I say? It surely wouldn't help if I told him the truth—that I was checking we hadn't been followed.

But I was being crazy, I thought.

The man in the long black Mercedes didn't have to follow us—he'd left Oliver's broken bicycle in our driveway, so he must already know where we lived. Not that the thought was particularly encouraging.

"Nothing, darling," I said.

I restarted the car, turned the lights back on and drove home.

Not that my worries were over. Not by a long way.

The house was in darkness and I imagined all sorts of evils lurking in the deep shadows cast by the solitary streetlight across the road. It was as much as I could do not to drive away altogether, and I had to force myself to park the Mini in the driveway.

No sooner had the wheels stopped turning than Oliver was out of the rear passenger door with Toby close on his heels.

Had they no idea of the potential danger?

No, of course not. It was me, not them, who was paranoid.

Needless to say, we all made it safely inside and I went around double-checking that the doors and windows were all properly closed and locked.

The boys started watching a DVD on the television in the sitting room while I sat in the kitchen wondering what the hell I should do now.

Should I call the police?

But what could I tell them?

GRANT ARRIVED HOME after ten o'clock and found he couldn't get in through the front door. So he rang the bell and made me jump.

"Why did you double-lock it when you knew I was still out?" he demanded when I let him in.

"Have you had a nice evening?" I asked, ignoring his question.

"No," he said. "Complete waste of time. It was meant to be a working supper, a brainstorming session, but as soon as the wine came out it degenerated into a gripe session about the company. I knew we should never have had it at a restaurant."

Grant was cross.

It had been his idea to have the evening session in the first place, so that the design team couldn't drift off back to their workstations rather than participate in the discussion. It had clearly not been the success he had hoped for.

"How about you?" he asked. "How was your day?"

"Busy," I said.

"What have you had to eat?"

He always asked.

"Not much," I said.

"What did you have for supper?"

"The boys had a McDonald's on the way home."

"And you?"

"I was going to have some fish," I said. "But I didn't feel like it."

"Chris," he implored, "you really *must* have something to eat. You know what Stephen Butler said. Do you want to end up back in that hospital?"

"Of course not."

"Then you must have some supper. I'll make you an omelet."

I smiled at him. "That would be nice."

Grant put his head around the sitting-room door.

"Bedtime," he said to the twins, and received the usual howls of protest in reply.

"Come off it, Dad," they complained. "Can't we watch the end of the film?"

"No," he said firmly. "It's time for your bed. You can watch the rest tomorrow."

Reluctantly, the boys switched off the DVD and went up the stairs.

"I'll be up in a minute," I shouted after them. "Do your teeth."

How things change in life. No teenager ever wants to go to bed early, I certainly hadn't, but now in my forties there was nothing better than an early night. As a family, we had almost reached the point where the parents went to bed first, leaving the children to lock up and turn out the lights.

Role reversal.

But that didn't only apply to the boys.

Over the past couple of months my mother's health had begun to fail and she'd had a couple of TIAs—transient ischemic attacks, also known as ministrokes. Even though most of the symptoms rapidly disappeared, the attacks had left her somewhat confused and very frightened.

After many years of stubborn independence since the death of my father, she was now forced to rely on me more and more. And, whereas in the past I might have resented this intrusion into my own freedom, I discovered a newfound tolerance, even love.

So I had started caring for her as if she were a small child, as she had once done for me.

Perhaps that is why we humans are so keen to have children— we instinctively know it is the best way of being looked after when we get old.

But that is assuming we actually do get old and our children aren't run over in the meantime by a long black Mercedes with dark-tinted rear windows.

The very thought made me shiver with fear.

I went into the sitting room and peeped through a crack in the curtains, out toward the driveway, checking that there was no dark-suited chauffeur with big biceps lurking between the rosebushes.

"What are you doing?" Grant asked from behind me.

"Just checking," I said.

"Checking for what?"

I turned and looked at him, trying my hardest to keep the

worry out of my face. But he could read me all too well and he knew straightaway that something was wrong.

"What is it?" he asked anxiously.

"Nothing," I replied, but I had difficulty holding back the tears. I needed to tell him. I needed his reassurance that everything would be fine.

But he wouldn't give it. He couldn't.

IN FACT, Grant was cross when I told him. Very cross indeed.

"Why did you ever even go near them?" he demanded. "I knew that working at that bloody racecourse was a bad idea. I wish now I'd stopped you going. It's been nothing but trouble."

We were in the kitchen.

While I'd been up to say good night to the boys, Grant had made me an omelet. Now I sat with it only half-eaten in front of me.

I pushed it away.

"And you won't bloody eat either. Do you realize what that does to our social life? We haven't seen any of our friends for months."

"Keep your voice down," I said. "The boys will hear you."

"I don't care if they do," he said, louder than ever. "If you had an ounce of sense in you, you'd put their welfare first rather than starving yourself to death and pursuing this ridiculous notion you have."

"That's not fair," I said. "And it's not a ridiculous notion. Do you really think there would have been this reaction if it wasn't true?"

He threw his hands up in frustration. "There you go again. It's none of your bloody business. Leave it alone."

He turned away from me and leaned on the sink.

But it surely was my bloody business.

As a doctor, I was obliged to call in the police if I suspected a patient had been the subject of serious abuse or assault. That didn't apply in this case but, as a responsible citizen, was it not at least my moral duty to report wrongdoing to the authorities?

"I don't want you going back to the racecourse tomorrow," Grant said without turning around.

"I have to," I said. "Adrian Kings says they need me. There were only three doctors there today and that's the absolute minimum required by the rules. Without me, there will be no racing."

"Then there will be no racing," he said adamantly, turning back to face me. "You're not going."

"Oh yes, I am," I said equally adamantly. "I have to. My reputation will be ruined if I don't." To say nothing of my prospects of ever being asked to be a racecourse doctor again.

"What if you were ill?" he said. "Then what would they do?"

"But I'm not ill."

"I don't care. Call in sick. You're not going, and that's final."

How dare he tell me what to do?

I bit my lip not to answer him back. It would have only fanned the flames.

We didn't normally argue. In eighteen years, only twice had we gone to bed without speaking and, for both of those occasions, neither of us could now even remember why.

But something about this current row made me apprehensive.

Was Grant finally getting fed up with me?

Would it actually be best if we took some time away from each other?

Best for whom? For him? Or me? Certainly not for the boys. I had seen too many friends break up with early-teenage children and it all too often ended in disaster. Happy, confident youngsters became insular and withdrawn and neither parent ever regained the trust of their children that they had enjoyed previously.

Maybe that would be a step too far, but inside I was seething with annoyance that Grant thought he could *order* me not to do what I wanted.

However, he may be right.

Perhaps it would be better if I didn't go to the races the following day. But I resented him laying down the law in such a manner, and he knew it.

For the third time in our married life, we went to bed without speaking.

Not that I could get to sleep.

I kept churning things over and over in my head, trying to decide what to do, and not just whether I should defy Grant and go to the racecourse the following morning.

I still couldn't get the dead man out of my mind.

Dick McGee had simply corroborated what I already believed to be the case, and Jason Conway's reaction had only confirmed it further. There was no question in my mind that he and Mike Sheraton had been involved in spot-fixing races by jumping the first fence in front on instruction from the man in the black Mercedes.

That knowledge, and the fact that Rahul Kumar had been an investigator for a racing authority in India, where gambling on anything was endemic, plainly threw the "misadventure" verdict of the inquest into doubt.

Misadventure implied accidental death precipitated by unintentional, ill-advised or reckless actions of the deceased. It certainly didn't cover murder and, the more I thought about it, the more convinced I became that Rahul Kumar had been killed to prevent him exposing the corruption.

So what should I do about it, if anything?

No one else seemed to think that anything untoward was going on in the first place. But that was surely the key feature of the most ingenious frauds—no one even noticed they were happening.

THINGS WERE hardly better in the morning.

Breakfast was a very quiet affair with both the boys sensing that Grant and I were at loggerheads. Either that or they'd heard the exchanges the previous evening and had decided that keeping quiet was the best policy.

My cell phone rang to break the silence.

It was Adrian Kings.

"You are coming in today, aren't you?" he said with a touch of panic in his voice. "I managed to get a fourth doctor, from Warwick, but Jack Otley has now called me. He's been ill all night and he's unable to make it so we are back down to the minimum."

I looked across at Grant.

"Hold on a minute," I said to Adrian.

I covered the microphone with my hand.

"They desperately need me at the racecourse today," I said. "One of the other doctors is sick."

Grant wasn't happy but he waved a hand dismissively, which I took to be a reluctant acceptance.

"OK," I said to Adrian. "I'll be there."

He was relieved. "Great. I'll still try and get someone else but it's such short notice and in school holiday time too. Try and be here by twelve. The first race is at one-fifty."

We disconnected.

"What about the boys?" Grant said acidly.

"They're at a cricket coaching course all afternoon," I said. "I'll take them in early before going on to the races. Can you collect them after?"

"Do I have a choice?"

"They could wait for me like last night."

He shook his head. "I'll do it."

"Good," I said. "We're all sorted then. I'll try and be home a bit earlier. How about if I cook you a steak with peppercorn sauce?"

His favorite. A peace offering.

He smiled and it lit up my life. "That would be lovely."

Shame he didn't get it.

31

The only good thing to say about the Thursday of the April Meeting was that it was less busy than the day before, at least as far as the medical team was concerned. However, the sunshine of the previous day had given way to overcast skies and a steady drizzle, interspersed with heavier showers as a cold front moved in from the west. Definitely an anorak day.

I dropped the boys off at their cricket-coaching course at eleven. They didn't mind the rain, as they would be inside anyway, using the indoor nets in the college sports hall.

"Don't wander off," I told them seriously. "And wait inside for Dad to collect you. He should be here by six."

"Yes, Mum," they said, rolling their eyes in unison. "We could have caught a bus home, you know. We're no longer little kids."

Catching a bus would have involved walking down the hill from the college to the bus station in the town center, as well as along our road in Gotherington at the other end, and, for reasons I didn't explain, I wasn't keen for them to be out wandering the streets alone. Not just at the moment.

Indeed, I checked all around to ensure I couldn't spot a lurking long black Mercedes before I was happy to leave them and go on to the racecourse.

AS ON THE DAY BEFORE, I was the first doctor to arrive at the medical room, but there were already three jockeys waiting in there for clearance to ride.

One of them was Mike Sheraton with his stitched right knee, and he wasn't pleased to see me.

"I'll come back," he mumbled to no one in particular, walking back out into the changing room.

Go ahead, I thought, taking off my coat.

I didn't want to see *him* every bit as much as he clearly didn't want to see me.

The other two were straightforward and I removed their Red Entries from RIMANI.

Next, I helped the nurse go through all the medical supplies, checking that they were all back in order after busy use the previous afternoon.

Adrian Kings arrived as we were finishing off.

"Ah, hello, Chris," he said. "Thank you for stepping into the breach. Don't know what we'd have done today without you."

"I'll remind you of that before the Festival next March," I said with a laugh.

Mike Sheraton came back into the medical room and presented himself to Adrian.

"Can you clear me, Doc?" he said.

Adrian was busy working out the doctor and ambulance positions for each race, writing them up on the whiteboard on the wall ready for his briefing.

"Chris," he said to me. "Can you do it?"

Mike Sheraton wasn't happy, and nor was I, but neither of us had much choice.

He pulled up his right trouser leg and put his foot on a chair while I removed the dressing and inspected the knee.

The nurse really had done a good job with the suturing and healing had clearly started.

"That's fine," I said. "Healing well. You will need a support dressing over it but otherwise you are fit to ride."

He looked at me with distaste.

"I could have bloody ridden yesterday. You cost me a winner in the last."

"My job is simply to ensure you receive the best possible medical care," I said. "No other considerations are important. Today you are fit to ride, yesterday you were not. I will confirm to the Clerk of the Scales that your Red Entry has been removed."

He didn't thank me. He just pulled down his trouser leg and walked out without even waiting for the dressing to be replaced. I wasn't going to call him back. If he landed on his knee and split it open again, he would have no one to blame but himself.

Did I care?

Not a jot.

THANKFULLY, there was not a single faller in any of the first three races, which allowed me to remain in the dry of the Land Rover as much as possible.

However, the third race was not without some interest.

I was in the center of the course for the start of a two-and-a-half-mile handicap hurdle with thirteen runners.

I confirmed to the officials that the medical arrangements

were in place and then watched as the horses circled, having their girths tightened by the starter's assistants.

Mike Sheraton was riding horse number one, the top weight, and he jumped off fast when the flag dropped, skipping over the first hurdle in front of the other twelve.

They're at it again, I thought.

They must be very sure of themselves.

Mike Sheraton had known I was there, he'd seen me at the start. Perhaps they still didn't realize I knew what they were up to, or maybe the bets had already been laid and it was too late, and too expensive, to cancel.

Either way, I considered it a personal insult.

But it was none of my business, right?

I HAD A CUSTOMER in the fourth race, a pretty young lady jockey called Jane Glenister, who fell at the open ditch at the top of the hill while leading the pack of nine runners.

"Hi, there," I said when I reached her. "Dr. Rankin here."

She was sitting on her haunches, groaning.

"Where does it hurt?" I asked.

"Where doesn't it?" she said. "Got kicked around by all of them like a bloody soccer ball." She started to get slowly to her feet. "But I'll be fine."

"Did you bang your head at all?" I asked.

"No," she said, taking off her racing helmet and shaking free a huge bundle of bouncing red curls. "Thank God."

I walked with her away from the fence toward the inside rail.

She winced as she ducked under it.

"Are you sure you're OK?"

"Nothing a couple of ibuprofen and a long stretch in the sauna won't cure. I'm just sore, that's all."

"Make sure you report to the medical room when you get back to the weighing room," I reminded her. "You'll need to be checked over there."

"Sure will. Thank you, Dr. Rankin." She smiled at me with a set of gleaming-white perfect teeth before climbing into the jockey transport that had stopped to collect her. I stood for a second and watched her go, wondering why such a beautiful face wanted to gallop over fences at thirty miles per hour with the inevitable injuries that would surely come. Had she not seen the men in the changing room with mouthfuls of gaps and dentures?

But, I suppose, if she loved the excitement of racing and the surge of adrenaline in her veins that it produced, then maybe it was worth the bumps and bashes. I just hoped she still thought the same in the years to come. If I had teeth like that, I'd take up something safer, like BASE jumping.

I returned to the Land Rover and rejoined the chase of the remaining runners on their second circuit, but there were no more fallers and I made my way back through the rain to the weighing room.

Jane Glenister was there, lying on one of the beds. She watched me come in.

"You OK?" I asked her.

"Sure," she said. "Just resting my aching bones until the ibuprofen kicks in. I'll be fine in a bit."

"No more rides today." It was more of a statement than a question.

"No," she said. "Just the one. All this way just to get my arse walloped."

"Where's home?" I asked.

"In Devon, near Plymouth."

"Are you driving back tonight?"

"That's the plan. Straight down the M5."

I turned to the nurse. "Has she done the concussion tests?"

"Passed with flying colors," the nurse said with a laugh. "She didn't just know which jockey won the Gold Cup but also his extra-large condom size."

"That was meant to be a secret between you and me," Jane whined in mock complaint.

"Too much information," I said, laughing. But I was satisfied that she wasn't concussed. "Lie there for as long as you like. But promise me you'll tell us if something doesn't feel right, and don't drive home unless you're well enough. Better to stay somewhere locally."

"OK, OK," she said, waving a hand at me. "Don't make a bloody fuss." She closed her eyes. She was clearly in more pain than she was letting on, but there was nothing unusual about that in racecourse changing rooms.

"Jockeys, five minutes," announced the loudspeaker

Time for me to go out again to the Land Rover.

THERE WERE TWO MORE FALLERS in the remaining races but neither of the jockeys was injured, one of them getting up from the turf beyond the second-last fence and running off so fast that I was left gasping in his wake.

"No strenuous exercise." I could almost hear my GP's stern warning ringing in my ears.

I gave up the chase, watching him disappear into the distance. I'd done my best to attend to him within one minute. If he was able to run all the way back to the weighing room, I reckoned I could safely assume he was unhurt. Not that he wouldn't still be tested for concussion when he got there.

I returned to the medical room more slowly to find that the two beds were now empty.

"What happened to our patient?" I asked the nurse.

"She went for a sauna. She said it would ease her aches and pains."

I smiled.

Jane Glenister was clearly quite a girl.

Cheltenham Racecourse hadn't yet run to a separate sauna for the lady jockeys, the only one being in a corner of the men's room. Perhaps Jane's knowledge of the over-endowment of the Gold Cup winner had been acquired in appropriately steamy surroundings.

The day concluded with Adrian giving his debrief about an hour after the last race. I had already called Grant to ensure he hadn't forgotten about picking up the boys from their cricket course.

"Of course I haven't forgotten," he'd said rather tetchily. "What time will you be home?"

"Seven to seven-thirty," I'd replied.

"Did you get my steak?"

The route to a man's heart.

"It's in the fridge. I went to the butcher's early."

After the debrief, I switched my racecourse doctor's coat for my anorak and went into the jockeys' changing room to find Whizz. He and the other valets were busy finishing the loading of all the equipment into three huge wicker baskets.

"Where tomorrow?" I asked.

"These two are for Fontwell," he said, indicating toward the baskets nearest to him, "and the other one's for Southwell for evening racing. I just hope I get the right stuff in each."

I was confident that he would.

"I gave your bags to Dick McGee and Jason Conway," I said.

"I know. Jason discharged himself from the hospital and was here first thing to collect his car keys."

"How is he?" I asked, not that I cared much.

"Like a bear with a sore head," Whizz said. "And still a bit confused, I reckon. I didn't fancy him driving so I arranged for my lads to drive him home. He only lives in Cirencester. But, I tell you, he's not happy with you medics. He's furious that he can't ride for seven days."

One had to wonder why, after such heavy falls, jockeys were so keen to do it all over again. But that was what they were all like.

"Seven days is the absolute minimum after a concussion," I said. "He'll have to pass two separate assessments, including one with a specialist neurosurgeon. Ten to fourteen days is much more likely, or even longer."

"Don't tell him that," Whizz said. "He's angry enough already."

Didn't I know it.

THE MEDICAL TEAM all went for tea together in one of the tented restaurants near the exit to the parking lot.

The season at Cheltenham was almost over for another year, with just the Hunter Chase evening meeting to come in another week or so, when the jockeys would all be amateurs and the horses have to qualify by spending days out hunting. The course would soon hibernate for the summer, with only the Best Mate enclosure being used as a trailer park, before racing returned in October.

I sat at the table for quite a long time relaxing and drinking tea, while the others ate ham, egg and cucumber sandwiches and slices of a delicious-looking fruitcake.

I just watched.

Not that I wasn't hungry. I was. Very.

It was a state I was used to. I spent most of my life these days being desperately hungry but trying to blot it out of my mind.

Yet, in spite of my hunger, I still couldn't eat anything because the voice in my head was telling me not to. It told me that terrible things would happen if so much as a single mouthful passed my lips. The house would burn down. Or Grant would leave me. Or my boys would get run over by a long black Mercedes.

I called Grant to check again that he'd picked them up and all was fine.

"Safe and sound," he said. "Oliver's up in his room playing computer games and Toby has gone along to the village sports ground for a team practice before their last game of the season on Saturday."

"You let him go on his own?" I asked incredulously.

"Why not?"

Why not!

"Please collect Oliver and both of you go down to the sports ground to watch Toby."

There must have been a degree of desperation in my voice because Grant didn't argue.

"All right," he said. "We'll go right away."

"Please call me when you're there. I'm going to leave here now and I'll come straight to the ground."

I disconnected and stood up to go.

"Oh, Chris," Adrian Kings said, putting a hand on the arm of my anorak. "I've just had a call from the weighing room. Seems our lady jockey, Jane Glenister, is now not feeling very well. She's asked if you could go back and see her."

Now what did I do? I wanted to leave, to get to Gotherington, to check on my babies.

"Can't you go?" I asked.

"She apparently asked specifically for you and I promised my wife I'd be home early."

Hell, I thought.

Grant would be at the sports ground before me anyway, even if I drove there at breakneck pace. It would be all right, I told myself. I'd eaten no sandwiches nor any cake so Toby would be fine. Surely he'd be safe with all the other members of the soccer team around him?

"OK," I said with resignation. "Where is she?"

"She's waiting in the changing room."

I hurried back toward the weighing room.

It was now raining hard with the few remaining racegoers hurrying to their cars with coat hoods pulled up against the elements. I skipped up the steps into the weighing room and went to collect the keys to the medical room from the key safe in the Clerk of the Course's office.

They weren't there.

How odd, I thought.

I went into the changing room, which was deserted. The jockeys and valets had all gone home. The door to the medical room was wide open and the lights were still on. Adrian must have forgotten to lock up.

I walked over and went in.

The blue privacy curtains were pulled around one of the beds.

"What's wrong, Jane?" I asked, pulling the curtains open.

But it wasn't Jane Glenister in there.

So preoccupied had I become with the safety and security of my sons that I had neglected my own and walked straight into a trap.

Behind the curtains was the man I'd last seen sitting in the long black Mercedes, the driver with the bulging biceps.

32

I turned to run back out into the changing room but Big Biceps and I were not alone.

Mike Sheraton had been standing behind the door and he now pushed it closed.

And he was smiling.

"You're a real bloody menace, you are," he said.

I rushed toward the door, mistakenly thinking that I had a better chance against the smaller man. But jockeys are probably the strongest sportsmen around, pound for pound. If Mike Sheraton could control half a ton of horse with just his hands and heels, an alarmingly underweight doctor should be a pushover.

But that didn't mean I wouldn't fight.

I was still wearing the heavy hiking boots that I habitually used to run around on the muddy racecourse, and I kicked Mike Sheraton with one, hard onto the point of his right knee, exactly where he'd had the stitches inserted the previous afternoon.

He screamed with pain, clutching his leg while I made a dive for the door.

If I thought he was angry before, he was more so now, and

his chum arrived as reinforcement, grabbing me around the neck from behind with his arm across my throat in a chokehold.

I kicked back at him too but I couldn't get the leverage. He simply tightened his grip, so much so that I was worried he would strangle me.

Physical assault is an unfortunate occupational hazard for emergency staff in our hospitals and, consequently, there were many self-defense courses available for doctors and nurses to attend. In my younger years, I'd been on two of them, and how to get out of a chokehold had been at the forefront. But this was the first time I'd had to put the theory into practice in a real life-or-death situation.

I took a deep breath, then, as I'd been instructed, I turned my head away from the man's elbow and bent down, moving my legs backward and rotating my body so that my head slipped out below his shoulder and I ended up behind him.

It worked!

But that was only the start of my troubles.

Two strong men against an undernourished female should have been a "no contest," but desperation delivers resources beyond logic.

And I fought dirty.

I kicked and punched at places on their bodies not permitted under Queensberry rules, I elbowed and head-butted, scratched and even bit.

Their plan seemed to be to prevent me reaching the door but, otherwise, to let me run out of steam, which would be pretty soon at this rate.

"Don't mark her," Big Biceps said at one point, which I took to be both an encouragement and a concern. What other torment did they have in mind?

If I couldn't get out the door, what else could I do?

Phone for help?

My cell phone was in my anorak pocket.

I pulled it out and got as far as dialing the second of three nines before Big Biceps made a lunge forward and knocked it out of my hand, then he stamped on it in his size twelves. Even if the components inside still worked, the touchscreen had shattered into a thousand pieces, rendering it useless.

How about the landline?

Every racecourse medical room had to have a dedicated landline, one that couldn't be blocked by an incoming call, in case of an emergency.

Surely this *was* an emergency.

The phone here at Cheltenham was attached to the wall beneath the television monitor and I took my eyes off the two men for just a fraction of a second to look at it.

"She's after the phone," Mike Sheraton said, and he inched farther to his right to prevent me reaching it.

So, there would be no summoning up the cavalry, not yet anyway.

Slowly but surely, they were forcing me back to the far side of the room such that my back was almost up against the medical store cupboard.

I reached behind me and opened it.

Big Biceps made a move toward me and I aimed a kick at his groin. He reached down and tried to catch my foot but I was wary of that, pulling it away sharply.

I was losing this game of cat and mouse, I thought, and I was certainly the mouse. One of the men would come forward and, while I was dealing with him, the other would try to outflank me. It would be only a matter of time before they succeeded.

I reached behind me into the cupboard.

I knew what I was after and I found it immediately without having to look. A box of ten size-11 disposable scalpels.

We'd only recently been required to have them, in case we had to perform an emergency tracheotomy on a jockey who had an obstruction to the airway.

I ripped open the pack and suddenly I had a scalpel in each hand.

Now it was the men who were on the back foot as I waved the highly honed blades at their faces. The scalpels may have only been short, but what they lacked in length they made up for in sharpness.

Now I began to circle, working my way back toward the door.

And, if I couldn't use the phone because it took two hands, I could at least use my voice.

"Help!" I shouted as loud as I could muster. "Help! Help!"

I went on shouting, the noise bouncing loudly off the walls of the room. Surely someone must hear me? Why didn't Whizz and the other valets come to my rescue? Because they were already on their way home in a van full of wicker baskets.

By now I had my back to the door but I daren't turn around or let go of one of the scalpels to open it. The two men were getting inventive, with one of them using a pillow from the beds to try to smother the blade in my left hand, while the other had picked up a wooden leg splint and was using that to try to hit the one in my right.

I shouted even louder, terror causing the frequency to rise.

"Help! Help! Somebody please help me!"

The door opened against my back.

Thank God.

"Call the police!" I shouted.

"What the hell is going on in here?" said a voice behind me.

"Call the police!" I screamed again. "I'm being attacked."

The door was pushed fully open, causing me to have to take a step forward. Then I moved backward through the opening, never taking my eyes off my assailants. It must be safer for me out of the medical room.

Suddenly I was gripped from behind in a bear hug, my arms pinned down by my sides.

My savior, my knight in shining armor, was no such thing.

I tried to lash out behind me with the scalpels but the hug was too low and too tight. And I could hardly breathe let alone fight or shout. My resistance was over and the men in front quickly moved forward and twisted the blades out of my hands.

"What's wrong with you two?" said the voice behind me crossly. "A feeble woman against two strong men. You should be ashamed of yourselves."

"Sorry, Chief," said Big Biceps. "She's a slippery one, that's for sure."

Chief? Indian chief?

Against two, I had held my own, but three were too many. The two in front and the one behind lifted me bodily onto one of the beds and pinned me there.

For the first time I saw the face of the third man.

Rupert Forrester, managing director of the racecourse. Geronimo, the English fixer. One and the same.

And he clearly wasn't happy with the other two. Perhaps he'd hoped that he would remain in the shadows, unseen and unrecognized.

"Get on with it," he snapped.

With what?

Nothing good, I thought, at least for me.

"Did anyone else hear her shouting?" Big Biceps asked.

"No," said Forrester. "I sent everyone away and I've locked up. The rain is hammering on the roof anyway. No one's about."

Big Biceps pulled a small bottle from his trouser pocket, a little bigger than a spirit miniature but smaller than the quarter bottle they had obviously used last time. The bottle was half full with a pale golden liquid. More cocaine dissolved in whisky, no doubt.

I wasn't going to just lie there and let them poison me. I managed to pull a hand free and tried to grab the bottle to throw it against the wall, anything to break it, but Forrester was too quick.

"Get something to secure her hands," he said, forcing my arms back onto the bed.

They used a roll of white adhesive bandage tape that they found in the medical store, binding both wrists together behind my back so that I ended up lying on them. Now I really was in trouble.

Mike Sheraton was at the foot of the bed and I tried to kick out at him but he had his hands on my ankles and pushed them firmly down. With Forrester doing the same with my shoulders, I was almost totally immobilized.

But my head could still move.

I twisted my neck to my left and bit Forrester's knuckles. I wanted to tear his flesh and draw his blood—to leave some evidence, perhaps some of his DNA between my teeth, something a pathologist could find on my cold dead corpse and deduce who was responsible for my death.

"Bitch!" he shouted, pulling his hand away and striking me across my face with his open palm.

"No marks," Big Biceps said sharply. "Remember?"

Did they really think that a second cocaine-induced death at the racecourse would again be considered as misadventure?

Apparently so.

While Forrester and Sheraton held me down, Big Biceps attempted to pour the liquid down my throat.

Needless to say, I resisted.

First I turned my head from side to side so that he couldn't get the bottle near my mouth.

"For God's sake, keep her bloody head still," Big Biceps said to Forrester.

He let go of my shoulders and held my head instead, placing one hand on my forehead and pressing down, while his other one gripped my hair.

Secondly, I kept my mouth firmly shut, clenching my teeth and lips together as if my life depended on it, which it probably did.

But one has to breathe and Big Biceps pinched my nose closed.

I tried to draw air through a tiny opening on one side but Big Biceps forced the top of the bottle into the gap while putting his free hand on my chin and forcing my jaws apart.

I could feel the sharp burning sensation of the alcohol in my mouth.

I spat out what I could but I could also feel a trickle go down my throat. What had the pathologist said at the inquest? *Only a single teaspoonful of the liquid ingested orally would have been sufficient to cause death.*

How much of it had I ingested? Not as much as a teaspoonful, I thought, but Big Biceps wasn't finished yet. He forced the neck of the bottle back between my teeth and emptied the rest of the contents into my mouth. I could taste the sharpness of the alcohol and the bitterness of the cocaine, strangely mixed with an increasing numbness of my tongue and gums.

I tried to spit it out again, but, this time, he was wise to that, gripping the base of my chin and forcing my jaws together.

Initially, I didn't swallow but I knew that both alcohol and cocaine were absorbed into the bloodstream much faster directly through the mucus membranes of the mouth than via the stomach and intestines.

What was best?

I was already beginning to feel the effects of the drug on my brain. The overhead lights of the medical room were dancing, with shooting colors at their edges. They were sensations I had once welcomed as a distraction from the agony of my depression but now I was terrified by them.

I managed to eject quite a lot more of the liquid by blowing it through my teeth and allowing it to dribble down the outside of my cheek onto the bed, but I still swallowed far too much, not out of choice but as a natural reflex that eventually I couldn't resist.

I wasn't sure exactly how much I'd consumed, but probably more than the single teaspoonful required for a fatal dose.

"How long?" I heard Rupert Forrester ask. "I have to go. I'm speaking at a charity dinner at the Queens Hotel in town. I've got to change yet and I'm late already."

"Not very long," Big Biceps replied. "She had it in her mouth for ages. That will speed things up. She'll be unconscious soon and dead in an hour."

"Dead?" Sheraton said with some alarm. "I thought we were just frightening her."

"Shut up," Forrester said. "You're in this as much as we are. We need to silence her permanently. And there'll be no damn cleaner to find her alive this time. This place won't be cleaned now until tomorrow and I'll be in by then anyway. But I want us to get out. Security will be locking the gates soon."

Good old security, I thought. Where were they when you needed them?

I closed my eyes but that didn't stop the bright lights exploding in my brain like fireworks on New Year's Eve.

But I could still think.

Play dead, I told myself. *They have to get out before the gates are locked. The sooner they think I'm unconscious, the quicker they will go.*

I forced all my muscles to relax and Sheraton must have felt the change in my legs.

"She's going," he said.

"Untie her hands," said Forrester, releasing his grip on my head and hair.

They rolled me over and I sensed the tape being removed from my wrists. Then I felt Big Biceps take my fingers and wrap them around the empty bottle.

Fingerprints, I thought.

"Right," said Forrester. "Let's get out of here."

"Are you sure you really want to kill her?" Sheraton asked. He was clearly in this way over his head.

"I told you to shut up," Forrester said sharply. "It's too late now anyway. There's enough cocaine in her system to kill a horse. She's already dead."

Someone lifted my right eyelid.

It was as much as I could do not to look at him. I had rolled my eyes up in the fraction beforehand and I concentrated on keeping them there, only seeing him peripherally. It was Big Biceps.

"Definitely unconscious," he said. "Dead soon."

"OK," Forrester said. "Let's go."

I heard the door open and their footsteps receding but I continued to lie as still as I could. However, if I didn't move soon, I really would be unconscious and dead soon after.

I opened my eyes and swiveled my head.

They had gone.

I was euphoric. It felt like a victory. But I wasn't so far gone that I didn't realize that the euphoria was more to do with the drug rather than any sense that I was now safe.

I wasn't. Far from it.

I was in mortal danger and I could already feel a quickening of my heart and a rise in my body temperature. If I didn't do something very soon, I would be dead for sure when the cleaners arrived to find me in the morning.

33

Perhaps there was nothing I could actually do to save myself, but I wasn't going to die without trying.

My first instinct was to rid my body of the toxin.

Everyone knows the old wives' tale that a concentrated salt solution is an emetic—that is, it makes you vomit. But, not only is excess salt an extremely dangerous poison in itself, any emetic effect due to surplus sodium takes far too long to occur— up to thirty minutes rather than the immediate response as depicted in a James Bond movie.

I would probably be dead in thirty minutes.

As every sufferer of bulimia knows, the only sure-fire method of making oneself instantly vomit on demand is to use the gag reflex.

I inserted my forefinger into my mouth, and, stretching it in as far as I could, I pressed down hard on the back of my tongue.

I retched and threw up the meager contents of my stomach into the washbasin in the corner.

Then I washed my mouth out, drank some water from the tap and repeated the whole process twice more until I was sure nothing remained in me.

But had I been in time? Had too much of the drug already passed through the intestinal membrane into my bloodstream?

The physical effects were certainly becoming more noticeable.

I was sweating profusely, my heart was racing and I was experiencing slight chest pain as a result.

I had been here before.

What had Rahul Kumar taught me that I could use to save myself, whereas I'd been unable to save him?

Cocaine is a short-acting SNDRI, a serotonin-norepinephrine-dopamine reuptake inhibitor. Hence, a cocaine overdose is a double whammy. Not only is the drug a powerful stimulant but it also restricts the body's natural ability to regulate its metabolic rate. So my body had gone into overdrive and, with the brakes also removed, it was running downhill out of control. Whether my heart would give up the struggle first or my other organs would fail due to increased body temperature was anyone's guess.

Either way, I'd be dead. And soon.

There is no specific pharmacological antidote to cocaine poisoning but what I needed was a sedative, something to counteract the drug's stimulating properties.

And fast.

I shook my head as if to clear it.

"Think," I said out loud. "Think!"

I went over to the medicine store cupboard and looked in.

In spite of my body going into top gear, my brain seemed to be stuck in neutral. I knew what I was after but I couldn't find it—a benzodiazepine called diazepam, known almost universally as Valium.

I dug through the basket of drugs. I knew there was some in here; I'd checked it myself earlier in the day. Diazepam was an injectable sedative and we had it available in case a jockey had a severe case of muscle spasm, or a seizure.

"Come on," I said. "Do you want to live or to die?"

Maybe six months ago I wouldn't have cared either way, but now I did.

I finally found what I was looking for, a small glass ampoule of milky-white liquid containing thirty milligrams of diazepam in solution.

"I want to live," I said excitedly, but getting the drug from the ampoule into my veins was another problem because my hands had started to shake.

I managed to attach a hypodermic needle to a syringe and carefully broke off the glass top of the ampoule. How much? Ten milligrams was the recommended dose for acute muscle spasm.

But this was more of a crisis than that.

I decided on an initial twenty. That would leave another ten if I needed it later. Overdosing on diazepam was not a worry, no one ever successfully committed suicide by swallowing all their Valium pills at once, not unless they mixed them with other drugs or very large amounts of alcohol.

"Be careful," I kept telling myself as I inserted the needle into the ampoule. "You cannot afford to drop this on the floor."

I drew the diazepam up into the syringe.

It could be injected into muscle but, to be effective quickly, it needed to go straight into the bloodstream, into a vein.

Using my right hand and my teeth I applied a rubber tourniquet to my upper left arm and tapped the inside of my elbow. One of my veins stood up nicely and, with ultra-care and by stressing both my arms against the table, I managed to insert the needle and slowly depress the plunger.

Initially, I could feel nothing and I panicked that I'd gone straight through the vein and injected the drug uselessly into the joint cavity.

But then I remembered the tourniquet.

I released it, allowing the diazepam to progress up my arm toward my heart and beyond. Within a minute or two I could detect a soothing sensation, not that it seemed to do anything to reduce my rapid pulse.

And I had a worrying pain in my chest.

Not a bloody heart attack now, I thought.

"Come on, body, give me a break," I said out loud.

I laughed. Fancy talking to myself. I must be mad. Or high. Both, in fact.

"Get a grip," I said. "This is the cocaine talking. Concentrate!" I slapped my thigh with my hand. "Concentrate and you live. Waver and you die. Think of your boys. Live for them."

Also in the medicine store we had a glyceryl trinitrate spray in a small red bottle with a white top. *Glyceryl trinitrate* was simply the medical name for *nitroglycerin*, the high explosive that Alfred Nobel mixed with crushed sedimentary rock and washing soda to produce dynamite.

Apart from its explosive properties, nitroglycerin reduces blood pressure by causing the blood vessels to dilate. The effect was discovered by accident when those making dynamite found that it gave them headaches and also that their blood pressure dropped alarmingly at work. Nowadays, it was widely used by angina sufferers to alleviate pain and tightness in the chest by spraying it under the tongue.

I picked up the bottle and removed the top, but then I hesitated.

One of the other actions of nitroglycerin was to increase heart rate and mine was quite high enough already. But the pain in my chest implied that my racing heart was getting insufficient oxygen and, if Rahul Kumar was anything to go by, my blood pressure was probably too high as well.

Would it do more harm than good?

To spray or not to spray? That was the question.

The pain in my chest was definitely getting worse.

Maybe I would die whatever I did or didn't do. But surely action had to be better than inaction? At least I would then die knowing I had tried, and whoever found me would know that I had wanted to survive.

I squirted a single shot of the nitroglycerin under my tongue and instantly felt a reaction. The pain in my chest subsided but I became very dizzy and I sat down quickly on a chair.

Now what?

My heartbeat was still up in the stratosphere, but, even if I'd had any adenosine, I knew from past experience that it wouldn't work.

How about more diazepam? Or perhaps some oxygen?

We had an oxygen cylinder and I attached a mask to it, turned it on and breathed deeply. Next I drew half of the remaining diazepam into a fresh syringe and injected that into the same vein as before.

I sat on a chair, took more deep breaths of the oxygen and measured my pulse using the second hand of the clock on the wall. It was still very high at 180 beats per minute but I sensed that it was down a little from its maximum.

Was I over the worst?

Was there anything else I could do?

Just sit still and let nature take its course.

I knew from a study I'd read at medical school that ingesting cocaine orally didn't produce its maximum result for an hour or more after consumption, but I rather hoped that the reactions I had experienced were more due to the relatively small amount of the drug I'd absorbed through my mouth lining, and that I had expelled most of what had actually made it down to my stomach.

If that was the case, then I could be out of the woods.

I'd beaten the bastards.

I giggled uncontrollably.

Cocaine may be nicknamed *paradise powder*, and perhaps some of my current elation was still related to the drug, but I felt surreal and fantastic, even invincible, with a crystal-clear head.

And with revenge on my mind.

TEN MINUTES LATER and my pulse was down to 150 and I considered that I was past the critical stage. I decided I'd live.

I glanced up at the clock. It was only twenty past eight.

It felt like I'd been fighting for my life for several hours but it was only sixty minutes or so since I'd rushed back to the weighing room from tea.

I looked down at the remains of my cell phone lying in pieces on the floor. Grant had probably been trying to call me on it.

I stood up and went over to the landline phone on the wall and picked up the receiver.

I stared at it.

Maybe I should have used this to call an ambulance for myself, to ask for help. But I was so used to actually *being* the help that the thought had never crossed my mind. It was no good me dialing 999 and asking for assistance whenever a critically ill patient arrived at A&E.

I was 999.

On this occasion, it had simply been me who had been the

critically ill patient, and my "you alone have to deal with this emergency" mode had instinctively kicked in.

Did I call for help now? And how about the police? Should I call them too?

Of course you must, said the sensible half of my brain. *Someone has just tried to kill you—again.*

The police surely couldn't *not* believe me this time? Could they?

But I was the madwoman with the crazy ideas and suicidal tendencies. I had form—at least in their eyes.

"She's only making it up," they'd say.

"To justify her delusion that Rahul Kumar was murdered," they'd say.

"Wasting our time again," they'd say.

Wouldn't they?

Perhaps I had to die to convince them. Maybe not even then.

I dialed a number—Grant's cell phone—and he answered at the first ring.

"Where are you?" he asked with more than a touch of worry in his voice. "I've been trying to call you for ages."

"I'm still at the racecourse," I said. "Sorry. I dropped my phone and it broke."

I wasn't quite sure why I didn't tell him the truth. Maybe the influence of the cocaine was still with me more than I appreciated.

"What are you doing there? I thought you were coming straight to the sports ground." He now sounded more angry than worried.

"I had to deal with another patient," I said, without telling him that the patient had been myself. "Are the boys all right?"

"They're hungry," he said.

Nothing new in that, I thought. At least they weren't kidnapped or run over. But why would they be? They were perfectly safe because Forrester and the others believed I was dead.

"Are you coming home now?" Grant asked.

"Soon," I said. "Take the boys and get some fish and chips from the chippy in Bishop's Cleeve."

"What about my steak and peppercorn sauce?" he whined.

"I'll do it for you tomorrow," I said. "I promise."

"How about you?" he said. "Can I get you something?"

"No. I'll get myself something when I get home," I said. "I may be quite a while yet. I have to go into town."

He wasn't pleased. "That bloody hospital."

I didn't enlighten him that I had no intention of going anywhere near that bloody hospital.

I was invincible, right?

I was off to a charity dinner at the Queens Hotel.

34

I found driving my Mini under the influence of cocaine was curiously easy.

Whereas the drug had a profound psychoactive impact on the mind, it left the motor cortex remarkably unaffected.

Getting out of the weighing room had been my first problem. As Rupert Forrester had said to his henchmen, he had locked up. Tight.

In the end I had used the push-bar-to-open fire escape door in the laundry room to make my escape, but not before I'd made a couple more telephone calls and acquired a few supplies from the medical-room drug inventory.

My next obstacle was how to get out to my car with security having by now closed all the exit gates from the racecourse enclosures. And it didn't help that it was now dark, the evening spring twilight being cut short by the low cloud and the persistent rain.

I suppose I could have gone in search of a roving security detail but then I'd have had to answer questions about why I was still there and where I'd been.

Could I be bothered? In this rain? No way.

Instead, I dragged a large rubbish bin twenty yards across the tarmac to the gate, climbed up on it and swung myself over, making sure not to snag my plastic bag of supplies on the top.

If nothing else, cocaine clearly gave one confidence.

I might need it.

THE QUEENS HOTEL in Cheltenham had an elegant and imposing neoclassical porticoed façade overlooking the formal Imperial Gardens. Its style was firmly in keeping with the grandiose reputation of the town as a former upmarket and fashionable spa resort.

The mineral springs were first tapped during the reign of George III and the King reportedly spent five weeks in the town drinking the foul-tasting medicinal waters in an attempt to cure his madness.

Perhaps I should try some.

The hotel itself dated from the time of Queen Victoria, after whom it was named, first opening in the year of her coronation in 1838.

But I wasn't interested in the aesthetics or history of the place. Not tonight. All I wanted to know was where in the hotel the charity dinner was being held.

I may have been confident, bold even, but I wasn't reckless.

The last thing I wanted to do was to park my Mini alongside a black Mercedes only to discover that Big Biceps was sitting in it.

Hence, I stopped some distance away on Bath Road and covered the last few hundred yards on foot, pulling the hood of my anorak up over my head not only as protection from the rain but also so that I couldn't be recognized by any lurking large-muscled chauffeur.

Maybe the cocaine wasn't going to kill me but it was still clearly affecting my system. The lights around the Town Hall, reflecting off the wet sidewalk, appeared to shimmer and dance delightfully with multicolored tails as I went by, and my feet seemed to be somehow disconnected from my legs.

I couldn't feel them on the ground.

Were they, in fact, someone else's feet?

I giggled. Of course not, you fool. Who else would have lent me their feet at this time of night?

I walked in through the rotating front door of the hotel and across the black-and-white-checked lobby floor to the reception desk.

"Where is the charity dinner?" I asked the young man standing there.

"Is that the one in aid of the Injured Jockeys Fund?"

"I want the one where Rupert Forrester is speaking," I said.

He looked down at some papers.

"Yes," he said. "That's the one. It's in the Regency Suite, our banqueting room."

"And which way is that?" I asked.

"Straight down the corridor to the end and then turn right," he said. "Do you have a ticket? It's Black Tie."

He looked at me in the manner of something he had picked up on his shoe. I clearly wasn't properly dressed for the occasion in green anorak, blue waterproof trousers and a pair of muddy hiking boots, and I was carrying a bright orange plastic grocery bag as my purse.

"No." I laughed. "I just have a message for one of the guests, that's all. I won't be staying very long."

I could see him waver as if he was deciding whether he should call hotel security to get me thrown out.

"I'm a doctor," I said quickly. "I've been on duty at the race-course this afternoon and haven't had time to change."

The reception man relaxed a little.

"Can you find your own way, then?" he asked. "I'm afraid I can't leave the front desk unattended and my colleague is on a break."

"I'll be fine on my own, thank you."

Better, I thought. Much better.

I turned to go but then turned back.

"Where is your bar?" I asked.

"Just to the right, madam," the man said, holding out his arm.

I glanced across toward where he pointed.

"My name is Dr. Chris Rankin," I said. "I'm meant to be meeting someone in your bar at ten o'clock."

The man and I both looked at the grand timepiece set high on the wall next to the main door. It read nine-forty.

"Instead of meeting in the bar, could you please ask him to go down to the Regency Suite as soon as he arrives and wait for me there?"

"Certainly, madam," the man replied. "And the name of your guest?"

"Filippos," I said. "Detective Constable Filippos."

BACK IN THE JOCKEYS' MEDICAL ROOM, I had made two fur-ther telephone calls after speaking to Grant. One had been to directory inquiries to find the number of the reception desk at Cheltenham Police Station, and the second had been to the desk itself.

"Cheltenham Police," the man who'd answered had said. "How can I help?"

"Can you please put me through to DC Filippos?"

"He's not here at the present time."

"Do you have his cell phone number?" I had asked in my most charming tone. "It's very important. I did have it in my phone but that's now broken and I can't access it."

"I'm sorry but I can't give out his number," the man had replied.

"Then can you please call him and pass on a message? My name is Dr. Chris Rankin. I am an A&E specialist physician at Cheltenham General Hospital and the matter is one of utmost urgency. It is crucial he gets the message as soon as possible."

"What's your message, Dr. Rankin?" the man had asked.

"Tell DC Filippos I have some vital new information concerning the case of Rahul Kumar and he should meet me in the bar at the Queens Hotel at ten o'clock precisely."

"Rahul Kumar. Bar. Queens Hotel. Ten o'clock." He'd repeated it as if he'd been writing it down. "Is that tonight?"

"Yes. Tonight."

"Do you want him to call you back at the hospital?"

"No. Just tell him that he must be at the Queens Hotel tonight at ten o'clock sharp."

The man hadn't questioned why. But he had promised to pass on the message immediately.

I WALKED DOWN THE CORRIDOR toward the Regency Suite with some trepidation.

Was my confidence now deserting me?

Had the cocaine stopped working when I most needed it?

There were one hundred and fifty guests at the Injured Jockeys Fund dinner on fifteen tables of ten. I could tell because there was a seating plan placed on an easel in the vestibule outside the actual banqueting chamber.

I studied the guest list closely.

There were quite a few names on the list that I knew or, at least, knew of, including several racehorse trainers and even a sprinkling of ex-jockeys, not that I could spot any of the current crop. Lavish midweek Black Tie dinners were no doubt not ideal for keeping their riding weight down for the weekend.

I specifically searched for any mention of Mike Sheraton and I don't know if I was pleased or disappointed that he wasn't in there.

Big Biceps could be, but I wouldn't know it from the list. There was no point looking under the *B*s or even the *BB*s.

Rupert Forrester was included of course. He was at table five, which was, according to the plan, right in front of a stage set up on the right-hand side of the room.

"Can I help?" said a voice behind me.

I turned around.

A waitress stood there holding two jugs of water. She was not in her first flush of youth, probably nearer seventy than fifty, and she was wearing a small white lace-fringed apron over a black dress. Very traditional.

"How far have they got?" I asked, nodding toward the door.

"Dessert," she said.

"When are the speeches?" I asked.

"Very soon, I think," she said. "I heard the guest speaker say he had to leave quite early. The auction is now going to be after his speech rather than before. Are you here to collect him?"

"No," I said with a laugh.

Collecting him was not exactly what I had in mind, not in that sense.

Forrester probably wanted to leave early so that he could be back at the racecourse good and early in the morning to deal with any problems—like a dead body found in the weighing room.

"I must get on," the waitress said. "They're waiting for these."

She lifted up the jugs of water.

I held the door open for her and glanced inside as she went past me. It was very noisy and everyone seemed to be having a good time, with plenty of laughter. But I didn't linger with the door open. I didn't want a certain guest to spot me—not yet anyway. And not before DC Filippos was present.

The door reopened and the same waitress reappeared, this time with two empty jugs.

"That was quick," I said. "Thirsty, are they?"

She laughed. "These are from different tables." Then she looked closely at me. "Don't I know you from somewhere?"

"What's your name?" I asked.

"Doris," she said. "Doris Meacher. What's yours?"

"Chris Rankin," I said.

It didn't seem to help. "What do you do?" she asked.

"I'm a doctor. I work in A&E at the hospital."

"That's it," Doris said with a big smile of success. "You looked after my son when he came off his motorbike. Over a year ago now."

"How's he doing?" I asked, not actually remembering and hoping he hadn't died as a result.

"Fine," she said. "Almost back to normal. All thanks to you, Doctor."

While we'd been talking, two women had come out through the door and went off down the corridor chatting and giggling away, presumably off to powder their noses. I really didn't want

Rupert Forrester walking right into me on his way to the men's room.

"Well, Doris," I said, "I could do with a little assistance from *you* now."

"Anything, Doctor. How can I help?"

"Is there another way into the Regency Suite apart from this door?"

"Only the staff entrances," she said. "They're what the waiters use. I'm only using this door to get water from the bar. It's easier than fighting past all the rest of them at the servery."

"Can you show me the staff entrances?" I asked. "I want to listen to the speeches but I've been on duty, so I couldn't actually come to the dinner. If I could slip in a staff entrance when the speeches start, it would be less noticeable than going in here."

I shrugged my shoulders and made a face at her as if it were an amusing conspiracy.

"Sure," she said. "Why not? I'll even lend you an apron. No one ever looks at the face of a waitress, least they never did when I was young."

She walked me back along the corridor toward the reception, but, before we got there, we went through a door into a staff corridor that led into the hotel kitchen.

"Come on," Doris said, taking me by the hand and leading me past the lines of stainless-steel chefs' stations.

There were two staff entrances to the banqueting suite from the kitchen, or rather one entrance and one exit such that the flow of personnel was circular past the kitchen servery and back into the room, and the doors were on either side of the stage.

"Perfect," I said to Doris.

I removed my anorak and waterproof trousers, which Doris

took away to the staff changing area. Underneath I had on a black sweater and a pair of black trousers. Doris then gave me a spare white lace-edged apron to tie around my waist. Apart from the hiking boots, I looked every inch a waitress.

"How about your bag?" Doris said. "Shall I put it with your coat?"

"No, no," I said, clutching the orange plastic tightly to my chest. "I'll keep that with me."

"OK," she said. "Will you be all right now? I've got those water jugs to fill." She laughed and went off leaving me there just inside the door feeling very conspicuous. I simply smiled at the other waiting staff as they rushed past me and out to serve the guests with coffee and petits fours.

I looked at my watch. Just gone ten o'clock.

Had DC Filippos arrived? Was he even now in the Regency Suite?

I hoped so.

"Ladies and gentlemen," said a female voice loudly and clearly over the audio system. A hush descended within the suite. "We are very fortunate to have our guest speaker with us here tonight. For the last two days he's been busy ensuring that everything has run smoothly at the racecourse for the April Meeting."

That's not all he's been doing, I thought.

"Please join me in giving a warm Injured Jockeys Fund welcome to the managing director of Cheltenham Racecourse, Rupert Forrester."

There was loud applause and the overhead crystal chandeliers were dimmed.

I slipped in through the door and stood in the shadows to one side of the stage, which, in fact, was little more than a raised dais about a foot high with a lectern now lit up by a bank of overhead spotlights.

Rupert Forrester walked to the lectern and raised his hands in thanks.

Just watching him standing there smiling at the assembled guests, lapping up their admiration, made my blood boil. As far as he was aware, I was still lying alone on a bed in the jockeys' medical room at the racecourse, my life slowly draining away to nothing.

I reached into the orange grocery bag.

"Ladies and gentlemen," Forrester began. "What a magnificent welcome. Thank you. It is a real joy to be here tonight supporting racing's favorite charity."

I've heard more than enough of him already, I thought.

I walked briskly over to the dais, stepped up onto it and stabbed Rupert Forrester in the side of the neck.

35

There was no gushing of blood from a severed artery, no rasping of breath through an open windpipe, indeed not much to show at all.

I had stabbed Rupert Forrester not with a knife, or even a scalpel, but with a hypodermic needle.

Almost as if in slow motion, he turned his head toward me, recognition, disbelief and realization blending almost instantaneously into raw panic in his eyes.

I could almost taste the fear in him. It was as if he'd seen a ghost.

And he had.

I was that ghost, resurrected from the dead.

Then I saw in his face that fear of me turn rapidly to fear of what was to come—exposure and disgrace. The loss of not just his liberty but also everything he had worked so hard to achieve.

It was a delicious moment, one that I relished.

I was both smiling and licking my lips.

Revenge, I thought, really is sweet.

I depressed the plunger of the syringe that was attached to the needle in his neck and injected forty milligrams of morphine straight into his jugular vein.

THE EFFECT OF MY ACTIONS was dramatic, to put it mildly, and not just on Rupert Forrester. There was pandemonium in the Regency Suite, with many people shouting and a few even screaming.

Forrester collapsed at my feet as his legs folded beneath him, I suspected from a combination of the morphine and blind terror.

Now he knew what it felt like to have a deadly drug forced into you.

I stood above him, rather pleased with myself, that was until one of the more athletic dinner guests took me down onto my back in a rugby tackle that smacked my head hard against the floor. It also left me gasping for breath.

The lights were turned up and I could hear a familiar voice above the other commotion.

"Police, police," DC Filippos shouted. "Make way. Let me through."

He came quickly into my field of vision and I smiled at him.

"What did you inject him with?" he asked, looking like thunder.

I lay there wondering why he didn't smile back at me.

"What did you inject him with?" he asked again, this time shaking me violently by the shoulder.

"Cocaine," I said, but I knew immediately that I'd got that wrong. "No. No. Not cocaine. That was me."

What was it?

"Morphine," I said, recovering some of my senses.

"How much?" asked the policeman.

Enough. *Morphine* gets its name from *Morpheus*, the mythical god of dreams and sleep. Apart from its pain-relieving properties, a large dose also depresses respiration and lowers blood pressure, sending the victim into a deep sleep. Forrester was better off asleep, I thought, or dead.

"How much morphine?" DC Filippos asked again, shaking me once more.

"Forty milligrams."

"Will it kill him?" he demanded.

I wish.

"No," I said, but I was only guessing at what was or was not a lethal dose because I'd never actually tried to kill anyone with morphine.

DC Filippos should have asked Dr. Harold Shipman, I mused. As one of the most prolific serial killers of all time, Shipman had used morphine overdoses to kill at least two hundred and fifty people in the seventies, eighties and nineties, and he remains the only doctor in the history of British medicine ever to have been convicted of murdering his own patients.

"There's more of it," shouted a man. "Look!"

I did look, up from my horizontal position. The man was one of the group standing around me and he was holding up another fully loaded syringe that he'd removed from my orange grocery bag.

"Please leave that alone, sir," DC Filippos said, without making any impression on him whatsoever. Instead, the man went on waving the syringe around high above his head so that everyone could see it.

"Naloxone," I said.

"What?" asked the policeman, leaning down close to my face.

"That syringe contains naloxone," I repeated. "Antidote to morphine. Inject Forrester with it."

He seemed to dither, looking back and forth from the syringe in the man's hand to my face. I had clearly given the young detective a serious dilemma. For the first time since I'd known him, DC Filippos obviously didn't know what to do.

"Inject the naloxone into Rupert Forrester," I said again. "It will counteract the effect of the morphine."

"Inject it where?" he said.

Intravenous was best, but it could also be administered into a muscle.

"Anywhere will do. Stick it into his arm or his leg."

He hesitated.

But so would I have done in his position. He only knew that the second syringe contained naloxone because I'd told him so, and I was the person who had caused the medical crisis in the first place. He only had my word for it that the second syringe would lessen the impact of the morphine, and not simply reinforce it, maybe even enough to kill.

Fortunately for the policeman, he didn't have to make the decision because at that point two ambulance paramedics arrived in their green uniforms.

I knew them. The same pair had collected me from Cheltenham Police Station the previous November, when my blood sugar had been too low.

I sat up and watched as the paramedics set to work on Rupert Forrester, removing his bow tie and opening his white shirt wide.

One of them glanced in my direction.

"Hello, Dr. Rankin," he said.

"Hi, Derek," I replied.

It all seemed surreal.

"He's been injected with morphine," PC Filippos said.

"Give him naloxone," I added.

They should have some of their own, I thought. Naloxone was also the antidote for a heroin overdose and ambulance crews were all too used to dealing with those.

"How much morphine?" Derek asked.

"Forty milligrams," I said.

He sucked air in through his teeth in a manner that worried me. Maybe forty milligrams was a lethal dose after all. I hadn't actually meant to kill Forrester, just make him go to sleep.

Primum non nocere—Primarily, do no harm.

Not actually part of the Hippocratic Oath, as some believed, but, nevertheless, a maxim to which all doctors were expected to adhere.

Had I done harm? Permanent harm?

Derek dug into his large red medical kit and pulled out a sterilized pack containing a syringe and a hypodermic needle. He filled the syringe with naloxone from a small bottle and then injected the drug into a vein on the back of Forrester's hand.

The results were remarkable.

One minute Rupert Forrester had been lying comatose on the dais, the next he was sitting up seemingly fully aware of what was going on around him.

The big question that no one had asked yet was why.

Why was I here?

Why had I stabbed Forrester with the needle?

Why had I injected him with morphine?

Why? Why? Why?

Those questions had been set aside due to concern over his

welfare, but, with him now seemingly well on the way to recovery, they became the main focus.

Not that I was yet in a fit state to answer.

Two more policemen arrived, this time in uniform, and they moved the crowd back from around the dais, asking them to return to their places at the tables so that a list could be made of their names prior to them being sent home.

There was anger too, with all of it directed firmly in my direction.

"Inconsiderate bitch," I heard someone say.

I suppose I should be sorry for ruining their evening—the Injured Jockeys Fund was close to my heart too—but the thought hadn't even crossed my mind.

One of the major effects of cocaine was that the world outside one's "self" became irrelevant. *Me, me, me* was the mantra of the cocaine addict, and to hell with everyone else.

Both Rupert Forrester and I were still sitting on the dais together with the paramedics and DC Filippos, while the other two policemen went to the tables to start taking down details of the guests.

And into this bizarre scene walked Big Biceps, no doubt arriving to drive his boss home.

I happened to be looking at the main door as he came through it.

Even the sight of him made the hairs on the back of my hands stand up in fear. But he hadn't seen me because PC Filippos was still crouched between us.

I watched as he asked something of a man sitting at the table nearest to the door. Then he looked over toward Rupert Forrester, who was now being helped up onto a chair by the paramedics.

Big Biceps clearly hadn't seen the two uniformed policemen who had made their way to the back of the room.

He walked over toward the dais and now the hairs all over my body were standing up as the adrenaline teemed into my veins. My caveman fight-or-flight reflex was running at full power.

"That man tried to kill me earlier this evening," I said clearly and quietly to DC Filippos, hardly able to contain an urge to stand up and run.

The detective turned and looked, and only at that point did Big Biceps notice me sitting there.

The color drained out of his face like sand out of an egg timer, from top to bottom, only faster, and he stumbled.

He looked quickly from me to Forrester and back again, and then he saw the two uniformed policemen.

He turned for the door and ran.

"Stop that man!" shouted DC Filippos loudly, leaping to his feet.

The two uniformed officers were too far away, but, still, Big Biceps didn't make it. Three men from the table near the door stood up and blocked his way. Their evening had already been ruined and they were in no mood for forgiveness.

The man turned round and round twice, looking for an alternative escape route, and then aimed for the nearest door to the kitchen but he was too late, far too late.

DC Filippos caught him from behind when he was still several yards away from it, dragging him down to the floor.

But he wasn't giving up that easily.

Big Biceps punched the young detective full in the face and threw him off as if he were a child, before starting again for the door to the kitchen.

By now the other two officers had responded, and, between them, they managed to manhandle Big Biceps back to the floor.

It took all three policemen to cuff Big Biceps's hands behind his back but he was still not giving up, kicking out at them as they dragged him over to one of the robust-looking central-heating radiators to which they shackled him using a second set of handcuffs. Even then, he tried to escape by attempting unsuccessfully to pull the radiator off the wall.

When the officers eventually stood up they received a rousing round of applause from all the guests in the room who had witnessed it all. More entertaining, I thought, than listening to the racecourse managing director.

I, meanwhile, had been watching Rupert Forrester's face, searching for some reaction to the fact that his muscular sidekick was captured, but there was only hopelessness and despair written into his features.

"Now," said DC Filippos, dabbing with a handkerchief at a trickle of blood coming from his nose. "What the *hell* is this all about?"

36

I spent almost the next three hours with the police, first in the
hotel and then at the police station, where I was formally
arrested on suspicion of assault causing actual bodily harm.

I had my fingerprints taken and the inside of my cheek
swabbed to provide a DNA profile. I also insisted on being seen
by a police medical examiner to have samples taken of my blood
and urine.

DC Filippos had called in his boss, DS Merryweather, and he
in turn had requested the presence of a detective chief inspector.
The incident at the charity dinner was clearly deemed important
enough to bring in the top brass.

The four of us sat together in an interview room, I having
waived my right to a solicitor in order to speed things up. Why
did I need legal representation when I had nothing to hide?

DS Merryweather started the recording equipment.

"Now, Dr. Rankin," said the chief inspector, "please tell us
why you assaulted Mr. Rupert Forrester."

I told them the whole story from the time I'd arrived back at
the racecourse medical room right up to the instant I'd stuck the
needle into Forrester's neck.

I could tell that none of them believed any of it.

They didn't actually say that my story was far too implausible and far-fetched to be true, but I knew it was exactly what they were thinking.

"I am not making it up," I said yet again. "And I'm not mad."

I implored them to go to the racecourse and do a forensic search. I told them they'd find traces of cocaine-laced alcohol on the bed in the medical room where I had managed to spit out some of the deadly stuff, plus the small empty bottle with my fingerprints on it.

I even showed them the faint marks on my wrists where I'd been tied up with the bandage tape.

Gradually, after more than an hour of trying, during which I had to go through the whole story at least four more times, I began to feel that some of what I'd said was at last breaking through their skepticism.

"Get my blood results," I said. "It will have cocaine in it. Or there will be benzoylecgonine in my urine, which will prove I've had cocaine in my system. And why did Forrester's driver try to run if it hadn't happened? He obviously had something to hide."

They didn't answer but DC Filippos nodded in agreement.

He knew.

He had been there, and he'd received a black eye and a bloodied nose for his trouble. And he had also witnessed the color-draining reaction when Big Biceps had first seen me.

The three policemen left me alone in the interview room for quite a long while as they went outside for a conference.

I thought back to what had happened in the Regency Suite after Big Biceps had been restrained.

Much to their annoyance, the dinner guests had to give not

just names but also their addresses to the police, something that seemed to take forever.

Six more uniformed officers had arrived to assist in the mammoth task and also to take away Big Biceps, who was formally cautioned and arrested for assaulting a policeman.

He had continued to stare at me throughout, perhaps disbelieving that I was even there and wishing he'd done a better job at bumping me off.

I was extremely thankful the handcuffs had remained in place and that he'd been surrounded by four burly boys in blue as he was taken out to a waiting police van, still resisting by kicking out at his captors.

All the while, Rupert Forrester had been attended to by the paramedics before being placed on a stretcher and taken away in an ambulance. The naloxone had a much shorter half-life in the body than the morphine, so, as the effects of the antidote wore off, those of the morphine would return. He would probably need another dose of naloxone at the hospital.

I had watched him depart with huge trepidation.

"Please don't let Rupert Forrester go," I'd begged DC Filippos.

"Why not?"

"Because he also tried to kill me."

The detective had looked at me as if I were a crazed old lady with a persecution complex, accusing anyone and everybody of trying to kill her.

"Forrester and that other man. They did it together. Why else do you think I stabbed him?"

I didn't for a second think that the detective had been convinced, but, nevertheless, he had called over one of the uniformed policemen, who'd been taking names and addresses, and told him to go with the ambulance instead, and not to let Rupert Forrester out of his sight.

"Has he been arrested?" the copper had asked.

"No. But keep your eyes on him anyway."

I suppose it was better than nothing but I'd have been infinitely happier if they'd locked him into the police van with Big Biceps, and then thrown away the key.

The three detectives finally came back into the interview room and sat back down on their chairs.

"Dr. Rankin," the chief inspector said in an almost embarrassed tone. "We are now inclined to believe you."

Hallelujah, I thought.

He went on. "A test on your urine sample has proved positive for you having had cocaine in your system at a significantly high concentration."

"So now what?" I asked.

"You will need to make a detailed statement and then you will be bailed and allowed to go home."

"Bailed?" I said. "For what?"

"Assault," the chief inspector said. "You remain under arrest."

"But Rupert Forrester tried to kill me," I said. "It was self-defense."

"He was not trying to kill you when you assaulted him," he said dryly.

I looked at the three of them with astonishment. DC Filippos wouldn't meet my eye.

"So am I being charged?" I asked.

"Not at this time," he said. "You will be bailed to return to the police station at a future date."

"And how about Sheraton, Forrester and his driver? Are they

under arrest too?" I tried hard to keep the sarcasm out of my voice.

"The driver is already in custody in connection with his assault on DC Filippos. He will now be arrested and interviewed concerning this other matter. Rupert Forrester will be detained at Cheltenham General Hospital and an arrest warrant will be issued for Mr. Michael Sheraton. That will be executed by Thames Valley Police at his home in Wantage as soon as possible."

I'd only be happy and feel safe, I thought, when all three of them were under lock and key.

"And how about Jason Conway?" I said. "He's up to his neck in this as well. He'd have probably been there too if he hadn't been concussed yesterday."

"We can't arrest someone just because they would have *probably* been there but weren't," the chief inspector said.

"But you could surely arrest him for conspiracy to murder Rahul Kumar."

AT ONE O'CLOCK IN THE MORNING, I was taken home in a police car, again abandoning my Mini. At least I hadn't been charged with driving away from the racecourse under the influence of drugs.

Grant was still up, beside himself with a mixture of worry, sympathy and anger.

When I hadn't arrived home by eleven, he had tried calling both the hospital and the racecourse but without any success.

In desperation he had then phoned the police to report me missing, only to discover that I was under arrest.

"At least I wasn't dead," I pointed out.

He and I sat at the kitchen table and I went through the whole story again.

He was shocked and outraged in equal measures, as well as feeling a little uncomfortable, I imagined. He had been one of those who hadn't believed me.

"Thank God you're safe now," he said, stroking the back of my hand.

It was the first act of tenderness he had extended to me for many weeks, and that, plus the release of tension in knowing that it was all over, made me cry.

"How are the boys?" I asked, dabbing at my eyes with a Kleenex.

"They're good," Grant said. "I didn't let on to them that I was worried you weren't here. They went off to bed with no trouble. I told them you'd be back in the morning."

The twins were well used to me not being there at bedtime. It was one of the prices they paid for me working shifts.

"Let's go to bed," Grant said, glancing at the kitchen clock on the wall above the window. "It's five past two."

The house phone rang loudly in the night stillness.

"Who on earth's calling at this time of night?" Grant said as I picked it up.

It was DC Filippos and he sounded breathless.

"Dr. Rankin," he said quickly. "I'm afraid there has been a development. Rupert Forrester has disappeared from the hospital after giving the constable there the slip."

My heart missed a beat.

"When was this?" I asked.

"About an hour ago. I went there to arrest him and he was gone."

An hour ago!

"Why didn't you call me before?"

"Because we had no reason to believe you were in any danger."

It was his use of the word *had* that worried me.

"But now you do," I said.

"I am currently at Mr. Forrester's house and I've just spoken to his wife. She wasn't at the dinner and knows nothing of the events of this evening at the Queens. However, when her husband arrived home a while ago, he told her some nonsense about there being vermin at the racecourse that he had to deal with immediately, and he left again in his wife's car. And he took his shotgun with him."

My heart missed another beat.

"I explained to Mrs. Forrester that I had come to arrest her husband and why. She is now deeply upset and very anxious that he intends to use the gun to kill himself. But I thought you should know."

"I want protection," I screamed into the phone. "I want it now for me and my family."

"I will dispatch a patrol car to your house right away," he said, and disconnected.

I looked at Grant. "Forrester has escaped and he's got a gun."

"Surely he won't come here," he said.

I wasn't so certain.

Revenge is a deep and powerful emotion. I knew. It had been revenge that had forced me to survive the cocaine and then to drive to the Queens Hotel when I'd had no right to be on the road.

In Forrester's warped logic, he would believe that I was the reason for his downfall and, even if he did intend to kill himself, I feared he would want to take me with him.

"I'll get the boys up," I said decisively. "We're going somewhere else."

"Where to?"

"I don't care, but away from here," I said. "Forrester knows exactly where we live. It was either him or his driver who drove over Oliver's bike and put it back on our driveway."

I walked down the hall toward the stairs but was only halfway there when there was a long shrill ring from the front doorbell.

That was quick, I thought, assuming that it was the police.

I almost had my hand on the latch before I realized it might not be the police after all.

The bell rang again.

I went into the dark sitting room and glimpsed out through a tiny gap in the curtains.

Rupert Forrester was standing there with the shotgun raised to his shoulder, aimed directly at the door, waiting to shoot whoever opened it.

My heart was now racing almost as fast as it had done earlier, but it was no longer due to cocaine. Mortal danger was a much more potent stimulant.

Keeping low, I slipped back into the hallway and down the corridor toward the kitchen. Grant was still there and he didn't need to ask me who it was. He could see the fear plainly writ in my eyes.

"Call the police," I whispered urgently at him—but how could anyone get to us quicker than the patrol car already dispatched by DC Filippos?

Grant had just been put through to the emergency operator when there was an almighty bang and crash from the front door.

Forrester had obviously become fed up waiting for someone

to answer the doorbell and had decided to expedite matters by shooting the lock off completely, sending shards of glass and wooden splinters right down the hallway into the kitchen.

I screamed.

"Out the back," Grant shouted at me. He made a beeline for the back door and disappeared out into the darkness.

What? And leave my boys alone in the house with an armed madman?

It was surely my life he wanted, not theirs, and I'd gladly die if it meant my twins were saved. I stayed exactly where I was.

Down the hall, I could hear as Forrester pushed open the remains of the front door.

But what if he first went up the stairs? Up toward the boys?

I couldn't allow that to happen.

"In here, you bastard," I shouted. "I'm in here."

I searched around for a weapon, but even the carving knife from the block on the kitchen counter would be unlikely to be much use against a double-barreled 12-gauge shotgun.

Not unless I threw it.

I drew the sharp blade out of the wood and raised it above my right shoulder, ready to fling.

Then I awaited the inevitable, my respiration becoming shallow and fast as awful trepidation twisted my stomach into knots, making me feel sick.

The first sign of my impending doom was the sight of the long barrels appearing through the kitchen doorway, the twin circles at their ends moving from side to side like eyes seeking me out.

I was literally shaking with fear.

I threw the knife as soon as I saw his head, wanting to catch him unawares before he had a chance to shoot me.

He was surprised, so much so that he jerked the gun up in

front of his face to protect himself, loosing off both the barrels as he did so.

The noise in the confined space of the kitchen was horrendous and debilitating. The lead shot slammed into the wall above the window, detaching huge chunks of plaster and totally destroying the kitchen clock. But the knife had failed to reach its mark too, falling harmlessly to the floor.

I stared at him as he dug into his coat pocket for more cartridges to reload, snapping the gun closed before I even had a chance to react.

"What's happening, Dad?" one of the boys shouted down from the landing, the terror clearly audible in his voice.

Forrester half turned toward the sound.

"Go back into your room and stay there," I shouted back.

Forrester continued to turn.

"No. No!" I screamed at him. "It's me you want, not my boys."

I rushed him, grabbing his arm and pulling hard.

He turned back and threw me off him with such force that I ended up sprawled on the kitchen floor.

"I'll kill them too when I'm done with you," Forrester said, sending an icy chill down my spine.

Oh God.

I started to cry, not so much for my own death but for theirs.

He raised the gun and pointed it straight at me so that I could clearly see down the barrels. At least I wouldn't feel anything. The shot at this range would probably take my head clean off.

I stared straight up at him. If he expected me to cower away or to beg for mercy, he would be disappointed.

He closed one eye to aim, looking right down the length of the gun.

This is it, I thought.

Good-bye, world.

There was suddenly a primeval shriek from behind him.

"Noooooooo!" screamed Grant as he charged through the open front door and down the hallway with one of his golf clubs held high above his head.

Rupert Forrester started to turn to meet this new threat but he was too slow, much too slow. The long barrels of the shotgun made it unwieldy and they got stuck in the doorway as he turned. And so intent was he on keeping hold of the weapon that he didn't even raise his arms in self-defense.

The toe end of the golf club caught him just behind his right ear and Grant had put all his considerable strength into that one shot. The cracking noise of the impact was impressive. Indeed, I was surprised that the metal hadn't gone right through the skull and embedded itself deep into Forrester's brain.

Now who thought golf was a silly sport?

Not me.

For the second time in only three hours Forrester's legs folded beneath him and he went down onto the kitchen floor like a rag doll.

Grant stood over him hyperventilating, the golf club ready in his hands in case a second swing was needed.

It wasn't.

Rupert Forrester was totally unconscious and he had blood coming from his right ear—a sure sign of major problems inside.

I stood up and carefully removed the gun from his senseless hands, breaking it open and removing the cartridges. I amazed myself with my calmness and control, not just now that it was over but also when I'd been convinced I was about to die.

Where was a panic attack when you expected one?

I went back down on my knees next to him and felt gently around the point of impact. The bone moved under my fingers.

"His skull is fractured," I said. "And the blood from his ear indicates a likely brain injury beneath. He will probably die without immediate hospital treatment. Call an ambulance."

"Are you crazy?" Grant shouted at me. "The man just tried to kill you. Let him die."

"No," I said firmly. "I'm a doctor. Saving lives is what I do."

PART 4

OCTOBER

37

Horseracing at Cheltenham returned for what was known as the Showcase Meeting in late October but the talk of the town did not concern the horses.

The revelations, currently appearing on a daily basis from the trial of one Fred Harris, known on the streets of east London as Crusher Harris and by me as Big Biceps, were making all the headlines in the *Gloucestershire Echo*.

Harris's defense strategy was simply to blame everything on Rupert Forrester, a tactic almost guaranteed not to be questioned by the man himself.

Forrester had survived the brain injury caused by the golf club, due to the prompt arrival of an ambulance and his immediate transfer to the hospital.

If *survived* was the right word.

An initial CT scan of his head had shown severe bruising to the right side of his brain and a critical swelling within the cranium cavity.

Emergency surgery had removed a section of his skull in order to relieve the pressure in his head but not before it appeared to have caused major damage to the part of the brain that juts down through the foramen magnum, the hole in the base of the skull where it joins the spine.

Forrester had remained completely unconscious in an induced coma for almost two weeks before the swelling had subsided and the neurosurgeons had decided to try to wake him up.

And he *had* woken up, after a fashion, insofar that his eyes had opened and he was able to move them up and down.

But he had, so far, not regained any other movement whatsoever and, after six months, the neurologists thought it unlikely that he ever would.

So this particular Geronimo would never again be leaping from great heights.

"Locked-in syndrome," one of the brain surgeons had said to me. "Cognitively awake but unable to move or speak. In fact, unable to do anything other than flicker the eyes. Very sad."

It wasn't the tiniest bit sad as far as I was concerned. Indeed, it was nothing less than he deserved.

I'd looked up locked-in syndrome in my medical textbooks.

It was a rare condition, caused by damage to a part of the brainstem known as the pons, a sort of neurological junction box between the brain above and the spinal cord below, through which all motor-nerve messages pass. When the pons was damaged, none of the signals could get through, leaving patients completely paralyzed except for the eyes, the motor nerves to which branched off the stem higher up.

Most sufferers were fully aware, seeing and hearing perfectly normally, and they even retained full sensations throughout their body as the sensory nerves were left mostly unaffected.

So Forrester got itches that he couldn't scratch.

"He'll probably never stand trial," DS Merryweather had informed me confidently some time after the diagnosis. "Not in that state. He needs twenty-four-hour care, and no prison could cope with him anyway."

But he was in prison already, I thought, a prison created by his own body, and serving a full-life sentence with no hope of parole.

BIG BICEPS, however, did stand trial, at Gloucester Crown Court, charged both with the murder of Rahul Kumar in the racecourse restroom and the attempted murder of me in the jockeys' medical room. The police had decided that there was insufficient evidence to prove that he had also tried to push me under a bus, but I knew—I was sure of it.

Mike Sheraton and Jason Conway acted as key witnesses for the prosecution—along with myself, of course—and both jockeys had seemingly done deals with the Crown Prosecution Service, even though everyone denied it.

Sheraton had pleaded guilty at a previous court appearance to the lesser charge of ABH, assault occasioning actual bodily harm, claiming that he hadn't known that Forrester and Harris had intended to kill me. In my opinion, however, he must have had a pretty good idea because of what had happened to Rahul Kumar, but his plea had been accepted by the court and he'd been given only a suspended sentence, presumably on the condition that he testified against Fred "Crusher" Harris.

Which he had done with great gusto, telling the jury exactly how Kumar had been lured by Rupert Forrester to the gentlemen's restroom, where Harris had been waiting. Sheraton swore that he didn't know Kumar had been killed until he saw the photos of him posted up as a dead man at the racing festival in March. Forrester had then assured him that the death had been an accident, something he now believed was untrue due to the attempt to murder me in the same manner.

Jason Conway, meanwhile, had seemingly got away scot-free as far as the full force of the law was concerned.

Both jockeys had admitted their part in the spot-fixing of races, but it was clearly part of their deal that no legal proceedings would follow. The police claimed that proving any corruption would be impossible without knowing who had placed the bets, with which bookmakers and whether it was the bettors or the bookies who were the beneficiaries. And that information was "locked in" elsewhere.

The racing authorities, however, had not been quite so compassionate and forgiving, their burden of proof being somewhat lower than the required "beyond reasonable doubt" of criminal proceedings. They were satisfied that there was "clear and convincing evidence" that spot-fixing had occurred—namely, the jockeys' own admissions—and had banned both of them from riding in races for two years, a punishment that many, including me, believed was far too lenient.

THE TRIAL was now in its second week, and, for the past two days, it had been my turn in the witness box.

Grant had been there throughout, providing moral support from the public gallery.

Since that fateful night in April, he and I had undoubtedly moved back closer together. Maybe it was the realization that what we had was so precious—and the knowledge that we had come so close to losing it made it even more so.

We were lucky. Most people don't appreciate what they have until it has gone forever. In our case, just the threat of that loss was enough and we were able to build new bonds in our relationship, sat firm on strong foundations.

But our boys had been seriously traumatized by the events. They had heard the shots and later seen the damage to the front door and in the kitchen. And they'd watched from the upstairs windows as both Rupert Forrester and his shotgun had been carried out of the house.

Their young minds were sharp and they had quickly worked out how much danger their mother had been in, not to mention themselves as well.

We had not hidden things from them, spending time talking through what had happened while also doing our best to play down the worst horrors. It had been a living nightmare and one that I did not want to recur for them throughout their lives in bad dreams.

I'd told them that Grant was not just their father but also their hero, a true white knight, and he had saved us all by slipping out the back door to fetch a five iron from his golf bag in the garage to ward off the evil, just as Saint George had slain the dragon with his sword. What more could they ask for?

It had made them laugh, but, even so, there remained a vacant blankness in their eyes as if the mental image of their dead mother, her head blown clean away, was still large in their imagination.

As it was in mine.

Only time would be the healer.

Much to Grant's irritation, the police had also taken away his prized five iron. It was his favorite club, and mine too now—I would never again complain when he spent his Saturday mornings at the local golf course.

My eating had improved, not yet back to what others might

refer to as "normal" but definitely improved. And that too, I was sure, was down to the events of that traumatic night.

To have had my mortality so manifestly paraded in front of my eyes, only to have the gift of life miraculously restored, provided me with a totally new perspective on relative values. I had finally reached a place of serenity and peace where I was more comfortable in my own body—a place where I no longer always needed to be the thinnest person around.

And the fact that Grant had risked his own life to save mine gave me a trust in him that had been absent previously: a trust in his love, a trust in his faithfulness and a trust in his intentions.

I no longer lied to him, and I stopped breaking my promises.

Instead, I started believing that Grant really did want me to get well and I became determined not to disappoint him. I'd even put on a couple of pounds without yearning to lose it again, and sex between us was back on the agenda, albeit occasional and tentative.

I had also recently cut down on my medications but there was still quite a long way to go in that regard.

Perhaps you never really recover from depression or an eating disorder, you only learn to live with them, keeping them under wraps like badly behaved dogs, hoping they won't escape and bite you, your friends or your family.

Except that the dogs are within you and can't simply be muzzled or sent off to a rehoming center. The trick is controlling *them* rather than letting them control *you*.

I CAME OUT OF THE COURTROOM after another particularly grueling session of cross-examination to find Detective Constable Filippos waiting in the lobby.

"How do you think it's going?" I asked him.

"Very well," he said, smiling. "The defense counsel made a huge error there in attacking your credibility over your depression. I was watching the jury. They were obviously sympathetic and believed your every word. Harris is going down, no doubt about it."

I admired the policeman's confidence, and shared it—even I couldn't see how Big Biceps was going to beat this rap.

Mike Sheraton came out of the court and, for a second, we stood facing one other, only a couple of feet apart. The last time I'd been this close to him, he'd been holding my legs down on a bed while Fred "Crusher" Harris and Rupert Forrester forced cocaine into my mouth.

He said nothing, just nodded at me once and turned away.

I stood silently staring at his back as he walked toward the exit, without so much as the slightest tingle appearing in my fingers.

"Dr. Rankin," said DC Filippos with concern, "are you all right?"

"I'm fine," I said.

I really was.

TURN THE PAGE FOR AN EXCERPT

Harrison Foster, a crisis manager for a London firm, is summoned to Newmarket after a fire in the Chadwick Stables kills six very valuable horses, including the short-priced favorite for the Derby. There is far more to the "simple" fire than initially meets the eye . . . for a start, human remains are found among the equestrian ones in the burnt-out shell. All the stable staff are accounted for, so who is the mystery victim?

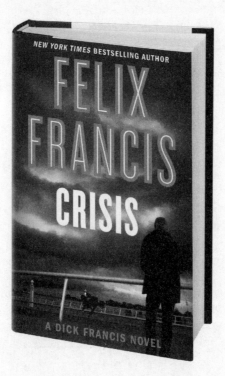

1

According to my business card, I was one Harrison Foster, Legal Consultant, but I was known universally as Harry and my speciality was crisis management.

And today's crisis involved a murder—not that anyone knew it at the time.

"NEWMARKET!" I SAID. "But I know nothing about horseracing. I hate it and don't even enter the office sweep on the National."

"No matter," ASW said. "You know about business and you're needed."

ASW was Anthony Simpson-White, founder, chairman, chief executive, owner, and driving force behind the Simpson White Consultancy Ltd—my Boss with a capital "B"—and he was standing in the doorway close to my desk.

"Can't one of the others go?" I asked. "Rufus loves the horses. He spends most of his salary at the bookies."

ASW shook his head. "Rufus is stuck in Italy with the wine people. You're my best available man."

I looked around at the other desks in what was called the Operatives' Room. Each of them was unoccupied.

Even on a Monday morning, I was his *only* available man.

"And, anyway," he said, "the client has asked for you specifically."

"Oh," I said somewhat surprised. "Who is the client?"

"It will all be in the brief. I'll send it to you by e-mail while you're on your way. Take a fast train from Kings Cross to Cambridge."

"Not Newmarket?" I asked.

"Cambridge is better. You'd have to change there anyway to get a local service. I'll get Georgina to arrange a car and driver to meet you."

Georgina was his PA—fifty-four years old, divorced with two grown-up sons, she was always smart, bright, and happy. She was also ASW's mistress, not that either of them would ever admit to it. But we operatives knew. Of course we knew. As the Boss was always telling us: *I expect my operatives to know everything about everyone.*

"Whose stables in Newmarket?" I said.

"That'll be in the brief, too. I'll get Georgina to book you a room. Now get going, Harry, there's a good chap."

In spite of his genial tone, it was an order not a request.

I immediately closed the laptop on my desk, stood up, put on my jacket, and collected my already-packed roll-along suitcase from the cupboard in the corner where it sat, permanently on stand-by, primed for an instant departure to anywhere in the world, hot or cold.

How to pack a suitcase was one of the first things taught to new operatives at Simpson White.

The main rule was that the bag had to be small enough to fit into the overhead bins on an airliner—waiting at baggage claim was considered to be time that could be spent more productively with the client.

Two clean shirts, a change of underwear, washbag, hairbrush, razor, phone, and laptop chargers were all essentials; chinos, trainers and a polo shirt were optional, while shorts and flip-flops were frowned upon. Operatives were expected to always wear a suit and tie to the office to reduce the need to pack them.

My suitcase also contained a small first-aid kit—scissors removed—a pair of swim-shorts and a small rolled-up Union Jack.

One never knew when that might be useful.

Anything else that an operative might need on assignment was expected to be bought "in theatre," as ASW called it, and he provided us with a company credit card for the purpose although any purchases were tightly scrutinized to ensure that they were absolutely necessary.

Not that Simpson White was exceptionally mean towards its employees. In fact, quite the reverse. Operatives travelled business class on long-haul flights so as to be rested and ready for work immediately on arrival, and provision of a comfortable car with a driver was the norm, as were four- and five-star hotels.

"I need my staff fresh," ASW would say, and he would charge his clients accordingly.

Retired colonel, Anthony Simpson-White had established Simpson White Consultancy Ltd in the mid-1990s partly with his gratuity paid on completion of eighteen years exemplary service in the British army. But ASW had not been a fighting soldier. He was a lawyer.

He had served as a senior officer in the advisory branch of the

Army Legal Corps, dispensing advice on military and international law to Prime Ministers and the High Command, including during British wars in the South Atlantic, Persian Gulf, and Bosnia.

"I spent most of my time telling the bigwigs what they really didn't want to hear," he'd once said by explanation of why he had finally resigned his commission even when tipped to be a future Director General of Army Legal Services. "Not that things have changed much since," he'd added with a laugh, "except the bigwigs now pay me more for the privilege."

He'd started as a one-man operation, giving legal advice and opinions to companies in financial or operational difficulty using the same authoritative and blunt manner that he'd employed at the Ministry of Defence. The company directors might also have not liked hearing what he had to say but he had an uncanny knack of cutting through the chaff to the meat of a problem before offering a lifeline, palatable or otherwise. It was then up to the company to decide whether to accept or reject his recommendations—to survive or go under.

Over the years his reputation had grown and so had his business, so much so that he now had ten operatives working under his watchful eye, and there was talk of recruiting numbers eleven and twelve.

Most of us were lawyers but there was also an ex-special forces sergeant plus two financial wizards enticed from the city not so much by a huge paycheck but by the promise of a more varied and exciting life.

And varied and exciting it had proved to be.

I was operative number 7—007, I liked to think—and I had been with the company for almost seven years having become bored with conveyancing houses, drawing up wills and submitting divorce petitions—the staple diet of a local high-street solicitor in rural Devon.

One particular wet and tedious Wednesday afternoon in Totnes, I had spotted a small, understated advert in the corner of the jobs section of the *Law Society Gazette*.

Vis mutare aliquid magis excitando tuum? was all it said with a London telephone number alongside.

Vis mutare aliquid magis excitando tuum?

I'd done a year of Latin at school but, clearly, not enough.

I typed the words into an online translator and it spat out: *You want to change to something more exciting?*

On a whim, I called the number.

"Can you come to our offices for an assessment?" asked a female voice immediately without so much as a "hello."

"Certainly," I replied. "When?"

"As soon as possible," said the voice.

"Where?" I asked.

"That is your assessment. Don't call this number again or you will have failed." She had then hung up, leaving me baffled but intrigued.

I remember having sat staring at the mobile phone in my hand, quite expecting it to ring as the woman called me back. But she didn't. It remained silent. There had been no name offered, not even the name of the firm. The voice hadn't even asked for *my* name.

Was it a scam? Or was someone just playing silly buggers?

Or was it actually for real?

But where did I start? There were over ten thousand law firms in the UK, almost half of them in London alone. Did I go through the legal directory looking for a telephone number to match? But this number seemed to be just for the advert not the one for the firm's switchboard.

I entered it into Google but, predictably, it gave no clue to the number itself, though it did provide some pointers. By inserting only the first seven digits, the search results showed various entities including a string of foreign embassies, a medical practice, and several restaurants. All were in the London SW1 postcode area, and most in subsection SW1X.

I Googled SW1X—Knightsbridge and Belgravia—the smartest parts of west London, but both with thousands of addresses.

Hopeless.

I had sat at my desk idly staring out the window at the people hurrying up and down Totnes High Street in the rain rather than getting on with my work, wondering what sort of idiot would place such a stupid advert.

But it made me determined to find out.

So I called the office of the *Law Society Gazette* and asked for the classified-ad department.

Sorry, they said, they were not at liberty to give out the details of who had placed the advert, data protection and all that. Indeed, the man I spoke to seemed quite amused by my request as if it was not the first time someone had asked him the same thing.

Then I searched on my computer for law firms in London SW1X and made a list. There were just eight of them.

Things were looking up.

Next I compared the telephone number in the advert to those of the eight firms. None were identical but three had the same initial seven digits even if the last four were all significantly different.

Now I felt I was really getting somewhere.

I called back to the *Law Society Gazette* and asked to be put through to their finance department.

"How can I help?" asked a female voice.

"I'm chasing an invoice for an advert placed in your jobs section," I said.

"For which firm?" asked the woman.

"It could be one of three," I said. "We act as a recruiting agent for a number of firms." I gave her the name of one of the firms on my short list.

"Sorry," she said after a few seconds. "No record of that one."

I gave her the name of the second firm.

"Ah, yes," she said, raising my hopes. "They advertised with us two years ago for a legal secretary. Is that the one?"

"Is there nothing more recent from them?" I asked, trying to keep the desperation out of my voice.

I could hear her tapping on her keyboard.

"No, nothing," she said.

I gave her the third name.

"Sorry. Nothing from them either."

"How odd," I said. "I'm sure it was one of our firms in the SW1X postcode. Could you please check again?"

"SW1X, you say?" I could hear her tapping the postcode into her system.

"We only have one other record of an invoice going to an address in SW1X, but that wasn't to a law firm."

"When was the invoice sent?" I asked quickly.

"Last week. It's for the current edition. But it was sent to an individual rather than a firm."

"Could you tell me the individual's name?" I asked in my most enticing tone. "It must have been a mistake."

"I can't," she said, sounding almost apologetic. "Mistake or not, it's against our rules."

"Could you give me the full postcode then?" I asked. "I can work out which firm it was from that."

She hesitated, obviously debating with herself whether that was also against the rules. She decided it wasn't.

"SW1X 8JU."

"Right, thanks," I said, jotting it down. "I'll get on and check."

I disconnected, smiling. Surely that was it.

But the postcode didn't match any of the eight law firms I had on my list.

Hence, two days later, I had found myself walking up and down Motcomb Street in Belgravia, a road of designer shops, art galleries and fashionable restaurants, wondering which of the unlikely twenty-eight addresses that shared the postcode SW1X 8JU was the one I wanted, assuming that it was one of those addresses anyway.

None of them looked remotely like a legal firm and there were no helpful brass plaques on any of the doors, so I went into each of the shops, galleries and restaurants to ask the staff if they knew of any law offices in the vicinity or anyone who might have placed an advert in the *Law Society Gazette*. None did. But it at least eliminated half of the addresses on my list.

Most of the buildings in the street were fine examples of Georgian architecture, three stories high with intricate wrought-iron railings surrounding balconies on the upper floors. They had originally been built as single-family homes but each had long since been converted into a self-contained retail space on the ground floor with accommodation above accessed through a narrow front door squeezed alongside the shop and opening directly onto the pavement.

I looked up at the high windows, trying to see someone sitting at a desk or to spot some other clue that would indicate a place of work rather than a residence, but the angle from street level meant that mostly all I could see was the reflection of the sky.

In the end I resorted to simply knocking on the front doors or ringing the doorbells and seeing who was in.

By the time I got to the last one, I was beginning to feel disheartened. At eight of the fourteen properties there had been no reply, while at five others the occupants obviously had no idea what I was on about when I told them that I'd arrived for my assessment.

"Get lost," a man shouted at one property. "I'm not buying anything."

While at another, the door was opened on a security chain by an elderly woman. "Are you from the council?" she asked through the crack.

"No," I replied. "I'm here for my assessment."

"I'm the one who needs assessing," she said. "Are you sure you're not from the council?"

I explained that I was absolutely certain I wasn't from the council, and she was clearly not pleased at having come all the way down the stairs to open the front door for no good reason—"not in my condition."

So when I pressed the cheap plastic bell on the very last door, I was thinking more about the times of the trains from Paddington back to Totnes than anything else.

The door was gray with grime. I imagined it had once been white or cream but time had not been kind to the paintwork, which was flaking off badly at the top. The small brass-surround letterbox was corroded green, and the central doorknob had several screws missing such that it hung precariously to the wood.

"Yes?" asked a voice through the tiny speaker situated above the bell push.

"I've come for my assessment," I said once more, with no hope or expectation.

"Good," said the voice. "Come on up." And a click from within opened the door.

And so I had stepped into the world of Simpson White.

No one ever asked me *how* I found them. Only the fact that I *had* was important, not the means I'd employed. Three hours later, I had an offer for a job. Although at the time, I'd little or no idea what the job actually involved.

"We are definitely not a law firm," ASW told me seriously, "and we're not a PR company either. But we do deal in public relations, and we do need lawyers." Indeed he spent more time telling me what they were *not* rather than what they *were*, as if he wasn't entirely sure himself. But I liked him and he clearly liked me too. "So, do you want the job?"

"How much does it pay?" I asked.

He seemed slightly irritated that I should ask about anything as sordid as money.

"How old are you?" he asked rather than answering my question.

"Thirty-two," I replied

"Married?"

"No," I said, wondering if that was a suitable question for a job interview.

"Engaged?"

"No."

"Any relationship at all?"

"Not at present," I said, although that was surely none of his business.

"Then why are you worried about how much I would pay?"

It was my turn to be slightly irritated.

"I have to live."

"You'll do that all right," ASW replied with a laugh, "and you'll also never feel so tired, so excited, or so important, all at the same time."

"So what would I actually do in the job?" I asked.

"Anything and everything," he replied somewhat unhelpfully. "We are basically an advisory service and we give legal and other advice to everyone from presidents and prime ministers to CEOs of major international companies. Anyone, in fact, who is in need of our help and is prepared to pay our fees."

He drew breath and I sat quietly looking at him waiting for him to go on.

"We are specialists in crisis management. Crises will always occur, either man-made or from natural disasters, and the perception of how the crisis is managed is almost as important as the relief effort itself. Our job is simply to ensure that, when things are bad, they are not made worse by insensitive or downright stupid words and actions by those who are meant to be making things better."

"Like *Deepwater Horizon*," I said.

"Exactly."

Deepwater Horizon was a BP oil-drilling rig that exploded in April 2010 causing an environmental catastrophe in the Gulf of Mexico. BP bosses initially claimed it was only a small problem and that it was not their fault. For BP, the public relations disaster was almost as destructive as the physical one.

"We sit on shoulders whispering advice into ears and hope it's listened to although, thankfully, we weren't involved in that one."

"Okay," I said.

"Okay what?" ASW replied.

"Okay, I'll take the job."

SO HERE I was seven years later leaving through that same grey, grimy front door on my way to King's Cross and then on to Newmarket.

Horseracing! God help me.

FELIX FRANCIS

"Felix has proven a champion storyteller."
—*Mystery Scene*

For a complete list of titles and to sign up for our
newsletter, please visit prh.com/FelixFrancis